THE ACT OF LOVE

Howard Jacobson is the author of nine previous
novels and four works of non-fiction. He won the
Everyman Wodehouse Award for comic writing in
1999 for *The Mighty Walzer*.

HOWARD JACOBSON

The Act of Love

VINTAGE BOOKS
London

Published by Vintage 2009

4 6 8 10 9 7 5 3

The author is grateful for permission to reprint copyright material
from the following: *Eroticism* by Georges Bataille, translated by Mary
Dalwood, reprinted by kind permission of Marion Boyars Publishers.
Flowers of Evil by Charles Baudelaire, translated by Jacques LeClercq,
reprinted by kind permission of Peter Pauper Press, Inc.

While every effort has been made to obtain permission from owners
of copyright material produced herein, the publishers would like to
apologise for any omissions and will be pleased to incorporate
missing acknowledgements in any future editions.

First published in Great Britain in 2008 by
Jonathan Cape

Vintage
Random House, 20 Vauxhall Bridge Road,
London SW1V 2SA
www.vintage-books.co.uk

Addresses for companies within The Random House Group Limited
can be found at: www.randomhouse.co.uk/offices.htm

The Random House Group Limited Reg. No. 954009

A CIP catalogue record for this book
is available from the British Library

ISBN 9780099526735

The Random House Group Limited supports The Forest Stewardship
Council (FSC), the leading international forest certification
organisation. All our titles that are printed on Greenpeace approved
FSC certified paper carry the FSC logo. Our paper procurement
policy can be found at
www.rbooks.co.uk/environment

Typeset by Palimpsest Book Production Limited, Grangemouth,
Stirlingshire
Printed in the UK by CPI Bookmarque, Croydon, CR0 4TD

To Jenny — my one and only

The fever of the senses is not a desire to die. Nor is love the desire to lose but the desire to live in fear of possible loss, with the beloved holding the lover on the very threshold of a swoon. At that price alone can we feel the violence of rapture before the beloved.

Georges Bataille, *Eroticism*

'I'll tell you . . . what real love is. It is blind devotion, unquestioning self-humiliation, utter submission, trust and belief against yourself and against the whole world, giving up your whole heart and soul to the smiter — as I did!'

Charles Dickens, *Great Expectations*

Prologue

FOUR O CLOCK SUITED THEM ALL — THE WIFE, THE HUSBAND, THE LOVER.

Four o'clock: when time in the city quivers on its axis — the day not yet spent, the wheels of evening just beginning to turn.

The handover hour, was how Marius liked to think of it.

Marius the cynic. Marius who held that natural selection gave the lie to God, and humanity the lie to natural selection. Marius who anticipated no more big adventures for himself, not even that last adventure left to modern man — ecstatic, immoderate, unseemly, all-consuming love. Marius who took pride in being beyond surprise or disappointment, there being nothing to expect of anybody, least of all himself. Marius the heartbroken.

He was thirty-five — though he looked and sounded older — tall and hazardously built, with a face suggesting ecological catastrophe: lost city of Atlantis eyes, blasted cheeks, a cruel, dried-up riverbed of a mouth. Women found the look attractive, mistaking their precariousness for his. Me too, though I was in every respect his opposite. I was the ecstatic he thought the world had done with. I am the one whom love consumes.

We're all fundamentalists now, regardless of whether we're believers or we're atheists. One way or another you have to be devout. Marius worshipped at the altar of Disbelief. I at the altar of Eros. A god's a god.

Faith is said to make you strong. My faith was of a different sort. I believed in order to be made weak. Love's flagellant, in weakness I found my singularity.

I

Four o'clock it was, anyway. The handover hour. A conceit so lewd I can barely breathe imagining Marius imagining it.

As for who was handing over what, that is not a question that can be settled in a sentence, if it can be settled at all. The beauty of an obscene contract is that there's something in it for everyone.

The wife, the lover, the husband.

I was the husband.

PART ONE

MARIUS

Here he is. In his black velvet jacket sumptuously lined with dark fur, he is a proud, handsome despot who plays with the lives and souls of men . . . Under his icy gaze I am again seized with a deadly terror, a premonition that this man will capture and enslave her, that he has the power to subjugate her entirely. Confronted with such fierce virility I feel ashamed and envious.

Leopold von Sacher-Masoch, *Venus in Furs*

I FIRST SIGHTED MARIUS, LONG BEFORE I HAD ANY INKLING I'D HAVE USE FOR him – or he for me, come to that – at a country churchyard funeral in Shropshire. One of those heaving-Wrekin mornings the poet Housman made famous – rain streaming on stone and hillock, the gale plying the saplings double, a sunken, sodden, better to be dead than alive in morning. It didn't matter to me, I was from somewhere else. I could slip on galoshes before I left my hotel, put up an umbrella, endure what had to be endured, and then be gone. But others at the graveside chose to live in this hope-forsaken place. Don't ask me why. To assist in their own premature interment, is my guess. To be done with life before it could be done with them.

Such a lust for pain there is out there. Such apocalyptic impatience. I don't just mean in Shropshire, though Shropshire might have more than its fair share of it, I mean everywhere. Bring on the dirty bomb, we cry, and publish instructions for its manufacture on the Internet. Blow winds and crack your cheeks: we scorch the earth, pitch our tent at the foot of a melting iceberg or disturbed volcano, sunbathe in the path of a tsunami. We can't wait for it to be over. The masochists we are!

And all the while we have the wherewithal to suffer exquisitely and still live, if we only knew where to look. In our own beds, for example. In the beloved person lying next to us.

Love hard enough and you have access to all the pain you'll ever want.

Not a thought I articulated at the time, I have to say, not having met, not having married, not having lost my heart and mind to the woman

5

who would be my torturer. Marisa came later. But in the vegetative dark that preceded her, I never doubted that my skin was thinning in preparation for someone. Easy to be wise after the event and see Marisa as the fulfilment of all my longings, the one I'd been keeping myself for; but of course I didn't fall in love only *provisionally* before I met her. Each time I lost my heart and mind, I believed I had lost them for good. Yet no sooner did I regain my balance than I knew that the woman who would finish me off completely – make me hers as I had never so far been anybody's, a man possessed in all senses of the word – was still out there, waiting for her consummation as I was waiting for mine. Hence, I suppose, my interest in Marius, before I apprehended the part he would play in that consummation. I must have seen in him the pornographic complement to my as yet incompletely formed desires.

It was impossible to tell from his demeanour at the funeral whether he was one of the principal mourners. He looked sulkily aggrieved, scarfed up and inky-cloaked like Hamlet, but somehow, though he gave conspicuous support to the widow – a woman I didn't know, but to whom there clung a sort of shameful consciousness of ancient scandal, like a fallen woman in a Victorian novel – I didn't think he was the dead man's son. His distress, assuming it to have been distress, was of a different order. If I had to nail it in a word, I'd say it was begrudging – as though he believed the mourners were weeping for the wrong person. Some men attend a funeral jealously, wishing to appropriate it for themselves, and Marius struck me as such a man.

I'd known and done a spot of business with the deceased. He had been a professor of literature with a large library. I had travelled up from London to value it. Nothing came of our negotiations. The library was ill-cared for and crumbled into dust before I could come up with a figure. A fortuitous event in its own way, since the professor did not really want to part with his books, whatever their condition. He was a sweet man, out of time and place, who expostulated against life's cruelties in a squeak, like a mouse. One of life's, now one of death's, disappointees. But I hadn't known him so well that I could move among his family and friends and ask them who the Black Prince was. As for striking up an acquaintance with him directly, that was out of the question. He was as obstinately sealed from eye contact or introduction as the corpse itself.

Observing him later, in the little centrally heated village hall to which we'd trooped after the service, plied double like the saplings, I wondered whether the bleak weather had been responsible for his appearance at the graveside, so much less saturnine was he, divested of his coat, his scarf and, if I wasn't mistaken, the widow. To say he was merry would be to go too far, but he'd turned animatedly unapproachable, as opposed to simply unapproachable. A cold fire seemed to come off him, like stars off a sparkler.

He was handsome, if you find high and hawkish men handsome. As a non-predatory man myself, I felt intimidated by him. But that's part of what being handsome means, isn't it: instilling fear.

He was standing by a table of sausages and pork pies, making access to it difficult for other people, flirting icily with two poochy-looking girls who, for no other reason than that he appeared to wish to divide them, I took to be sisters. He gave the impression, fairly or not, of a man who would cross any boundary if there was gloomy mischief in it. It was this same impression that made me wonder whether the girls were quite of an age to be spoken to with such freedom, all things considered. Exactly how old they were I couldn't tell — when you don't have children of your own (and I am not a breeding man) you lose the power to distinguish twelve from twenty-seven — but they wore the nakedly raffish expressions of girls who know they can get you a prison sentence.

For his part, though Marius allowed them to feel they had exclusive use of his attention and were exclusively the beneficiaries of his brilliance, he succeeded at the same time in holding them up as a sort of reproach to the gathering, as though it was their dullness that reduced him to whiling away his time with chits in black lipstick and nose rings. But I might have misread him. Perhaps he was deeply affected by the funeral, consumed by a grief which only indiscreet intercourse with the young and the provocative could assuage.

What did they see in him, I wondered, that dissolved the usual indifference young girls feel towards lugubriously clever men nearly twice their age. They laughed with a responsiveness that would have been flagrant at a coming-out ball let alone a funeral breakfast. They raised their bare, flushed, perilous pixie faces to him, ablaze with the consciousness that there was an audacity in his starry attention that demanded a reciprocal boldness from them.

Quite suddenly, as though he feared a scene, he called it to an end, recalling himself to what he owed the dear departed and his widow, however dull their conversation. But in the moment before he left the girls I caught him mouthing a phrase at them – half secretly, half not. I, for one, had no difficulty interpreting the communication, but then I miss very little that has a promise of impropriety in it. And yes, I admit it, will find impropriety where impropriety isn't. Not this time though.

'Four . . . o' . . . clock,' he said without making a sound.

So what was he doing? Arranging to meet them after school?

Four o'clock.

The tremble hour.

If it *was* an assignation, he didn't keep it – that was my guess. The jail-bait, yes; one, or more likely both of them, each egging the other on as they stood at whatever corner Marius had instructed them to meet him, pulling back their frilly sleeves to consult their Mickey Mouse watches every other minute, laughing into their handkerchiefs, while their pulpy hearts pounded inside their blazers. But not Marius. What he wanted from the girls he had already taken.

How you can tell on so brief an appraisal (and most of it from behind) that a man is an absentee libertine, that he lights fires and doesn't stop to see them blaze, that at the last he'd sooner withhold a sexual favour than confer one, I can't explain. Perhaps that sort of sadism shows in the curvature of the spine. Perhaps I'm just good at seeing what I want to see. However you account for it, I felt, in advance, the 'sting of his disregard'

— I steal the phrase from Leopold Bloom, Bloomuponwhom, the patron saint of the subjugated and deceived — as acutely as those girls would have felt it at four o'clock on whatever day in whatever place Marius did not turn up to meet them.

My territory — sexual insult. I'm a connoisseur of it. I could write you a treatise, a thousand pages long, and in a dozen languages, some of them dead, on the difference between a sting and a smart. It comes, partly, from an extensive and perhaps over-collaborative reading of that category of classic novel (English, French, Russian, whatever) whose subject is humiliation. I'm tempted to ask what other category of classic novel is there. But I accept — if with bewilderment — that there are some readers who open books in order to be mystified by extravagant event, or stirred by acts of prosaic heroism. I must have been born without a taste for mystery or heroics.

Love, that is all I've ever cared to read about. Love and love's agonies.

Love afflicted me.

I draw no distinction between literature and life. In the stories I precociously devoured I gravitated naturally to the pain — to the sorrows alike of Young Werther and the older Alexei Alexandrovich Karenin, to the easily bruised boyish prickliness of Julien Sorel and the deep womanly contemplative sadness of Anne Elliot. But it had never been any different for me in life. I was born lovesick — unrequited, highly strung, quiveringly jealous, with a morbid yearning to give my heart long before there was anyone to give my heart to.

That I too would be spurned, left to pine away like the heroes and heroines of my reading, I never doubted.

The first girl I could ever truly call a girlfriend — the first girl whose fingers I was allowed to interlace with mine — betrayed me the second time I took her out. We went into the cinema together and she left two and a half hours later with someone else. How and where she found him when there appeared to be only she and I sitting alone in the darkness and I had never once let go of her hand, what she saw in him with the lights down wherever she found him, why she preferred him to me, what I lacked or had done wrong that could explain that preference or her cruelty in making it so plain – none of this I understood. I was fifteen, she the same. She had a cascade of black hair, eyes like a fortune-teller's and long, slender brown arms which I imagined wrapped around me twice. She had kissed previously, I had not. But she came from a family of teachers – her father taught cello at the Royal Academy of Music – and she said she would enjoy teaching me to kiss. Now, inexplicably, she was enjoying teaching another pupil more.

I stood outside her house after school for weeks, imagining that she would relent, that what had happened had been a mistake, a confusion that conversation or just the sight of me would clear up, but she never showed her face, not even at a window. I hoped her father might come out. As a cello teacher he would surely have understood my desolation. But he too never appeared. Eventually a girl emerged from the house, I assumed Faith's sister, to inform me of the situation. 'Faith says she's going out with Martin now. She says would you please go home and leave her alone.'

I put my satchel down as though I meant to stay rooted to that spot forever. What did I want? The earth to open up and take me? A retraction from Faith of her sister's words? A glimpse of Martin that would at least show me what I didn't have?

The sister must have been moved by the spectacle of thwarted love I presented because she found a kinder tone in which to say, 'These things happen. You'll get over it.'

I never did get over it. What I suffered in the loss of Faith, reason told me, was quite disproportionate to what I'd felt for her on the mere two occasions we'd gone out and the time I'd thought about her in between. But reason was no help. Nothing helps against jealousy. I began to idealise her beauty. Her arms grew longer and more slender. Her kisses, which had been no more than tentative and toothy, were now deep probings, as fathomless as the sea and as desperate as drowning, only someone else was swimming in them and I was drowning in their absence. I was unable to eat. My schoolwork suffered. My head ached. I felt murderous, not to Faith or Martin but to myself. Had I possessed more of whatever it was that girls wanted this could not have happened. And it was too late to acquire that mysterious whatever it was now, because there was no future in which to put it into practice.

I rubbed at the pain in my heart. Probed it, polished it, until there was no skin left between my heart and me. Was it Faith I missed or was it myself, the self I'd been when she'd wound her lovely arms around me twice? Where to locate the hurt exactly – in the kisses that had been stolen from me almost before they'd begun, or in the insult of her preferring Martin? What was it she saw in him? What was it she didn't see in me? What was it, what was it, what was it . . . ?

It made me careful thereafter – in the thereafter I never thought there'd be – never to hurt as I'd been hurt, never to leave the cinema with anyone other than the person I'd gone into the cinema with, never to show that I preferred kissing someone else. How to survive jealousy became the study of my life. How to accept that someone you love might not love you in return. How to bear her kisses going elsewhere. How to face up to abandonment – the knowledge that you are and will remain unloved, cast out, not just because you are not worthy in yourself, but because you stand in the way of two other people's happiness. Made lonely for all eternity so that they can be for all eternity together.

'You know my motto,' my father said in a cloud of cigar smoke. 'If you miss one bus there's always a second.'

He was disgusted by my weeping. I was disgusted, plain and simply, by him.

'What's the use of a second bus when you've been knocked down by the first?' I replied.

He shrugged. 'You'll have a few broken bones,' he said, 'no more.'

'Bones!'

My mother was more sympathetic, though of no more help. I did not visit her in her room, which for as long as I could remember had been a chamber of private grief, for she too had been abandoned. But she came to me one morning as I lay disconsolate and motionless on my bed, looking up at the ceiling, nursing a sadness which day by day had been making a permanent home for itself in my body – a molten river of acid and scalding honey that moved with slow deceptive sweetness through my veins.

'Is it always like this?' I asked her.

'Betrayal?'

'Love.'

She thought about it for some moments, pulling her brocade dressing gown around her. She had always appeared to be from another age, my mother, as though abandoned into an earlier time. 'I wish I could tell you it isn't,' she said. 'But you will find someone else, and then you'll forget what happened this time.'

'And when it happens again?'

She touched my hand. A gesture of unusual warmth in my family where touching was reserved for impropriety or rejection. 'You might be lucky,' she said. 'It might not happen again.'

'What might make it not happen again?'

'You might learn to love the next person a little less. Or at least invest a little less in her.'

'But would that then be love?'

'Ah, now that,' she said, gathering herself up, 'is the big question.'

I might only have been fifteen, but I knew the big answer. If you wanted to be in love – and I wanted nothing else – then you had to welcome into your soul love's symptoms and concomitants: fear of betrayal which was no less potent than the fear of death, jealousy which ate into the very marrow of your bones, a feverish anticipation of loss which no amount of trust would ever assuage. Loss – loss waited upon gain as sure as day followed night, that's if day would ever follow night again. You loved not only expecting to lose but *in order* to lose – this my favourite books had told me and now I'd put them to the test in life I knew them to be right. You loved to lose and the more you loved the more you lost. Fear and jealousy were not incidental to love, they *were* love.

The molten river sluiced through my body, as though it had found its natural course there and would never leave me.

Good that *something* would never leave me.

I didn't take the train back to London after the funeral as I'd meant to do. Some impulse or other kept me in Much Wenlock. Not a desire to hit the town even though it was a Saturday night. I ordered sandwiches and ate them in my hotel room. Everything in the hotel was on a slant. The sandwiches slid off the tray. My bottle of beer slid off the bedside table. It was only by holding on to the mattress that I was able to avoid sliding out of bed.

But the crookedness of the place went with my mood. I'd been disarranged.

I was woken by the sound of Sunday church bells ringing. A mocking sun was streaming in through the curtains. The old man was buried and now life could begin again. I decided to take advantage of what could be the only sun Shropshire was going to see for a hundred years and dressed quickly. I needed breakfast and wasn't prepared to risk a fried egg sliding on to my lap, so I went looking for a café. After that I mooched around, taking in the priory, a few half-timbered buildings, at last finding a couple of bookshops of the sort I make a point of investigating when I'm out of town. I rarely find anything of value but I never fail to buy a book or two, simply as a way of expressing fellow feeling. Of all the forms of that premature interment I've talked about, selling books in the provinces is the most pitiable. They sit behind their wooden tables, pretending to read – though they've read their entire stock a dozen times already – entering their few sales into a ledger with a blunt pencil. Could so easily have been me, I always think, but for the worldly far-seeingness of my ancestors, making sure our destiny would be in Marylebone, London's city within a city. Felix Quinn: Antiquarian Booksellers — in the quiet assurance of our name I believe you hear the confidence of a family that couldn't imagine ever living more than a few hundred yards from everything the soul and body of man requires: art galleries, concert halls, good restaurants, suppliers of wine and cheese, infirmaries, bordellos.

Others must travel to satisfy these needs; we had only to stretch out a hand.

Indeed, it was one of my father's recurrent malodorous jokes that at his age happiness resided solely in being able to reach out his hand and feel under a woman's skirt. He didn't mean my mother's.

By the time I'd searched the shelves of the bookshops and made consolatory, not to say condescending, conversation with their hapless proprietors I needed lunch. It was gone three when the taxi slid me out at Shrewsbury station. All the trains were late. I pounded the far end of the platform in irritation, looking for somewhere to sit in the sun, wondering whether to pick fights with people who took up seats with their luggage. People with backpacks always the worst offenders. Walkers! Those masochists who think their minds are healthy. At last a seat fell empty and I bagged it. When I looked around me I saw that I was sitting next to Marius.

He was still dressed funereally. I thought I could see traces of cemetery clay on his shoes and even on his jacket. But that was probably fanciful. I glanced at him a couple of times, hoping for one of those half smiles that invite conversation. I was curious to know why he'd been at the funeral, what his relations were to poor Jim Hanley and his widow. Maybe, if we were travelling to London on the same train, he'd tell me about his penchant for picking up and then letting down underage schoolgirls. Explain the appeal of sadism to me.

'Such a beautiful afternoon,' I said at last, accepting that if I waited for him I'd wait forever. 'Weather like this makes one wish one were somewhere else, don't you think?'

He favoured me with the quickest of looks, such as a wild animal might throw a man he's not afraid of, but doesn't want to eat. It was evident that if I wished to be somewhere else, he wished I'd go there. It was equally evident that he didn't recognise me from the funeral.

I threw my head back and screwed my eyes against the sun to make it easy for him if he didn't want to reply. Let it never be said that I'm not a complaisant man.

Deciding not to be rude to me, he looked at his watch. 'Time of the day, squire,' he said.

I wasn't sure I understood him. Was that a question? Was he wondering if his watch was slow? 'What about the time of the day?' I asked.

'It's the reason you want to be somewhere else. Nuffink to do with the weather,' He consulted his watch again. 'You're smelling somewhere faraway. Four o'clock has that effect.'

I was surprised to detect a faint accent. I mean under the faux cockney or whatever it was he was affecting. Not West Midlands quite, but nearly. I hadn't imagined him accented. It disappointed me. I wanted him pristine. I viewed him, as I have said, pornographically and pornography is a picky medium. It permits no extraneous material or tomfoolery. Just the clean, chill sepulchral lines of sexual violation and the silence that comes after.

'And which faraway place does four o'clock smell of to you?' I asked.

'Ah!' he said, as though that were a question that reached deep inside his soul. He drummed his fingers on the briefcase he carried on his lap and appeared to let his imagination roam worlds real and fanciful. I waited, expecting Petra or Heraclea, the Galapagos Islands or the Fields of Troy. I knew a pedant when I saw one. They always are, these queasy, tyrannical men. They ease their disgust by reading the classics.

'Thanatos,' was what he finally came up with. Proving me right. He was a tyrant.

I pulled a face. 'Thanatos?'

'You're wondering where that is? Greek for death, matey.'

It took all my restraint not to tell him I'd rather he didn't treat me as one of his schoolgirls. 'I know what Thanatos is Greek for,' I said. 'I'm only surprised to hear you call death a place.'

15

'What would you call it?'

'The end of place.'

He rubbed his hand across his mouth as though to stop himself from laughing at me, or from ripping me apart with his teeth. I understood how those girls had felt. It was exciting to be near him. Dangerous, somehow, as though the death he spoke of was an entity he had power over. I felt I was sitting on Shrewsbury station with a vampire.

I wouldn't be surprised to learn I'd covered my throat.

'You'd probably argue no less prosaically, then,' he said with undisguised scorn, 'that deff ain't a person neither. But the Greeks wouldn't have agreed with you. They made him a beautiful young man and shoved a butterfly in his hands. Wherever you are at four o'clock, you hear the bu'erfly beating its wings for the final time. That's why – since you brought the subject up – your heart aches, as every heart on the planet aches, in sympathy with the dying day as it faints in the embrace of desire. *Comprendez?*

I didn't say I knew all about the fucking bu'erfly, thank you. I was too affected by his prose style. 'Yours would appear to be the cosmology of an incurable romantic,' I countered, showing I was not without a bit of style of my own. But by that time he was on his feet. There was no train coming, but he wanted to be certain that when one did, he would not be on it in my company.

This might be hard to credit, but Marius was travelling to London to clear a few matters up with people and one of the people he was travelling to clear a few matters up with was me. Not me personally, but me as in the business.

Not as coincidental as it sounds, given that his errand was connected to the death in which we were already bonded. I don't mean his Thanatos twaddle, I mean the actual death that had taken me up to Shropshire in the first place. It appeared that the professor had been ill for some time and that in the course of his illness his mind had begun to wander.

Someone, he believed, had stolen the most precious volumes of his library. He kept a diary which contained all the information necessary to track the thieves who had come up from London in the night and emptied whatever books they could lay their hands on into a pantechnicon. They hadn't tied him up or harmed him, but they did warn him with threatening gesture against doing anything to hamper their getaway. Fortunately he'd had the presence of mind to take down the name of the driver. Felix Quinn: Antiquarian Bookseller. A reference in his diary to an appointment which he himself had made with Felix Quinn in person, and a subsequent entry describing the meeting as 'highly satisfactory from one perspective', suggested a different version of the story. But those who cared about him – retrospectively, that is – and who might just have been worried for their inheritance, thought it would be for the best to clear this up. A bit soon after the funeral, but it was not for me to pass judgement. Country people are more suspicious than we who live trustingly in cities.

As for those who cared about him, they comprised his wife who had run off with a much younger man – a favourite student of the professor's – and the much younger man in question, who was Marius.

Nothing, as I say, coincidental about any of this, except the fact of one of my assistants, Andrew – who dealt with Marius when he turned up on Monday morning – knowing him from university. I wasn't in the shop when Marius and Andrew renewed their acquaintance, but I was told it went off as amicably as any encounter involving Marius could. Marius left, grumpily satisfied the old man had not been swindled out of his George MacDonalds and Christina Rossettis, after which Andrew – a breathless, book-mad fellow in a ponytail which I insisted he cut whenever it reached low enough to threaten his safety on the library steps – agreed to tell me all he knew about Marius over lunch in a New Zealand restaurant that had just opened on the High Street.

He had eloped with her, the prof's wife, that was the juiciest bit. We say 'run off' when all we mean is set up house elsewhere. But this was truly an elopement. He twenty, she fifty. The story of it, to which further researches of my own have added a degree of colour that Andrew's rapid narrative of necessity lacked, was this:

She was the wife of an emeritus professor, working part-time and with only half his wits active, who befriended Marius in his second year at university, seeing in the young man a precocious and perhaps ill-fated genius that reminded him of his own. Before settling for a life of academic ignominy, addressing what was left of his thoughts to empty lecture theatres – empty of everyone except Marius – the professor had held out hopes of being an essayist, mythopoeist, and epigrammatist of wit. Now, lame and hard of hearing, he imagined that same future for Marius who became a frequent guest at his house, where he met – as it was always written that he should – Elspeth, old enough to be his mother, not quite old enough to be his grandmother. She was beautiful, silvery in that seemingly ageless style of middle-class Englishwomen who get the business of looking old over with while they're young. At fifteen she looked about a hundred. For the following thirty years she looked about fifteen. Now she was poised, equinoctially, between assurance and desperation, her day not yet spent, the wheels of her evening just beginning to turn – and Marius, whatever the arguments in favour of circumspection, to say nothing of decency, was not, as I was to learn, proof against the equinox.

He talked to her, openly – by his standards of uncommunicativeness – and in the hearing of the professor, of his love for her. His language, as I now imagine it, somewhere between Gatsby's and Schopenhauer's, grasping at dreams, beating on, boats against the current, towards the most certain dissatisfaction and unhappiness.

'What would you know of love or its unhappiness?' she challenged him, her voice all bells, like a Christian village on the morning of a coronation.

They were in the garden, drinking Pimm's. It was one of those soft English summer days that make one think of eternity.

'At your age love is just a word,' said the professor. 'You cannot yet have fathomed its miseries.'

When the professor spoke it was as though dry paper rustled in the trees.

'On the contrary,' Marius objected, 'I have fathomed *only* its miseries.

I agree that what Wittgenstein calls "pathos" attaches to a man in love regardless of whether that love makes him happy or unhappy. "*Aber es ist schwerer gut unglücklich verliebt sein, als gut glücklich verliebt*" "But it is harder to bear yourself well when you are unhappily in love than when you are happily in love."'

Now the trees sang a song of forever.

The professor exchanged glances with his wife. See, the old man's eyes said, is he not as brilliant as I told you he was?

Elspeth nodded. Yes, yes she saw.

They eloped. They may have been the last people in this country *to* elope, elopement being an act of desperation for lovers in a strict society. Now you just say you're going and whoever doesn't like it can lump it. In fact they would have met no resistance either from the professor, whose life was already such a disappointment that the loss of his wife (which could, anyway, be seen as the gain of a son) barely impinged upon his melancholy, or from Marius's father who looked down on his son and needed no further evidence that he was a fool. Marius's mother, it embarrasses me on behalf of human psychology to report, had eloped herself just a year after Marius was born. A proper elopement, pursued by a husband with a gun. Marius and Elspeth, pursued by no one, eloped because they wanted to elope.

Marius, in a borrowed car, waited outside her cottage in the Shropshire village of Quatford. He was twenty, she was . . . but it didn't matter how old she was in actuality; in expectation she was twenty too. It was four o'clock in the afternoon, an hour when her husband the professor was either lecturing or taking a nap, or, as Elspeth joked, her voice as merry as a young girl's, doing both things simultaneously. She would have preferred to be driven away at night, with only the moon as their witness, but Marius couldn't borrow the car for that long.

Marius tried to kiss her the moment she appeared carrying an overnight bag and with a scarf around her shoulders, but Elspeth insisted they make haste.

'Drive,' she said. 'Just drive.'

He enquired after the rest of her luggage.

'Just drive,' she ordered him.

No one was following but Marius did as she said and just drove.

Occasionally she would lean across and look into the rear mirror to be sure they weren't being tailed. She grew nervous at traffic lights and appeared startled whenever someone overtook them. But they were safe. No alarm had been raised and no one was in pursuit. Having ascertained that his library was intact and that they hadn't run off with a single one of his lectures, the professor sighed and left them to their fate. For this, Elspeth never forgave him.

They hadn't discussed where they were going. Elspeth wanted it to be a secret. Marius assumed he would be taking her back to his digs in Sutton Coldfield, no matter that he shared a bathroom with four other students. But Elspeth expected a transitional passage in a place that belonged to neither of them. When Marius explained he had to get the car back before night fell she warned him that in that case he'd have to get her back before night fell too.

'If you can steal a wife from your professor and protector,' she told him, 'you can steal a car from your friend.'

It was at that moment that Marius realised what a crooked course he had embarked on. Henceforth he was to understand himself as an immoralist.

He drove without purpose or direction until Elspeth saw a sign to Stratford-upon-Avon. 'Take me there,' she said.

Marius checked his petrol gauge. He believed he had just enough juice to make it.

Elspeth, who loved Shakespeare, loved Stratford-upon-Avon on his account. Instead of going straight to their room in the bed and breakfast Marius found them, she took him to the Royal Shakespeare Theatre to see, as luck would have it, *Antony and Cleopatra*.

'Do you know,' she whispered to him before the lights went down, 'I watched Peggy Ashcroft play Cleopatra to Michael Redgrave's Antony in this very house twenty-five years ago.'

'Before my time,' Marius whispered back, concealing his alarm at Elspeth's use of the word 'house'.

She held on to his arm. 'Nobody thought Peggy Ashcroft had a Cleopatra in her, but she was magnificent.'

Before his time it might have been, but Marius remembered that Kenneth Tynan had been waspish about this famously aberrant coupling. It was Marius's essay comparing Tynan and George Bernard Shaw as critics of the English stage that had first brought him to Elspeth's husband's attention. The professor was not a lover of the theatre, as was not Marius, and they shared a taste for those moments in theatre criticism when the great critics weren't that keen on theatre either. What Marius remembered was Tynan's joke that the only role in *Antony and Cleopatra* that any English actress was equipped to play was Octavia, Caesar's pallid sister. Somewhat sadistically, in the circumstances, he repeated this to Elspeth, along with Tynan's deliberately bad-form follow-up joke that 'The great sluts of world drama have always puzzled our girls.'

We will assume the worst of Marius's motives. Not only must he have wanted to reassert himself after the poor fist he'd made of the mechanics of elopement, but it must have excited something in his nature – the spitefulness and the sadism, let us guess – to use the word 'slut' in the company of his professor's wife, a woman of an age to scold him for his language, and who had this very day left the decorous safety of her old life for him.

For her part, Elspeth believed that Peggy Ashcroft had found as much slut in herself as was necessary to play the part of Cleopatra. In her heart she winced from the brutality of the word and didn't consider it apposite to Shakespeare. But she argued the case dreamily and without conviction, as though it excited her, in turn, to wonder, in this hallowed place, whether she would be able find as much slut in *herself* as would be necessary to play with conviction the part of Marius's mistress.

A story which – whatever else there was to say about it – explained why Marius had agitated me from the moment I'd set eyes on him. It isn't every boy of twenty who will entice a woman two and a half times his age away from her husband and get her to set up house with him. He was a crosser of lines, a disrespecter of the decencies, and I have a nose for such people. Never mind that (or do I mean precisely because) he was a disrespecter of me as well.

To say I have a nose for such people makes light of an instinct about which I should be more courageously forthcoming. Some men – and Marius was such a man – have always filled me with dread on account of their appearing to possess a quality I don't: the wherewithal to persuade a woman to abandon herself, against all reason and against all conscience, to unbridled lust. This is what I mean when I say I viewed Marius pornographically. Whatever the reality of him, he played an archetypal role in that book-fed theatre of riot and melodrama that was my sexual imagination. He lurked in darkened cinemas, invisible to everyone but the woman he would steal from you, kissing her unnoticed in the blackness even as you sat and held her hand. He was the eternal rake or roué who must make any man not a rake or roué worry about his potency. It doesn't matter whether or not you yourself wish to persuade a woman to abandon herself against all reason to unbridled lust, the knowledge that you can't and he can lies curled like a poisonous snake in the long grass of your self-esteem. And that's before you address the heated question of what will happen if you find yourselves going head to head for the same woman.

Freudian? Did I see my father in him, competing with me for my mother? I wouldn't bet against it. I see my father in most men and no doubt my mother in most women. She was permanently in distress, he was a swine – as archetypes go, you won't go far wrong in life with those to guide you.

Mystery of my absorption in Marius solved, anyway. He was one of *those*. He had what Sacher-Masoch saw in that dark-furred, shudder-making Greek – 'the power to subjugate'. It wasn't because I'd desired either of the underage girls myself that it had made me uncomfortable to watch him toy with them in the bone-freeze cemetery damp of Wooton-under-Whateveritwas; nor was it because I envied him the professor's widow that I felt her pain as he tormented her with his detachment. No doubt the latter was just part of their age-discrepancy ritual of cruelty and cringing anyway. No, what had got under my skin was that he'd done what he'd done because he could get away with doing it. They enjoy an exemption, these non-delivering libertines with sad faces. Or they do in my fears. Which might mean only that I'm the one who exempts them.

First I attribute almost impossible powers to them. Then I set them free. Free to do what?

Free to do whatever a pervert's delirious fancy wishes them to do. Free to do damage. Free to take what's yours. Free to whistle your wife away from you. Free to make a slut of her. Free to make a nothing of you.

Whatever else there is to be said about the subject, that was where my interest in Marius ended. He was a character in a salacious fiction I wrote in imitation of all the salacious fiction I'd ever read (and what fiction isn't salacious?) only when his image was before me. Once he was out of view, the fiction went unwritten. And it would have stayed unwritten had he not turned up entirely unexpectedly but opportunely some five or six years later – the years in which I'd fallen hard for Marisa – on an errand of the heart. Not normally where a normal person's heart takes him, Felix Quinn: Antiquarian Booksellers, but Marius was no more normal a man than I was.

He wanted us to retrieve a number of volumes of personal significance that had passed into our hands some years before. That was the gist of it. Not the volumes the professor had accused us of purloining on his deathbed, but others that had been the property of the professor's wife and which she had not had time to take away with her when she eloped. It wasn't with me that he made his appointment, indeed he had no reason to connect me with the shop, but Andrew, remembering my interest – he remembered everything: every book that anyone had ever wanted, every book that we have ever sold, every book that anyone had ever written – informed me Marius was coming in. I was in my office when he called and recognised him immediately, though heavy glass separated us and he was much changed. He carried his height differently, less imperiously, more as an excuse for abstraction. He had grown moustaches, great sea-lion excrescences which he wore, like a Swedish adventurer's, as though to give himself the look of someone with something to hide. But which to me gave him even more the look of a bodice-ripper sadist. From the number of times Andrew had to incline towards him, sometimes going so far as to pull his ponytail clear of his face and tug the tip of his ear, I gathered that Marius had become a mumbler too.

He didn't see me and if he had he would not have remembered me. I was beneath his notice, in all senses.

Though he'd already written to us with his request, there were still procedures to go through before we could find him what he wanted. We don't, at Felix Quinn: Antiquarian Booksellers, hurry clients, nor do we like them to hurry us. You come in, you talk, you go away, and then we send you a parcel or we don't. Even if the books you seek are visible on the shelves we still write out an order form and institute a search. In the age of Amazon these virtues are appreciated by our customers. Marius left us his address. Out of idle curiosity – another interpretation would say out of suicidal curiosity – I checked to see where he was living now. Surely not in sodden Shropshire still. And in this I was right again. The countryside was no place for a flower of evil such as Marius. What I hadn't expected, though, was to find that he'd moved to all intents and purposes next door, into the purlieus of my marriage.

For a moment or two everything went very still about my heart. Peace, was it? The peace the gods send you on the eve of certain destruction? Just to be sure I was not destroyed already I went up into the street and looked into the faces of people going about their business. Blank, most of them. Ignorant of the sort of secret I was carrying. But they might have thought the same about me. You never know what's lying still about the heart of anyone.

According to the Elizabethans, Fortune is a whore. You have to take that with a pinch of salt. The Elizabethans saw whores everywhere. They were besotted with the word's hoarse and poxy music and grew drunk on that disenchantment with women – indeed that disenchantment with the sexual life in general – which it denotes. Horn-mad and whore-obsessed, they fornicated, contracted syphilis, feared that every smile concealed a lie, and thought no woman chaste. I, who am no less intemperate but view the falseness of women differently – let us say as an opportunity rather than a bane, and certainly with greater understanding – see Fortune more as pimp than whore. Explain otherwise why Marius, with all the world to choose from, and at a time when I was in urgent need of his particular genius, was impelled to come and live so close to me that, even leaving aside our shared interest in antiquarian books, our paths were bound eventually to cross, and I was bound eventually to reel him in.

HE WAS LIVING, I DISCOVERED, ABOVE A BUTTON SHOP IN A LANE OF small romantic restaurants and chic boutiques at the epicentre of the action, as though to show himself each day what he was missing. To one side of him was a curtain-maker, to the other a stain removalist's. Left and he was in Wigmore Street, right he was in Harley Street. Day or night there was nothing a man needed that he couldn't immediately find – art, music, cheese, shoes, sausages, specialists of the spine, the brain, the cardiovascular system, new books, antiquarian books, the bored wives of retired professors – except that there was nothing he believed he any longer needed. Other than the stain removalist.

He was as disordered sexually as I was, in his way, only he couldn't get out of bed to enjoy it. It wasn't laziness, it was torpor. He had done a terrible thing and wanted nothing more to do with the world in which he'd done it.

He woke early, often before dawn, with a worm of bile coiled around his gut. Some mornings he wondered if the worm of bile *was* his gut. He would think of going to his desk to write something, epic or epigram, but automatically reached out instead to turn on his bedside lamp by the light of which he would go on reading whatever had occupied the previous night's vacant hours before he had slid, neither willing nor unwilling, into sleep. Usually what he read was modern foreign literature in translation – the chill eroticism of Czech or Italian rendered into plainsong English being all he could digest, like cold weak tea.

The sort of prose, incidentally, which I feel I should write when I describe Marius, rendering him as the type of heartless English libertine the French love to fantasise about, like Sir Stephen in *Story of O*, a man in whom O detects 'a will of ice and iron'. But that's one falsity of porno I cannot swallow: its chastity of expression. In my fear of Marius – in my greed for Marius – I teemed with words.

In fear of himself, however, he was not so productive. On his desk he kept a lined notebook which he'd bought when he was a student nearly twenty years before. In this he had intended to write an English version of Baudelaire's spleen-fuelled prowlings around late-night Paris. He had the title. *Four o'clock*. That was the hour that excited Marius. Never mind midnight. Midnight was obvious. If the twenty-four-hour day marked nothing but the fluctuations of our desires, four o'clock was, for him, the hairspring hour. Once upon a time it had affected him like a transfusion of vital fluids. He walked the streets and felt the oscillation between day and evening as a change in the temperature of his own body. He heard his blood heat. Now he merely observed it through his window above the button shop. Four o'clock in the city – the shop assistants looking at their watches; the waiters, with that violence of gesture peculiar to waiters, throwing their cigarette stubs into the street and laying out clean table-cloths; barmen polishing glasses and looking at their reflections in the bowls; men and women on the streets quickening their pace, their minds elsewhere, heading home to change, pausing only to buy flowers, choc-olate, wine, lingerie – as though the whole city were a lover thinking about its date, but a date which, for the cycle of expectation and disappointment to begin again, had to end unsatisfactorily.

His bed was narrow and uncomfortable, like a monk's. It had been the fourth-best guest bed in his previous life. But what did he need now? He wouldn't have admitted it was a penitential bed; it was narrow because that was all his new space allowed. But the discomfort served a purpose. His bed was for reading in only; he would not be bringing back any woman to sleep in it.

Other than to check the currency markets in the newspapers – and no other item in the newspapers engaged his interest, everything was predictable – he had nothing to do with the time at his disposal. No work. No function. On a good day the little money he had made selling a house he'd inherited made a little more. On a bad day he was brought to the point of having to decide again whether to keep it in dollars or in yen.

Once in a blue moon, when the money markets turned against him and he was able to summon the will to get out of bed, he sold Taiwanese copies of old masters on the railings outside Hyde Park. He knew a man who knew a man who knew how you could lay hands both on the space and the paintings to fill it. A pastiche of Michelangelo or Gainsborough slapped together in five minutes on an island off China appealed to Marius's sense of the ridiculous. It made a mockery of meaning. Nothing came from anywhere or had value.

Otherwise, he had no occupation. He had behaved as badly to his career, such as it might have been – teacher, critic, man of letters, chronicler of the daylit city turning into night – as to the woman he'd once loved. Because abandonment becomes a habit, he had left it to die as well.

What had caused this change in Marius's circumstances is simply told. Elspeth had died and he had not been with her. You can not be with someone when they die as a matter of accident or choice. Marius had not been with Elspeth as a matter of choice.

It had been evident at the professor's funeral that relations were not as they should have been between a couple who had run away for love – Elspeth to be with Marius every hour God granted, never to miss a moment's looking into his face or lying alongside his body; Marius, convinced her beauty would continue to enrapture him, making the wildest protestations of devotion and promising to adore her forever. It's possible Marius had not liked seeing her shedding tears over her ex-husband. Some people are jealous of the dead. It's also possible he was troubled by retrospective misgivings, whether of the 'I've been a bastard' sort, or 'I've been a fool'. Whatever the explanation, I had watched him with my own eyes behave abominably to the poor woman, tormenting her with philandering and coldness at a time when it was nothing short of a solemn duty to let her grieve and reprove herself in peace.

If things had been bad before the funeral they deteriorated quickly after it. Who knows, perhaps the death of the professor stripped Elspeth of what was left of her allure. It's inconceivable that Elspeth would not have charged Marius throughout their years together with falling for her only because she belonged to another, older, wiser man. And now, appalled and frozen, Marius would have wondered whether she was right.

Though the disparity in their years had moved and excited him at first – just as the theft of her had excited him at first – it had little by little been losing its fascination until at last he had to admit to himself that he could not bear, for her sake no less than his, to watch her age. Accordingly, though it must be said only after much pilgrimage of the soul and body (of which his removal of what was left of him to Marylebone was the final stage), he spared her the distress of his suffering and left her, to die with dignity, on her own.

Finis.

That was three years before. How long he'd been in Marylebone since was anybody's guess. He liked to keep his movements secret. It went with his cultivated air of accidentality. A Conrad of the Marylebone Archipelago. But he couldn't have been kicking about for very long or I would surely, as a conscientious not to say compulsive looker-out for erotic opportunity – not for myself; I am speaking maritally – have eyed him sooner.

Wherever he'd got to after Elspeth's death he'd been living as one of the dead himself, growing a moustache to keep the world at bay, communicating from his great height with almost no one, the few words he spoke now – to the staff at the button shop below him, to the newsagent, to anyone who bothered him at a pavement café, as I was to make a habit of doing until I was sure of him – inaudible behind his moustache.

'Barely a word of it,' was Andrew's answer, when I enquired whether he'd been able to hear anything Marius had asked him. 'But then he was never that easy to understand at university.'

An oblique man even before he had reason not to look life directly in the face, Marius, in his disgrace, was in danger of speaking a language spoken only by himself.

I the same. Though I claim universality for my condition I cannot pretend I know many people who find the words for it which I do. Except at the outer reaches of pornography, in the phantasmagoric chat rooms where the deranged whisper to the deranged, what I do is not talked about. So that was each of us speaking a language spoken only by ourselves. On which basis I believed we could converse. Or at least do verbal business.

He would, I was certain, be appalled by my language once he got to hear it. But I didn't mind that. I wanted to appal him.

No man has ever loved a woman and not imagined her in the arms of someone else – that sort of language. *No husband is ever happy – truly, genitally happy, happy at the very heart of himself as a husband – until he has proof positive that another man is fucking her.*

To say I kept Marius under surveillance aggrandises somewhat my efforts to become familiar with the patterns of his existence. There wasn't, when all was said and done, that much to surveil. He was in most of the time, trying to finish the book he'd never started. But thanks to conscientious staff, and domestic arrangements that can best be described as plastic, I had time on my hands and was sometimes able to catch him when he did venture out. Once or twice I saw him circling Manchester Square, as though unable to decide whether to brave the Wallace Collection. What kept him out I didn't know. Paintings, I discovered later. Paintings reminded him of Elspeth. Elspeth loved paintings. Loved them too much for Marius's temper. He met paintings eye to eye, squabbled with them, felt their power and wrestled with it – he didn't 'love' them. Music ditto. He listened, mused, resisted and gave in only after a struggle – he didn't 'love'. Which was presumably why I saw him loitering outside the Wigmore Hall in the same spirit. Elspeth died for music, too.

Art hung about her like a halo. She was transfigured by it. The refulgence, when she came home from a concert or a gallery, hurt Marius's eyes. Art was not the reason he left her; the deterioration of her body was the reason he left her. But who's to say that loving being around art, especially art of an overly imaginative sort – her most favourite exhibition of all time had been Pre-Raphaelite Fairy Painting at the Victoria and Albert, and she owned, or had owned, signed first editions of everything by Tolkien, a one-time acquaintance of her father's and husband's – who's to say that fevered art in whatever form she favoured it had not been instrumental in loosening her flesh from the bone?

Otherwise, Marius proved to be a difficult customer to tail. The one routine of his I could count on – four o'clock coffee at whatever tin table he could find vacant on the High Street, by preference one of those outside the Greek café opposite the travel bookshop – was too risky to take advantage of. I doubted he'd recognise me from Shropshire, but I couldn't take the chance. It was important, for what I wanted of him, that he didn't know of my existence.

I began to haunt the button shop simply in order to be beneath him. If the shop was empty and I listened hard I fancied I could hear him pacing the floor. Still searching for that opening sentence. I bought far more buttons than I needed in the course of this operation, but I felt I was getting the smell of him this way, and would subsequently know, if we happened to be shopping in the same supermarket, say, or visiting the same doctor, that he was near.

It could have been pure chance or it could have been his odour that took me to the local fromagerie one lunchtime when Marius was deliberating over cheese. That bread and cheese were just about all he ate I had figured out already. I felt certain there was no table in his flat. He would eat his lunch, I imagined, sitting on the edge of his bed, slicing the cheese with a sharp fruit knife and ripping the baguette apart with his hands. There was something satanic in this image, by virtue of its suppressed explosiveness. No man his size and temperament could go on living like that.

You could feel the tension he emitted in the fromagerie. Everyone fell quiet around him as he muttered into the cheese, asking for one rat-trap-sized portion after another, leaving increasingly long silences between each selection.

'Will there be anything else?' the young woman behind the cheese counter not unreasonably enquired, Marius having abstracted himself so completely at last that he appeared not to be there in mind at all.

The question produced a wheeze of broken-hearted merriment from deep inside his moustaches. '*Will* there be anything else? I certainly hope there will, but when there will, or what there will, I'm damned if I have an earthly. Time being unredeemable, what else there will be, no less than what might have been, is an abstraction remaining a perpetual possibility only in a world of speculation, as the poet he say.'

'That'll be seventeen pounds and thirty pence, then,' the young woman said. I gathered she was used to his nonsense.

Another of his tragic Old Man of the Sea wheezes, and then he peeled off a twenty-pound note from a wad he carried in the back pocket of his corduroy trousers, like an Oxford don who'd gone into the protection racket.

'Ta, doll,' he said, shining his icily heartache, opal-blue eyes into hers as she gave him his change. He had no desire to make a fool of her. On the contrary. The meek shall inherit the earth, Marius believed, the haughty having made such a mess of it. Then the meek shall do the same.

Doll, for Christ's sake!

Who called a woman *doll* any more?

I didn't know how she felt, but I turned a little queasy for her, hearing it. *Doll!*

I wasn't sure it was still allowed to address a woman in that way. I wasn't sure it should ever have been allowed.

He didn't buy his bread and cheese at the fromagerie every lunchtime, but he did so frequently enough for me to hope that they would see each other there eventually – he and Marisa – since she too was a cheese eater and the fromagerie, at least on the days there was no farmers' market, was the place to get it.

And eventually – though I had to keep my wits about me to ensure it – they did.

As an expert on them both, I saw what they saw. He, as dusty as a snake, a scarf about his neck in defiance of the warm weather – the eternal student, just down from Wittenberg, not going anywhere in particular, thinking about his satanic lunch. She, in a high-waist pencil skirt so tight he would have wondered how her skin could breathe inside it, her sunglasses in her hair, her earrings rattling as she paced the shop in her punitive stilettos, an alien presence in so organic a place. She was, to my heightened senses, more than usually absented, her lovely Diana-the-huntress head slightly to one side, as when she was weighing up a proposition. I knew when Marisa registered a man. I had watched her register enough of them. She cleared her throat. I had seen Marius only with prey that was too young and a mistress who was too old, so I wasn't sure what changes to look for in him. But I saw him take hold of the ends of his moustaches and shape them into a pointed beard. Short of his making goat's horns with them I don't know how he could have signalled his interest more plainly.

It was all over in a second – just a flicker of acknowledgement between them, such as high-bred cats exchange when they pass on the common street.

Had they been cats I could have left them to it. They would have known what the next move was. But they were an over-civilised pair. On their own, no matter how often they eyed each other off in the fromagerie, they would not have proceeded further. They were too alike – they stimulated the romance of impossibility in each other.

I, on the other hand, proceed more quickly than is considered decent from the subtlest intimations of sex to the grossest couplings. Jealousy operates at a speed beyond the capabilities of adultery, no matter how licentious the adulterers – from a dropped handkerchief to the act of shame a thousand times committed, all in the blinking of an eye. And jealousy when it is a hunger is faster still. No sooner did I remark the catlike hauteur of their exchange of glances than I leaped all intervening stages to Marisa quivering, head down, hindquarters raised; Marius, claws out, parting her fur, obscenely scarlet like a line of blood . . .

I was not insane. I knew I'd have to wait a while for that.

But at least we were up and running. And in the meantime I did not lack resource. I knew their weaknesses. In Marisa's case, conversation. In Marius's, women who already had husbands, and – so long as it was not wonder-touched, so long as there was corruption in it – art. All I had to do was get them to a gallery and start them talking.

PART TWO

MARISA

He didn't like dancing. He didn't like gambling. He didn't even like drinking. His only pleasure was jealousy. He loved it, he lived by it.

Joseph Roth, *The Tale of the 1002nd Night*

In the East Indies, though chastity is of singular reputation, yet custom permitted a married woman to prostitute herself to anyone who presented her with an elephant . . .

Michel de Montaigne, *Essays*

NO MAN HAS EVER LOVED A WOMAN AND NOT IMAGINED HER IN THE ARMS of someone else.

I repeat the sentence not only for the pleasure it gives me to imagine Marius appalled. I repeat it as a categorical, unwavering truth, though I fully expect it to be contradicted. You will sooner get a man to give away his money than admit he longs to give away his wife. (Or better still – for we are dealing, if only we'd come clean about it, in nothing but degrees of good – to have his wife give away herself.)

Of course imagining is not the same as longing; what you see in your mind's distempered eye you might not welcome in your heart. But then again you might. What else is imagination for if not to lure the heart away from safety?

Here's a simple test for husbands: Do I *fear* another man is fucking my wife or do I *hope* another man is fucking my wife? And of the two, which do I prefer?

Take as much time as you need to think about it. Close your eyes. Do a little picturing of the scene. You are filled with dread, of course. But what if part of what appals you is the degree to which you want the thing you dread? Are you not as much energised as terrified by what you see?

The more you love a woman the more you fear her loss. Is it not a sensible strategy – of the imagination *and* the heart – to *practise* losing her?

Call it self-protection: we do it in every other sphere, we shore up against tragedy and destruction, we take out insurance, we make provision.

If you know you cannot bear what is going to happen, if your heart is pulp – and what man's heart is not as pulp? – then surprise it before it surprises you.

Against the swollen river of molten jealousy there is, as far as I know, no other defence. Throw yourself in. At least that way you have a hand in your own destiny. And sink or swim, it may prove exhilarating.

A great endeavour lures me on – the words are not mine but those of another deviant on a moralising mission. Pervert Pervert, as I recall a sneeringly buttoned-up English teacher calling him when I mentioned I'd been reading *Lolita* in the vacation. Takes one to know one, was what I should have said, but I didn't want to lead him on. In my school you only had to look at a teacher to have him leaving you love letters in your satchel. His – Pervert Pervert's – great endeavour bore on girls even further below the age of consent than Marius would have been prepared to entertain, though with Marius it was more a case of being horrified by old flesh than revelling in young. My endeavour, which is strictly legal, is less threatening to society. It is to make the case for cuckolds, though I have to say I hate the comicality of the word. And when I say 'make the case' I don't mean win publicity for our cause. I'm not looking to form an association. What lures me on is an altogether more pastoral ambition – to extend the great arm of brotherhood around the millions upon millions of husbands who would invite their wives to wrong them if they could only find the courage for it. Cuckolds of the World Unite! You have everything to lose but your chains.

By someone else – the someone else whose arms we imagine wound around our wives – I mean another man. The fancy which some husbands entertain of seeing their wives carnally embracing another woman is something else entirely. I'm not such a puritan as to deny titillation its place in the erotic life, or to pretend that the sight of two women kissing isn't sometimes pretty – my father more than once announced he had a taste for it – but titillation is not what I'm about. Hell doesn't wait on the soft-focus experimentalism of an age that will try anything once and in the process let all danger (other than disease) drain clean away from sex. The nymphs climb off the bed, bow gracefully to their audience, get dressed, and normal life resumes, unless they discover they like too much where they've just been, but that too is another story.

No, the love of which I speak, love desperate and bloody, the only love that *deserves* to speak its name – the last erotic adventure left to us as we await extinction – requires another man. A rival. Not a companion in enjoyment of your spouse's favours, not a Jim to your Jules or a Jules to your Jim. Not a vacation from you or a variation of you, or even the Heathcliff-if-all-else-perishes rocky-eternity beneath you, but the dread, day and night and in all weathers alternative to you. You as it hasn't fallen to you to be. You who might efface you and make you as though you had never been.

But such imaginings come and go, sometimes acted upon, more often not, until the imagination cools and finds other errands for itself outside obsession. For the lucky (or the daring) few, fancy is transfigured into fact. You unlatch your nature. You welcome Pandemonium into your heart. You do not have to wonder, you know. You do not have to beg, as Othello begs, ophthalmic proof. You have the proof. And now the love you bear the woman who betrays you – except that it is no betrayal, for a consummation cannot be called betrayal – flowers into adoration.

No man has ever adored a woman who does not know her to be lying in the arms of someone else.

No man ever adored his wife as I, Felix Quinn, adored Marisa Quinn, already the lover of other men, but soon – soon, soon, if desires have wings – to be the mistress of Marius.

The surprising thing is that I was the other man – the rival, the dread alternative to the man she had – before I became her husband. The best cuckolds are always those who have cuckolded first. They know from the inside the enormity of that betrayal which is no betrayal, though in our case it *was* a betrayal since the other party was unable to take any pleasure in my supplanting of him. In the psychopathology of everyday life there are such casualities: men who miss out on the most exquisite sensations love has to offer because they cannot accommodate jealousy in their hearts.

He was a collector of antiquarian books. I am a seller of antiquarian books. I found him what he wanted and we became friends. Let that be a warning: don't befriend the antiquarian who satisfies your bibliomania, for the next thing is he'll be satisfying your wife.

I'm aware that my tone of voice changes when I remember myself as the lover. I get taken over by a gross levity which I frankly don't much care for. This proves – had it needed proving – that the role of seducer, or however else you choose to describe the offending party, doesn't suit me. I am myself only when I am the offended. In this one instance, however – perhaps because I foretold where at last it would take me – I played the cuckold-maker.

It was impossible to tell from Marisa's demeanour when I first met her whether she was happy in her marriage or she was not. She looked imper-manent, that was my strongest impression of her. She looked as though she hadn't settled, as a butterfly never settles; indeed had someone told me that, like the butterfly which accompanied Thanatos, she would die before the afternoon was out I'd have believed it possible, for all that she had the bloom of health upon her. Though absolutely of the here and now in her dress, never not elegant in the steely heeled, city-woman style, a powerhouse capable of taking on any man at his own game, she somehow wasn't with us. When she smiled at something one of us said – we were just the three, Marisa, her husband and I, taking tea at Claridge's, the four o'clock ritual – it was as though she were playing catch-up, smiling at something that had been said the last time she was here. She wasn't slow, far from it, she was simply operating in another dimension, thinking her thoughts and saving up whatever was said for an hour when she would be more receptive to it.

Women who slip time in this way find a direct route to my heart. Their slippage suits my desire to be expected by them before they know me, and then to be postponed by them once I am known. They deny me temporal reality in a way that excites and energises me. They bear the promise that I will at last be lost in them.

And, to be plainer about it, they solicit my pity. In the split second before I imagine being lost in them, I imagine doing them some good. Protecting them from I don't know what. Terrorists, the melting ice caps, cynicism, Marius, myself.

It's wrong of me to speak as though such women had trooped through my life. They had not. If I generalise from Marisa it's because I learned from her, in the very first moment I saw her, what I had all along been looking for in woman, or, to put it another way, I no sooner saw her than I saw my fate.

What was it that I saw? A grey light in her eyes. Not ruthlessness exactly, but a sort of surety born of seriousness. She smiled, she laughed, she looked elsewhere and wasn't with us, but no one could have given less the impression of frivolity. Was she a puritan? I believed she was, and only puritans are worth bothering with sexually, for there is no eroticism where there is not a grave weighing of consequences.

I had been aware, also, when I gave her my hand, that she had taken it as though it were hers by right to possess. There was nothing remotely forward or flirtatious about this, nothing of what my father used to call the 'old whore's claw'. It simply appeared natural to her to accept what was on offer and hold on to it for as long and with as much sense of proprietorship as she chose. Whatever mine she touched hereafter, would be hers. I sat there, watching her, enumerating my losses.

'The way a man takes off his jacket tells you all you need to know about him,' my grandmother used to say. 'If you can't do it with confidence, keep it on.' When Marisa took off her jacket – beautifully tailored it was, single-buttoned with wide revers and a peplum that graced her hips – she told me all I needed to know about *myself*. I was gone. In fact a waiter helped her out of it, a test of confidence in itself, but she responded to his movements – leaning into him and then shaking herself free – as though men had helped her out of jackets all her life. Under the jacket she wore a filmy, lovesick satin shirt that seemed more to haunt her body than to clothe it. No cleavage. She was not, as I was to discover, a cleavage type. She owned nothing low-cut. There is always something desperate about women who want you to look down into their breasts. Marisa carried hers with a full-on assurance, knowing that the beauty of her chest was frontal not abysmal, a matter of the harmonious interrelation of thorax and abdomen, of arms and back and shoulders, not the mere shape and protuberance of her mammaries. I stress this because I have never been particularly moved by breasts as discrete objects, to be enjoyed independently of the woman to whom they belong. It was the way Marisa carried her chest as a sort of introduction or frontispiece to herself – at once soft and sculpted, the breasts themselves not large, though the general effect luxurious – that moved me. At the moment of her sitting down, anyway, I had to look away. It was that or go blind. Whether that was why she laughed I couldn't tell, but she was one of those women who know they must laugh at the disturbance of which their voluptuousness is the cause. And hers was a rich contralto laugh, full of depths, like everything else about her somehow material and evanescent all at once, evoking the laughter of summers long gone or summers yet to be.

Of her husband Freddy – a successful media musicologist who advised radio listeners on their record collections and popped up on television as well on account of the lightness with which he wore his learning and the frenetic way he moved his hands, a man who made too much conversation and tore his food before he ate it – she was absently tolerant, sometimes remembering to brush crumbs off his lap, or to wipe cream from his face, but always with the back of her hand, and without looking at him, in the manner of a mother busy with too many children. Of me, her husband's bookseller, she took no apparent notice, whatever her treatment of my offered hand (as though it were hers to shake or sever) portended . . . Saving me for another day.

Whether the clandestine appointment she made boldly with me some months later really was about buying her husband a birthday gift of

Berlioz's *Treatise on Modern Instrumentation and Orchestration* in as beautiful an edition as I could find, or whether it was me she wanted to see, I never asked, even after we married. We were to exchange many confidences that were obscene by the usual marital standards, and it's true that I subjected her to interrogations for which many a person would have said I deserved to burn in hell, but we were never gross in the intrusive sense. That's to say she always led me away from intrusion when intrusion threatened the secrecy necessary to a successful union.

I begrudged Freddy his Berlioz, whatever Marisa's motives in buying it for him. Not the book itself but the circumstances of her giving it – the fact of her putting her mind to what would best please him, her conscientiousness in seeking my advice on the matter, her not caring how much it would cost, and her meaning to present it, as she told me, at a dinner in Freddy's favourite Roman restaurant to which she was secretly flying out their closest friends. This was a wife with a grand sense of marital ceremony, who meant well by her husband, who followed his passions and cared about his happiness, even if she did have half an eye on another man. Principled, I called that, and only women of principle have ever aroused me.

Man for man – setting aside his modest media fame – there was not a great deal to choose between us, Marisa's then husband and me. I had more money, he had a more demonstrative presence; I was better-looking, he had a more powerful build, but neither of us was what you'd call a Byron. What I believe swung it my way was talk. I've said that Freddy was a conversationalist, but a conversationalist will often leave a woman lonely. Marisa wanted to converse, not be conversation's recipient. And I was all talk of the sort she needed. Talk that was dramatic, observational and of the moment, talk that was amusing but more importantly amusable, talk that was fed by talk, talk that was listening to talk. I am said to be womanly in this regard, though I confess to not quite knowing what that means.

Oceanic, perhaps. Not rigidly structured. Amniotic. I liked starting without knowing where I was going to finish or be led, I liked letting the current of talk carry me along, wishing neither to deliver a lecture to any woman fortunate enough to find herself ensconced with me (as Freddy always did), nor to curtail her in a flight of her own because I had more pressing matters to attend to (as Freddy always had). I made myself an agreeable but above all an available companion. On days when we'd made no arrangement to meet, Marisa always knew she could ring me up and ask me to accompany her to a gallery opening, to the theatre, to a concert, or to dinner. It helped that we were near neighbours, both residents of Marylebone. Everything we needed for a life of civilised, incipient adultery was there for us to extend a dainty pair of fingers and pluck without appearing obvious or greedy. We looked at art a lot, but we ate out even more. Food was our milieu, restaurants more the medium of our courtship than hotel bedrooms. Marisa's favourite restaurant – the one to which Marius would one day win the right to take her, the scene of their first kiss (hear the deranging sibilants in it: *first kiss*) – was *my* favourite restaurant first. It was part of my appeal – how many more restaurants I knew than she and Freddy did, and how many more restaurants knew me. I must have appeared sybaritic to her: a man wholly given over to the three great sedentary pleasures – reading, eating, talking. And women like men who sit still for them.

But Marisa also liked men who would, at other hours, dance with her. I was reluctant at first. Not because I couldn't dance but because dancing was an activity I associated with my mother and my aunts and never remembered I enjoyed until I did it. It was her telling me that Freddy had never danced with her that changed my mind. Whatever Freddy wasn't, I was. Whatever Freddy didn't, I did. And the dancing school, incongruously housed in the vaults of a grey steepled Victorian church, was virtually on my doorstep. When Marisa rang me out of the blue and asked me, even in the middle of a working day, whether I was free to dance, I could be quickstepping with her in under twenty minutes. Sometimes she would already be there when I arrived, in the arms of one of those apache dancers she could conjure up out of a room of cleanly shaven bank clerks. Then I would sit – a more than willing wallflower – on one of the plastic chairs arrayed on one side of the room, among the discarded anoraks and day shoes, and let the man and the movement claim her.

If she left her body when she danced, I left mine just watching her. She wasn't like the many careworn Japanese dancers who attended the school, precise and anxious in their foot movements, as though dancing was something the body had to learn from scratch and happened only in an area between the ankle and the toes, at the behest entirely of the brain, but nor was she one of those Corybantes who thrash their hair about and wave their hands. Hers was a much more measured frenzy – concentrated, never not aware, as though the mind she was escaping from was always in the room waiting to escort her home again. So that in the end this state of possession was a sort of defiance – of herself not least. And, I liked to think, of me. She would close her eyes and let her head fall back – and I'd be gone from it.

On summer evenings I allowed her to seduce me into gentler exercise. We walked in Regent's Park – a home from home for both of us – not hand in hand, not like lovers but like old friends with catching up to do. We sat on benches and watched the ducks, we identified flowers, we got to know the men who fed the birds, the Sikh with his black bin liner filled with crumbs, the squirrel man who held his hands out like a scarecrow, showing the squirrels the nuts he'd brought for them and for which, with only the quickest nervy look around them, they ran up him as though he were a tree. We observed other couples with tenderness as though we were past all that and fondly recalled ourselves in them. Sometimes I contrived to walk behind her – pausing to tie up a shoelace or throw litter in a bin – so that I could admire the strength of her legs and have a moment to myself to swoon over her. But openly I made no show of what I felt and did not press myself upon her.

This role of friend to Marisa was one I found pleasurable – for Marisa was herself a vivacious talker once unloosed – long before *we* kissed, and regardless of what would come of it. Indeed, had Marisa offered the two men in her life the compromise of continuing to lie with the one so long as she was permitted to talk to the other, I for my part would have accepted it. Was I not, after all, destined to accept a much poorer bargain on the face of it when it came to Marius, a man with whom Marisa would both lie *and* talk?

But Freddy was not framed as I am framed. Though the mere thought of eating out alone with his wife, discussing the nothing very much of their domestic life (and no third party to appreciate the vivacity of his talk), made him apoplectic, the thought of another man discussing anything with her made him more apoplectic still. You can hurt some men, it seems, by stealing from them what they are not aware they want.

He visited me in the shop when he found out what had been going on, shouting, even before I'd come out of my office, 'So these are the thanks I get.' Most angry husbands would not have remembered their grammar. 'This is the thanks' is the usual locution. But Freddy was as punctilious in his usage as I am, and indeed as Marius would be, which must say something about Marisa's preference for precise men.

'I'm not sure,' I said, 'what it is I owe you thanks for.'

'For my wife for one thing.'

'You haven't given me your wife.'

'You're damn right I haven't.'

'Then what are these thanks that you have come to collect?'

'I haven't come to collect anything. I've come to punch your nose.'

Hearing the commotion, my staff emerged in no great hurry from their cubicles. Had Freddy wanted to make a fight of it he'd have had them to contend with as well. Not a terrifying sight, four antiquarian booksellers in worn bookworm suits (ponytailed Andrew the most macho of the lot), and an easily upset secretary in an ankle chain – I will come to the ankle chain – but then Freddy wasn't a terrifying sight either. And I knew he would not make good on his threat to punch me on the nose. His hands were too important to him. Not because he feared particularly for his piano playing, which even he knew was execrable, but because he needed them in his profession as expressive television pundit.

'It's all right, go back to work,' I told my staff. To Freddy I said, 'We do no more than meet in restaurants some afternoons.'

Not quite true, but true enough.

He breathed through his nostrils at me, like a horse. I got the feeling that had I told him we no more than met at the Savoy and fornicated some evenings he'd have been less disgusted.

'I didn't ask,' he said, 'for you to meet my wife in restaurants some afternoons.'

'No, you didn't,' I conceded.

'And no judge is going to believe that story anyway.'

'No judge?'

'What — you think I'm not going to name you? You think I'm going to go for irreconcilable differences or whatever they call it now when I've got the evidence of her adultery staring me in the face?'

'We just talk, Freddy.'

Not quite true, but true enough.

'*Talk*. I've seen your *talk*. I've got photographs of your *talk*.'

'I doubt,' I said, 'that photographs of talk will cut much ice with a judge.'

A flippancy I regretted no sooner than I'd spoken it. But I've said that being the lover didn't suit me. It turned me into a person I neither recognised nor liked. A jeerer. I even felt differently inside my own skin, as though I inhabited myself lightly, I a man who had always understood himself as heavy.

The husband burned his eyes into me. He too, perhaps, was playing an unaccustomed role. He lit a cigarette and threw the dead match on the carpet. I bent to pick it up.

'We'll see then, shall we,' he said. 'We'll see what *cuts ice*, as you so elegantly put it. No doubt you are more familiar with the divorce courts

47

than I am. But my feeling, for what it's worth, is that what you mean by *talk* would get you a life sentence in some parts of the world.'

Which parts of the world was he referring to? Saudi Arabia? The Yemen?

'I'm sorry,' I said. 'I didn't think this would be a divorcing matter.'

'That's good of you. What would you have done *had* you thought it was a divorcing matter? Made shorter sentences?'

He was waving his arms about so violently I wondered if he might punch me, inadvertently, after all.

'I'm sorry,' I said.

'Nothing like as sorry as you will be. Rest assured, Quinn, I will take you for every penny you have.'

He made an operatic gesture with his hand, meaning, I supposed, say goodbye to all this: your shelves of modern first editions, your locked mahogany cupboards of illuminated bibles, your Berliozes, the pampered lifestyle which allows you to go out to restaurants some afternoons with other men's wives. I even thought I knew the tune. *Non più andrai, farfallone amoroso . . .*

I shrugged. What else could I do? I had no instinct for being the other man.

'And I'll be sending back every book I have ever bought from you, together with every book you seduced my wife into buying for me – buying for *me*, ha, there's a joke I'm glad I was not privy to – for which, for which I give you fair warning, Quinn, I expect to be reimbursed with interest.'

I inclined my head. Something told me that now was not the time to remind him that we operated, as Felix Quinn: Antiquarian Booksellers had always operated, a strict no sale or return policy.

He was done with me. Breathing hard, he ascended the stairs, but before he was at street level he turned to face me. I had seen him negotiate the identical pantomime swivel on television, before delivering one of his famously saltatory pieces to camera. He tossed down what was left of his cigarette. With one hand he made a gesture suggestive of the wildest largesse, casting his five fingers to the wind, with the other he made a sort of sucking sea creature with spidery tentacles, tugging obscenely at the viewer's attention.

'I have one more thing to say to you, Quinn,' he said. 'A woman who betrays one man will betray another. That is the immutable law of woman. So: you are welcome to her. Enjoy her. Take her to your bed. Wrap her in your arms and talk to her all you like. But never forget this: tomorrow she'll be in someone else's arms, drinking in his words, abandoning herself to his conversation exactly as she abandoned herself to yours. Words are cheap, Quinn. As you should know. As cheap as is a woman's love, which you should also know. That's my gift to you and, no, I expect no thanks for it: a woman whose loyalty you will never be sure of, not for a single fucking second of a single fucking minute of a single fucking hour . . .'

He got over it. That is the immutable law of man. The immutable law of that sort of man at least. He and Marisa were divorced without any judge having to look at photographs of the co-respondent discoursing with the wife, and shortly afterwards Freddy married his research assistant – a woman, if he was right in his assessment, of whose loyalty he would never be assured.

I envied him his uncertainty. Not because I lacked uncertainties of my own, but because I believed you could never have too many.

At the time Marisa and I were putting him through hell I envied him still more. For her part, Marisa didn't believe a word of his every single fucking second of every single fucking minute oration. But that, I think, was because Marisa didn't understand how minutely jealous even an indifferent man could be. I never doubted it. Whenever I escorted Marisa to the theatre or the opera I imagined Freddy imagining us in the dark. When we strolled together through the park I imagined him wondering how many of his friends saw us, what they thought, what conclusions about our intimacy they drew, how our togetherness on benches throwing breadcrumbs to the ducks reflected on him. Conversing with Marisa in a restaurant, I imagined him at a nearby table in disguise, still as a hare, watching, listening, inhaling, no grain of infidelity in a single syllable lost to any of his senses; or outside taking photographs to show the judge, proof tangible of that betrayal which talk in the abstract represented for him.

Remember, he had no sense of humour. And men with no sense of humour, who fear and loathe the intimacy which laughter brings because it is unknown to them, experience a jealousy beyond the range of men ordinarily amusable. Or at least – because I admit no rival in jealousy myself and I am, I hope, amusable – they are without the resources to convert it into an emotion from which they might garner consolation, even pleasure. You need wit to get the best out of being a cuckold. For Freddy, the thought or, worse, the spectacle of Marisa and me joking together must have been as scorpions in his brain.

The lucky devil! (Had he only known how to enjoy it.)

It might seem strange, my envying a man for what I put him through, but nothing that bears on sex should surprise us. And besides, what is envy of the sort I have described but imagination in the service of humanity? I placed myself where Freddy was because it pleased me to; not triumphantly but sympathetically. Is this not precisely the act of fellow feeling which the world's religions exhort us to perform? Art, too. We enter into the consciousness of someone not ourselves. As Mozart entered into the clownish jealousy of Masetto, as Shakespeare entered into the fastidiously witty jealousy of Leontes, as Tolstoy entered into the demented Beethoven-driven jealousy of Pozdnyshev. Had they not sought, at the moment of creating these tortured figures, to suffer what they suffered, these artists would not have made the consummate art they did. Of course envy is not the word for it in art. Just as art is rarely the word for it while we envy. But it felt like art, sitting there with my thumb and forefinger looped at last around Marisa's wrist, creating the turmoil of poor Freddy.

We married soon after the divorce. They came apart easily, Freddy and Marisa. So easily that it was difficult to see what they had been together for. 'He was good company when I first met him,' Marisa told me. 'And he knew the words of every song I liked.'

She sat quietly with me in a coffee shop on the morning before our wedding, running her hand through her coppery hair, going through his qualities. 'I admire him, actually. He has always persisted in what he's good at. And he did it for himself. I was born into advantage, of a sort, he wasn't. He had to create himself.' She raised her eyes to me, serious as always, 'I won't hear anything against him,' she said.

I nodded. I didn't feel I had to defend myself against an unjust accusation. It was clear what she was doing. She was putting one house in order before she moved on to the next. She could hold more than one loyalty in her head, she wanted me to understand. One nail did not drive out another.

I didn't ask too many questions. I'd peeled her relatively effortlessly from him, no matter that she admired him still, but was not so vain as to attribute my success to something overwhelmingly irresistible in me. Either she'd been unbearably lonely with him, in which case I would make it up to her; or she'd fallen into the habit of solacing herself elsewhere, in which case I wasn't yet ready to learn with whom. Whom other than me, that was.

I'd never previously married. Faith was not the last girl or woman to cause me to weep copious tears. But though the memory of their rejection stayed with me, the memory of them did not. Whether that meant I was a lukewarm lover after all, heated only by the pain they caused me, or I was simply holding myself in reserve for Marisa, I was unable to decide. But at least there were no feelings of earlier spouses or children of earlier unions to consider. The Marylebone villa which had been in my family for generations, witness to the unsuccessful marriages which my father and his father and his father before him had all made — unsuccessful because not a one of them had found a wife with an amused attitude to her husband's bringing home the clap — was now mine and waiting to be warmed back into life by the latest Mrs Quinn. 'Bring home the clap to me and neither you nor it will be left standing,' Marisa had said with a laugh when I'd filled her in on the house's history. Otherwise she seemed more than happy to move in.

It was, anyway, since Marylebone had always been her patch too, no more than a matter of packing up on one side of the road and unpacking again on the another. Everything she was used to was here, not only her conveniences but her obligations. Her hairdresser *and* the Oxfam book-shop which she worked in out of conscience. Her acupuncturist *and* the Samaritans to whom she devoted her Friday nights. The nail shop *and* the Wallace Collection to which she volunteered her services as a guide, when other guides to the collection fell ill. Even without me she had the wherewithal to pamper herself, and every time she did that she felt she had to make amends. Hairdresser to charity organisation, manicurist to beggar. Thus did she balance the scales of social justice. It was a good day for a seller of the *Big Issue* when he caught Marisa coming out of her favourite shoe shop. But then in my eyes it was a good day for anyone when he caught Marisa coming out of anywhere.

We solemnised our union quietly — what remained of both our fam-ilies being of no account to us — in a registry office round the corner and honeymooned in Florida. Why Florida? Because after more than a year of near-chaste talk we felt we owed each other the swamplands of sensu-ality. We wanted to smell the Everglades. We needed to run with sweat in each other's company.

Five days into our humid honeymoon Marisa fell ill. We had estab-lished a routine: every afternoon we returned to our hotel, I peeled her dress off her sticky body, then we showered the bad-egg odour of mangrove off each other, then we went to bed and stayed there until it was time for her to shake herself into something even more diaphanous for dinner. No woman I had ever known inhabited tropical fabrics better than Marisa; some women bulk them out, some disappear inside the folds, Marisa wore them as a second skin. Which made peeling her out of them a slow and laborious business, in the course of which I some-times had to sit on the edge of the bed to get a second wind and look at her, the dress over her head, still caught on her arms, her glistening thighs and belly unprotected from my stare. But on the fifth afternoon she was too feverishly weary for any of this conjugal horseplay. At first I took it to be merely one of those butterfly malaises to which she was subject. Lassitude. Loss of temporal bearing. Not unhappiness exactly, more a mislaying of happiness, as though she was happy in some other place but couldn't remember where. The fever, however, was real enough. And she wasn't sweating for my pleasure. The hotel called a doctor who examined her in our suite. He was a Cuban with an avaricious mouth, brown teeth the length of a horse's, and exaggerated good manners. I wondered if he wanted me to leave the room. He put an arm around my shoulders, noticing my concern. 'Stay,' he said. 'Pour yourself a drink. And pour me one while I see to Mrs.'

He had, I observed, the most beautiful long hands, with inordinate fringes of silky fur on every knuckle, and a wedding ring on both his little fingers. I poured us a drink then sat myself down in an armchair and watched as he took Marisa's temperature, shone a light into her ears, looked deep into her open mouth, felt under her armpits and examined her chest. The moment was decisive. Not the beginning of a new sensation but a revelation of it in its entirety, like coming out of a dark room and being met by the brilliant orb of the sun. Whoever I had been before – whatever luxuriating oddities had marked me out from other men in the matter of love and loss (and I had only ever felt marginally odd, just a trifle too given to losing my heart and ending up at the suffering end of passion) – all equivocations were finally at an end: I was now someone who was aroused by the sight of another man's hands on the breasts of the woman he loved. Henceforth, given the choice, I would rather Marisa gave her breasts to a man who wasn't me. That was to be the condition, the measure, of my love for her. At a stroke I was freed from the fascination of Freddy's jealousy. I was now liberated into my own.

You know it when you walk into the torture garden of your own disordered nature. You recognise the gorgeous foliage, overgrown and fantastical. You know the smell. The smell of home.

'Overexposure to the sun,' the doctor told me, looking round but keeping longer than was necessary I thought, his hand on my bride's breast, allowing the nipple to swell unseen inside his palm.

Did he exchange a glance with me, in which the proprietorship of those breasts passed briefly from me to him, or did I imagine it? I am not blind to the politics of a woman's breasts; I knew then, as I know now, that Marisa's breasts were the property of Marisa and no one else. But familiarity confers the illusion of possession, however impertinent, and it might have been the rights to that familiarity that we exchanged. The sight of those silken-furred fingers on Marisa's breasts precipitated in me, anyway, the desire to see them elsewhere on and, yes, *in* her body. A generalised desire which, over time, took on a less opportunistic, more sophisticated colouration. Marisa did not have to be feverish or otherwise at the mercy of a man. We did not have to be in Florida smelling the Everglades. And at last I did not have to see with my own eyes. Hearing about it, learning about it, and ultimately simply *knowing* about it, would be enough.

ON TOP OF THE TWO AFTERNOONS A WEEK SHE GAVE TO PRICING ART BOOKS at the Oxfam bookshop, the four Friday nights out of five on which she manned a hectic phone line for the Samaritans, the occasional day she put in at the Wallace Collection, not quite telling visiting ladies from the provinces what she thought Fragonard was really painting, Marisa read to a blind man once a fortnight and four times a year bundled up the clothes she no longer wanted to wear and gave them to a local hospice. Though she believed she was good at what she did – twice, for example, she had found books which had gone on to fetch in excess of £1,000 at auction at Christie's; the blind man, she felt sure, was enraptured by her reading; art lovers thanked her for showing them what they could never have seen without her; and God only knew how many deep depressions she lightened at the slit-wrist end of a Friday night – she was unable to recognise herself in these activities. She didn't begrudge the time (how could she, given the amount of time at her disposal), nor did she resent the neediness of those she helped (in their need, she believed, she found her purpose). But she wasn't personally engaged in what she did. The only time Marisa felt she was anyone she knew was when she danced. 'You say you find yourself dancing,' I told her once, 'but to me it looks more as though you lose yourself.' She smiled in recognition of the paradox. Outside herself was where she lived. Other than when she danced she was in some foreign place, speaking in a voice that wasn't hers, though where that foreign place was, and whose voice she borrowed, she couldn't have said.

'Where are you, Marisa?' – her mother calling.

'Hiding.'

'Marisa, you are always hiding.'

To which Marisa knew better than to say, even at that early age, 'That's because I'm trying not to be found by you, Mummy.'

Apart from the charity work she did – that's if it really was her who did it – and all the dancing she could crowd in, she was not what could be called a busy woman. Though well educated – well finished, might be a better way of putting it, but then I'm a snob when it comes to education – she had not, in her words, 'achieved anything'. No need. She had always been well provided for. Her father, who had owned most of the bed shops on Tottenham Court Road, walked out on her mother when Marisa was five years old. The child could perfectly well see why. Her mother lacked judgement. True, it was her father's fault for leaving her mother alone as much as he did, but that didn't excuse her mother for falling for every man she met and introducing all of them to Marisa as her new daddy.

'Why does Mummy love everybody?' she asked her father.

'She doesn't love me.'

'But she used to, didn't she?'

'Yes, and I used to love her for loving me. Then I realised she would have loved me no less had I been a cloth bag stuffed with marbles. Or with beans, like your frog Frenchie.'

So would her mummy have liked *her* just as much had she been stuffed with beans like her frog Frenchie, Marisa wondered, hiding in her wardrobe.

Hiding became at last their only medium of communication. To lure Marisa out of the wardrobe, her mother had to hide presents for her, hide her clothes, hide her supper. 'See if you can find what I've made you, Marisa.'

'What have you made me?'

'You'll have to find it to find out.'

'See if you can find me, Mummy,' Marisa said. The difference being that while she wanted to find supper, she didn't want her mummy to find her.

'I wish she'd hide my new daddies,' she told her old daddy, 'where they can't be found.'

She remembered the day her father left, she remembered him lifting her up on to his shoulders, she remembered looking down into his strong chestnut-polished baldness and seeing her own forlorn reflection in it, she remembered his words: 'Whatever she tells you, Daddy is leaving Mummy, whom he doesn't love or see the point of any more, not you, whom he does.' In proof of which, though she only infrequently spent time with him again (it had to be in secret, everything always in secret, because his new wife didn't like to be reminded that there'd been an old), he paid for her to go to a good school, to have singing and ballet lessons, to hide as far away from her mummy and her armies of new daddies as she could get, to drive her own car while she was at university, to rent a flat in Venice for a year after graduating, to enrol for every fine-art course that took her fancy in Florence, Spoleto, Siena, she had only to name it – to live, in short, the life she pleased.

She grew up secretive and well off. Looking good, always in expensive clothes, which were the grown-up version of being in hiding, keeping herself to herself – sometimes keeping herself *from* herself – with time on her hands.

Because of her looks she could not entirely and forever remain her own property. Boyfriends insisted themselves on her, each of whom she hid from the other, followed by first one and then – again initially in hiding – a second husband. She never thought of herself as adulterous. Simply close. It was no one's business but hers. One way or another, though, the indulgences she'd been used to from her father continued. For the reason that she looked spoiled already, you could not see Marisa and not want to spoil her more. Just as you could not be with her, even when you were perfectly entitled to be with her, and not feel you were stealing her from someone else. Sometimes in Marisa's company I could not escape the sensation that I was stealing her from myself.

And to commemorate that theft, I, like everyone else, showered her with gifts – perfume, jewellery, underwear, whatever you buy to perpetuate the illicit.

But always I sensed I had not found the gift that was adequate to her temperament. Grey beneath the eyes, with a long reflective countenance and a Roman nose such as you see on statues of Roman goddesses in Italian gardens, Marisa looked too sombre, however tight her skirts, for perfume or underwear. Wouldn't the collected dialogues of Plato have made a better present? I asked her once. Of course she said she wanted nothing. But the impression I formed was that the ideal gift for her was the dialogues of Plato *and* underwear.

Never the necessity to make provision for herself, there was the problem which no amount of social or community work could solve. Yes, she could have filled her days with the deeds her morality pressed her into doing; but that wouldn't have left her sufficient time to improve her own lot as a thinking being, and if she wasn't any good to herself then how could she be any good to other people?

She didn't complain, repine or moon, she just mused a lot. Which men, of course, find provocative. A woman musing on something other than them piques their *amour propre*. Especially predatory men who muse a lot themselves, with time to hang around outside art galleries and museums, singing tirra lirra and waiting for just such a woman to emerge, so that they can shatter the mirror of her concentration. But that's to anticipate Marius.

Men apart, they pay a high price for their own beauty and fortune, these women for whom self-improvement is a necessity, and achievement is a goad. Marisa would have gone further in any career she chose for herself had she looked less as though her clothes had been cut for her by a glove-maker, and had she not known how to please the absent daddy in any man. No bitterness intended. If anything, Marisa rather admired the way men could tell lies, take off whenever the fancy pleased them, or instal a woman like her in a fine villa in Marylebone, with every confidence that she would play the part of lady of the house to perfection. In her head, she lived as though she had been born a man herself. Whenever one of her half-sisters phoned her for advice (she had as many new sisters as she had new daddies) the advice she gave was always practical, forward-looking and iron-hearted

– 'Leave him, darling' or 'Go get him if you want him, just don't tell your husband' – much as she imagined a man would have given. She walked like a man. Her clothes, in particular her suits, were ironical references to what men wore for the City. Even when she showed her legs, which in all honesty were too good not to show, she showed them as a man – say a fencing master or a *danseur noble* – might, as evidence of her suppleness and strength. She followed her fancy, drank hard, declined motherhood with fervour, doted on no man, and wasn't averse to being looked over in the street. Only in actuality was she kept as more feminine, less ambitious women had been kept for centuries. Though even 'in actuality' things weren't actually as they seemed. Contrary to what the great man said, all happy families are not alike.

THOUGH I SAY THEY WERE REVELATORY, I WAS NOT A COMPLETE STRANGER to the emotions which overcame me in the hotel room in Florida. At least I was not a stranger to the fact of their existence in the human heart.

In my sixteenth year I was befriended by an associate of my father's, Victor Gowan, a once successful publisher who, in the brief period I knew him, moved from a lightless, noisily ramshackle office opposite the British Museum to a silent house with a great glass window overlooking the Thames in Cookham – Stanley Spencer country. The move felt like a retirement to me, though whether Victor saw it that way I didn't know. But he couldn't have been more than fifty at the time of his migration, and when I saw him in his offices he was voluble and merry, and when I saw him in Cookham he was introspective and sad.

Looking at a river all day can do that to you, of course, but I didn't think the river was the cause of it. Some misfortune that wasn't talked about must have befallen him, anyway, because his association with my father began with the selling off of his library almost book by book. Not the books he published – we wouldn't have been much interested in those – but a rather fine collection of classical texts, both in the original Greek and Latin and in translation. It is, as I have said, a melancholy business for a person who loves books to have to sell them. Each book you part with is a little death. Which is why a shop like ours is necessarily a funereal place. We are to all intents and purposes undertakers. We wear black suits, tread softly and try to make the extinction of a lifelong passion, the passage of an old friend, as comfortable and dignified as possible.

In Victor's case my father recognised that solemn rites were not appropriate. Victor put a brave face on his losses and trusted it would be only a matter of time before he was in a position to buy back from us what he'd sold, a fantasy which my father considered it in our interests to foster. To that end – though I must not be too cynical, for I think there was genuine friendship in it too – my father saw a lot of Victor, sometimes calling on him in his creaking Dickensian offices with me in tow, and later, after Victor's melancholy move, inviting him to have dinner with us when he was in town. It was in the course of one of those dinners that Victor suggested I visit him in Cookham.

Classics were the pretext. He had studied classics at Balliol in his youth, and there was talk that I would do the same. It was presented as being for my future benefit, anyway, that I should spend a weekend with him in the country, see his library of which much remained, dine with him in the evening, talk literature, perhaps go rowing, and meet his wife, a one-time beauty and biographer of the Fitzrovia set, rumoured in her younger days to have been the mistress of more than one Fitzrovian scoundrel, but now, sadly, confined to her bed. Though too infirm to enter society or to engage in those researches necessary to her profession, Joyce Gowan still loved having visitors to her home.

I won't pretend that I viewed the prospect of a weekend with my father's disconsolate associate and his sick wife with any pleasure. At sixteen you don't want to be close to people whose hopes have all but ended. But though I couldn't picture anything that wasn't dismal happening when I got there, the act of going felt like an adventure. I packed a bag, remembering to take a blazer and a tie for dinner and summer flannels for rowing, caught the train from Paddington to Maidenhead, and extended my hand like a seasoned traveller when Victor came along the platform to meet me. In a flash I saw my future, travelling on trains from one end of the country to another, getting off at rural stations, extending my hand to downcast book-collecting men who were getting on in years and reduced to selling what was precious to them. Already, though I hadn't met them all, I felt a bond with them. Men whose feelings of loss were etched into their faces.

In the car to Cookham Victor told me about Stanley Spencer, the presiding genius of the place, who was famous for some wonderful murals, in Victor's view, showing local people rising from the dead, and also for a small number of shockingly fleshly paintings of himself and a woman called Patricia Preece with whom he had been wildly in love, though it was thought his relations with her were never consummated, if I understood his meaning. Wanting to show I understood his meaning perfectly, I wondered whether it could have been the fact of the non-consummation that rendered these paintings so shockingly fleshly. 'Frustration is the midwife to imagination,' I said, 'and having to give body to what is denied you is a powerful inducement to art,' though I might not have said it in quite those words. And even if I had I would only dimly have understood what I was talking about. Of the world of the passions I still knew nothing. I'd read a lot, that was all. And I'd gone out with the daughter of a cello teacher who threw me over for someone she met while I was holding her hand in the cinema. But like many boys my age, I bluffed well.

Victor, I remember, praised me for an astuteness beyond my years and couldn't imagine how I wouldn't sail into Balliol. (As, indeed, though it isn't strictly relevant to this narrative, I did.)

Thereafter I caught him looking at me sideways on many occasions, as though not sure he'd done the right thing inviting me. Alternatively he was thinking he'd done exactly the right thing inviting me.

When he wasn't looking sideways at me, I was looking sideways at him. He had a grand profile that appeared unrelated to his body, which was almost dainty. Only his head seemed to matter. But it was run spectacularly to seed, pouches under his eyes, hair growing in bunches from his ears and nostrils, the veins in his red cheeks broken as though from exposure to country life, the back of his neck beginning to pleat over his shirt collar. For reasons I couldn't then and cannot now explain I hoped I would grow to look like that myself. A little tired of the world. A little weary with the effort of carrying around so large a head. And with a secret sorrow that was also an inexplicable cause of satisfaction.

I didn't meet Mrs Gowan on my first evening in Cookham. She wanted to say hello, Victor explained, but wasn't up to seeing me. The house was quiet with the quiet of a woman who wasn't up to seeing anybody. Everything was put away and tidy, the curtains closed in a way that suggested it was a long time since they'd been opened, a faint covering of dust on the furniture, none too fresh flowers in the vases, an air of distraught disuse pervading everything.

But in another sense Joyce Gowan was ubiquitously present. There were photographs of her everywhere – Joyce as a little girl laughing with other little girls, even then lovely to look at, dark, intense and knowing; Joyce masterfully leading her pony; Joyce as a young woman in a London pub, surrounded by poets, with her lipstick smudged; Joyce in the act of becoming Mrs Gowan, sculpted into her bride's dress, throwing back her head, her throat long like a swan's; Joyce the biographer of wild times signing one of her books at Foyles, dazzling the signee with the brilliance of her smile . . . Joyce, Joyce, Joyce. In the living room a grand society painting of her in her glory days, her hands, one of which held a black fan, crossed in her lap and a faraway expression in her eyes. On the stairs a cruder oil showing her in a plunging evening gown, her breasts more rouged than any serious painter would have made them, a dog too obviously representing male besottedness at her feet. And in the bathroom assigned to me a frolicking sepia nude dancing with curtain drapes, by Russell Flint: not definitely her, so stylised was the pin-up, and so unlike her, given how else she had permitted artists to represent her – but if it wasn't her why was it there? And if it was her, why was I permitted to see it?

For the sake of her beauty, maybe, and nothing else. For the sake of the beauty she had been.

Victor took me to a pub for chicken in a basket and asked me questions about myself, about my closeness to my father, about the books I liked to read. He was reading *Don Quixote* for the umpteenth time and wondered if I knew it. I told him I'd started it umpteen times but could only get so far before I had to give up. It was when the novel departed from its own narrative to relate stories that were strictly speaking extraneous to it that I lost interest. 'Like the story of Anselmo and Lothario,' he said. I told him I didn't think I had got as far as Anselmo and Lothario. 'Ah,' he said. 'Then you should.'

The following morning we went rowing on the river as he'd promised, though we never strayed far from the riverbank. Then we had lunch in another pub, went to see one or two of Stanley Spencer's paintings – though nothing that struck me as either shocking or fleshly – in the little village museum devoted to his work, and returned home for tea. Because the weather was fine we were able to sit out on the lawn and watch more able-bodied rowers power up and down the Thames. A gentle wind blew through the trees. A succession of creamy, calming clouds floated across the sky. Again, Mrs Gowan was too indisposed to join us.

At around about four o'clock my host nodded off in his chair. On the grass by him lay a copy of *Don Quixote*, which he'd presumably brought out so that he could read an extract from the story of Anselmo and Lothario aloud to me. While he slept I leafed through the novel to see if I could find their names, which proved not to be too difficult as many of the scenes in which they appeared were marked. Their adventure, if it could be so called, appeared to be another version of a plot in a Shakespeare play I'd read at school – one man inviting another to try the fidelity of the woman he loved, to tragic or near-tragic effect. According to the notes in my Arden Shakespeare, the 'fidelity test' was a recurring motif in medieval Italian novellas, from which Cervantes too must have borrowed. I was too young to know anything for sure, but something told me that a fidelity test was more likely to be a literary device than a strategy much resorted to in real life. But it could only have cropped up frequently in literature if it answered to something that gave real men cause for concern: namely, the character of their wives when subjected to overwhelming temptation, for where, as Anselmo says to Lothario, is the merit in her being virtuous 'when nobody persuades her to be otherwise? What mighty matter if she be reserved and cautious, who has no opportunity given her of going astray?' A fear which once acted upon, it occurred to me, must surely stimulate a curiosity that is never to be assuaged. Why should Anselmo stop with a Lothario no matter how true this Lothario proves his wife to be? Indeed it would be illogical to do so. For is there not always to be encountered a Lothario more persuasive than the last? Will there not always be an 'opportunity' for disloyalty greater than the one before?

Victor awoke as I was turning the pages. 'Ah,' he said, when he saw which pages those were.

Joyce Gowan never did descend from her room. On my final evening in the house, after just the two of us had eaten a cold dinner at his kitchen table, Victor suggested I accompany him upstairs to take his wife a nightcap. A terror immediately seized my heart. Was I to play the part of Lothario to his Anselmo? Was this all the weekend had ever been about, a preparation to my trying the virtue of a sick old lady by making love to her? Was my father himself a party to the scheme? I wouldn't have put it past him. He was of that class of men who sought to further their sons' worldly education by taking them to brothels and ensuring they got their first dose of syphilis where it could be treated by a London doctor, rather than in Abu Dhabi where the medical attention was patchy, though I have to say he hadn't yet gone that far with me. I could even have been part of a business deal between the two men, Victor reclaiming a number of his books in return for his wife, or my father laying hands on the rest of Victor's library in return for me. It all depended on how you calculated the favour.

I say a terror seized my heart, but desire was not unmixed with it. The two are rarely separable in me. When I thought of the invalid in her bed and what she or her husband or indeed my father might have been expecting of me, I felt giddy with apprehension and disgust; but when I remembered the Russell Flint nude doing a striptease with curtain drapes, the rouged breasts on the society oil painting, and the smudged lipstick in the photograph of Joyce carousing with literary men and painters with loose morals in Fitzrovia, I felt giddy with longing. I was still a virgin. Whatever was about to happen to me had not happened before. Whatever I had to do, I did not know if I could.

I followed Victor up the stairs. He was a carrying a tray with a bottle of port and three glasses on it. Joyce Gowan's bedroom door was closed. Her husband paused, put an ear to it, then pushed. The room was in semi-darkness, just one small bulb burning, not by her bedside but in a far corner of the room. I thought I could smell medication, but it was possible I'd brought the smell up with me, indistinguishable from my apprehension.

'I'm not sure,' Victor said in a whisper, 'whether she's awake.'

I stood half in the bedroom, half on the landing. In the dark I could make out only shadows, the shape of a window through which were thrown a couple of fine diagonal bars of citrus light from the garden, the outline of a chair, the immanence of the bed but not its occupant.

'You can come in,' Victor said, again in a whisper.

But I barely had the courage to proceed. I'd been brought up to respect the privacy of a woman's room. I must have seen my mother in her bed when I was an infant, but I'd never seen her in her bedroom let alone her bed thereafter, except to see her die. My father, I suspect, was kept out of there as well. A woman's bedroom was a revered and frightening place to me. I didn't know what happened there, other than that it was where women wept. And this wasn't a boudoir consecrated to a healthy if embittered woman's mysteries, it was a chamber of sickness and decay. God knows what I would walk into and knock over in my fear if I did as Victor suggested. I hovered at the threshold.

Suddenly, there was more light. 'There,' Victor said.

Not brilliant light but light enough to make out more than just the bulking outline of the bed, and then yes, yes, to discern Joyce Gowan herself, still asleep on it, or apparently asleep, but not hidden by the bedclothes, indeed not hidden by anything, but disposed as a painter such as Russell Flint might have disposed her, for the titillation of the buyer, not quite on her back but not quite on her side either, her nightgown rucked up as though by an accident of sleep to reveal the undulation of her thighs and buttocks – silvery and slender in the half-light – and fallen off her shoulders by the same careful disarrangement of accidentality to show the spillage of her breasts, in profile only, not with that startlingly grand fullness and frontality celebrated in the oil painting on the stairs, or with the same attention to the rouge (unless the pallor was just an effect of the lighting), but the more tremblingly desirable, it seemed to me, for being a gentle intimation rather than a bold assertion of themselves.

Whether her pose was artful or artless, Mrs Gowan would have found a path to any man's heart, let alone a frightened boy's. It was impossible not to imagine what it would be like turning her over and gathering her into your arms. Was that because her limbs were truly slender, or because they were wasted? Was it because she had retained her beauty even in her illness, or because, with the help of careful lighting, the illness itself was beautiful? I didn't know. How could I know? I was too young to know.

'If you come closer,' Victor said, but I could not.

I wanted to look but I could not. All thoughts of what would follow, or what *should* follow, fled my mind. There was no right or wrong of what came next because there could be no next. This was wrong enough. Whoever was its instigator – and I didn't exclude myself from blame, for desire is instigation too – this was an unpardonable abuse of a woman's helplessness. She was an invalid. A man's rapacious eye will take every kind of liberty with a woman's body and permit no actual or moral obstacle to be a hindrance to his seeing, but Joyce Gowan's sickness was a hindrance I could not overcome. Never mind that you would never have known from the lovely shape of her that she was ill. Never mind that her being desirable in despite of that illness made her if anything more desirable still. And never mind that she was a woman who had been admired for her beauty all her life and perhaps wanted to go on being admired whatever her age and health. Enough had passed between us for me to be sure it had been Victor's idea to get me up here, not his wife's; that it was he who, in an act of desperate love, sought to exhibit her one more time to someone who could never have beheld such beauty before; and that, no matter whether she had willingly gone along with him in this, *his* will – his need, the rather – had been the stronger. But it didn't matter for whom I had been brought here. For myself I wanted to look, but I did not. Desire dissolved in sadness.

'I will go downstairs now,' I said to Victor.

A few days after my return to London I received a package from Victor with an accompanying letter of explanation and apology. 'I cannot imagine what you must think of me,' he wrote, though the fact of this apology proved he could imagine it only too well. 'I plead – but what right have I to plead anything. I did not mean unkindly by you. I realise now how alarmed by the Cervantes story you must have been. Trust me, I had no such errand as Lothario's in mind for you. Your youth would have persuaded me against such a course had I ever considered it, but I have never doubted Joyce and of course, tragically, can have no cause ever to doubt her now. I am unable to explain what prompted me to dredge that story up. If your answer is that I dredged it from my unconscious there is nothing I can say to you, since my unconscious is of necessity unknown to me. But I do beg you not to view my situation – for yes, I confess it to be a "situation" – in that sinister light. It is not in order to be forgiven, only to be understood, that I send you as a sort of corrective the enclosed. It is, I think, a truer account of the respects I bear to you and the love I feel for my dear wife.'

The 'enclosed' was a facsimile of the 1502 first printing of Herodotus' *The Histories* in the original Greek, bound in calfskin and bookmarked at the passage which tells of how Candaules, King of Lydia, a man disordered by the love he bears his wife, arranges for another man, Gyges – a well-regarded subordinate, but a subordinate all the same – to spy upon her nakedness. Outraged to discover this liberty taken with her person, the queen (to whom Herodotus never gives a name) offers Gyges a terrible

68

choice – either he pays with his life for what he has unlawfully seen, or he assassinates her husband and succeeds as King of Lydia in his place.

Not knowing the state of my Greek, Victor included a translation of this famous story, for all that he was sure, given my precocious cleverness, I had 'no need of it'. I say 'famous' but in truth the tale of Gyges and Candaules is well known only to classicists and to men of my strain for whom, despite the unfortunate ending, it enjoys the status of a sort of founding myth.

This much I can say about it today, but at the time I was out of my depth. I might have been a precocious turner of sentences but I had only briefly kissed one girl; to ask me to draw fine distinctions between degrees of wife-mongering was to ask too much. Now, of course, water having passed beneath the bridge, I get what Victor wanted me to understand: that there is a world of difference between the everyday torments a jealous husband suffers and that desire which is so overwhelming you have to share it. Love was at the bottom of it for both of them; but whereas Anselmo shrank into his own terrors under the alchemy of love, Candaules so could not contain the ardour of his desire that it spilled over into a thing it would not be fantastical to call philanthropy.

From the opening lines of Herodotus' narrative – and I quote from the popular translation by G. C. Macaulay which Victor sent me – Candaules appears uxorious beyond the common run of men.

> This Candaules then of whom I speak had become passionately in love with his own wife; and having become so, he deemed that his wife was fairer by far than all other women; and thus deeming . . .

. . . thus deeming, he contrives to have Gyges hide himself where he can see the queen disrobing for bed.

Is not the idea of a man *becoming* passionately in love with his wife intriguing? We must assume, else why would the opposite be remarked on, that husbands in the kingdom of Lydia neither married for love, nor found it after marriage. So this is a love story before it is anything else. First the rare and unexpected love which King Candaules bears his wife, then the conviction of her superlative beauty, then the wish to have it seen. To my mind an ineluctable progression.

Ask why King Candaules couldn't have been content with Gyges beholding the queen clothed and you enter into the unconditional nature of his passion.

'It was the completeness of my wife's beauty I fell for,' he will tell you from whichever circle of lovers' hell he inhabits. 'Not the colour of her eyes or the turn of her neck, but the sum total of her parts, the harmony of her, and that harmoniousness, you must surely see, can only be appreciated *naked*.'

Ask why he couldn't have been content to enjoy the totality of this beauty for himself alone and you touch upon the nature not only of romantic love, in one of its extreme forms, but of art as well.

'The instinct to share that which we find beautiful,' he will go on, 'lies deep within our natures. It is not only for ourselves, but for others to look at too, that we hang paintings we care for upon our walls. The man who hides his artworks in a vault is considered to have deprived the world of a pleasure, some would go so far as to say an entitlement. Though I would lose my kingdom and my life for it, I could not deny the world its entitlement.'

Before succumbing to Candaules' feverish persuasion, Gyges voiced the conventional man's objections. 'Master, when a woman puts off her tunic she puts off her modesty also.'

An observation seconded by Herodotus himself. 'For among the Lydians as also among most other Barbarians it is a shame even for a man to be seen naked.'

But a man as mad in love as Candaules was in love, a man who had committed the folly of falling in love with his own wife, who found her nakedness too beautiful for himself to gaze on all alone, such a man knows shame only to court it. The greater wrong it was for a Lydian woman to be seen naked, the greater the necessity for Candaules to bring that wrong about.

I don't condone it. I tremble before its imperatives as he must have done, that's all.

Though the story isn't officially over until the queen discovers what has happened and delivers Gyges her fearful ultimatum – kill him or die yourself – it's over for me the moment Gyges sees, as I imagine it, how right Candaules was to estimate his wife's beauty so highly. For those who like a moral, the moral is on the side of modesty. But for me it is not a cautionary fable about impudicity. For me it is a tragedy. What *is* a husband to do when his wife's beauty is such that he cannot find enough ways of honouring it?

None of this, as I have said, meant anything to me when I was sixteen. Yes, Faith had sought the kisses of another boy, and I could still taste something scalding sweet sluicing through my stomach when I remembered it, but I made no connections. I read the story Victor had marked for me, saw it as an attempt to put a classical gloss on lewd and dishonourable behaviour, blushed a few more times for my own close shave with shame, and thought no more about it. But that doesn't mean it was not all the time quietly eating at my soul, preparing me, without my knowledge, for Marisa.

Had I known what its effects would be I would have thanked Victor in person.

Not that those thanks would ever have reached him. About two months after my visit a fire consumed the house in Cookham. Neither Victor nor Joyce Gowan survived it. The fire took everything – the people, the photographs, the paintings, and all that had been left of Victor's library.

THIS IS NOT, IN THE CONVENTIONAL SENSE AT LEAST, A FAMILY STORY. IF anything it is an anti-family story, the whole point of me, I have come to understand, being the example I set of how a man might win freedom from the evolutionary imperative. Never mind, I say, what happens to your seed. Let others overleap yours with their own if their biology dictates it. My seed is going nowhere. This is how I answer Marius who thought mankind was finished. Behold in me the promise of a brave new humanity, heroically careless of selection or extinction, come out of Darwin's swamp at last.

So how does this heroic new humanity continue?

Questions, questions. It isn't only the cuckold who's forever wanting an answer to the question what happens next.

We stand on midgets' shoulders – that's how we prosper. We continue because we are parasitic on life's common seed-bearers. And 'Your parasite,' as Mosca, parasite of *Volpone* exults, 'Is a most precious thing, dropped from above, / Not bred 'mongst clods and clodpolls here on earth.'

Similarly your cuckold: callous, vain, as slippery as an eel, but a most precious thing. An example to future men, for the very reason that no future can proceed from us. We burn up like the phoenix. What's bad in us, dies with us. We have no followers and belong to no sects. And we are fools to no belief systems, unless a wife is a belief system.

But I come from family even if I won't be having one of my own, and I don't think I compromise my exemplary refusal of evolution by saying a little more about the family firm of which I am the sole director. Though my father opposed my taking over the business, crediting me with no aptitude for any line of work other than 'weeping into pillows', my uncles honoured me with a trust I went out of my way to justify, even long after they'd died and my father was declined into a life of weeping into pillows and otherwise wetting beds himself, playing canasta in an old persons' home from morning to night with elderly ladies who sat with their legs apart, on which account he made them promises he could not keep.

We have been selling antiquarian and rare books for more than a century and a half, never once moving from the same discreet premises, barely noticeable to the naked eye and closed to you unless you have an appointment, in a quiet square to the north-west of Wigmore Street. People with an appointment look to the right and the left of them when they enter and do the same again when they leave, like men afraid of being caught loitering in the vicinity of a brothel. This is how we like our clients to feel. We encourage an atmosphere of underhandedness and dubious intent, no matter that the great majority of the thousands of books which pass through our hands are works of the utmost probity.

I grew up among old books and feel in sympathy with them. In particular I enjoy the buying of them, an activity which has taken me – exactly as I foretold it would the day Victor collected me from Maidenhead – to the most picturesque parts of the country and acquainted me with human nature in some of its sweetest and most melancholy aspects.

The selling I leave mainly to my employees. These days technology looks after most of it. But buying libraries is a business of the senses as well as the intelligence. You can smell the quality of a collection in advance of perusing it, as you can smell what you are going to get from a lover before the kissing starts. Sex inheres in everything, in books and their histories no less than in humans – at times more than in humans. Do we not, on a bus or a train, see people turning the pages of a book with a sensual expectation that reminds us of nothing so much as the act of undressing another person? And where the book is consecrated by age and experience, the turning of those pages is rendered the more delicious by the thought of the number of fingers which have been there before you. This, I grant, is not everyone's taste. Some prefer that odour of brand-newness which comes off paper covers, as some prefer an unperforated virgin. We are all sick in our own way.

No doubt I inherited this fascination with promiscuous prior owner-ship from my disreputable father and his no less disreputable brothers. Until me, however, no member of the family had taken that conception of the erotic to its natural conclusion. Only I have turned out to be a true voluptuary of the second-hand.

Which, among other things, means I am sensitive to a similar volup-tuousness in others. I don't push anyone into selling, even if I've travelled far to buy. Few of those who decide they must part with their books genuinely wish to do so. Easier, for some of them, to part with their wives. The elderly and long-retired professor without whose funeral I'd never have met Marius was a case in point. He was pacing up and down the drive when I came in answer to his summons, made distraught by the idea that I'd be arriving in a pantechnicon at the appointed hour and begin loading immediately. Seeing me turn up in a bumpy taxi from the railway station and discovering I was going to do no more than look at what he had, calmed his agitation considerably.

'Oh,' he said. A high piping sound such as a mouse might make when you tread on it. 'Then I don't have to hide things from you after all.'

He made me tea with shaking hands, an old scholarly fusspot aban-doned to his books and bookish thoughts by a wife who, as he explained it, had been unable to bear their musty smell. 'Or mine,' he laughed, the laughter rattling his chest.

I liked him. I liked his long bent silhouette, his boniness, and the fact of his wearing a tie knotted he didn't care where, so that the narrow end was twice the length of the broad. In my business I meet a lot of men who knot their ties this way, a coincidence I ascribe to the loneliness of book collecting.

I have a soft spot for abandoned men. I enter into their feelings. Perhaps because I've always feared that one day I'll be an abandoned man myself.

And yes – since we are entertaining perhapses – perhaps because I hope to be one too. Left to sob out the rest of my days, while the woman I love . . .

There are more unfathomable desires.

After tea there ensued a terrible passage in which, emboldened by the lack of anything like rapaciousness in me, he began removing what he thought to be priceless editions from a cupboard underneath his stairs, George MacDonalds, Christina Rossettis, 'Monk' Lewises, each ceremented in ancient newsprint, only to discover that the Shropshire damp had got to them long ago, as it had got to him, and turned their brilliant pages into compost.

'Oh,' he said, his voice more piping than the first time, as though I'd trodden on him again. 'Then you won't be wanting these.'

But there was relief for him even in a disappointment as sharp as this. He laughed an old man's dry and bony laugh. I wouldn't be taking his books because his books weren't worth taking.

I clasped his arm. I was happy to be travelling back to London empty-handed.

He sent me the occasional greeting card after this, expressing guilt and gratitude, out of which motives he bought a few things from our catalogue – the odd George MacDonald, Christina Rossetti, 'Monk' Lewis. After his death, his executors arranged for us to purchase the little of his library that was of value, which happened to be the very books he'd bought only recently from us. Time's whirligig and all that. But it wasn't for business reasons that I attended his funeral. Sometimes the heart must lead you. And mine led me to Marius. So you could say I hadn't travelled back to London empty-handed after all.

I was careful not to discuss the Cuban doctor with Marisa on her recovery. It's possible she remembered nothing of her illness or his visit and would not even have known who I was talking about. We flew home from Florida as soon as Marisa was strong enough to travel and took an immediate second honeymoon in Suffolk. After the swamplands we felt the urge to be somewhere chillier and more bracing. I am not one who subscribes to the hot and cold shower theory of marriage, but we needed to clear our heads.

In the event, I didn't succeed in clearing mine. Today I'm at peace with the knowledge that I never will, that it cannot ever be quiet or uncrowded in there, but at the time the mental congestion I suffered whenever I embraced my wife alarmed me. I am a moralist in the matter of intercourse. You sleep with whom you're sleeping with, I've always believed. It isn't necessary that you love every woman you invite to share your bed, but you must do each of them the honour, at least while you're inside them, of thinking of no one else. If another woman's face rises up before you, you withdraw and make your apologies. But my morality floundered when the face which rose up before me was not another woman's but another man's – not someone I wanted to kiss more than I wanted to kiss Marisa, but someone I wanted Marisa to kiss more than I wanted her to kiss me.

I opposed the presence of this phantom with all my will. He made himself known to me initially on that second honeymoon, indeed on the very first occasion of our making love in Suffolk on an iron bedstead from which we could see – or should have seen had another not intruded – the vast greyness of the sea. I took long walks in the morning, sometimes before Marisa had so much as stirred, convinced that the wind which could make such startling transformations to the Suffolk sky would blow away my unwanted guest. But the moment I returned and moved my face close to Marisa's, there he was again, the Cuban doctor with his long brown horse's teeth. No matter how tightly I pressed Marisa to me he was always able to make sufficient space to slide his silk-fringed knuckles between us and find a way to her breasts.

This action, I must stress, was not that of a man who meant to replace me. The part he played was more that of my assistant, in the sense that a magician has an assistant. But doesn't every magician's assistant want to be the magician in the end?

$\backsim$

As I hadn't raised the Cuban doctor with Marisa, I saw no reason to raise his ghost. Though I had virtually talked her out of her previous marriage, though conversation was our medium and words were our caresses, some things we were too discreet ever to speak about. Direct verbal engagement with our feelings for each other was not our way. I'm not saying that our relations were cold – far from it. There's a heat in inexplicitness which couples who live in a state of mutual erotic candour know nothing of. Our eyes met furtively across signals barely made and scarcely half-perceived and in the exchange of guesswork and intuition we found our space.

Had I spoken of the Cuban doctor's presence in our bed, had I proposed finding another man to do what he'd done when he'd examined her, or suggested to Marisa that she find one for herself, I might well have lost her. There was a streak of severity in Marisa that I feared. Make no mistake: I loved her for it. It excited me to be married to a beauty who was also a moral philosopher. Not every man gets to lie simultaneously with Salome and Socrates. But the disadvantage, if it can be a called a disadvantage, was that I thought twice before opening to her the sewer that was my mind.

And to myself, too, I knew to be careful about bringing up the Cuban doctor. I didn't want to murder in me a sickly hankering which had a way to go yet before it flowered into a monstrous appetite.

There are some desires which are too elusive and undefined ever to be put satisfactorily into words: utter them and they lose their trepidation, call them by their name (supposing that you know their name) and you forgo that oscillation between the possible and the unthinkable, between what you rub at in your imagination and what you fear ever coming to pass (or worse, not coming to pass) in reality. If that oscillation made us giddy it also made us the more in love. Perhaps I shouldn't speak for Marisa. It was part of our unspokenness never to be certain how in love the other person was. For me, though, the not knowing what was permissible, what Marisa made of my odd nature, how many of my dreads and fancies she had become aware of and would ever allow to come to pass, threw me into a frenzy of waiting and wondering that conventional people would regard more as servitude than love, but which for me was love's very image, love without surety or promise, love in an eternity of suspense.

There are men in whom the masochistic impulse takes the crudest forms. They want a woman to strike and abuse them, to spit in their faces, to thrash them like children. It was otherwise with me. Marisa's knee would surely have been a fine place on which to take one's punishment, but it was her mind I wanted to lie across. And there, in the wordless quiet, to wait for her to think her worst.

I glowed with the suspense of it. People I ran into in the impersonal way of work commented on my appearance. My staff suddenly enjoyed my company and seemed to want to talk to me in the morning rather than scuttle off into their cubicles. Defencelessness, I suppose, was what they saw. That aura of being unprotected and unguarded we love in infants or young lovers, as though they are in their milk skin still, waiting for the second layer to grow. Isn't that, half the time, all we mean by beauty? A translucence of the flesh through which the quaking nakedness of our souls is visible.

I rarely visited my father. We didn't like each other. I had deposited him in an old persons' home in Hertfordshire where, as I have said and will say again because it gives me pleasure to hear the words, he played canasta with elderly women with sick minds, making them promises he couldn't keep. He had done the same with my mother. Me too, in a way. He had promised I would never get the business but here I was in charge of it. For which he promised he would never forgive me. But even he, the one time I did go to see him, was struck by how well I looked.

'Anyone would think,' he said, spitting into a bowl, 'that you'd found someone to get your leg over at last. It's not a man, is it? I recall your mother had a brother who went in for that. It wouldn't surprise me if it's in the genes.'

'No,' I said. 'It isn't a man.'

Though of course strictly speaking . . .

My doctor went so far as to offer it as his opinion that marriage so agreed with me it had extended my life by at least ten years. My bad cholesterol had gone down, my good cholesterol had gone up, my blood pressure was lower than at any time since I'd been his patient, I had lost weight and if I allowed him to measure me I would probably discover I had grown taller by a couple of inches.

'Whatever it is she's giving you, Mr Quinn, it would save the National Health Service millions if we could bottle it.'

'I visit you as a private patient,' I reminded him.

'Think altruistically,' he said.

I fear I must have blushed, so altruistically was I thinking.

I have said Marisa was severe but I must not give the impression that she was prim. Of the two of us, though I was the more criminally insane, I was also the more censorious. It is not uncommon to be simultaneously perverted and puritanical. For only the pervert knows how rank it gets inside his head. Had I been the judge charged with trying me for crimes against the hearth, I'd have sentenced me to hang at first light and let the birds peck my bones clean.

Marisa, on the other hand, was unshockable in matters of sex, passing judgement on nobody, least of all herself. Prior to me, whether married or single, she had taken lovers freely. Not always when she wanted them, for there were other people's feelings to be considered, which made her hang back or go ahead not quite in accordance with her desires. But as a woman who admired the freedoms open to a man, and who was herself, psychologically speaking, the triumphant product of those freedoms, she had no choice but to reach out and take a lover so long as there was no compelling reason not to. Men helped themselves to what came along; she did the same. The experience neither inflamed nor depressed her. It was possible she was not in it for the sex. Yes, the act first of making, then of keeping an assignation energised her: being taken to a restaurant she did not know, deciding what to wear, choosing what to eat, wondering what might happen next, where and in how much secrecy and danger. Hotels she liked, provided they were comfortable, the beds warm and large, the hot water plentiful and the room service efficient. Four star was about as low as she could tolerate. Anything less and she would rather forgo sex altogether. Was she in it for the linen? She sometimes wondered. Things went best when she saw to the arrangements, who would sign in first, how one would know the other was in the room, in what fashion (meaning in what manner and in what garment) she would either open the door or knock on it. The social-organisation side of adultery – its Women's Institute, bring-and-buy-sale aspect (helping *out* rather than helping herself) – she found engrossing; thereafter – the kissing, the unbuttoning, the penetration, the apologies, the thanks, the excuses and the fabrications – she could take or leave alone.

Once, someone she worked with in the Oxfam shop suggested she accompany him to a wife-swapping club he had himself, in other circumstances, frequented.

'But I'm not your wife,' she'd objected, mildly. She was not being prudish about it; merely precise.

'Wife-swapping is a manner of speaking,' he explained. 'It's more fetish.'

'Fetish as in voodoo?' She couldn't help herself: she could only imagine he was proposing taking her to West Africa or Haiti.

'More as in chains and leather.'

She explained she owned no leather clothing, other than shoes and belts and a jacket that was too good to wear for clubbing in Haiti. And her only chains – the only chains she kept – were eighteen-carat white gold necklaces bought by lovers from Asprey's or Garrard's.

He offered to find her something on the rails at Oxfam. She told him she had never worn second-hand clothing. 'In that case just select a skirt and jacket from your own wardrobe,' he suggested, 'then lose the skirt.'

'I look my best in skirts,' she told him. But met him halfway, losing the jacket.

He hadn't told her stilettos but she assumed them. She could do stilettos. And liked wearing them. They made her taller than most men.

The club was in fact the living room and kitchen of a semi-detached Victorian house in Walthamstow. Some of the men wore shorts with crossed leather braces, a bit like lederhosen; others hero shirts and riding breeches. A few had dog collars round their necks. One had come as a Druid. The women, by and large, wore what she imagined prostitutes must wear under their coats. A tall blonde girl in a diamanté eyepatch and choker danced by herself in a pink and purple rubber cocktail dress which Marisa thought she'd like to own were she to do this more often, which she didn't suppose she would. The atmosphere made her think of a taxi drivers' Christmas party, though she'd never been to one.

She danced with an unattached young black man in PVC trousers who put her hand on him and proposed intercourse either where they were or in the bathroom. She didn't mind what he did with her hand. She was dancing and what happened when you were dancing was not governed by any of the usual laws of good behaviour. He wasn't a bad dancer either. But intercourse, in either place he'd suggested, she was not up to. She had seen the bathroom and would not have wiped her nose in it. As for where they danced, she was reminded of a boarding house in Bournemouth to which her mother and one of her faux-daddies had taken her not long after her real daddy walked out. The carpets were green and there had been bowls of crisps and peanuts on the mantelpiece. 'Don't ever,' her mother had admonished her, grasping her wrists, 'take crisps and peanuts from a bowl where God knows who have had their fingers.' Marisa, wishing her mother were only half as particular about herself, cried the whole time they were there. The carpets in Walthamstow were green and there were bowls of crisps and peanuts on the mantelpiece. Marisa left her hand where the young black man had put it but shook her head. 'Let's just dance,' she said.

He shook his head. If he'd wanted to just dance he'd have gone to the Hammersmith Palais.

'Then I can't help you,' she apologised. 'It's not personal. I can do debauch, I just can't do crisps and peanuts.'

She went looking for the Oxfam colleague who'd brought her. A very fat woman in a riding coat was sitting astride his face, reading the racing pages of a newspaper.

'Home time,' Marisa called down.

He wasn't able to answer.

'Don't worry,' she said, 'I'm perfectly happy to leave on my own if that's what you'd prefer. Just bang once on the floor if you're staying, twice if you want me to wait for you.'

The man banged once. 'Then I'll see you in the shop next week,' Marisa said.

She wasn't in the slightest bit scandalised. No vagary of the sexual life was ever scorned or rejected by Marisa. What people did they did. But for herself, as she wrote in her diary, where she was unable to feel free with the savoury snacks, she was unable to feel free with her body.

She wasn't at all frigid, withholding or non-orgasmic. She didn't wonder whether there was any experience of the senses she was going without or needed to experiment with further. What women were supposed to feel she felt. What *she* was supposed to feel – which might have been a different matter – she felt. But none of it occupied her beyond the moment in which she felt herself feeling it. As a discrete event, she looked neither forward to congress, nor back on it.

In so far as she anticipated with eagerness any aspect of this nether-world of her existence, it was the conversation. She liked verbal fluency in men and would not have sought physical intimacy with anyone, no matter what his rival attractions – unless he was the best dancer in the world, of course – whose mind was not a source of interest and amusement to her. She had to like a man to exchange bodily fluids with him, but she had to have exchanged intellectual fluids with him before she could like him.

Some nights she found herself thinking about someone she had stretched out alongside in the day, some nights she did not. The 'thinking about' bore no correlation to any sexual excitement she'd happened on. Something they'd said about their lives might have intrigued her, an idea they'd had, a sentence they'd formed. She quite enjoyed hearing about their work. Or where they'd been. She didn't at all mind hearing about their wives so long as they were not demonised or airbrushed to spare her feelings. She could sleep with a man who loved his wife. If pressed, she would probably have accepted that a man who loved his wife was the better option. Less chance of his turning up on her doorstep with his eyes moist and his cases packed.

In this way, you could think of her as conservative, not to say reactionary, where the institution of the family was concerned. She wanted everybody to stay together. It was not unknown to her to think about her lovers' children if she'd been shown photographs of them or they had in others ways been made vivid to her. So much so that on more than one occasion she considered 'doing something' for them – contributing to their schooling, say, or opening a small trust fund for their later years. This, as a means, perhaps, of compensating for the absence in her of anything like a maternal instinct, which absence she of course attributed to the poor example of parenting to which she herself had been exposed.

Thus, the men she had the leisure to devote the secret hours of her life to were secret only in the literal sense, and didn't answer to any unconscious needs or unacknowledged longings in her. Other than the pleasure she took in being secretive. They were consistent with the rest of her life; they could have been invited to her dinner table but for the conventions that said they couldn't. When they were out of her sight, they were out of her mind. She might have reflected on their marriages, their children, and even their job prospects, but the one thing she did not find herself going over when she was unable to sleep was *them*: how much she did or didn't love them, how much they did or didn't love her. She loved her husband. Then she met me. Another husband. And loved him. End of story.

Or should have been end of story.

In so far as I didn't know whether it was or it wasn't, I was happy. As I have said, the uncertainty suited me.

And yet it didn't.

My skin shone all right, but within the tense cocoon of silent expectancy which passed as contentment, I yearned for some repetition or equivalent of the scene I'd beheld all trembling at Marisa's bedside. If she was not to be touched by other hands just yet, could she not at least be seen by other eyes? Though I was not yet Victor Gowan's age, I understood his desperation. Marisa was not running out of time, nor was I come to that – indeed I'd been told I'd gained time – but you never know what's going to happen. I feared that the comfortable unblemished conventionality of our life together, with much promised but nothing ventured, would swallow us if we weren't careful. A wife can grow accustomed to her husband not undressing her for another man.

So how did we ever get to where at last we got to? How did we negotiate our silences into an action as loud and incontrovertible as Marius?

Impossible to trace a progression – some, I acknowledge, would call it a descent, though they'd be wrong – as infinitesimally refined as ours. You might as soon attempt to paint the second by second changes in light that mark day's disappearance into night.

But every day has its pivotal four o'clock and a marriage is no different. Imperceptibly but decisively we yielded to those equinoctial hours when relations between lovers quiver on their axes. And where we didn't quiver as perilously as I wished, I applied my weight. An old acquaintance of mine would come to stay and I would feign indisposition in the middle of the evening, leaving Marisa to do the entertaining. I would make myself scarce at Marisa's Oxfam and Samaritans parties, watching from the shadows while she talked and laughed with whom she chose, to all intents and purposes a woman who had only her own engagement book to consult. I danced with her less than in the days of our courtship, either missing out on the school's social nights, so that she could mingle freely with those against whom she'd earlier pressed her body, or arriving opportunely late for one of our periodic classes, in the hope of finding her tangoing like a mare on heat with the newest teacher, an Argentinian with punched-out eyes and a ponytail.

Nothing was referred to during and after these events, if they could be called events, but a change was mutely noted – that change being my removal by another notch, like a fading ghost, from the adventurous scene of Marisa's life.

Ghostly as this progression was and had to be, we could not avoid discussion of sexual turbulence altogether. We went to the theatre, the cinema, the opera, the ballet, we bought tickets to hear singers sing and writers read from their work. You cannot live a civilised life and not have your nose rubbed in art's eternal telling of inconstancy and sorrow. But we did not crudely apply what we had seen to who we were. Only in the discursive and purely intellectual aftermath of some masterpiece of erotic despair such as *Dido and Aeneas* or *Winterreise*, only in language as impersonal as it was chaste, did we lay down what was necessary to our comprehension of each other.

One occasion in particular comes back to me. We had been out with Marisa's youngest and least pleasant half-sister Flops and Flops's husband Rowlie to see *Othello* at the National Theatre, a passionate and uncomfortable production because the actor playing Othello gave such energy to the jealousy that it was difficult to imagine how any man could think himself alive who did not suffer the torments he did. Very much my interpretation, I concede, but if I had to hold back at the theatre as well as in the bed, when was Marisa ever going to know me for who I was? But it was not only *my* interpretation, hence the heated discussion between the four of us in the Mezzanine restaurant afterwards – 'Anyone would think from the performance we've just seen,' Marisa's half-sister's husband protesting, 'that Othello *wanted* Desdemona to be unfaithful to him, which I have to say isn't the play as I understand it.'

I liked Rowlie, partly because his wife didn't, and I didn't like her, partly because there was nothing about him to dislike. I wasn't sure what he did.

Real estate, I think. But what he did was of less importance than where he'd been. Rowlie was one of those Englishmen about whom the only thing to be said was the school he'd gone to. There was a touch of that about me too, only I was several thousand pounds a term less interesting. And I no longer carried around with me what Rowlie carried around with him, in his clothes and in his hair – not just the good manners and the assurance of being somebody in particular, but the odour of housemaster and prep and school song and chapel and playing fields and fagging and flogging.

Flops raised a ginger eyebrow to him – that was part of what I disliked, her peppery aggression – as though to say 'And since when have you, my dear, had an understanding of any play?' From which I deduced that jealousy in some form was an issue between them, hers of him, I thought, but you can never be sure.

'Isn't it in the nature of the marks jealousy leaves upon your soul,' I ventured, 'that you are unable at last to remember what it was like to be without them?'

'That doesn't mean,' Flops said, blinking – she was a blinker, too – 'that you don't long for the time before jealousy began. Othello's tragedy, as *I* understand it, is that he knows he will never again enjoy the peace of mind he used to.'

'Not poppy nor mandragora,' Marisa said dreamily, 'shall ever medicine thee to that sweet sleep which thou owedest yesterday.'

A tremble of apprehension, as though of a joy or pain to come, ran through my blood and pricked my heart.

'Yes, but that's Iago,' Rowlie objected. 'The Othello we've just seen didn't want sweet sleep.'

'Who does?' I managed with great difficulty not to ask.

'Funny, though, don't you think,' Marisa said, 'that Iago should be both the architect and the poet of Othello's fall. I'm always struck by how poignantly he speaks of his victim and how much sorrow for him he feels.'

'But isn't he talking about himself?' Flops replied. 'Isn't it his own sweet sleep he's missing?'

'Because he too is jealous?'

'Yes, of what Othello has been up to with *his* wife.'

'I never believe that,' Rowlie said. 'It sounds like rationalisation to me.'

'It would,' his wife said.

'No, I agree,' I said. 'It is almost as though Iago has to try out the causes of what makes him who he is. His jealousy, if that's the name for it, is half-hearted. Confronted by Othello he realises he falls far short of the real thing. He knows envy and resentment and spite, but his mind is nothing like dirty or capacious enough to do jealousy on the grand scale.'

'What's so grand about jealousy?' Rowlie wanted to know.

But Marisa was wondering about something else I'd said. 'Does Othello have a dirty mind?' she enquired, as though from another room.

'He did tonight,' Rowlie said. He seemed put out, as though it was something he would need to speak to Othello about if he persisted in it.

'He should do every night,' I said. 'All Shakespeare's best heroes have dirty minds.'

Flops looked up at the ceiling of the restaurant, where she seemed to see something invisible to the rest of us. 'I think our husbands, Marisa, are telling us something about what it is to be a man.'

Her husband snorted. 'Othello's heart is broken. That's why the play's called a fucking tragedy, isn't it? What we've just seen was more like black comedy, excuse the pun. An Othello almost frantic to be proved a cuckold.'

'I don't see why you object to that,' I answered him evenly. 'Unless you object to it in the play. "I had been happy if the general camp had tasted her sweet body," Othello says. "Her sweet body", for God's sake. I grant you he puts that in the conditional tense, but there's still no getting past how vividly he conjures up the scene, as good as undressing Desdemona not just for the general camp but for Iago too.'

'Why would he want Iago to taste her sweet body?'

Unwise of me, but I laughed. 'Iago, Cassio, Roderigo – it doesn't matter. Paradise for Othello is for Desdemona to be enjoyed by as many people as are able to enjoy her, and for him to be hidden where he can see it. I'm not saying it wouldn't also be a hell. There's no sweet sleep for the man whose wife has a sweet body. But it's a hell he invites.'

'Oh, come on!' said Flops and Rowlie in a rare show of marital unanimity. They come together when they feel threatened, the wives and husbands of Middle England.

Whereupon conversation turned to other matters.

But later, as we were preparing for bed, Marisa said, 'You cheated a bit there, as I recall. Doesn't Othello say he'd have been happy for the camp to taste Desdemona's body *provided* he knew nothing about it?'

'Desdemona's *sweet* body,' I corrected her, since we were swapping emphases.

'But knowing nothing about it.'

'That's what he says, yes.'

Marisa appeared to reflect on this. 'You would, I suppose, argue that he does not wallow in the idea of Desdemona's defilement any the less for imagining himself ignorant of it.'

I nodded.

'I think I'd go further,' she said, her eyes suddenly become hooded. 'I think the not knowing turns the screws of jealousy even more exquisitely.'

'As long as you know you don't know – is that what you're saying?'

'As long as you don't know whether there is anything *to* know.'

Pleading tiredness, I wished her good night, wanting to take her words with me into sleep. Though of course I did not sleep.

LOOKING UP FROM HIS FISH SOUP LUNCH AT THE ZUNFTHAUS ZUR ZIMMER-leuten, a favourite Zurich restaurant on the right bank of the Limmat, Felix Quinn – not me but a young man bearing a remarkable resemblance to me (same soft mouth, same shy, hooded eyes) and after whom, like my father before me, I am named – finds himself meeting the bold stare of a comely, not unfashionable, but indefinably common woman (ours, as I have not attempted to conceal, is a family of unapologetic snobs) who could at a guess be twice his age, sitting with a pigeon-chested, half-blind man who at a guess could be her husband. Felix has seen the pair before, once at a performance of *Troilus and Cressida* at the Pfauen Theatre, once while walking by the lake. On those occasions, too, he had stared and been stared at. The idea that they will think he has been following them humiliates him. The alternative idea – that they have been following him – embarrasses him in a different way.

The year is 1919 and Felix Quinn, who happens to be my grandfather, is in Zurich on family business, inspecting the library of an industrialist who would like to sell up and move to Paris now that Europe is safe again, but does not want to take his library with him. Felix blushes to the roots of his hair, as I would have done in his place, when he realises that the excessive interest he's been taking in the woman at the table opposite – it is her air of indolent accessibility, and yet not, that he finds fascinating – is being observed by the man he assumes to be her husband.

He lowers his head and tries to concentrate on his fish soup. But it is impossible for him not to raise his eyes every once in a while, and whenever he does so he finds the woman and her birdlike companion staring at him with expressions he does not have the language to describe.

At last, to his relief – that was how he always told it, anyway, *relief* – the woman leaves the table. Felix hears, but does not see her go. A moment later the man is on his feet before him, civil but highly agitated, wondering if there is any objection to his sitting down and discussing how things stand between them, as they seem to be seeing a lot of one another but have not yet exchanged words.

'Please,' my grandfather says with a gesture of the hand.

'I would like,' replies the gentleman, his cigarette describing a circle of gallantry in the air, 'to extend the same invitation to you.' Whereupon he sits, coughs a number of times, and fastens Felix with a stare of such inordinate intention that he fears he will burn up beneath it.

When Felix had seen this man in the park, swathed in a grey coat, he had taken him for a revolutionary. In the theatre, in his patent pumps, he resembled a dancing master. Today he looks like someone from the music halls. In fact he is an Irish exile, a language teacher in Zurich and a writer of some growing renown but of whom Felix is ashamed to admit he has not heard. 'I have been here less than a week,' he explains.

Felix loves plays and novels and they talk literature awhile – Ibsen, Flaubert, George Bernard Shaw. Once the husband picks up that Felix, like all the Felixes in our family, is classically educated, he begins to pepper his conversation with a Latin which my grandfather finds alternately Jesuitical and of the schoolyard. He does not understand everything that is said to him but grasps that the husband has begun to deliver intimate, not to say obscene confidences about his wife. Because he lacks the assurance to object, to demand that the husband recall himself to propriety, to plead his own fastidiousness or plain bashfulness, he can only go on smiling feebly as the absent woman's living flesh is appraised and parted for him in a dead tongue.

'You will sleep with her, then?' the husband asks at last, as though their whole conversation so far has been heading to this point and this point only.

Felix does not know what to say. He cannot, after what he has so far allowed, offer to take offence. He cannot, without giving offence himself, refuse the wife. And to wonder whether she has been consulted on the matter, as would be only proper, is tantamount to agreeing to sleep with her if she has. In the end there is only one thing he can say, and that is, 'I'll think about it, yes, of course I will, I am honoured to be the recipient of such a magnanimous request.'

'Muchibus thankibus,' says the writer, lighting a cigarette. 'It will be of inestimable value to me in my researches.'

The following day, after deciding without seeing it that the industrialist's library is not suitable for us, my grandfather packs his bags and returns to London.

And that, if he was telling the truth about any of it, was as close as any member of our family ever got to granting the inventor of Leopold Bloom his earnest wish to have another man cohabit with his wife.

Whether that meant Joyce had to try again with someone else, or simply had to make it up, is one of those literary mysteries that no amount of reading and rereading *Ulysses* will solve.

There is no saying, had my grandfather only held his nerve and hung on in Switzerland a little longer, that he'd have made it into literature, but he might at least have got to see a performance of Joyce's *Exiles*, a play in which Joyce investigates the 'baffled lust' that makes a husband the agent of his own dishonour.

Who knows – Joyce might have sat him next to Nora in the stalls.

Marisa and I saw a production in Dublin which we were visiting for an Antiquarian Booksellers Association dinner, not long, coincidentally, after our *Othello* evening – coincidentally, because *Othello* stimulated Joyce and was plainly a work to which he felt indebted.

Taking my wife to see one play about willingly jealous husbands after another was not, I must say, part of any campaign I was waging to make her aware of where I stood. The apparent continuity of theme is simple to explain: this is what literature is about. And more than that, this is what drives the making of literature. Not all literature perhaps, but I think the best literature. Or at least the best literature written by men. Employing a suspense identical to the suspense of the husband who waits to be betrayed, the writer (in Henry James's words a person 'on whom nothing is lost', and therefore upon whom, if he is any good, everything is visited) puts himself in a position to observe, as God the immortal cuckold has been observing from the moment He divided light from darkness, the ever recurring disloyalties of his creations. Knowing what He must have known would be our natures, not least our propensity to go whoring after lesser gods, Jehovah's great creative founding act was of the essence masochistic. The writer's creativity is no different, engraving, in loving detail, the infidelities of characters dear to his heart. Anna Karenina, Madame Bovary, Tess of the D'Urbervilles, Molly Bloom – what do they have in common? Simply this: that each yields to minutely observed seduction at the hands of unworthy men, and in the process subjects her creator, who loves her better than any other man ever could, to the torments of the damned.

We sat silently through *Exiles*, not exchanging glances, though if Marisa knew anything of me yet there was much in the comedy of the husband's lewd catechisms ('On your mouth?' 'Long kisses?' 'And then?') to exchange glances with me about. But the closing lines of the play took us back to where we had left off. 'I have wounded my soul for you,' the would-be cuckold husband says, 'a deep wound of doubt which can never be healed. I can never know, never in this world. I do not wish to know or to believe. I do not care. It is not in the darkness of belief that I desire you. But in restless living wounding doubt.'

We did not say a word to each other, but our eyes met in a nakedness of knowledge that was rare between us. *A restless living wounding doubt* . . .

Marisa did not ask me whether that was the condition of wounding doubt in which I had no choice but to long to live. And I did not ask her

– how could I? – whether, like the wife in Joyce's play, she would create or permit the circumstances in which my living with that wound would be allowable. Not that she would have told me, anyway. She was a hider, as I have said. Not dishonest, just wedded by the circumstances of her nature to concealment. But I thought I detected something akin to a resolution in her eyes – a resolution which, now I think back to it, was sombre to the point of tragedy – that I was who I was and she would not seek to change me, but that I would be bound to the logic of my desires. If desiring her in the darkness of belief, as men usually desire women, was not my way, if I chose the rather to live restlessly in wounding doubt, then I would have to live in doubt of whether she was wounding me or not.

Thus did the early years of our marriage pass in a sort of cliff-hanging harmony, with every conversation we almost had or refused to have pressing in on our precariousness, but without any resolution in event. For my part I did not solicit salacious circumstance, and for hers Marisa gave me no cause for jealousy: a freedom from anguish which, until I grew accustomed to it, was anguish enough. But there is a hunger to know whereof you don't know, which no amount of tearing at the wound of doubt can ever satisfy.

And so, at last, I *did* solicit salacious circumstance. A better way of putting it might be this: seeing it coming, I met it halfway.

A relative of mine, a Quinn but too far removed a Quinn for me to work out how exactly we were related, wrote to me requesting a period of work experience in the firm. Though I was unimpressed both by his handwriting and his manner of expression, I had no choice but to agree. In matters of business a Quinn does not refuse a Quinn. A queer loyalty, given what brutes the men of my family have all been to their wives, but then the wives weren't born Quinns.

Quirin was his name. Quirin Quinn. QQs were not unknown in our family, I suspect as much for the elegant gold monograms they made on leather suitcases and trunks as for any other reason. I had heard mention of at least three different Quentins among us, a Quinton, a Quintus, an earlier Quirin, and, though it is hard to credit, a Quilp. This Quirin turned out to be from the tall branch of the family. There are no half measures if you're a Quinn – you're tall or you're short. And you scintillate or you don't. Quirin flashed like a lighthouse. Which marked him as from the lazy as well as the tall branch of the family. He was as gold as his mono-gram, personable, handsome in a languid, milkmaidish sort of way, with soft skin and yellow curls, a penchant for bootlace ties and floral jackets, and an utterly untrustworthy air. He wasn't a student, as I'd feared from his reference to 'work experience', though after a stint in advertising and public relations, he was still unable to decide what to do with himself. Some cock and bull story about his being kicked out of a house he shared with an old girlfriend was the prelude to his asking if he could lodge with us for a day or two while he sorted things out. No, was my first response, then something made me say yes.

Ours was a big house, built in the 1770s by an architect called Johnson in the Adam style, but much interfered with since then, primarily by my grandfather, who returned from cruising to New York on the *Queen Mary* – I believe he was on the maiden voyage in 1936, by that time a more grossly sensual man than he'd been in 1919 – with the conviction that a house should resemble a ship. Hence the loud, louche semicircular saloon staircase he installed, its extensively patina'd brass bannisters, the vast tinkling chandelier swaying above it, all of which no member of the family had since been able to find the money or the will to tear out. Though the house looked, on this account, far more spacious than it actually was, there were still bedrooms enough to sleep a handful of puppyish relatives with QQ on their luggage and not notice they were there. So how could I say no to Quirin?

I checked, of course, with Marisa first. She shrugged. She didn't expect him to be in her way. She had a lot on that week: a hair appointment, dinner with a girlfriend, her once a month all-nighter for the Samaritans, a reception at the art gallery, another reception at her favourite shoe shop

94

– that was how they sold Marisa her shoes: over a martini and canapés – and an all-day and all-evening course that was in some way related to her Samaritans work and for that reason not to be discussed. By the time she was able to look up, he would be gone, would he not?

What she didn't say was that it would be nice to have some young company about the place when she was home. But then there was much Marisa didn't say.

When it was that I decided Quirin would be light relief for Marisa, and heavy exercise for my imagination, I don't recall. Perhaps the minute he moved his stuff in. There is something about the sight of a flaxen-haired stripling unbending himself from a taxi with a leather grip on his shoulder, looking for somewhere to lay his head, and trying a little too hard to please, that is bound to move a man like me. Move him on behalf of his wife, I mean.

He went his own way for a couple of evenings – he claimed he was talking to people about accommodation – then Marisa went hers for a couple of evenings more. He must have been in the house a week before we all sat down to eat something together. As a consequence of my grand-father's desire to feel at sea when he was at home, we had to ascend the staircase for drinks, a jest which Quirin entered into by taking Marisa's arm (Marisa in a belted, short-sleeved linen dress, the colour of squashed plums) before they began the climb.

'The captain awaits,' he laughed, and Marisa, though she could not have found that funny, laughed with him.

I felt as the hounds must feel before the kill. But as the fox must feel as well.

When we reached the top I remembered aloud I had a catalogue to proofread before morning. I drank a claret with them, made my apologies, and descended.

Leaving my study door open, I was just able to hear the ebb and flow of their conversation, not anything that was said, only the music of their intimacy. Any silence was of course interpreted by me as an embrace. You do not, when you are as I am, grace people with the usual build-up to impropriety. They talk. They stop. They kiss. Anything longer you do not have the patience for. Yes, waiting is of the essence. But you have already waited an eternity to get to this. Now the actors are assembled, it's action.

As it happened, the silences were few and far between. Unless they were kissing while they were speaking, they were not kissing at all. Once or twice I stepped into the hall and listened hard. I thought I could hear Quirin quizzing Marisa about her work with the Samaritans and Marisa, as always, giving little away. Secrecy was in the nature of what she did and she did it well. If I wasn't mistaken, Quirin asked if she knew how many people she had lost in her time manning the lines. I didn't catch Marisa's reply, but Quirin said, 'Gosh.'

After about two hours I went upstairs. All talking had stopped. I would not look into the room where I had left them should the door to it be closed. But it was open. Marisa had retired. Quirin was stretched out on a chaise longue once favoured by my mother, reading a magazine. He laughed when he saw me, his laughter like water overflowing. 'Great woman, your wife,' he told me.

The familiarity cut through me like a blade. At the same time I willed him to be more familiar still. Why 'great' woman? Why not 'beautiful' woman? Why not 'seductive' woman? Though I loathe the word 'sexy' I'd have taken that from him as well. 'Sexy woman, your wife' – the vile little neologism closing like hair-fringed fingers over Marisa's honour.

Three nights later I left them to each other's company again. This time Quirin talked about his life, painting himself, so far as I could hear, as lovably beyond the pale. Occasionally the name of a woman would float down to me, followed by a snort of incorrigibility, as though this was another one he'd either let escape or let down. I wondered how the roll call affected Marisa. Did it make her jealous? Was she retrospectively slighted by it?

But again when I went upstairs I found Quirin on his own, drinking my brandy and going potty, he told me, looking for a radio or disc player. 'I've never lived in such a silent house,' he told me. 'What do you listen to all day?'

'I'm out,' I told him.

'And Marisa?'

'Ask her.'

'But don't you play music when you're home?'

'Sometimes, but I doubt it would be what you mean by music.'

He didn't bother to rise to the insult. It's possible he didn't hear it. 'I couldn't live without music,' he said.

'Well I can,' I said – disingenuously, for I did not add that I had music enough to listen to in my head.

A day or two after that conversation he collared me as I was leaving the house in the morning – he in a jute dressing gown, I in my business suit – to enquire if I intended being at home that evening.

'Shouldn't I be the one asking you,' I said, 'whether you intend being at work today? Work experience is what you are here for, is it not?'

He smiled his irresistible, sapling smile at me. 'Finalising my accommodation today,' he said. 'By tonight we should all have reason to celebrate. I'm going to crack open something expensive.'

Something expensive of mine? I wondered.

He clapped an arm around my shoulder. An odour of flagrant youth came off him – cologne, hair gel, new skin, marijuana, optimism, music, sex. 'Marisa has told me what she likes,' he said, 'so I'll be picking up a bottle of that.'

'Have you checked whether she'll be in?' I wondered.

'I have,' he said. 'And she will.'

When, I wondered, this being eight thirty in the morning, had he checked whether she'd be in?

When Marisa and I met for lunch that day, as we tried to do at least twice a week, I mentioned I had work to do again that night – indeed might not manage to get away until quite late – and would therefore, I was sorry, have to leave her to toast Quirin's good news without me. She narrowed her eyes. 'Anyone would think,' she began, but then stopped herself. We were careful where we let any tetchiness lead us. But even curtailed, this was further than Marisa normally went.

'Anyone would think what?' I asked.

She took her time. 'Anyone would think you're trying to avoid him.'

'I am.'

'Why? He's all right.'

'How all right?'

Impossible to tell whether the question irritated her. She was used to dealing with people about to throw themselves off a ledge. 'As all right as a boy his age can be,' she said.

'I suppose so, if you mean by that pretty, and with an eye for the older woman.'

'He doesn't have an eye for me, Felix.'

'He has an eye for your chest,' I said, calling for the bill.

I stayed at work until nine then made my way slowly home. It was a moony night, the sky very high. On nights like this when you are young you imagine a vast life for yourself. Life felt vast again for me, pregnant, infinite. But what it was pregnant with I couldn't have said.

Because our house sits at a watchful angle at the end of a terrace on the corner of a square, you can enjoy commanding views from any of its front windows; conversely you can enjoy commanding views of the house long before you reach its door. I approached it from the opposite side of the square with the trepidation of a traveller returning home after years abroad, unsure what he would find but hoping to tell from the number of lights burning what was happening within and what reception he might receive. This was a nonsensical calculation. They were not going to plunge the whole house into darkness because they needed a circle of darkness round themselves; nor were they going to turn on every lamp to let me know it was safe for me to return. But what did sense have to do with anything? I wanted evidence of an event and yet I did not. I wanted to see and yet I did not know whether I would be able to live with what I saw. Sense? Sense vanished from my vocabulary the day the Cuban doctor put his hands on Marisa's fevered breasts and claimed them as his own.

Unless it vanished when Victor led me up the stairs to see his sickly wife.

Unless it vanished the night I first read a novel.

Unless it vanished the night I was born of woman.

Though the curtains of the upstairs room into which I stared were closed, I could see silhouettes behind them and they were not the silhouettes of people behaving in any way out of the ordinary. I don't know how long I waited for the scene to change, but at last I crossed the square and took my keys from my pocket. I inspected them with a curiosity that amounted almost to nostalgia. Keys? Did I still possess keys to this house? I fumbled at the lock, not expecting it to work. Before I could open the door I heard singing. Whatever I expected of this evening – and much of what I expected I did not name even to myself – Marisa and QQ singing to each other was not part of it.

Here was a very different sort of jealousy from that for which I had prepared my mind. I took a couple of steps back to listen. Quirin was piping, 'My luv is like a red, red rose.' If he thought to win her that way, he was mistaken. Marisa had told me many times, in the intervals of operas and recitals, that she did not much care for tenors, let alone tenors who faltered in the falsetto register. True, that was Marisa sober, but when her turn came to sing she did not sound drunk. Like all women of her class and education, she had a vast repertoire of Scottish and Irish sentimental ballads of the Barbara Allen sort which she performed with trembling sorrow in her voice and a misty, exiled from the islands of her childhood look in her eyes. Quirin was welcome to those. It was when she started on Dido's Lament that I became upset. The first time Marisa did Dido for me I wept. 'When I am laid, am laid in earth, May my wrongs create / No trouble, no trouble in thy breast.' I had no defences against those words, no defences against the idea of a woman laid in earth, whoever the singer. But swelling in Marisa's throat they touched feelings I did not know I possessed. On many an evening since then I had called for it and Marisa had obliged, taking an artist's satisfaction in my tears, and also, it sometimes seemed to me, a mother's, cradling me until I had sobbed myself out. Was the song, in that case, not sacred to our marriage?

After Dido the house went very quiet. I did not know whether to let myself in or not. I decided to walk once around the square, allowing my competing jealousies to find their own equilibrium. By the time I returned I had decided that the silence meant they were now in each other's arms. How else do you follow Dido?

I looked up at the window but there was no sign of them. The lights still burned, but nothing, no one, not a shadow, moved. Did that mean they had left the room? If so, to which room had they repaired?

Not a murmur from the house. I turned the key in the door and went inside. It was not my intention to spy or listen in; all I wanted was to be under the same roof as them. The house was as quiet within as it had seemed without. I trod quietly, but not so quietly that they shouldn't know I was back. You will not be disturbed by me, I hoped my tread would say. You are not to hold back on my behalf.

I sat in the leather chair in my office – a chair which had exuded authority for generations – uncertain what to do next. You can never know how you are going to feel in a situation such as this. I was elated as I expected to be, but I had no employment to which to put my elation. You cannot stay elated, waiting in a silence which might be a silence of something or nothing. Exclusion had all along been my object, but now exclusion was achieved I felt excluded from the exclusion I had sought.

The wife-besotted artist Pierre Klossowski – a photograph of whom, acting out his besottedness, I had on my desk – wrote a novel on this very subject. *Roberte Ce Soir*. Not much read on account of the erogenic subtlety of its subject matter. How, Klossowski wondered, do you take a woman in your arms when you want it to be someone else who takes her in his arms, and you aspire to see him at the very moment he sees you? The conundrum that had troubled Candaules and Anselmo both: how to be simultaneously voyeur and actor, exhibitionist and stage manager, husband and lover. 'One cannot at the same time,' Klossowski wrote, 'take and not take, be there and not be there, enter a room when one is already in it.'

Or, conversely, leave a room that one has already left.

Once or twice I crept out into the hall, but heard nothing. All the lights were on as they would have been when the evening began, otherwise it was as a house shut up for the night, not a sound anywhere. I am not sure how long I kept up this vigil of pacing, listening and not listening, but I must at last have fallen asleep in my chair because a cry and then a thumping sound, as though something had fallen off a wall, and then a second cry reached me as from some other dimension. By the time I was out of the chair there was more commotion. I ran into the hall and there was Quirin unconscious, if not dead, at the bottom of the stairs, and there was Marisa, frantic, in her nightgown, at the top.

Quirin was not dead. He was not even all that unconscious if you discount the wine. Blood was trickling from a small cut above his nose. He moaned when I kneeled by him and felt his shoulder. 'Christ,' he said, looking around, 'what's this?'

'A bloody miracle,' I said.

He stared around him as though he'd never seen the place before. So that was two of us.

Above him, switched on by Marisa, a thousand starry shipboard lights began to twinkle. Quirin looked up with an imbecile grin on his face, as though he expected to see the dazzling countenance of God grinning back at him. 'Great chandelier, Uncle Felix,' he said.

'I'm not your uncle,' I told him.

Marisa was ringing for an ambulance. 'Tell him to lie still and not talk,' she called from the phone.

What was it she didn't want him to talk about? It couldn't have been the chandelier, so what then? The kiss at the top of the stairs that had been so dizzying he couldn't keep his feet? The erotic horseplay that made them careless of all danger? Had she pushed him to repel him? Had he fallen to escape her?

My questions were not of the Maigret sort. I wanted to know what had happened, but not to solve a crime.

How far had things gone?

I phrase the question with the bluntness it phrased itself to me at the time, despite there being more pressing matters to deal with. But there you have it: for me there was no matter more pressing than this. Yes or no? Suppose Quirin to have been in mortal agony, which, thanks to young bones, soft carpets, and all-round insensibility, he was not, I would have ordered my thoughts no differently. Had the thing happened, and if it had not, what chances were there of its happening still?

You are meant to be returned to your senses when an accident occurs. That is what accidents are for. The madness goes and sanity reasserts itself. But my elation had not been dampened by events. Baulked, yes, but not extinguished. The night was not over yet.

The doorbell rang. I could see a blue light flashing outside. 'I think,' I said, taking Marisa to one side, 'that you should go with him in the ambulance.'

She stared at me. 'Felix, this is not a joyride. The boy's fallen down the stairs. He might have broken every bone in his body for all we know.'

'That's why I think you should go with him.'

'He's your relation.'

'Yes, but distant. You're much closer to him.'

'I?'

'You.'

She backed away from me. Something she had never done before. 'You're insane,' she said. 'Are you sure it isn't you that's fallen down the stairs?'

I didn't say I had no reason to fall down any stairs because it wasn't I who'd been locked in a wild embrace at the top of them. 'I can't see what's insane about my suggestion,' I said instead, which better proved my mental stability. 'If you won't go with him I will, but I don't know what I've said that's insane.'

She shook her head. 'Does it never stop for you?' she asked.

Shocking in itself, for what it posed, the question shocked me still more for being put at all. This was the most direct Marisa had ever been with me on a subject that burned between us, but which we had tacitly agreed never to address in words.

'I don't know what you're talking about,' I said, not looking at her. Had I met her eyes they would have roasted me alive.

'Yes, you do, Felix. Does it never stop? Does nothing more important ever intervene?'

It was a great temptation to seize the moment and admit it – no, Marisa, nothing more important ever intervenes because nothing more important exists. But that would have been the end of everything. She already thought I was crazy and she didn't know the half of it. When the moment presents itself to a masochist he dare not seize it unless he wants to pull his world down around his ears, which he thinks he does and boasts he does, but which of course he doesn't. More even than the sadist, the masochist craves infinite repetition.

I took a step back from the precipice so that I might stand over it again.

THINGS WERE BOUND TO BE DIFFERENT BETWEEN US AFTER THAT.

But not on the surface. And not all at once.

I'd gone with Quirin in the ambulance and could see there was not much wrong with him. Not in body, anyway. He was released from hospital after a couple of days of observation, and was thereafter, so I heard, to be seen limping around town with a silver-topped cane. He didn't show up for further work experience. He dropped us a card to thank us for our hospitality and conversation – the word conversation underlined for some reason which I thought only Marisa would understand – and sent round a friend with an even more untrustworthy air than his own to collect whatever he'd left lying about our house (toys, as far as I could tell) and return the key. The end. Marisa did not mention him and nor did I. Our conversation sealed over him, as it sealed over the dangerous eruption of frankness he had precipitated. He hadn't taken a suspicious tumble down our grand triumphal staircase. I hadn't asked Marisa to travel in the ambulance and hold his hand. Marisa hadn't said to me what she'd said.

We were in good shape. We denied it all to each other, therefore none of it had happened.

But, whatever we pretended, our precious pact of implicitness had been broken.

And with it our still more precious pretence that the wounding doubt in which I lived was no figment of my disordered brain but answered to an actuality – Marisa's wounding, never to be mentioned infidelities.

When my love swore that she was false, I did believe her though I knew she lied.

Not any longer.

Now Marisa would have to be false to me in earnest.

Hard to explain the moral logic of that, but we both sensed it was how it had to be. It was as though we accepted the necessity to move down a philosophic plane – as it were from the beauty of abstractions to the ugliness of deeds – and would be coarser with each other from now on. Not because Marisa had to punish me with who I was – hers was not a punitive or vindictive nature – but because there was nowhere else for us to go.

Without doubt, she could not have done what she went on to do had she not been an adventuress with a deep instinct for concealment. But she could not have done it had she been an adventuress only. What she did she did because she loved me. I see her forerunner not in Guinevere or Messalina or Moll Flanders, not in Sacher-Masoch's fur-wrapped Wanda or any of the libertine women in de Sade's *The One Hundred and Twenty Days of Sodom*, but in the highly respectable Mrs Bulstrode in *Middlemarch* who stayed loyal to her disgraced husband. Good wives do this. They shoulder the burden of us, they espouse our sorrows. I wasn't disgraced, but I wasn't weighted down with moral honours either. Mrs Bulstrode took off her ornaments and put on a plain black gown; Marisa touched up her lipstick – otherwise they were acting out of the same sense of duty. That Marisa didn't suggest the separation route, and that I never threatened her with it – that divorce never entered into either of our minds – proves how devoted to each other we remained.

In recognition of which, and again without words, we threw ourselves into a period of the most intense, romantic love. It was like the honeymoon we had never quite managed to have. We woke smiling into each other's eyes. I wouldn't let her leave the bed, whether to go into the kitchen or the bathroom, without me. I watched her dress. I watched her apply her make-up, her head tilted slightly backwards for the final application, as though she were putting eye-drops in her eyes and was careful not to spill any. When she did this her nostrils narrowed and the muscles in her neck tightened. From this angle, too, the grey tea-bag stains beneath her eyes shone silver. Fascinating. I didn't want to miss a moment of any of it. Which of course made her self-conscious, though that too I didn't want to miss. Brusque in her dressing normally, like a man, she would slide more sinuously into her clothes with my eye on her, until this struck her as preposterous and she would put the finishing touches to herself hurriedly, without looking in a mirror. Wonderful to me – how colourful and variegated she could look with so little ceremony. Even in her younger days my mother had rarely descended before lunch, so much was there to do to her person before she was ready to face the world. Marisa skipped into the day still warm from bed, as though she couldn't wait for her life to start.

On the afternoons she worked in the Oxfam shop I'd visit and pretend to browse through the books, though all I wanted was to see her, to observe her with other people, to hear her voice and make her smile when I appeared from behind a stack. She was the same. She walked to my premises with me. And she was there, as though she'd never left, her face illuminated, when I came up out of the basement six hours later. We paused somewhere for tea. Then we paused again for a drink, like lovers not wanting to part, though there was nothing to stop us going straight home and following each other round the house. We burst out laughing for no reason, and this time Marisa laughed in the present tense, overjoyed by the state we were in. We went for long walks all over London, our hands glued. People smiled when they saw us. I am not a person who normally invites conversation from strangers. I am not saying my face repels it, but I don't make it easy for people to break in on my concentration. Marisa, too, can be forbidding. Though where my face closes down, hers is full of sharp intelligence which you think twice before you brave. But together in this mood we seemed to suck whoever came anywhere near us into our happiness. Old ladies sat close to us on park benches. Children too. Dogs played around our feet. We were not just innocently and good-naturedly in love, we were the cause of innocent, good-natured love in others.

And every day while it lasted Marisa grew more lovely to me. The stains beneath her eyes faded. Her stern, Roman nose lifted infinitesimally. Her lips relaxed and grew softer. A light seemed to have turned on inside her. On one particularly restorative spring morning we went out walking in St James's Park early, while the trees were still damp with night. One of the pelicans was sitting on a bench, as miraculous and cumbersome as an angel, clacking its plastic salad-server beak. Marisa made me join him and put an arm around his shoulder. 'Smile,' she said, as she photographed us with her mobile phone.

And I swear that that was exactly what the pelican did.

'It's difficult to say,' Marisa laughed, 'which of you looks more incapable of flight.'

'He does,' I replied.

I spoke only the truth. This morning I was lighter than any other living creature in the park, Marisa excluded.

A magpie crossed our path. 'Hello, Mr Magpie,' Marisa said. 'How's Mrs Magpie?'

I asked her what she meant by that. She was surprised I didn't know the superstition. A single magpie was bad luck. You had to make the pair of them present.

I wanted to weep for her. Other people's superstitions affect me in this way. It is as though all their long-ago childhood fragility is distilled into the moment of their revealing them. I love seeing the girl in the woman. It breaks my heart. And that was how I suddenly saw Marisa – as a little girl, skipping through the park, being taught by her skittish mother to say, 'Hello, Mr Magpie, how's Mrs Magpie?'

We kissed under the minty, maiden leaves of a willow tree, breathing in their newborn greenness with the rapture of parents smelling for the first time the freshness of their infant's hair. When we left the shelter of the tree I saw that minute diamonds of moisture hung upon Marisa's eyelashes like seed pearls. The image is Thomas Hardy's. Tess in a rare moment of happiness. And that was how I saw Marisa in all her harmed innocence. Enjoying a reprieve.

And then, just as suddenly as it began, it stopped. It was as though we'd been embracing for the last time at the foot of the scaffold, and now one of us had to ascend.

Before the willow tree came into full leaf she had a lover.

As for how I knew – well you just know. You cannot be all in all to each other as we had been, and then admit another person, and not know.

To the eye of an outsider we must have looked the same: still a solicitously loving pair, no space between us, at fault – if it could be called a fault – only in our closeness. Certainly there was nothing in Marisa's appearance, her dress or her demeanour, to suggest her life was even microscopically different to how it had been. I have seen men oblivious to the fact of their wives' fall from virtue while all the world notes with cruel amusement the shortening of their skirts, their teetering heels, the expansion of their décolletage, their longer nails, their more swollen and empurpled lips. Marisa was not a woman of that sort. She had not departed from any of her customs or from her essential idea of herself in the course of her dishonouring Freddy, nor was she other than she had always been now that she was dishonouring me.

So what did I see that others didn't?

A new compassion for me was the start of it. A sorrowing look, almost as if she feared what the future held for me – an apprehension of my loneliness – would cross her face, not when we were alone, but in any sort of gathering, wherever our eyes met from opposite ends of the room, across a dinner-party table, or when waving a second goodbye in a crowded street. One sunny afternoon in her half-sister Flops's garden in Richmond, with Flops's unpleasant ginger children playing all around us – no hint of Rowlie in their offspring, all Rowlie's genes obliterated by the bitter pungency of Flops's – Marisa held me through the smoke of the barbecue in a glance of such lingeringly melancholy regret that it was all I could do not to burst out crying. Day by day her tone of voice to me altered also. No one else would have noticed, but I lived in Marisa's voice, as a child lives in its mother's. And that was precisely the alteration I detected: a sorrowing tone to match her sorrowing looks in which I read the diminution of my status – as a loved person – from all husband to all child. Given everything, she owed me no apology as a wife: as a husband I was the author of my doom. It was in her duty of care – parentally, so to speak – that she was prepared to acknowledge dereliction. An acknowledgement that implied a countercharge, the merest whispering of a reproach: for who, if she was failing to care for me, was caring for her?

That was what I heard in the new music of her tenderness to me – the sad and unexpected reasoning of our arrangement, that when the husband abdicates his responsibility to protect, another must take his place.

And someone had.

Eventually, of course, for all Marisa's exquisite precautions, he became present to me: an invisible but tangible replacement, on the other end of Marisa's now too busy phone, at the arrival point of Marisa's now too many taxis. Late for the theatre one evening and fretting because she'd mislaid the tickets, she used a pet name for me I'd never heard before. She assured me, on the way out of the house, that it was a name she'd given Freddy. Short of ringing him, which was out of the question, I had no way of confirming the truth of this. But she did not appear concerned whether I believed her or not. Once upon a time, had anything been amiss between us before we took our seats, Marisa would have squeezed my knee during the performance. But on this night she kept her hands folded firmly in her lap.

Had anyone asked me, even in the interval, what the play was about I would not have been able to answer. Perfidy, I'd have guessed. What else is any play about?

Two or three weeks after this freeze-out at the theatre I found an expensive fountain pen I didn't recognise on a side table in our living room. 'Had visitors?' I asked. 'No, why?' she replied, not looking up from her book. And that evening she turned her mouth away from me when I tried to kiss her.

There'd been no room for doubt before, but now certainty was screaming in my ear. A lover. Marisa had taken a lover.

The precise locution was important to me. She didn't have a lover, she had *taken* a lover.

Had I imagined I would riot orgiastically in the moment when it came? No. I had anticipated it, correctly, as the eventualisation of terror, as when, hearing noises in the dead of night, you descend the stairs and discover that there is indeed a stranger ransacking your home. But I had not anticipated just how devastating this eventualisation would be. In the moments after Marisa refused me her mouth I shook with fear. A bar seemed to lodge itself inside my chest. My rejected mouth dried up. Had someone cut my throat, or had I – as would have been more appropriate to the occasion – taken a knife to my wrists, I'd have bled iced water.

A *lover*.

A lover such as I had once been to her – and he who was first the lover of his wife knows better than anyone the treacherous transference of affections of which that wife, without betraying it in the movement of a single muscle or the disarrangement of a single hair, is capable.

It was here, what I had asked for: the wounding doubt that was doubt no longer, the wound itself, the gouge in the heart, and I was distraught.

Yet at the centre of my distraction, coiled like a baby's fist, was a promise of the immense and terrible bliss to come, not when I was calm, because I never would be calm, but when I at last learned to take possession of all my fears and accept them as my fate.

Very well then, I would learn and I would accept. A lover. A lover. Like a celebrant of some terrible religion of self-cruelty, I breathed the incense of deception and chanted the unholy words. *She has taken a lover. She has taken a lover. My wife Marisa has taken a lover.*

A lover – say it, Felix – for whom she was keeping her mouth pure.

And when, many months after this, emboldened by what seemed to me a change in our marital temperature – and remember, I measured on a scale of exactitude unknown to other men – I put out my lips to kiss her and was *not* rebuffed, I made the only rational deduction: *lovers*. Lovers in the plural. Too many now to remember which one of them she was keeping her mouth pure for. Like Zelda Fitzgerald who maddened her husband with the boast that she had kissed thousands of men and intended to kiss thousands more. Only with Zelda it was all pampered, Southern States, jazz-age bravado, whereas Marisa . . . Marisa was a reflective being, a woman who didn't naturally jig about in body or in mind, a woman who weighed the significance of her deeds, who did nothing lightly, and the consequences of whose kisses, therefore, could only be terrible.

And here's an interesting and I don't doubt utterly reprehensible question. Was I stimulated in my hurt more by Marisa's taking many lovers than by her taking one?

Yes and no. That is not prevarication. I answered the question differently every day I woke with it on my mind, and as Marisa's unfaithfulness became the settled pattern of our life, I never did wake *without* it on my mind. Each provoked me in his own way, the lover and whatever the collective noun is for lovers. If we are talking simple jealousy, then of course the lover, singular, had me by the throat as the gaggle of them never did. He alone had Marisa's sole attention, therefore he alone had what belonged to me. And on top of that he was the first. With him I had to learn from the beginning — the Cuban doctor could no more be called a beginning than Quirin could — how to bear what I had no choice but to bear. He took from me — whoever he was — my virginity.

But simple jealousy was only a small part, as I learned — and I was learning as I went along — of what this was all about. Yes, I was the mental voyeur of my wife, lying alone in our vacated bed, picturing in relentless and unforgiving detail the progress of my rival's every finger as it adventurously traced its stolen ownership of Marisa's flesh. Pore by pore, I touched what he touched, lived inside his hands, took up residence in his mouth and followed his tongue wherever Marisa permitted him to thrust it. Where he went, I went. Must I go on? I was more him than he was himself. And perhaps more me than I had ever been. Had I ever entered Marisa as rapturously solus as we entered her together? And yet at no point in this intense familiarity I enjoyed with him was I curious to know who he was. I didn't want to see him, learn his name, discover what he looked like, or find out what he did for a living. I assumed we were not acquainted; Marisa would not have been so vulgar as to take her first lover (her first lover since *we* had become lovers) from among our friends. But even if we were acquainted I didn't wish to know about it and would not have reproached Marisa for her choice. This was about her not him. The story that engrossed me was the story of Marisa's reaching out and taking herself one, and then several, regardless of who any of them happened to be. A story which, in all its essentials, I would rather Jane Austen than de Sade or Sacher-Masoch to have written. How did Marisa feel it at her heart, with what quickening of emotion and perturbation of spirit did she depart from the straight path of our marriage and plunge into that initial infidelity? And with what tumult of feelings, what expectation of felicity or dismay, what augmentation or diminution of self-regard, did she do to Lover Number One – who must surely have been particular to her – exactly as she had done to me and betray him in the careless distribution of her favours now to Lover Number Two, now to Lover Number Three, now to however many more of them there were? Which was the greater indecorum? Which, if any, shamed her more, assuming that shame was what at any time she felt? And if not shame – for she was, as I have said, a serious and reflective being – then what? Love? May the thought perish in the utterance, but could she have lost her heart a little to Lover Number One? Could she even have lost her heart to him a lot? And did the dissipation of her feelings for him, as she spread her net wider, cause her regret? Did she lament her infidelity to *Him*? Or was lubricity now the element she swam in?

Though I did not question her in this way to her face, I questioned her, in her absence, to her soul. And I do not scruple to call this line and intensity of questioning love. Not a mere crush or act of passing fancy, not the faint love-twinge Marisa might have felt for the man with whom she first unhusbanded me, but proper, indurated love – my sort of love, uncondi-tional, time-tried, morbidly steadfast and submissive, all absorbing and absorbed.

Until we are in love – my sort of love – we pass one another by. We take glancing notice when our interest is aroused, we half perceive or care-lessly wonder, but we do not truly observe or interrogate until we love. This is how we know love from its poor relations: by the greed with which we devour its object, not resting until we have ingested the loved one in his or her entirety. Only artists are as voracious in their gaze and curiosity. And of course the religious, who will eat their god to know him.

Art, religion, love – how closely allied in their baffled sensuality all three have always been. I was lover, artist, fanatic devotee of Marisa. And never more so than when, like those vanishing damozels in whose pursuit poets and painters wear out their lives, like the cruel, invisible deity whom the prayerful again and again entreat in vain, she eluded every attempt I made to enter her imagination as others were now permitted to enter her body.

I borrow that somewhat archaic way of putting it from Marisa herself. In my company, at least, that was how she described and (forgive me) performed the act of love – as a surprising and maybe even inappropriate intrusion. I am not saying she opposed it on those grounds. On the contrary, I think the more unintelligible she found the experience of being pene-trated the more it aroused her. At that moment when other women closed their eyes and tried to vanish from distracting consciousness altogether, Marisa would grow more alert and curious, raising herself up on to her elbows to look down, needing to see the mechanics of it – the actual penetrative moment – as if only then, when beholding it in all its un-accountable obscenity, could she admit that although she never understood why people, including her, enjoyed it, she did.

And if this was a spur to my understanding her when I was with her, how much the more so was it when I thought of her with someone else.

On the nights Marisa left me to myself, not saying whether she would return before morning or not (I always knew when she would not) I turned our bedroom into a cathedral. When I played music, it was always Schubert, the great agoniser –

> Ich frage keine Blume,
> Ich frage keinen Stern,
> Sie können mir alle nicht sagen,
> Was ich erführ so gern

– not asking flowers or stars to tell him what he burned to know because the thing he burned to know he burned *not* to know as well. But mostly my excruciations needed no accompaniment.

At about nine o'clock I locked the house up, not to keep Marisa out but to keep me in. For my cathedral was a prison too. Thereafter I didn't leave the room, or do anything except by the light of two church candles which burned on either side of the bed. Incense, too, I burned. Opium was the aroma that suited me best. By ten I liked to have changed out of my business suit or whatever I was wearing that attached me to any purpose other than Marisa. In the days before she'd taken ill in Florida, Marisa had bought me white pyjamas in a shop in Key West that sold only garments Hemingway might have worn. Hemingway's connection to white pyjamas was a mystery to us, but they were certainly more suited to the damp and heat than those I'd brought with me. Marisa had laughed, I remember, on discovering I had brought *any* pyjamas to Florida. Why pack such things to go on honeymoon? 'So that you can laugh at me,' I told her. There was no laughter associated with my white pyjamas now. These were sacrificial garments, the vestiture which signified the abnegation of my virility and independence. I was Marisa's to do with as she willed, and let my icy blood stain the garments I wore in her service until every corner of them was incarnadined. Thus robed and eviscerated, I lay myself down to keep vigil through the night.

There is a word used by those who practise suspensefulness as a calling: subspace – the ritual abandonment of your will to another's sexual caprices, the nirvana stillness of complete submission. In subspace you receive with joy and gratitude whatever punishment is meted out to you – a private insult, a public humiliation, a flogging, a blade, a flame, the torture of your choice or your torturer's.

The subspace I entered was ruled over by Marisa's absence. With joy and gratitude I suffered her being somewhere else, and that cut deeper than any blade.

Sometimes I got some sleep – short, fitful lapses of moral duty – most nights I did not. When I did sleep I woke in guilt, believing that not to have stayed awake was disrespectful and ungrateful to Marisa who was out there labouring, in a sense, for me. But I forbade myself sleep on other grounds, too, for you do not squander subspace on unconsciousness. You are alert or you are nothing when you choose submission to your wife's caprice as your vocation. You are Henry James's novelist on whom nothing dare be lost. And every second I slept was a second lost of the torture of being awake. Sleep through the nights of your wife's unfaithful absence and you might as well embrace the consolations of common men – drink, gambling, sport, suicide.

Besides, I could never be sure which night of wounded wakefulness would be my last. Not in the suicide sense, but allowing, as I had to, for the volatility of human passion. Marisa might do anything. Might take it into her head to return to our life as it had been, in which case no more sickly vigils kept by me. Or might do the very opposite and leave me altogether, in which case again my devotions would be over. For make no mistake: this ritual was a celebration of our singular togetherness, a marriage sacrament that would lose all point and savour were we to part. The exquisite peace of subspace – the peace that passeth all understanding – was predicated on a happy union.

As for the other privation which I owed Marisa in the course of these cathedral nights, I will not speak of it here. Whatever else it may be, this is not a fluidal narrative. But no is the answer, I did not. To have done so would have been to take from Marisa what was, by the terms of our marriage contract, hers whether she had use for it or not – more hers, paradoxically, the less use she did have for it: hers to declare void.

In the blackest corner of my soul I would have wished her to secure me against treasonable temptation before she left the house, perhaps by binding my hands behind me. Or even – for there was nothing in my fever I dared not contemplate – by hacking them off at the wrists. And that wasn't the end of it either. Once you allow amputation into your erotic imagination there is only one conceivable conclusion. The man must be constrained, the man must be unmanned, the man must die without a trace of manhood left. But if Marisa knew of these longings, she never satisfied them. Perhaps on the grounds that she was doing enough for me already.

And so I lay there, in the stretched silence, as on a slab of stone, imagining how it would be when one day, as a gift, she consented to dismember me, though she had to all intents and purposes gifted me dismemberment already, by virtue of her absence. I held myself very still, impatient of any noise or movement that wasn't Marisa's. As if attached to her by tenuous threads of love, like a fly caught in the web of his desiring, I vibrated to every sound she made and every thought she had. Marisa whispering, laughing, confiding, gasping. Marisa opening her body – it didn't matter to whom, it mattered only that she felt the shock, the shame, the rapture or whatever of it, and sent the silken message back to me, from however far away she was.

I would not be true to the condition – neither to myself nor to the love I bore Marisa – if I did not admit that even so complete a trance as this was subject to whimsicalities. Strange fits of passion did I know . . .

What if something bad should happen to Marisa when she was out on the wing? What kind of husband allowed his wife to wander unprotected through a feral city? Erotic transport even when it is as extruded as mine enjoys close relations with superstition in its moral guise. Centuries of puritanism cannot be thrown off in a single night. How could I not ask myself, under pressure of that puritanism, whether Marisa wasn't courting danger? Didn't she *deserve* to come to harm? And didn't I deserve to lose her, whether to mishap or another man? You cannot play fast and loose with the conventions of a disapproving, vengeful world and not expect it to exact its payment in dire consequences. The wages of dull sublunary sin is death. What then the price of wickedness as weird as ours?

My compunctions, as you see, were of a moralising, omen-mongering nature, never sexually visceral. I did *tremor cordis* but I did not once do *nausée*. Of course I rose some mornings from my sleepless victim's bed with a keen, English sense of the preposterous. I would throw off my white vestments and look with irritation at my reflection in the mirror – a man closer to his middle than his early years, with tired eyes and yet an expression of almost beatific innocence on his face, a washed boyish gratitude which made me angry with myself. But I took this to be a necessary revulsion if I were to get on with the other, lesser business of my life. And it never lasted more than a day or two, or spilled over into a revulsion from Marisa and the dog's life she was leading me.

The famous words from Dostoevsky's great novel of moral inversion *The Brothers Karamazov* – 'What the intellect regards as shameful often appears splendidly beautiful to the heart' – are profoundly true. But one can rearrange their thrust. 'What to the heart appears splendidly beautiful the intellect must not regard with shame.' I have always made it a matter of principle to encourage the intellect to go wherever the heart dares. If it is beautiful enough to feel it, it is beautiful enough to think it. And let reason – which is so often no more than awkwardness before the heart's excesses – go hang. So, though I turned briefly from the spectacle I was making of myself, I was not for long disgusted by what my life with Marisa had become.

As for the love I bore her, it increased the more reason she gave me to admire her boldness. With every infidelity – actual or imaginary (for the imagination does not suddenly stop working just because reality becomes a match for it) – my devotion to her deepened. No man truly loves a woman, I have said, who does not know her to be lying in the arms of someone else. I do not retract a word of this. When she was away from me, I pictured Marisa in the greatest, and that is not necessarily to say the grossest, detail. I counted the hairs on her head. I measured the skin between her fingers. I heard the sound her eyes made when she closed them and then again when she opened them. She was so vivid to me I could have put her together, vein by vein, had imagination been gifted with the wherewithal to re-create a human life.

Love, of course, does not reside only in the veins. And it wasn't only the look and feel and touch – the presence – of Marisa that made my heart grow fonder in her absence. I thought longer, too, about the style and courage of her – for hers were no ordinary acts of marital deception. It took strength of mind and intuition and kindness – kindness to me, at least – to balance her affections and loyalties as she did. It required exquisite tact and knowledge of herself, acuity, breadth of understanding, judgement – the quickest discernment of character if she was not to play fast and loose with people's feelings, not excluding her own.

So add admiration to my devotion. An esteem for her that grew with every infidelity which in her became infidelity's very opposite: the proof of how much, how well – how *intelligently* – she loved me.

Practically, of course, these loving infidelities did not consume all our time. Whether she was rationing herself or rationing me I did not know or care to know; but I must not give the impression that Marisa's life was nothing but one amorous adventure after another. To the eye of an outsider the life we lived must have looked pretty much like the life we'd always lived. We still ate out most nights, still went to the theatre and the cinema, still kept up our dancing lessons (for which I continued to be obdurately late), still saw our friends. I worked every day as usual, Marisa read to her blind man, priced art books at the Oxfam shop, made jam to sell at fund-raisers, guided art lovers into the light of comprehension, and on Fridays sweet-talked the desperate out of the deep dark of their despair. Months could go by without a third party intervening in our marriage. But the fact of her unchasteness, however well spaced the incidences of it, did not leave me. I was never for a single moment not conscious of it. And therefore never for a single moment not in thrall to her.

I would stand at our bedroom window on those evenings which were consecrated to someone else and watch her climb into a taxi or go striding down the pavement with that lovely loose-limbed action, her skirt tight about her flanks, her heels making their characteristically precise attack upon the paving stones, her music case with her credit cards and make-up in it hot under her arm, and I could scarcely breathe for longing for her. Everything about her moved and stirred me in equal measure – the shine of her hair, the strength in her legs and back, the vibration which those clicking heels sent through her frame, and something lonely about her mission. This last always threatened to undo me. Oughtn't I to run out and bring her back? Oughtn't I to stop all this? Some nights I waved to her retreating form, wondering whether this would be my last goodbye to her. An apprehension of disaster that should have made me rap on the windowpane and plead with her not to go. But the thought of where she would soon be kept me motionless at the window. The general camp was tasting her sweet body, I knew it, everyone who saw her busy in the world without me knew it, and I was happy.

Whereas . . . Well, whereas if I had broken the silent spell that held us and said, 'Marisa, my beloved wife, my darling, enough now, I have supped full, I am satisfied and can take no more, come home,' who was to say that she would not have replied, 'My dear Felix, my dearest dearest husband, but what does any of this have to do with you? It never was and never will be about you and your wants. It is about me and mine. Now go back to your bed.'

And then where would I have been?

I SAW HER ONCE OUT AND ABOUT WITH A LOVER.

I hadn't followed her. There was no need to follow her. One way or another, by fair means or foul, sightings of Marisa at her impure devotions reached me. People dropped me hints. I read her diary. It is possible I was meant to read her diary. Letters which she left lying about I opened, as presumably I was invited to open, for Marisa was not a careless woman. Letters which were not left lying about I opened too, for Marisa did not hide things carelessly either. And I saw no reason not to listen to messages for her on the house phone. That I found no tangible proof of any love affair was itself no proof of anything. She would have wanted me to find no proof that she was having an affair as proof incontestable that she must have been. Spying on her in this way – entering her haunts on paper – had become our lovemaking. But I would never have dreamed of dogging her footsteps. It was a matter of honour to me that Marisa should be given the widest topographical latitude for her intrigues, and if that meant the whole of London then I would never leave the house.

Accidents, however, happen. This meeting – for it went beyond a sighting – was entirely accidental. Fortuitous or calamitous, depending how you view it. But not without a degree of embarrassment to all parties, in particular my secretary Dulcie with whom I was lunching when Marisa and her unknown friend entered the restaurant, not exactly with a show of intimacy, yet not as though they were there to discuss a business proposition either.

But then nor was I there on business. This wasn't a business restaurant. This wasn't a business restaurant. You went there to be seen. You made your entrance. You all but took the applause of the other diners as you were escorted to your table. And you seldom got there without having to kiss people you knew along the way. As Marisa had no choice but to kiss me.

'Felix,' she said, 'Miles.'

'Hello, Miles,' I said. 'Miles, this is Dulcie.'

They shook hands, I thought, as though they'd met before and looked embarrassed.

Marisa, of course, knew Dulcie who had been my secretary for years. So she wouldn't have supposed there was any impropriety in my taking her to lunch. Dulcie loved this restaurant but would not have been able to get a table without me. Every now and then I escorted her to it as a treat, or when there was a personal problem of which she needed to unburden herself, as was the case today. This, too, Marisa knew.

But Dulcie didn't know why Marisa was there with Miles. She blushed, not only on meeting Miles, was my guess, but at hearing herself say, 'Hello, Mrs Quinn,' as though she sensed that calling Marisa Mrs Anything with Miles standing possessively by her could cause a complication. Did she read that just from seeing them, I wondered? Were they *that* obviously coupled? Or were Marisa's infidelities common knowledge even to my staff? Did everybody know?

If I say I hoped so, I expect to be understood as meaning that I dreaded so, and therefore hoped so for that reason.

From his brief how-do-you-dos I took Miles to be an Irish millionaire. A horse-breeder, probably. He had good manners and was overdressed in the way of Irishmen trying to be Ivy League Americans, his suit more expensive than it needed to be, his pink tie knotted tightly at his narrow throat, just the right amount of double cuff showing when he extended his hand. His fingers, which I paused to look at fractionally in the moment before I took them, had a petrified, scalded appearance. There was not a germ on his body. At a guess I would have said he was Marisa's junior by seven or eight years. Which pleased me in ways it isn't necessary for me to go into. He gave me no sense that he knew or cared who I was. Which again pleased me in ways I'm sure I don't have to explain.

I held him in my gaze for as long as it was decent to do so. So here he, here *it*, was. The dread alternative.

I was face to face with it at last.

The dread alternative made flesh, and I could handle it. I could more than handle it: I thrived on it. Something moved in my stomach, presumably the transubstantiation of blood into water. But otherwise I felt wonderfully alive. *Felix Felicis.*

Felix Vitrix.

If Marisa, for her part, was discomfited she didn't show it. Peerless she was in her men's tailoring and effrontery. Not too much smiling, nor too little. No mention of coincidences. No denying me, but no effusive acknowledging me either. 'Well, enjoy your lunch,' she said, with no trace of anything but what the words implied, and they were gone.

It might have been better for Dulcie, if not for me, had Marisa and her Irish companion been shown a table far from ours. As it was, though we could not hear them, we could observe as much of their behaviour as we chose to. Of what I saw in the first ten minutes, it was the clinking of their glasses that transfixed me. They had, I could tell, clinked glasses before. They found privacy in the action, raising their glasses higher than is usual, and keeping them there longer, which I took to be the expression of a mutual impatience to hold each other's face in the reflection of the wine, away from the noise and publicity of the room. Marisa had looked at me through her wine glass in just that way when I was stealing her from Freddy. It was loving and impatient then, and it was loving and impatient now. I would say I smelled the impatience coming off them both were that not an insalubrious way of describing people enjoying lunch together. But then insalubrity is all in the interpretation and I have always been able to see it where less perceptive men see nothing. I must have turned a little white whatever I saw, because Dulcie asked if I was all right.

'Never been better, Dulcie,' I told her. 'And you?'

Dulcie, as it happened – and this had nothing to do with her seeing her

122

boss's wife out flirting heavily with another man under both their noses —
had never been worse.

A word or two about Dulcie, because her anxiety bore resemblances to
mine, or would have borne resemblances to mine had anxiety been a fair
summation of my state.

I have already alluded to the anomalous fine gold-linked ankle chain
Dulcie wore, though I was pleased to notice she wasn't wearing it for our
lunch today. This was not an ankle-chain-wearing clientele. But then Dulcie
was not by any stretch of the imagination an ankle-chain-wearing person
herself. She certainly hadn't worn one when I first interviewed her for the
job, a good twenty years before. Nor had there been anything in her character, her deportment, or her curriculum vitae, to suggest she ever would.
A trim and pretty woman, slightly catlike in appearance, with a turned-
up nose, wide-apart eyes on to which she applied too much mascara and
which for that reason had the appearance of being loose in their sockets,
and elegant charcoal-grey hair which she wore in a style that was once, I
think, associated with Doris Day, Dulcie Norrington was the daughter of
a clergyman with a liking for old books (hence her wanting to work for
me), the sister of a much loved Shakespearean actress (she played Emilia
in the production of *Othello* of which I've spoken), and the wife of a viola
player in a not very well-known or successful string quartet — a blissfully
happy union of which the issue was a son who had won a scholarship to
study Egyptology at the American University in Cairo, and a daughter
who was reading theology at Cambridge. To say there was no intimation
of an ankle chain in Dulcie's history or home life would be like saying
there was nothing in Dr Jekyll to prepare one for Mr Hyde. No, there
absolutely was not, but you never know what's going to turn up.

And turn up, suddenly one summer, it did. Dulcie without doubt had
a good figure still, and attractive legs, if a little too narrow and close
together to please the taste of someone for whom the airy separation of

Marisa's legs, slightly inflected at the knee, was the pattern of ideal beauty. So on fine days, when worn with slave-girl sandals and as an adjunct to floaty dresses, she could just about carry off her anklet. It was when she wore it under stockings, where at first sight it resembled a trapped centipede, that I began to worry seriously for her judgement.

She was the only woman who worked for me so she didn't have the benefit of fashion advice from a female colleague. And it would have been more than the jobs of the other employees were worth to pass manly comment. The staff knew my views on coarse allusions in business hours even to one another, and around Dulcie I had, as a responsible boss, erected a sort of cordon sanitaire. In my father's day no secretary or cleaner had been safe from rude comment or behaviour. Indeed it was in order to be rudely treated that they'd been employed. Once I took over, all that sort of nonsense came to an end.

Among the changes I instituted, for the benefit of every employee, was the installation of what I thought of as a comfort room or snug, not somewhere to drink coffee and catch up on one another's gossip – there were sufficient pubs and cafés above ground where staff could do that – but a place of meditation and quiet, almost like a hermit's cell only not quite so isolated. It was lit by a single pink lampshade and had a silvery pink Chinese rug on the floor. Originally there'd been a door so that my father and my grandfather (separately, of course) could lock themselves away in it and press their suits on willing or unwilling subordinates – a distinction, I regret to say, that was largely lost on both of them. I had the door taken off. Thus, if you'd repaired here in low spirits, you could count on a passing sympathetic glance, or even a concerned enquiry, if you simply raised your eyes to signal that you needed it.

It was here, not long after the first appearance of her ankle chain, that I found Dulcie doubled up like someone who had been shot in the stomach, sobbing like a child. Her right foot was stuck out in front of her. I saw that it was denuded of all ornament.

I popped my head in, gingerly.

'Everything all right, Dulcie?' I enquired.

It needed no greater prompting than that for the poor woman to unpack her heart to me.

I must have noticed, she began through her tears, that she had, these past three or four weeks, been wearing jewellery on her feet.

I lowered my head. 'No, Dulcie,' I lied, 'I had not.'

'Thank God at least for that,' she said.

For a fraction of a moment I wondered whether she might have taken my unnoticing to be an insult. A woman wears jewellery, when all is said and done, in order that its effect upon her be remarked.

She must have read my mind. 'It was not,' she said, 'my idea to wear the dreadful thing.'

Whose then? was the natural question, but I didn't feel I had the right to ask it.

She told me anyway. The whole sad saga of it.

Her husband Lionel, the viola player, had, while on a concert tour of the Midwest of America, encountered at a party he was loth to discuss in any detail an example, indeed several examples, of what Americans call a hot wife. Hot wives, Lionel had explained to Dulcie, were married women who, usually with the connivance of their husbands, announced their availability to men who were not their husbands by wearing gold chains around their right ankles. In the subculture where a semiology as subtle as this was recognised and acted on, a gold chain worn around the right ankle was as a promissory note of fornication with no strings attached, unless having the hot wife's husband looking on – as frequently occurred – could be called a string.

'It all sounds,' were Dulcie's first words to her husband on hearing about hot wives, 'appallingly blue collar. Did these people actually come to hear you play Janáček?'

'What you have to understand,' Lionel told her, 'is that they are in all other respects identical to you and me.'

Dulcie shuddered and feared the worst. Lionel had been seduced by one of these appalling women and had either fallen in love with her or brought home a social disease or both. Even if neither she was not sure she could forgive him. A woman with an ankle chain, from Detroit! Oh Lionel, Lionel, how could you?

But in fact – and Dulcie knew when he was telling the truth – Lionel had not fallen in love with anybody. He was as much in love with her, Dulcie, as he had ever been. In token whereof he had brought back from America an ankle chain for her to wear for him.

'To signal I am a hot wife?'

'Yes but only to me.'

'From what you've told me, Lionel,' she said, 'a hot wife is for other men to enjoy. Where would be the point of my showing you that I am available for other men's enjoyment when I'm not?'

He found that question, apparently, hard to answer. 'It's just the idea of it,' was the best, finally, he could manage.

'The idea that I am available to other men?'

'Yes.'

'Even though I'm not?'

'Yes.'

'Do you think you should see a psychiatrist?'

I had felt, even as she was talking to me, great sympathy for Lionel. I had met him a few times, either on the Antiquarian Booksellers Association's equivalent of a works outing, or at occasional recitals his quartet gave at the Wigmore Hall or other local venues which I felt we owed it to Dulcie to attend. I can't say I cared for him. He was at once a little too manly in the basso profundo, real-ale sense, and a little too womanly in the organisational way of things, ringing up unnecessarily to confirm dates and making lists of people's orders at restaurants – particularly Chinese restaurants where he liked to order by number – so as not to confuse the waiters, though his officiousness invariably confused them more. He had a long, Founding Father's face, marked by a sort of wolfish puritanism which he exaggerated by wearing what couldn't quite be called a beard, more a permanent five o'clock shadow which was sculpted into points on his cheeks and below his ears. There was something about the way he moved his mouth I didn't like either, as though it pained his teeth to talk to you. And he couldn't stop touching his hair. Even on stage, when he wasn't playing, his hair appeared to plague him. I'd have said it was a wig, except that no one would have paid good money for such a mildewed patch. But you don't have to like a man to feel for his predicament as a husband. He had been happily and conventionally married for too long. Nothing wrong with Dulcie. If you had to be happily and conventionally married for an eternity, Dulcie was probably the ideal person to be happily and conventionally married to. But the strain of keeping to the straight and narrow had begun to tell on him as it tells at last on everybody. It is too cruel, the way our society packages and sells the ideal of blissful conjugal normality. There is not enough room left for people to be peculiar. And by and large it is only by being peculiar that we achieve a measure of happiness. The majority of people who rang Marisa at their wits' end were not at their wits' end being peculiar. The peculiar are too busy being peculiar to have time to ring the Samaritans. It is not odd sex that drives people to the window ledge, it's no sex. We die of loneliness at the margins, not perversion. Perversion is exhilarating. The pervert might have second thoughts about himself sometimes but he knows he's alive.

Marisa told me this. Or at least I deduced it from the little Marisa did tell me. And I plied Dulcie with the essence of Marisa's wisdom. 'What do you think a psychiatrist might do for Lionel,' I asked her, 'that you, just by humouring him with an ankle chain, cannot?'

'Make his mind right.'

'Dulcie,' I said, 'there is no right.'

'You don't think it's wrong then that I should encourage his fantasy that I'm a hot wife?'

'I think it would be more wrong of you not to . . . so long as it doesn't otherwise entail your doing something you would rather not.'

'Wearing it is something I would rather not!'

'Well then,' I said, throwing open my hands, defeated by the perfect circularity of her logic.

'Would you ask this of your wife?' she suddenly asked.

I looked at the ground. 'An ankle chain, no,' I said. 'But that's just an aesthetic thing. And you have more slender ankles than Marisa.'

'Then, tell me,' she said, 'why a man would want this. Lionel says it's common. All over America, he says. And all over the Internet. If it's common, explain to me *why* it's common. What's happening to our society? I was brought up to believe a wife's job was to be faithful to her husband. Once upon a time Lionel went to bed and wouldn't speak to me for a month if I looked at another man. Now I'm supposed to be a hot wife.'

'Well I suppose the one is simply the other side of the other,' I said. 'If Lionel hadn't experienced the pangs of jealousy, he wouldn't be wanting to try them again in another form. No one who isn't by nature jealous is going to be interested in having a hot wife for a wife.'

She shook her head. They are very sad to behold, these well brought-up women with cat faces, when they are holding back the tears. And in the pink light of the snug she looked a very wan and melancholy sight indeed.

'You don't think,' she asked, 'that he is only wanting me to be a hot wife so that he can pay me back by being a hot husband?'

I told her I didn't believe there was such an animal, though thinking about his womanly side I didn't completely rule it out.

'Why don't you just humour him and wear the chain,' I said, 'on the understanding that the hot wife remains as fantasy. It's not an insult to you that he finds you an attractive woman and likes the idea that other men will find you attractive as well.'

'I did that. I humoured him. I wore the chain. Thank heavens you didn't notice, but I even wore it to work. But it's not enough. Now he wants to take photographs of me and post them on the Internet. Mr Quinn, I have children. What will they say if they open up their computers and find their mother smiling back at them in an ankle chain?'

'It's unlikely,' I said, 'that they would go looking on those sites.'

'You know those sites?' For a moment I thought she would tear her hair. 'You're my employer. What will *you* think if you find me smiling back at you wearing an ankle chain and, if Lionel were to have his way, precious little else? What if the trade sees me? What will that say about Felix Quinn: Antiquarian Booksellers?'

We both had the grace to laugh at that.

'So you've told him no?'

'I've told him no and removed the chain. He can like that or he can lump it.'

'And if he lumps it?'

Whereupon she cried upon my chest again.

And now here we were, six months on, lunching a mere three tables away from my hot wife, as Dulcie was bound to consider her, discussing the latest developments. We had got to the point of Dulcie's telling me that things had all got worse when Marisa and her Irish horse-breeder showed up. It took her a while to pick up her thread after that, so distracted was she by the horse-breeder, unless all that distracted her was what distracted me. Though she would not have dared, of course, to allude to it, she did put her hand on mind a second time and wonder if I wanted to call lunch off.

'No, Dulcie, why on earth should I?' I said.

She dropped her head and drank some water. 'What a world,' she said.

I waited and took the opportunity to ask the waiter to bring more bread.

'I have recently heard from my daughter,' she went on. 'She thinks she might be a lesbian.'

'Is that problematic for you?'

'It's problematic for her. She's studying theology.'

'Theology's different now,' I said.

'My family is going to pieces.'

'Because of your daughter?'

'No, just going to pieces. My daughter is part of the going-to-pieces process. When your mother wears an ankle chain you're bound to end up a lesbian, aren't you?'

I decided against asking her how her son was. 'You still haven't settled that, then?' I asked.

'Oh yes, we've settled it. The ankle chain is in the bin. But so is our marriage. Lionel has found me an admirer. He's an electrician.'

I didn't know why but I was reminded of one of my father's pisspot puns. *'Has Alec been in?' 'Who's Alec?' 'Alec Trician.'* So that was what I decided Dulcie's admirer must be called – Alec. But I kept the thought to myself.

'When you say "found you"?' I asked.

'I mean "found me". Picked him up off the street, for all I know. In overalls. Why couldn't he at least have found me a cellist?'

'You still wouldn't have been all right about it, Dulcie, if he'd found you Pablo Casals.'

She had a wonderfully droll way of enacting her despair, throwing her head back and opening the palms of her hands like a preacher. 'An electrician,' she said again. 'Lionel tells me he's bringing a friend home to dinner, asks me to wear something comfortable and cocktaily – wouldn't you think he'd know by now that no garment exists in which a woman can be both comfortable *and* cocktaily, let alone one in which she is meant to cook for her husband and his electrician friend as well? – and then shows me a Frank Sinatra CD he's just bought to "dance to later". We have never danced after dinner in our house, not ever. Lionel doesn't dance. But if I remind him of that I know what he'll say. "It won't be me that will be dancing." I am married to a sick man, Mr Quinn.'

'Oh, *sick*,' I said, waving away the word.

'What do you mean "Oh, sick"?'

'Only the sick are healthy,' I told her.

'That sounds cleverer than I think it is. What is healthy about being a paedophile or a rapist or a hot wife, come to that?'

'Or a lesbian?'

'I don't, now that I've had time to think about it, mind too much Phoebe's being lesbian. I'd have liked her to have children because I think she'd make a good mother, but if she's happy she's happy. Being lesbian isn't what I'd call sick.'

'People used to think it was. Time chips away at what we think is or isn't sick. In a hundred years' time the husband who wants his wife to wear an ankle chain will be considered the picture of health. And with a bit of luck they'll be locking up all those husbands who think their wives should cook the supper and love only them.'

'Thank God I'll be dead then.'

'But in the meantime,' I said, 'you can speed on the revolution. Dance with the electrician. And thank Lionel for the opportunity.'

'I don't need Lionel to find me an electrician, Mr Quinn. I can always find my own if I want one.'

'I don't doubt that, Dulcie. I mean thank Lionel for releasing you both from sex as a brute possessive instinct. It's a highly civilised thing he is asking of you. And of himself.'

'Civilised!'

She expostulated so loudly that half the restaurant turned to look. Though not Marisa and her lover who were too engrossed doing a civilised thing of their own.

'Yes. Civilised in the sense that it's a big step forward, for Lionel, from those old jealousies of his you've told me about. If he no longer has to put himself to bed every time you look at another man, be pleased.'

'I would be if it didn't mean that I had to put myself to bed with the other man.'

'Nothing's perfect. But at least you've now got a new post-phallic husband. The feminist in you should be pleased with that. Think that you've slain the patriarch, Dulcie.'

'And dance with the electrician? Better the patriarch you know, Mr Quinn.'

'He might be very nice.'

'But what if I don't want to find out?'

'Ah,' I said. The old *what if I don't want to find out* argument. How often modernity founders on that rock.

She could see I had no answer to it. You can't take people kicking and screaming over the sexual wall if they don't want to go with you. And yet it was clear Dulcie had hoped I'd be able to show her why she was wrong to refuse the climb. Wasn't that why we were having lunch?

So I had one more crack at it. 'There is this,' I said. 'If a man concentrates all his sexual curiosity upon his wife's capacity for misbehaviour, it stands to reason he will have neither time nor appetite for any of his own. Men married to hot wives are said to be as faithful and devoted as Labradors.'

She subjected me to one of her most precarious, eye-dropping scrutinies. 'You know that for sure, do you, Mr Quinn?'

'I deduce it. And I have seen the odd example of it for myself.'

'And do you think a woman wants that?'

'A faithful husband? Why ever not?'

'Not a faithful husband, a Labrador.'

'You don't like Labradors?'

'They dribble.'

I sighed. The old *who wants a dribbling Labrador for a husband* argument.

Dulcie sighed, too. She had, I noticed, been casting increasingly agitated looks in the direction of my wife's lover. 'I've been staring at him all through lunch but it's only just occurred to me who that gentleman is,' she said at last, with a quick glance at me to be sure I wouldn't mind her referring to him at all.

'Who is he, Dulcie?'

'My dentist. I've only ever seen him in a white coat.'

'Your dentist? You sure?'

'Sure.'

'Then I wonder if he's Marisa's dentist too,' I said, as much for my own benefit as Dulcie's.

Her green-grey eyes rested on me sadly. They were so wide apart it was almost like being looked at by two people, both of whom felt the same about me. At last, with a sweeping glance that took in the whole restaurant with all its garrulousness and glitter, all its gluttonous fantasies, spoken and unspoken, she asked, 'Where will it all end, Mr Quinn?'

'Where it always ends, Dulcie,' was the best I could say.

My lunch with Dulcie should have been, like Quirin's drunken imbecilic tumble down our staircase, a decisive event. To be sane as the world judges sanity is to know when there's a lesson staring you in the face. But then had I been a lesson learner I would long ago have looked at my father and given up being a man altogether.

I have not sought to hide my snobbishness, so it will surprise no one that I started from the association of my marriage with Lionel's as from a leprosy. Were we bonded in erotic necessity, that loose-toothed, ill-favoured, list-making, effeminately vulpine, vulgar viola player and me?

There is a contradiction here, I know. On the one hand I insist that what I feel all men feel, the only difference between us being that they will not admit it. On the other I no sooner see evidence of a commonality of sexual impulse than I turn against myself. If such wretches as one sees crawling between heaven and earth want what I want then would I not be better among the wantless dead? In the end you have to admit, to quote a foolish poet, that you 'share your knee bone with the gnat' or some such fatuity, and get on with scrabbling in the same slop bowl as the lowly. One must eat as other men eat, therefore one must desire as other men desire, too. But I found the idea of libidinal democracy impossible to accept when it came to ankle chains and hot wives.

Was there truly kinship between Lionel's cheap and cheerful fantasias for Dulcie and the austere religion of Marisa which I practised? I understood well enough Dulcie's revulsion from her husband's Americanised proposals. It wasn't the sex she hated, it was the Disneyfication of sex. I knew about hot wives. I had been to Minneapolis myself on book-associated business, I had even made an after-dinner speech at an Antiquarian

Booksellers Association conference in Milwaukee, and while I hadn't met anyone I could identify as a hot wife on those trips, I had a sense that they were out there, in the malls and in the shopping aisles of Wal-Mart. There is a significant subculture of wife worship in America, sometimes opportunistic in the way Dulcie feared – a pretext merely for trading an old wife in for a new – but more usually of the classically submissive sort, the husband wanting the wife to emasculate him, ideally, it is embarrassing to report, through consorting with a well-hung black man who pimps her out to his friends and in extreme cases having the black man's child. Perhaps because of the castrating times we live in, contemporary pornography has more of cuckolding in it than any other deviancy, and race-based emasculative cuckolding would seem, at least for Americans, to be the most popular fantasy of all. I was no stranger to the literature and winced from it: men who wished not to be men, husbands who called themselves wimps and sissies, husbands who could only be happy when their wives laughed at the ineffectiveness of their genitalia, husbands who dreamed of sucking black men's sperm out of their wives' vaginas. Was I on this continuum of castration? Was my dismembered trance just a dishonest man's metaphor for this same longing not to be a man at all?

No, is my considered answer. There is no continuum of aberration, except in the sense that every act of sex sits at a crossroads which leads to every other. We would all perish ecstatically in sex at last if we had the courage to go on travelling. 'In the end,' Bataille said, 'we resolutely desire that which imperils our life.' Otherwise, no, I was not companioned in the kitsch of being cuckolded with Lionel. I was a Frenchman, not an American, in my erotic life, seeking carnality's greatest prize – extinction. No one could have been further removed than I was from the breezy Disneyland of wife-swapping, cocktail nuts and ankle chains. No one.

But I kept an aloof eye, as it were, on these distant cousins in perversion, as an aristocrat enjoying perfect health might note with concern the incidence of rickets among the poorer branches of his family. Though Lionel and Dulcie were not family, I feared they had brought the affliction closer to me than I could tolerate. The thought even occurred to me as we were talking that Marisa and her lover were having the identical conversation about me. 'He's sick, Miles. He needs help.' And Miles, I was pretty sure, would not be championing me, as I'd vainly championed Lionel, as one of masculinity's pioneers, scouting for what was out there beyond the phallic pale. Dentists don't think like that.

Enough. To the degree that it was within my power to rescue Marisa from the category of hot wife, and me from the category of sperm-snuffling sissy, then I should do it. Enough. We had gone far enough. But no sooner did I make the decision to parley with Marisa and put it to her that we were in mortal danger of looking like the thing we both despised, that while morally we were sainted and heroic, aesthetically we had sinned, and so, my dear, enough – at that precise moment of resolution I heard the vitality leave my body in a rush. The psychoanalyst Theodor Reik describes what comes over a masochist 'patient' as he closes in on what might be termed 'recovery'. 'He notices that life loses some of its richness, its interest and colour. Life is felt as dreary, the day is trivial; life seems to have lost its substance. It becomes numb and meaningless.'

Which was exactly how 'recovery' felt to me as I envisaged it. *Enough*? I couldn't say the word.

Enough trivialised the day.

Enough made life numb, dreary and meaningless.

Enough promised nothing that had any richness, interest or colour in it.

There was no *Enough*.

Something else occurred that lunchtime which should have sent me in one direction, had I been a sane man, but which sent me once and for all, since I was not a sane man, in the other.

The something else was a look Marisa threw me across the restaurant, a look that bypassed her one-time Irish millionaire lover, now a dentist, bypassed Dulcie, and simply rested on me like a torch-beam in an empty room. Only two people who knew the complexions of each other's souls and knew what compassion the one could call on in the other, would have been able to exchange what we exchanged in a single glance. I read Marisa's meaning in her eyes, but it was the expression of her whole face that spoke to me. She opened her eyes wide, emphasising those serious tea-bag stains which I had always regarded as the site of all that was philosophic in her nature. Such a serious and reflective face, and yet kind and mirthful too in the wide, pearl-shadowed spaces above her eyelids. *How are you getting on with Dulcie?* her expression asked. *She looks as though she is having a hard time of it for whatever reason. I hope you are being gentle with her. You can be ironic and impatient, Felix, so please don't be. I don't think she is strong enough for that. Few people are. You underestimate the strength of your personality and will. I intend no reproach by saying that. What you will you will and what I do I do. You exercise no tyranny over me. Perhaps you try to, but in so far as I submit to it I do so for my own reasons which are not necessarily my own desires. You sometimes, I think, confuse the two but they are not the same. You can have a reason for doing something that doesn't answer to a desire to do it. I will say no more. I am a fictionaliser like you, and I know what truth can spoil. You look, by the by, very nice sitting there. It gives me immense pleasure to see you across a room, I don't always get the opportunity to see you in this way. And seeing you looking so nice I wish we were at the same table, you and I, talking. We have always talked so well together. Sad, isn't it, that we can't be doing it. Or at least that we can't be doing it at this instant . . .*

The way back. There it was – the retreat into normalcy.

As always, at such a time, the hobgoblins of the ordered world gathered to congratulate me on my narrow escape. *Thank your lucky stars you didn't get what you were after,* they gibbered. *Now you can live as the sane live. And be careful in the future what you ask for.* And just as reliably, the other voice – the voice of my addiction – shouted the impossibility, the undesirability (quite literally that which answered to none of my desires), of giving in to reason. I could even taste it on my tongue: the savourlessness of living as the sane live.

~

He didn't matter to Marisa, her Irish lover. If that wasn't what she was telling me, it was what I saw. Throughout my conversation with Dulcie I had kept track of Marisa and her lunch companion and no, they weren't tearing at each other's throats or grabbing handfuls of each other's flesh beneath the table. I took note of who put whose hands where, and no, they didn't. Call that crude, but there was necessity in it. I also took note of whether they whispered under cover of conversing about food, leaned cheek to cheek, met noses or kissed with their lips parted, and no, they didn't do that either. In most regards they looked no different from me and Dulcie. What I thought I'd seen when they raised glasses I probably hadn't. Maybe Miles was her lover, maybe he was just her dentist, taking her out to monitor her bite, maybe he was both – it didn't signify, one way or the other. This much I knew for sure: she wasn't hot for him. Very probably she liked him well enough – certainly she'd have approved his tailoring and spotless scalded fingers – but she didn't long to be with him, didn't conjure up his body or his features when he wasn't there or count the hours before she could be with him again or keep a curl of his hair in a locket worn around her neck. And certainly didn't tango with him like a mare in heat.

Excuse the frilly language, but that's jealousy for you. If you refuse to descend into the cesspit with Othello or roll around the comic brothel with Leo Bloom, snickering at the keyhole of your own cuckoldry – *Show! Hide! Show! Plough her! More! Shoot!* – then all you're left with is the bodice-ripper or the girly mags. Nothing I could do about it: the minute I put my mind to Marisa on the loose, I either had her swooning in the arms of a highwayman in tight breeches, or stripped naked and fucked until her brains bled. I accept no personal responsibility for this. When it comes to finding words for sex, the narrowest no-man's-land separates the most refined imagination from the coarsest. Literature and popular romance the same – the border between them is invisible and unpoliced. Is *Jane Eyre* a novel of serious intent or an exercise in sentimental pornography? At the moment Anna Karenina weeps over the loss of her honour to Vronsky, are we in a tragedy or a penny dreadful? We are in both, is the answer. Because desire itself inhabits that same narrow strip of unclaimed territory between sacrament and slush.

Consider this scene. A youth, sick with love for an unattainable woman, goes riding with his father. When they reach a 'tall stack of old logs' the father dismounts and tells the boy to wait where he is. Eventually, when the father does not return, the boy goes looking for him. At last he finds him, standing by the window of a small wooden house, talking to a beautiful woman. The woman, of course, is the object of the boy's unrequited love. Something – 'stronger than curiosity, stronger even than jealousy' – stops him from running away. (We know what that 'something' is: the ecstatic anticipation of proof oracular.) Then an 'unbelievable' event takes place before his eyes. The father lifts his riding crop and strikes the young woman a sharp blow across her arm, which is bared to the elbow. She quivers, looks silently at her assailant, then raises her arm slowly to her lips, and kisses the scar which 'glows crimson upon it'.

Phallic logs, sons sexually envious of their fathers, riding crops, crimson scars, women of spirit made to cower and quiver – of what work of monumentally melodramatic tosh is this the climax? Ivan Turgenev's *First Love*. And it is a masterpiece.

Great Expectations, of which my father once, for a small fortune, sold a copy signed by Dickens to his mistress Ellen Ternan, binds us into the same near-Gothic tale. In both novels a boy etherialises a woman out of her corporeal existence. In both instances he must suffer the spectacle of another man or men violently returning her to it.

Grand guignol, I grant you. But that's the temperature at which a man's erotic imagination functions. *Mal*functions, you might say. I won't argue the toss. But pity us anyway, clattering between the extremes of believing that a woman is beyond the gross contaminating touch of man, and fearing that the brute male assurance of which we are incapable is what she's really after.

But where was the brute male assurance in Marisa's life? Not sitting at her table – anyone could see that. Whatever else Miles had going for him, he wasn't mastering my wife the way mastering works in Turgenev and the bodice-ripper. Didn't have the muscles. Didn't have the dirty eyes. Didn't have what Henry James, that sad voyeur of one primal betrayal after another, called the 'sacred terror'. Good. For that relief, muchibus thankibus. Another hurdle in the steeplechase of dread negotiated.

But after the relief, the let-down. For if Miles was no threat to me, who was? What if all Marisa's lovers were like him, doctors or dentists or accountants, no more capable of wielding the riding crop than I was? Worse – what if Miles *was* all Marisa's lovers? My cathedral bed of jealous agony was a fraud in that case. I had no one to be agonisedly jealous of.

And perhaps that too was what I read in Marisa's expression across the restaurant – that she felt she'd let me down. That she'd done her best for both of us, but this was the limit of her iniquity. Reality had blown away illusion, and now the game was up.

I meant what I'd said to Dulcie about the faithfulness a wife can rely on from a husband who finds his fulfilment in her unfaithfulness to him. I didn't stop looking at other women when I first met Marisa. She hadn't, by simple virtue of her beauty and her presence, removed me from the field of promiscuous desire. But the moment I saw the Cuban doctor's fingers on her and conceived her infidelity, I became hers only. No other woman was remotely interesting to me. I neither looked at them nor thought of them. Not once. What could any of them have given me that would be anything like as engrossing – engrossing of every aspect of my attention – as *this*? False to me, Marisa occluded all her sex. I lived only to be faithful to her.

But fidelity of this sort – eroticised fidelity, by comparison with which the gadfly vacillation of the libertine is as gruel to wine – extorts its price. It aroused me to be faithful on the condition that she was not. I am not saying I would not have gone on being faithful to Marisa had she not gone on being faithless to me, but the arousal was in the inequity. For me to burn for her, Marisa had to burn for someone else. I could not lie transfixed in subspace, imagining her out in the abandoned night, if she were merely enjoying an orderly conversation with someone at the very sight of whom she did not go up in flames. If I were to continue extinguishing myself as a man, it had to be in a higher cause than this. Marisa had to frighten me with greater recklessness, of heart and body, and with a rival far more destructive of my peace of mind, and far more menacing to her erotic self-composure, than Miles.

Someone who would bring the both of us to our knees.

Enter, courtesy of that pimp Fortune, Marius.

Is it any wonder I made a grab for him? A vaguely troubling presence when I'd had no need for him, a distant figure agitating me at the margins of my masculinity, here suddenly he was, deranged and dangerous, an abstemious immoralist, a sadist at his wits' end, and on my doorstep. Just the man to save my marriage.

PART THREE

MARIUS AND MARISA

'Love her, love her, love her! If she favours you, love her. If she wounds you, love her. If she tears your heart to pieces . . . love her, love her, love her!'

Charles Dickens, *Great Expectations*

OF THE SOCIETY BEAUTIES WHOSE PORTRAITS HANG IN THE WALLACE Collection, the most palpitatingly lovely is Margaret, Countess of Blessington, painted by Sir Thomas Lawrence. She is positioned prominently, as she deserves to be, in a brothel-red damask and velvet chamber, to your right as you enter the gallery. I was introduced to her initially by my father who, whatever else there was to say against him, believed his son should have an art education, the more particularly as there was such a capital collection around the corner from where we lived. The old reach-out-and-grab principle.

His was, it's true, a fairly peremptory idea of what constituted aesthetic discourse – 'Now that,' he told me, pausing in front of Lady Blessington, 'is what you call a bosom' – but some fathers don't even get that far with their sons' education.

Lady Blessington was on Marisa's mind in the period following her eyeballing Marius in the cheese shop because, in her capacity as a volunteer guide and occasional lecturer, she had agreed to give a short talk about the portrait; and Lady Blessington was on my mind because, in my capacity as procurer for my wife, I thought Marius would get something out of hearing Marisa delivering it.

It wasn't to be a major PowerPoint presentation in one of the gallery's grand lecture theatres, just a gentle disquisition in front of the painting itself. Part of a series entitled *Meet the Ladies of the Collection* which the gallery was running. *Ladies* of the collection as in the aristocratic subjects of the portraits – Madame de Pompadour, Madame du Barry, Lady Hamilton, etc. – but also, by implication, allowing that women are not called ladies any more, as in Marisa and her fellow female volunteers. That was what the flyer advertising the series of talks showed: the six women lecturers standing in front of the six painted ladies – someone at the gallery, I fancied, hoping for a television series.

It wasn't one of Marisa's favourite portraits, perhaps because the Countess of Blessington wasn't one of her favourite subjects. Marisa, remember, was not a cleavage kind of person, whereas the countess was famous throughout Europe for the deep voluptuousness of hers. Nonetheless, she admired Thomas Lawrence's execution well enough.

I, on the other hand, though not a cleavage kind of person either, won't hear a word against the lady. That she makes the most of her famously esteemed chest (Lamb and Hazlitt, as well as my father, were among its admirers) in a gown which uplifts and accentuates it, and by adopting a pose in which she would appear to be showing how little it is subject to gravity – as though in her all flesh becomes as air – I'd see no reason to deride even if she hadn't been a woman of unpromising origins who had to make the most of what Nature had bestowed on her. As the ugly duckling of a none-too-particular Irish landowning family she was married off at an indecently early age to a drunken army officer who beat and imprisoned her. After three months of hellish marriage she contrived to run away. I don't hold with beating women, but I see this experience as important to the history of the woman she became: childless, prolific in her literary invention (no good writer was ever not beaten or otherwise maltreated first), and somewhat cold, not to say authoritative in her amours.

She was still not twenty when another officer took her, as they say, under his protection, transporting her from Tipperary to Hampshire, where she read long, studied hard, and we must suppose fulfilled, in private and in public, every expectation of a mistress since she soon became the object of a further transaction, passing from the captain's hands to those of Lord Mountjoy, later the Earl of Blessington, for the sum – more than princely by the measure of 1815 or thereabouts – of £10,000.

One has, as I recall saying to Marisa in the course of an argument about Lady Blessington, to be grown up about all this. We wouldn't barter a woman today, but we did once. Myself, I have this to say: if a lady with so much to recommend her, consented to be treated like an object that could be bought and sold, it must be fair to surmise that she had her eye on many of the attendant benefits, to wit the adoration of an influential man, as much jewellery as she could wear, a title she could call her own, entry into educated society, the opportunity to be listened to and read, and the freedom ultimately to enter the sexual commodities market herself, this time as a buyer not a seller.

However you view the compromises into which she was forced, Margaret, Countess of Blessington, having been several times a mistress, became at last what can only be called a master. Confident in her powers, she took up with a dandified French count some thirteen years her junior, and this in full public glare and while still married to the Earl of Blessington who, by all accounts, didn't seem to mind. To me it is obvious that the earl, a man renowned for his munificence, did not only 'not mind' but was active in his encouragement of the count. He loved his wife, therefore it stood to reason that he must love her no less when other men loved her, too, and she loved them in return. No doubt he was present when the countess put the little Frenchman over her knee and did to him what had too many times been done to her.

'You wish!' Marisa said.

In fact I didn't wish. Whatever worked for the Earl of Blessington would never have worked for me. It didn't excite me to think of Marisa touching fingers in the ballroom with a perfumed dandy. I'd already seen her touching fingers with a perfumed dandy over lunch and I was still alive to tell the tale. Nothing less than the devil taking her would do me now.

Read her as you will, the 'most gorgeous Lady Blessington', armed with husband and effeminised lover, continued to entrance the world of literature and fashion. 'She looked superb,' the painter Benjamin Robert Haydon wrote of her in 1835 when, by the standards of the day, she was to be accounted middle-aged. 'Her beautiful complexion engoldened by the luxurious light of an amorous sleepy lamp, her whole air melting, voluptuous, intellectual and overwhelming.'

To my mind, it is hard to conceive a more complete compliment being paid to a woman of any age, let alone one of forty-five, or, if you measure as Marius measured, rapidly approaching four o'clock, her day not yet spent, the wheels of her evening beginning to turn. She died of a heart attack in her fifty-ninth year, an age Marius found impossible to contemplate in the woman he had once loved to distraction. The count, however, was inconsolable. So not all young or younger men recoil from a wrinkle as though it is the plague.

Whatever our disagreements about Lady Blessington, I had no doubt Marisa would speak wonderfully about the portrait, both as it brought alive an extraordinary woman and as it related to other society paintings in the collection. I'd already heard her, for example, on the Henry Bone enamel miniature of Lady Hamilton as a bacchante on the opposite wall. The enamel had been done from an original – which it would have been a kindness to leave alone, Marisa said – by Vigée-Lebrun. So what is it you don't like about it again, I'd ask her, for the pure pleasure of hearing her say, 'Well, she's plump, soft, hairy and stupid, for starters. And as for that gauze nightgown, which leaves as little of her podgy flesh to the imagination as Lord Nelson presumably would have desired, I can't conceive where she found it given that Ann Summers hadn't yet opened up a shop in 1803.'

The one thing Marisa, as a woman, couldn't be expected to understand was the erotic appeal of gaucherie in a woman with a title. A society woman making such a bad job of being a bacchante finds its way into the excruciation system of a man, where getting it sexually wrong is transformed into getting it sexually right. Which is not to say one would want to frolic with Lady Hamilton looking like that for long. In the end – and I didn't doubt Marius was of my party in this – the intelligence in a woman's eyes is more provocative than any other part of her no matter what her state of undress. No woman could be seductive who wasn't clever – that, I was sure, was where we both stood.

So the sooner Marius got to hear Marisa in full aesthetic flow the better.

I had a word with Andrew, Marius's old college acquaintance, about persuading Marius to come along to Marisa's talk. They had the occasional drink together, I gathered, though Marius rarely stayed out longer than half an hour, leaving without a word the minute Andrew went to the bathroom or otherwise gave him an opportunity to escape. I made up some cock and bull story about my worrying whether Marisa would get a fair crowd for her talk. It was Andrew who'd told me about Marius's passion for Baudelaire, and since Baudelaire had written about the artificial in art, and woman's airs, and dandies, it was possible he'd be interested in what Marisa had to say on those subjects as they bore on the life of Lady Blessington. Could he suggest it to him? Not to say who Marisa was or anything. I didn't want to be seen begging my wife an audience. Just a discreet nudge. Not important. But I'd be grateful. And never of course to mention a word of this to Marisa whenever he next met her.

I gave him the flyer which had Marisa's photograph on it. If Marius bothered to look he would surely recognise her face and that would be that.

Perhaps Andrew did as I asked, perhaps he didn't. I think my interest in Marius piqued him a little. You never know where jealousy will surface. Perhaps Marius saw the flyer, perhaps he didn't. What I suspect got him to the lecture was more providential than planned: a tableau, as I saw it, of inevitable connection – Marius cooling his heels in Manchester Square, deciding whether or not he was yet ready, after Elspeth, to look at paintings again, and seeing Marisa going in and out of the gallery, sharper put together than your usual gallery-goer, everything about her equivocal, severe and yet seductive all at once, her leather music case gripped under her arm because she disliked the femininity of a handbag, but her earrings saying something else, her heels picking at the paving as though it were ice beneath her feet, or as though she owed the stones some injury, angry – he must have thought – much as he was angry around art, a woman who looked at a painting more in the way he looked at a painting, grudgingly, not gushingly, whatever the pleasure, like someone startled out of a pleasant reverie, resenting the painter or the paint for pulling so importunately at that something in the heart that wishes to be left alone . . . and in that instant seeing (just as I had seen) his fate. Remembering her from the fromagerie – you don't forget a woman you've looked over as comprehensively as Marius had looked over Marisa – he must have wondered what frequent business took her to the Wallace Collection, and found in that wondering his opportunity to enter a gallery again, to look at paintings again, and in the process discover who she was and what she did. The consequence of which was his appearing at the back of Marisa's audience, drinking in her words.

I too was standing at the rear but changed my position when I saw him enter. It felt like a changing of the watch. He stepped forward, I stepped back. A woman in front of me turned round to see what the commotion was, so loudly was my heart beating.

Marisa's talk was a success. That air she had of being somewhere else worked well when she spoke in public. She didn't try to please. She gave the impression of a person looking deep into a subject which both was and wasn't in the room with her. The right way, I have always thought, to address art. As something that is and isn't of one's time.

People went up to her afterwards to talk about this and that. I hung back, as I always did. Not a husband's business to be nosing into his wife's public triumphs. But I had more reason to stay out of the way this time because Marius, too, was waiting to say something to her. He let others go before him. I recognised the tactic. He wanted to be last. When he did have her to himself he ventured an observation he hoped she wouldn't find too personal.

'A very impressive act of concealment,' he said, touching his moustaches nervously.

She wondered what he meant.

'I feel I have been listening to someone speaking fondly of an enemy rather than a friend,' he went on.

'I don't think of Lady Blessington as my enemy. Why should I? She is past doing me any harm.'

He smiled a slow sad knowing smile. 'A person can harm you from the grave,' he said.

She looked up at him. She wasn't used to looking up at men. 'And what harm, even from the grave, is it that you think I fear? Not the harm of a comparison, I hope. I'm not competing with her for fortune, or for looks.'

His eyes went from her to the painting and back again. His expression suggested she had nothing to fear from any such comparison. 'On the contrary,' he said, 'I think you bear a striking resemblance to her, or she to you if you prefer it that way.'

'Well I wouldn't say no to her figure,' she laughed. Marisa had never needed me to teach her how to her flirt.

She coloured a little. So did he.

'I wonder,' he said, 'if the similarity isn't precisely the reason for your hostility towards her, if that isn't to put it too extremely. There's something in her eyes that might remind you of yourself. Something that would be direct and yet isn't. Not a pleading, exactly, but a half-sadness, and with it a sort of expectation of sympathy she isn't certain she deserves or even wants.'

Rather than look at Marius, who was becoming guilty of something very close to impertinence, Marisa looked at the portrait. He was right. Lady Blessington leans a little forward in her scarlet chair, lightly clasping her hands – a gesture of nervous ownership, of composure not quite attained. And yes, she didn't like the look. Though it had not occurred to her that she didn't like it because it reminded her of herself.

She turned to face Marius again. 'You know a lot about me,' she said, 'for someone I've never spoken a word to before.'

He mumbled what might have been an apology into his moustache. 'I was struck by your talk, for which I thank you,' he said. 'I listened hard. That was all. I just thought you weren't saying all you thought.'

'So you are privy to my intellectual life as well? I am an open book to you, evidently. You miss neither the words I don't say nor the sadness I don't feel.'

He stared hard into her face, noting the tea-bag stain pouches under her eyes, the site where the skin would turn from ochre to yellow and at last to brown, though as yet the pouches suited her, suggesting the play of seriousness, a capacity for philosophic amusement unspoiled by levity. He was like me in this regard: he loathed inconsequence. Or at least he did in the company of Marisa. No silly voices or foolish accents with her. A man who could be himself only with women, I noted. Or with women with whom he thought he could fall in love. 'I would much rather,' he said, lowering his gaze at last, 'that you gave me the chance to know exactly what it is you do feel.'

She shook her head – a rattle of razor blades. 'That won't be possible,' she said. 'I'm doing only one talk in this series. And I've just done it.'

He was about to say that wasn't what he meant but recovered his subtlety in time. He'd been up in Shropshire too long. Consorting with the under and the overaged.

'Perhaps, then, we could reconvene at the next person's talk.'

'Do you have an interest in Boucher's portrait of Madame de Pompadour?'

'I do if you do.'

'I don't.'

'Perhaps we could reconvene so you could tell me why.'

'Perhaps we could,' she said. With which she turned her body and her attention to other matters.

So was that a date or wasn't it?

Marius, for his part, wasn't sure. He strode back home with no spring in his step, his mouth set in a curl of hollow distaste. He told himself he was bored. What else was sexual desire but boredom turning in its sleep? However they started, these things always finished the same way. Her mention of Boucher reminded him of his precious Baudelaire, spleening it to the moon:

> I am an ancient boudoir filled with faded roses
> In which a ruck of long-outmoded gowns reposes,
> Where pastels all too sad and Bouchers all too pale
> Alone breathe in the scents that uncorked flasks exhale.

Marius, too, was an ancient boudoir, his sorry brain the repository of too many secrets, poems, love letters and golden curls. Worst of all, it held the fatal knowledge of what always comes next, the unmistakable finale heard in the overture.

He was ungrateful, it seemed to me. He was undeserving. It's a species of rudeness amounting to cruelty not to be able to accept an erotic adventure and maybe even the promise of erotic happiness when it's offered you, no matter that the offer has a few equivocations in it.

But I had to accept what was offered me as well. It was for his cruelty, when all was said and done, that I'd sought him out. It was for the trouble he was capable of causing. So I wasn't going to relinquish him for being himself. When you find a man like Marius you don't willingly let him go.

I happen to know that Elspeth clung to his legs when he told her he was leaving. It was a most terrible scene. A woman in her middle sixties and a man not yet forty, a mother and her son they might have been, except that mothers don't behave that way with their sons, except in the murderously pornographic novels – of which I have a signed set in mint condition, not for sale – of Georges Bataille. Though Marius had loved her so deeply in their first years together that he would sometimes weep over the transience of her mature beauty while she slept, afraid that each breath might be her last (and he the reason for it), unable to imagine any life of the senses without her, all he felt when she clung sobbing to his legs (unable to imagine her life without *him*), was revulsion.

'To despoil is the essence of eroticism,' Bataille wrote, which is why 'there is nothing more depressing than an ugly woman . . . for ugliness cannot be spoiled.' Old age with its indignities, similarly. It had been something for Marius to live for, profaning the elegance of this older woman by subjecting her to every act of loving and not so loving animality his fevered ingenuity could devise. But there was nothing left now to profane or despoil. Time had done it for him.

Her hands, he noticed, had grown square, the skin at the base of her fingers puffy, as grey as dough. And she was without wrists now. Her thumb was an extension of her arm. Fingers which he would once, and not so many years ago, have plucked with violence one by one from contact with another man, he found so loathsome that the effort necessary to pluck them from his legs was beyond him.

'It doesn't become you, Elspeth, to behave like this. Not at your age.' Did he actually say those words to her or did he merely think them? It's an unnecessary distinction. You cannot think those words in the presence of somebody who loves you without your face betraying them.

'At my age! Do you dare? How many times did I beg you,' she cried, 'that if you were going to leave me, to leave when I was young enough at least to make provision for myself? Now look at me.'

Look at her? That was the last thing of which he was capable.

'You were never young enough to make provision for yourself,' he might or might not have said. 'Not on my watch.'

'Didn't I say to leave me where I was if you were not sure you could love me forever?'

'How could I have left you where you were? You weren't happy.'

'I was happy enough.'

'Had you been happy enough——' But no, that he couldn't say. Instead, 'It doesn't fall to any man to be sure he'll love a woman forever, Elspeth.'

'Yes it does. Yes he can. And if he can't then he must leave the woman where she is. I had a life, didn't I? I was cared for. I was secure. I didn't need you to come along and do *this*.'

Her mouth, he noticed, had lost the fleshy fullness he had once loved. In her distraction it hung open, like a dog's, and he wondered if she would ever again be able to close it fully, or to keep it dry. The brows of her eyes, too, once so full of challenge, striking in the broad arch of their expressiveness, particularly when she laughed or conveyed desire, had fallen below the bone, making her look tired and bewildered, again like an old dog fearing the end.

When he drew his legs away from her clutches – yes, *clutches* – she fell forward on to the floor, striking her head. This seemed to suggest to her a last, desperate course of action. 'I begged you, I begged you,' she screamed, banging her head on the floorboards willingly now, blow after blow, causing blood to pour from her face, meaning to dash her brains out if she could. And to spill them at his feet.

'Elspeth!' he cried. 'Elspeth, please stop it.'

But he couldn't go to her. Couldn't touch her. Couldn't help her.

MARISA DIDN'T KNOW WHETHER THEY HAD A DATE EITHER. SHE, TOO, WAS out of sorts. She feared she'd been obvious, both in allowing Marius to see that the painting had got under her skin, and in showing him it irritated her to be found out. Wasn't this precisely what infuriated her in the portrait of Countess Blessington – a wealthy and successful woman, at the height of her influence and power, unable to conceal her vulnerability? No, not unable, *unwilling*. Marisa could perfectly well see why the painting, in Byron's words, had 'set all London raving'. It was what usually set all London raving in a woman: the persistence in her of the supplicating girl. A pettish and slightly crooked girl at that, beggarly even, despite the fur and finery; a suggestion, beneath the allure of her assurance, of uncertainty and neediness. Was this to be woman's indelible mark, no matter how far she progressed in the world of men – the wanting to be loved and rescued by them?

And she, Marisa, had betrayed this very neediness on her own face.

She couldn't forgive herself. She would show Marius a different expression the next time.

How did I know she was contemplating a next time? I lived inside her head, that's how I knew. Had we been Siamese twins my heart could not have been attuned more sensitively to hers. But it worked the other way, too. I passed my dreads to her along her bloodstream, where eventually – in her own time – she transmuted them into her own desires.

She didn't turn up the following week for the Madame de Pompadour talk. She wasn't going to be obvious. But the week after she lunched late with Flops at the Café Bagatelle in the gallery's sculpture garden – two hours sitting over a plate of rocket salad and parmesan shavings, a further thirty minutes looking harder at the urns than any urn could merit – being careful to return to the room where the next talk in the series was being held, at the stroke of four o'clock.

Marius was not there.

She was mildly disappointed. She looked good, she thought, in a not too short steel-grey tulip skirt and wide leather belt, high-heeled sandals that showed her painted toes, big metallic earrings and of course a white shirt in which when she moved she rippled. She coruscated, was her own view of herself. But he wasn't there to be dazzled. She was more surprised than hurt. Her instinct for these things was normally uncanny. If she expected to see a man she saw him. 'I conjure them,' she joked in an entry in her diary that might or might not have been left around for me to read. 'Some people bend spoons, I conjure men.'

This was no wanton boast. More a reflection on the cruelty of things. Conjuring men was her affliction.

But she did not, on this occasion, conjure Marius.

She tried to dismiss him from her mind. He was not important to her. For herself she could take him or leave him alone.

The next talk in the series she skipped. Two could play at touch me not.

But the final one she attended. As, by the marvellous synchronicity of warped desire, did Marius.

I missed them meeting. (I was loitering with intent – Marisa's intent – in Manchester Square. 'Leave the shop early,' she'd told me. 'Wait for me. Don't know how long I'll be.') But it must have gone off well, because afterwards they sauntered round the gallery together, Marius deferring to her expertise, Marisa thinking he might like to see how Fragonard's *The Swing* looked in its new position in the reinstalled Oval Room. My understanding is that they spent more time looking at this painting than a man and woman who are not officially betrothed should ever be allowed to spend. In my perhaps overexcited interpretation of events, what had of necessity transpired between them – given the painting, given the over-heatedness of their discourse – was this: in full public view, and on the basis of an acquaintance of no more than fifteen minutes' duration, including the look they had exchanged at the cheese counter, they had made Marisa's vagina the subject of their conversation. Indeed, had Marius kneeled before her, unzipped the pinstripe trousers she was wearing, pulled aside her underclothes and exposed her genitals to his curiosity, he could not have offended against decorum more. I make no judgements. I merely describe events as they occurred.

A shame I missed it.

That they were able to do this without causing a scandal I ascribe to education. Educated people, particularly those educated in literature or the visual arts, have more ways of talking about a woman's vagina than those who leave school when they're fifteen. The latter will claim they call a vagina a vagina – except, of course, they mainly call it something else – and that talking about it anyway is not what they prefer to do. Thus they miss out twice: first on knowledge, then on sex at its most refined – talking about it being an indispensable prologue to doing it with any grace. But then the uneducated are not taught to value grace.

I'm not sure how much Marius knew already about the happenstance of Fragonard's *The Swing*, originally titled *Les Hazards Heureux de l'Escarpolette*, but whatever gaps in his knowledge my Marisa found, my Marisa filled.

In fact you don't have to be educated beyond the common tittle-tattle of art history to know how Fragonard came to accept the commission for this most prurient example of rococo trifling, so innocently admired of the art-loving public that they have it reproduced on tea towels and table mats though it is about the pudenda and nothing else. I don't intend to repeat that tittle-tattle here. Suffice it to remind those who have forgotten that a lesser painter than Fragonard had been invited to execute the composition first, but declined the commission on the grounds that it was indecent. The commissioner of the painting – a French gentleman of the court – wished to have his mistress painted swinging in a bower, as high and as uninhibitedly as a bird. Pushing the swing was to be a bishop, and gazing up her skirts was to be the gentleman of the court. Why the bishop no one knows. As Marisa would have said to Marius, 'There is no plumbing the religious filthy-mindedness of the French.'

It's possible that for the painter – at the time enjoying some éclat in Paris as a religious allegorist – the bishop was the last straw. But it's also possible, as Marius might have surmised in return to Marisa, as they stared up at the painting together, 'That the invitation to throw the lady's legs as wide as the composition or his imagination would allow was not one he felt he could accept, bishop or no bishop.'

Fragonard, being less queasy, and no doubt with a quicker intuitive understanding of why a man might choose to submit the private parts of the woman he loves to the eyes of as many onlookers as possible, took over without demur, introduced a young voyeur – perhaps to double the nobleman's excitement – and painted what Marisa described as 'The most profusely arboreal excuse for a vagina ever seen.'

Thus was coition managed between them, as an act of purely intellectual indecency, in a room full of art lovers not a one of whom would have noticed that anything untoward had happened.

Except me, and I wasn't even there.

They took tea – as I was able to learn, deduce, or otherwise piece together later – in the courtyard where Marisa had expected him, but then again not, a fortnight before. Marius wondered, since their afternoon had been so educative, whether she would accompany him to dinner on an evening of her choosing in order that he might be educated some more. She told him she was a married woman. He asked her to name her favourite cuisine. She told him Italian. He said his was French. She asked him if he spent time in France. He said only in his head. She wondered what he had against going there in body. He told her he was more head than body, just as he was more past than present. *Je suis un vieux boudoir plein de roses fanées*, he said. Baudelaire, he told her. I thought as much, she said. Which was why, he continued, it was such a pleasure, *this* – stretching out his fingertips to her, which she didn't touch with hers, she being a married woman – to talk to someone in the living present. There were too many withered roses, and insufficient live ones. She laughed at him. He coloured. She apologised.

'I've never been able to take flower imagery seriously,' she said. 'The nuns used to beat me for laughing at Wordsworth. *Three years she grew in sun and shower* – and I had my head in the desk, imagining this little girl standing in the rain for three years.'

'The nuns! You were a novitiate?'

'Hardly. But I boarded at a convent for a year. My mother thought I needed a religious education. In fact it was she who needed a religious education. She released me into the hands of nuns to expiate her sins.'

'And did you?'

'No. Which must be why I am expiating them still.'

'Is that what you're doing? I thought you were agreeing to meet me for dinner.'

She made a pyramid of her fingers. 'You are a presumptuous man,' she said.

'You know a lot about me,' he said, echoing her earlier words to him, 'for someone you've barely spoken to before.'

She smiled, and no doubt flushed a little, to be reminded of his full-frontal attack on her the afternoon of her talk on Lady Blessington.

'I'll tell you what,' she said. 'Since you offered then to know so much about me, and offer now to be so certain I'll enjoy your company, I'll accept your invitation on one condition.'

'And what condition is that?'

She rose from the table, not coquettishly, but abstracted. Marius paid for their tea, put money into the collecting box at the door of the gallery, then led her out into the thundery dampness of the afternoon where I was waiting for them, as invisible and inconsequential as an ornamental bush. Above them a watercolourist's sky, great smudges of grey cloud breaking up no sooner than they'd formed, a wet brush inscribing the imperman- ence of things in charcoal marks which they would have been within their rights to suppose they could read, so like calligraphy was it. A more fanciful man than Marius would have made Marisa look up to see their names coupled in bleeding black ink – *Marius and Marisa* or maybe *Marius Loves Marisa* – but then Marisa was not, in turn, fanciful enough to have cooperated with him in this. 'I see no such thing,' she would have said, unless the marks had been incontrovertible, and I am not prepared to go so far as to assert they were.

'And what condition is that?' Marius asked again.

I pricked my ears, aroused by the word 'condition'. If there was already a condition between them, they were making progress.

'That you book the table at the restaurant of my choice any night but Friday, and then ring me to say you've booked it.'

'That's not a very stringent condition. Consider it done. Just tell me the name of the restaurant and give me your number.'

'Ah, but that's the condition. You have to find those out.'

'And how do I do that?'

'I will hide them.'

Ah, Marisa – hiding now for someone else!

'Hide them where?'

'In the gallery.'

'In the gallery as in at the enquiry desk or on a noticeboard?'

'No. In the gallery as in the art.'

'Art as in paintings?'

'Not necessarily, but not necessarily not. The Wallace Collection has a fine collection of European furniture and sculpture.'

'And will the information I seek come in a code I must crack, or in an expression I must interpret, or will I be looking for an actual object in a drawer?'

She thought about it. 'I'm still deciding,' she said. 'I'd say a combin- ation of all those. But yes, there will be a thing. Though I'm hardly going to tell you where to look for it, am I?'

'A thing?'

'You ask far too many questions for a man with such a quick intelligence. Use your eyes and you will find it.'

'Do I get any other clues?'

'None.'

'And when can I start looking?'

'One week today.'

'It will take you that long to hide it?'

'Keeping you amused is not all I have to do.'

'Amused is not exactly the word I'd use to describe my condition.'

Nor mine, I have to say. Not on this afternoon of words and hidings. Doubly false, I found it, the idea that Marisa would hide a thing from Marius, a man with whom she hid herself from me.

A *Big Issue* seller accosted them before they could shake hands.

'I don't see your badge,' Marius challenged him.

'It was nicked from me,' the seller told him. 'They nick things from you on the street.'

Marius put his hand into his hip pocket and pulled out a wad of notes – a costermonger flourish which I recognised from the fromagerie. 'Don't believe a word of it, old cock,' he said, refusing the *Big Issue* but handing the man a five-pound note all the same.

'You're having an expensive day,' Marisa laughed.

'As the poet says, "There is no pleasure sweeter than surprising a man by giving him more than he had hoped for."'

'Baudelaire, presumably.'

'Ah! I'm sorry. I have become predictable already.'

I thought so, but Marisa, I observed, did not.

From where I was positioned, it wasn't possible for me to hear every word they exchanged, but what I didn't hear for sure I lip-read or intuited or made up for them out of the intensity of my curiosity. I took it to be a good omen that Marisa had asked me to wait for her on the off-chance of her encountering Marius. It was a sign of how differently she felt about him that she could flirt outrageously with him in my presence – if you could quite call what I was a 'presence' (certainly I wasn't present to Marius) – without acknowledging me as she had somehow at all times acknowledged me the afternoon I saw her out with Dulcie's dentist.

Did it excite her to do this? Did it excite her for herself as well as for me? Was she, in Marius's company, able to remove me as effectively from her consciousness as she appeared able to remove me from her proximity?

I never asked. I knew my place. And Marius was not a name we dared so much as breathe to each other. We carried him as though he were a precariously loaded tray which a single badly chosen word would cause either one of us to jolt and spill. He was our precious secret, hers from me, mine from her, inadmissible and unpronounceable, even as I lurked in the shadows of my own making, a self-ghosted man, and watched him fall in love with my wife. And she – if my luck held – with him.

He apologised again for the Baudelaire which she told him she did not recognise. I did. It was from one of the Frenchman's prose poems. *La Fausse Monnaie*. But I was not able to demonstrate my cleverness. Ghosted men have no faces and no tongues.

'The person who does the giving in the story,' Marius explained, 'is actually passing on counterfeit – performing a pretend-charitable act and making a good deal at the same time, gaining forty sous *and* the heart of God. A piece of calculation Baudelaire finds contemptible.'

'You are not passing on counterfeit yourself, I presume?' Marisa wondered.

'Not knowingly.'

They looked each other directly in the eyes.

'Not knowingly,' Marisa repeated.

'Not knowingly,' Marius said, repeating her repetition.

Have I said I was as invisible as a bush? Think the burning bush.

SO WAS I SATISFIED YET?

No. Hungrier than the sea on which he's buffeted, a cuckold sighting land. They had gone further in one afternoon than I could contemplate with calm – enough had been said and done and promised to burn a thousand ordinary stay-at-home cuckolds alive in their beds – but I could look only forward, not back, and every act of lewdness vanished in its accomplishment and made me impatient for the next.

It also worried me that Marisa had told Marius there was no point in his starting looking for at least a week. A long time in politics, a week in love is an eternity, the more especially when one of the lovers was a man as easily stirred up and then as easily turned off as Marius.

One thing Marius didn't mention to Elspeth after her husband died was that he'd met another woman at the funeral and subsequently spent time in her company. In fact two women, and spent time with them both. Not women, strictly speaking, either. More girls. Sisters, as I'd thought. One fifteen, or so she said; one sixteen, or so *she* said. One with black lipstick, one with a ring through her nose. Marius wouldn't have taken the trouble to remember which was which.

It would appear that I was mistaken, then, the morning I observed him in the village hall in Shropshire and picked him for a man who arranged more debaucheries than he attended. He did, after all, keep his four o'clock appointment. And that is not the only surprise. The appointment was for that same day. And not more than a few steps away from where he'd made it. *Meet me among the headstones, girls*, he must have said, *at four . . . o' . . . clock.*

I don't know why I should have been surprised. Why not get on with it? What's owing to the recently dead aside, I suppose because it's beyond me to understand immediate gratification. Why come so quickly to the end of a pleasure you can spin out?

That, of course, is if he came to the *end* of it. Yes, he met them – I had been wrong about that. But who was to say how much of himself he gave? There is more than one way of withholding consummation.

Whether he did whatever he did with them one at a time, or whether they mucked in together; whether they found a patch of dry earth, if such exists in Shropshire, or whether they stretched out on cold sepulchral marble, and waited in the rain – I don't know. In his reporting of the event years later he was sparing of these details; unless the person reporting it in turn to me was sparing of the details on his behalf. No one ever tells the whole truth about sex. Something must always be added or taken away.

What interested me at that later time, lying listening to Marisa telling me about it in the half-light, unconsummated myself, was not the hows but the wheres, a cemetery not being everybody's idea of a love nest. No one seriously interested in the erotic life of men and women can be ignorant of tapophilia, that morbid fascination with burial and decay of which tapophobia is the opposite and vampirism and Gothic romances the direct if somewhat lily-livered offshoots. That the death instinct was strong in Marius, I already knew from everything I'd seen and heard from his own lips in Shropshire. But you can be absorbed in the poetry of expiry – especially your own – and still not care particularly for yew trees and sarcophagi, let alone choose them as the backdrop to pleasure. The truth about Marius was that he was not simply half in love with death, but invigorated and made potent by it. Did the sisters have clay from the graveyard on their feet when he did or did not embrace them? Did their fingers claw at bones? Was their youth perversely redolent of decay?

'There's this to say for blood and breath,' wrote Housman, the presiding spirit of that dispiriting cemetery, 'They give a man a taste for death.' Marius functioned according to the reverse principle. Death gave him a taste for blood and breath.

'I can't pretend it detracted from the violence of my enjoyment of them, or did anything but sharpen my recovered taste for life,' he was to tell Marisa, 'that they were Elspeth's nieces.'

So he wasn't sparing of *every* detail.

Marisa was quiet for a while. 'Or that they were not of an age to refuse you?' she wondered at last.

'Nor that,' he said.

What, I wondered in my own time, did Marius stand to gain from bragging to Marisa about these violations? 'In the end it wasn't their flaming youth in that garden of death that stirred me,' he told her, 'any more than it was their blood-relatedness to Elspeth or each other. It was the bruised commonness of their mouths.'

Why tell Marisa that?

And here's another question: were their mouths bruised before they met Marius, or after?

And another: if the bruising came after, was that all they took away from their encounter?

I knew nothing of this – if by knowing we mean having words for – when I fretted over the week Marisa had given him: a whole week in which to go cold, turn tail, or pick up a couple of goth schoolgirls on Marylebone High Street in the hope they'd fancy being shown around a cemetery. But I knew and feared it in my bones. I knew and feared *him* in my bones. Call that my version of tapophobia.

The week passed. The minute the gallery opened on the first morning of week two, when it was OK for Marius to start looking, I was in the square, enjoying the early sun through the plane trees, my hat pulled down above my eyes. But no Marius. Nor the next day. Nor the next. It amazed me how a man could know that a woman in whom he was interested had hidden something for his eyes alone – an erotic lure, an enticement to do God knows what – and yet not be in a raging fever of impatience to find it. Had it been me I'd have been banging at the gates of the gallery the minute Marisa told me I could. By the end of the first morning I'd have torn the place apart.

But then *I* wasn't afraid of admitting my dependence on a woman's whim. *I* knew what fun it was being led by the nose.

Whatever was keeping Marius, I decided not to wait for him. There was my own rampaging curiosity to consider. What Marisa had hidden, I reasoned, she had hidden for me as well. It was not spoken about between us, but hiding pertained to our marriage. Concealment had become the language of our love. By which logic the test she had set for Marius was as much mine as his. And it was imperative to me to know what she'd left and where she'd left it, even if it wasn't imperative to him.

I didn't go to the gallery as Marius's rival. I went as his alter ego. And in a sense as Marisa's alter ego too. I went looking for the thing she'd hidden so that I could enter the heart of their intrigue, but more than that I went looking to learn how the cuckolding of me felt, as it unfolded, from the other side; I went to roll in Marisa's falseness as she plotted it through the gallery, room by room; I went to taste on my tongue the dry mouth of Marius's excitement as he closed in on the knowledge, artefact by artefact, that though she had told him she was a married woman she was soon to be his mistress.

Yes, I had been in that position myself when Marisa finally proved false to Freddy. But what was false to Freddy compared to false to *me*!

Since there was little prospect of Marius and I doing the treasures of the Wallace Collection together in body – emeritus husband and lover-elect

– I made do with taking him along with me in spirit. We were nervous the first morning, not knowing where to start, wandering from room to room without any purpose, discovering meanings in paintings and messages in furniture that probably weren't there, unable to examine anything closely for fear of setting off an alarm. More than likely there was someone in a little room somewhere watching every move we made.

I ceded preference to Marius. I liked following him. It satisfied my sulphurous desire to be demeaned, the last in a line of obscene pursuit – Marisa laying down her scent, Marius tracking her, and I trailing in the rear of them both, like a wounded dog.

It was a shame, I thought, that he wasn't there enough to converse with. 'Do you not think it wonderfully Venetian,' I would have asked him, 'our looking together for we don't know what, but which in my mind's eye, as I'm sure in yours, resembles a parchment letter or a scroll, a ribboned summons to a carnivalesque rendezvous posted in an item of rococo furniture, which, if we never find it, could remain hidden here for centuries until some other lover in pursuit of an evasive mistress comes upon it and believes it is for him? Do you think Marisa might entice a man into her arms three hundred years after she has died? Knowing how you are around mortality, I must suppose you are even more inflamed by that idea than I am.'

I will be quick about our search, for it lasted several days. By the end of it perhaps no one knew the loot in that salacious temple to luxuriance better than we did. Eighteenth-century inkstands made of pinewood and walnut with boulle marquetry, French cabinets supported by bare-chested blackamoors, oak and ebony writing tables, escritoires veneered with satiné and purplewood, console tables, chests of drawers with griotte marble tops, wardrobes, roll-top desks, coffers on stands, pearwood book cabinets, secretaires – whatever had a drawer, ostensible or secret, a compartment that might just open or give a little, a ledge, a surreptitious niche, that could with ingenuity be employed to hold the thing we looked for, we tried (him first, me after) but tried in vain.

As though to recall to us the immemorial indecency of our errand, wherever we looked classical mythology was there before us, playing out its exemplary carnalities. Ornamental satyrs raped and carried off their plunder, bacchant fire-dogs rolled their eyes, deep pudendal inkwells dared us to explore their blue-black darkness with our fingers (first mine, then his), Venuses chased and suckled Cupids, a gilt-bronze, imperturbably bare-breasted Diana stroked the head of a snarling hunting dog, while at her feet a pair of less pacified curs ripped out the throats of deer. I permitted Marius to stand a long time studying the Diana, struck by the impassivity of her bloodlust, wondering if there was some communication for him here. Whatever he was looking for, he guessed that Marisa must have concealed it in or by an artwork that spoke eloquently about her feelings for him. So was she warning him to beware her cruel Diana chastity? Was he, Marius, intended to find a reflection of himself in the wounded deer?

I'd have liked him not to move for an eternity so that I could go on attributing to his heart the palpitations which shook my own. At last, when I did move him on, I paused to see if we were being watched, then tested the drawers of the cabinet on which Diana and her dogs stood, but to no avail. Two cupboards held catalogues for the Wallace furniture collection – works to which I felt I could by now make an informed contribution – but these too, though a perfect hiding place, were inaccessible.

On we went, from untouchable walls of pink-nippled Psyches and Ariadnes painted by the breast-besotted Greuze, through dense rooms of armour and ormolu, and out again into the indolent frivolities of Boucher, I never so far behind that I couldn't inhale the heat of him, wondering what he was wondering, doubly tense for I was pursuing not only Marisa, I was pursuing his pursuit of her as well.

At last, for this could not go on forever, much as I wanted it to, we were led – as to our destiny – to Marisa's hiding place. But first something curious happened. I got rid of Marius. It was the third day and I no longer welcomed his presence in my head. I grew selfish, suddenly. I wanted to savour the moment all by myself. Call it a marital impulse. As

I neared the naked proof of my wife's adulterous intention, I wanted her to share it with me alone.

A milky Sicilian marble Cupid set into a Minton-tiled recess at the far end of the Smoking Room holds the attention of all visitors to the Wallace Collection whatever their mission. The Cupid is a youth, lavishly winged, taking an arrow from his quiver. *Love Triumphant* the work is called, though a flighty Cupid has never seemed to me an adequate metaphor for the way love clubs you into submission. Around the base of the sculpture runs a paean to love's stranglehold, itself far from flighty, written by Voltaire:

> *Qui que tu sois voici ton maître.*
> *Il l'est, le fut, ou le doit être.*
> (Whoever you are, here is your master.
> He is it, or was, or must be.)

Here is your master, but in fact this was not the place. No conceivable hiding room here for a communication directly from Marisa's hand. But to the immediate left of *Love Triumphant* was a staircase that gave the impression of being private, or at the very least rarely used. Certainly I had never before noticed it on my visits to the gallery. I sniffed Marisa's presence here at once. It was unmistakable. It overwhelmed me like a perfume. Men mastered by a woman can tell to a certainty when she has been in a room; for them her impression lingers long afterwards like warm breath on a mirror, or the recollection of a dream which daylight can't shake off. Obsession manufactures ghosts, and Marisa's ghost was here in all its restlessness. The ghostliness not only of her person but of the deadly game that she was playing. That was what, over the perspiration of my own nervousness, I could smell: not just her clothes and hair and breath but the delinquent purpose that had brought her. Up the stairs she'd gone, up into the ill-lit gloom, one step at a time, in full possession of what she was about, knowing what she meant to leave, where she meant to leave it, and what would ensue once it was found.

I fought against my own impatience. It was getting late. I didn't want bells ringing to warn that the gallery was closing just as I was on the point of laying hands on what was not for me. But even had the afternoon been less advanced I'd have done the same, resisting the smaller temptation for the greater. For the greater temptation was to remain in ignorance another night.

Subspace beckoned me – that nirvana stillness of utter submission which hitherto I'd practised only in Marisa's absence but which tonight I would enter with her by my side. There was a sort of blasphemy in it, but it was blasphemy in the name of a higher form of worship.

The following day, though I had barely slept (subspace, as I've said, is not for sleeping), I was at the gallery before the doors opened. With a heart beating violently enough to keep ten men alive I nosed my way where Marisa's adventuresome feet had been, breathing in, as though it were a poison I was destined to take, the flagrancy of her resolution.

Among dross not worth discussing, two small, and in the circumstances arresting paintings – arresting by virtue of their contrast – confront each other on opposite walls above the stairs; both of insufficient value to warrant tight security, and both with space enough behind their frames to hide a card, a letter, maybe even a small package. One, entitled *Reading the Bible*, by the nineteenth-century French painter Hugues Merle, shows two young girls in Quakerish bonnets being read to from scripture. Jailbait, both of them, if you are so minded. So arresting in that sense, too. Otherwise nothing to get excited about if you leave out what hangs on the opposing wall, and if you didn't know that the young Marisa had studied the Bible.

Opposite, as conceived by the academic painter Thomas Couture, an exact contemporary of Merle, the poet Horace partying with his mistress Lydia. *A Roman Feast*. The poet, reclining on a couch, holds out his goblet for a servant to refill. Naked down to her toes, Lydia snakes into her lover, one arm flung about his neck, her breast pressed into his chest, her flanks arced in sinuous luxuriance towards our scrutiny. The opulence of her haunches is shocking. Though she is bold and faithless in Horace's Odes to her, she hides her face in Couture's painting, embarrassed by the proximity of her lover's water boy. For a woman is of necessity more naked in the presence of two men than she can ever be with one.

Let me be plain. Nothing in the lusciously immodest shame of Lydia's posture would have made any man not intimate with her think specifically of Marisa. But if one started from the other end of the proposition, anyone who knew Marisa only in her clothes and imagined her without them would have pictured her much like this. Of a flowing voluptuousness that was beyond bearing.

Whether one of these paintings would have been enough, without the other, to stop in his tracks a man hunting down a love token, I doubt. Manchester Square is swollen with erotic invitation. But together, eyeing each other from opposite walls of the staircase, they were irresistibly garrulous.

I caught my breath when I found myself between them. Without a shadow of a doubt this was the place – hidden from the eye of any other person – where Marius's searching, if he could be prised out of his den, would come to an end.

But I was uneasy. Uneasy for Marius, and by extension – for my future happiness waited exclusively on his – uneasy for myself. There was a choice on offer here, between a chaste virgin to be educated in the ways of God, and an insatiable mistress to be peeled naked before the eyes of men. I knew where my preference lay; but it mattered that when Marius's time came he should not be made to feel he'd chosen grossly.

What I proceeded to do, I did with the best intentions. It wasn't intrusion. It was kindness. For their sake I could not leave anything to chance. They were not the sort of people you could rely on chance to help. They were both too easily knocked off course.

I slid my fingers behind *A Roman Feast*. No bell went off. Nor was there anything from Marisa. Only a thread of spiderweb. I turned to *Reading the Bible* and did the same. Still no bells. But this time my fingers found a folded sheet of plain A4 notepaper, defiantly impersonal, on which Marisa had written the name of her favourite restaurant, her mobile telephone number, and a brief message. Had the painting been alarmed it would not have been my hand that set it off, it would have been my heart. The message was: *There is no pleasure sweeter than surprising a man by giving him more than he had hoped for.*

I won't pretend those words weren't hurtful. Jealousy, as I have remarked before, is incalculable in its ferocity and reasoning. Though I had imagined them in each other's arms a thousand times, the thought of them joined in Baudelaire disgusted and upset me. Did she have to cuckold me in literature as well? The word-fucker she was! I breathed hard, as green-eyed as the next man. But no jealousy ever remained itself for long in me. Soon I was able to picture them in each other's arms reading Baudelaire together, and to feel again in the pit of my stomach the grief I'd learned to alchemise into gratification.

I could see why Marisa had decided against posting her offer of *more than he had hoped for* behind the Roman orgy. Too brazen. Without doubt the better joke — and in its own way the lewder invitation to violation — was the one she'd made, reminding Marius of her as a young girl in convent clothes. But there was something I knew which she didn't. She didn't know that Marius had an inclination, albeit a mortuary inclination, for the underaged. Who was to say that the allusion, however unintended, wouldn't sting him into a retreat? There was risk either way. Invite Marius to take his fill of an unclothed Lydia and he might well turn prudish on you. Like all sadists, he feared forwardness in women. But of the two I thought the Quaker girls carried the greater offence. It's possible I was rationalising my own preference. I could not see past Marisa offering Marius the promise of her company at his table, peeled naked to her toes.

Whatever my motives, what I did was not so terrible. How big a crime was it to move an already outrageously immodest come-on a mere armstretch from one wall to another, and have Marisa inflame Marius with the prospect not of a Bible class but a debauch? A debauch that contained the prospect, what is more – for it was not my intention to deny Marius anything – of the Bible class deferred.

IT WAS DISAPPOINTING TO COME OUT INTO THE CLEAN AIR OF THE ACTUAL world and to realise that in fact nothing had changed. I had inhaled the poison of their adultery in the gallery – sucked on it and emerged alive – but out on the streets Marius and Marisa were still far apart, orgiasts only in a future I'd been rearranging for them.

If leaving things a week had been a bad idea for him, it had been a bad idea for her as well. A game was fun for Marisa, and then it wasn't. A man was hot, and then he wasn't. The two great lessons of her childhood. This is not to say it didn't irk her not to hear from him the minute he had her number. At first she'd have enjoyed the idea that he was having trouble finding it, going through the gallery on his hands and knees, a fool to her ingenuity – he who thought he knew what made her tick. But when a further week went by, and then another, she had to face the possibility that he didn't have her number because he hadn't put himself to the trouble of looking for it.

I was sorry for her. I am, as I have said, a connoisseur of fine insult. 'Well I had fun finding it, anyway,' I'd have liked to tell her. But I too was a prisoner to our subterfuge.

The wondering didn't agree with her. She no more cared for being toyed with than did Marius. I bloom under indifference, she turned pale. I glow, she looked sicklied over. She would go out, forget what her errand had been, return home and then immediately go out again. She had her nails painted, decided she didn't like the colour, and had them painted again that same afternoon. She bought shoes she didn't need, and started letters to friends she hadn't corresponded with in years.

I grew seriously worried for her when one of my staff mentioned he'd seen her entering a church. It turned out she had gone only to hear an organ recital. I say *only* but in fact her being there was still a matter for concern. She hated the organ.

At last her native impatience with infatuation took over and she was out dancing again, spiking the paving stones with her shoes, and reading an extra morning a week to the blind man.

I entertained a fancy about Marisa and the blind man. She read to him, I believed, naked. She would be naked beneath her coat when she arrived. He would help her off with it, not a word exchanged. He knew that she was naked. The blind can smell such things. I don't refer to the body's natural odours and secretions, or to Marisa's perfume; what he would smell was her nakedness itself. In the dark — in his dark but also in the darkness of the room, for we always conceive the rooms of the blind as being sightless too — he would smell the abstract idea of it. But wouldn't touch her. Then she would read to him. Softly, beneath her words, she would feel the ebb and flow of his breath on her flesh. 'And her erectile tissue?' Reader, you ask too many questions.

An hour later the blind man would help Marisa on with her coat, his fingers careful not to touch her skin, and she'd go home, forgetful. Marius? Who was Marius?

More to the point, as far as I was concerned, *where* was Marius. He didn't leave his flat for days, not on my watch anyway. There was no sign of him at the fromagerie and on the couple of occasions I nipped back to the gallery, there was no sign of him there either. I asked Andrew whether he'd seen or heard anything, but he had nothing to report. They were not, he reminded me, bosom friends. Marius didn't do bosom friends.

A taxi called for him one morning when I was ambling in the lane.

Presumably to take him to the railings at Hyde Park. He descended with a number of framed paintings in cardboard boxes, looked at the weather, appeared to smell rain, or simply the disillusion in his soul, and sent the taxi away. Later that day – the rain having cleared and a clean, sunny breeze blowing through Marylebone – I found him drinking coffee on the High Street. It was four o'clock – Marius's vampire hour. His face looked sealed off from human commerce. It was not impossible that the taxi driver he'd sent away was the only person he'd spoken to since Marisa had thrown down her challenge to him.

Since death and desire had been our subjects the only other time we'd talked, and I could smell death on him today, I made no bones about sitting myself at a table next to him and steering us towards desire. Talk of desire, I mean, not actual body-to-body desire of a sort neither of us could possibly have felt for the other.

(A word about that. I accept that I must ask myself, for someone else is sure to ask it if I don't, whether I didn't at some subterranean level – and maybe not all that subterranean – lust vicariously after Marius through my wife, or at the very least hanker for him to call me, as he'd called the fromagerie woman, 'doll'. I registered it after all, and have drawn attention to my doing so. All things considered, and allowing that I'm in some respects more passive than a man is meant to be, I have to say I doubt it. I recognised in myself no ambition to lie with Marius or have him call me 'doll' – no ambition to have a doll, to look like a doll, or to be a doll. I am not a doll-associated man. But as homoerotic feelings are sometimes adduced as the underlying motive for my brand of deviancy, I wish to show I've given that diagnosis its due consideration. Could have been, but no – always granting that every deviancy contains the seeds of all the others.

But that I was more substitutively sensitive, so to speak, to the slights and caresses implicit in Marius's vocabulary than was good for me – yes. Ask me how I'd have felt about Marius trying 'doll' on with Marisa and I'll confess it would have been like having someone with long fingernails feeling around in my stomach. Not something you ever think you want until it happens. And then you start thinking about wanting it again. But it was a hypothetical sensation. Marisa would never have allowed him to address her in that fashion.

More's the pity.)

'And which faraway place of the senses are you inhabiting today?' was how I tried my luck this time.

If a look could kill, I would not be alive to tell this story now. 'I think you've mistaken me for someone else,' he said. 'You appear to be continuing a conversation we've never had.'

'Well, it was a long time ago,' I said. 'You told me about Thanatos.'

He shook his head. 'Thanatos? Nah. Never been there, guv'nor.'

I was tempted to tell him he didn't talk in this goonish fashion to my wife. Though that would hardly have served my cause. Interesting, though, in the light of what has been said about homoeroticism, that he reserved his serious self for women. Unless it was only me he chose to fool about with, and was perfectly direct with other men. In which case was his manner with me something I invited? Did I want him not to take me seriously?

'How about Eros, then?' I persisted.

'Wrong again, squire. 'Aven't been up to the West End in years.'

'Every man,' I said, pietistically, because his needling skittishness left me few conversational options, 'knows something of love and death.'

'Before you start – if you're looking for someone to discuss your marriage or your love affairs with, I'm not your man. I dwell alone.'

'But I've seen you in the company of women, I think.'

He turned in his seat to look at me, his face tight. 'Do you want me to knock your block off?'

I laughed one of those crazy laughs that hangers-on in Dostoevsky laugh. A beat me, hurt me, humiliate me, do whatever you want with me but you'll never shake me off laugh. Pavel Pavlovitch is probably who I'm thinking of, the Eternal Husband in the short novel of that name.

'I was merely making polite conversation,' I said. 'You look like a lover of beautiful women to me. I am a lover of beautiful women myself, in my own way. I felt like a talk.'

'Have it with your friends. Though it will come as no surprise if you tell me you have no friends.'

'I have no friends.'

'Then count yourself a lucky man. Friends only ever let you down. Women too . . . Will that do you for the talk you wanted?'

'Your experience is different from mine. No woman has ever let me down.'

He sat back in his seat, stretching out his legs and chortling – that was the only word for it – into his moustaches. Disconcerting in its incongruity, Marius's chortle, as though some crazy half-aquatic creature were suddenly to snort at you in a zoo, a sea lion turned mad by too long a confinement, a walrus with a bitter sense of the ridiculous.

'I hope you aren't expecting me to ask the secret of your felicity,' he said.

'Putting oneself at all times in the wrong. If you're in the wrong you can't *be* wronged.'

'Giving up all expectation of a happy life must work just as well.'

'They aren't the same. I *have* a happy life.'

'Then why are you stalking me?'

'Who said I was stalking you? I mentioned I'd seen you with a beautiful woman, that's all.'

'And what's that to you? Are you a private investigator?'

'No. I'm more what you'd call a pervert if you really want to know what I do.'

'And you think telling me this will make me feel better about talking to you? What would you do if I told you to get lost?'

'If I thought you meant it, I'd get lost.'

'*If you thought I meant it!* Is this what a pervert does? Hangs around people who tell him to get lost while he decides whether or not they mean it? Why don't you just call yourself a glutton for punishment and have done.'

'A glutton, yes. But not so much for punishment, more for the suspense.'

'Would that be suspense in the hanging from a rope around your throat sense, or suspense as in being kept wondering whether anyone is going to cut you down?'

'Well in the literature the two are not always to be distinguished,' I explained. 'But as in all art, the wondering and daydreaming are of the essence.'

'*Art?* I must have misheard. I thought you told me you were a pervert not a painter.'

I shrugged. 'So when did you hear of a perversion that didn't tend to art? Only sadism is anti-aesthetic.'

He slapped the tin table in mirth, making his coffee spill on to my shoes. 'Anti-aesthetic! Do you talk like this to every stranger you sit next to in the street? Hombre, you're not only pompous you're wrong. What do you think art is – pretty pictures? Let me tell you – every artist is a sadist. He creates life in order to annihilate it as the fancy takes him. As, in this instance, the fancy may take me to annihilate yours.'

'Aha!' I said, daring to point a finger at him. 'The violence of your feelings towards me proves me right. You're a man of artistic temperament yourself – I can see that – but in the brutal reiteration of your impatience I doubt you're able to stay still enough to make art. Annihilation is not art, it is the opposite of art. What you call art I call spilling blood.'

'And why does that frighten you? "Of all writings I love only that which is written in blood" – Nietzsche he say that.'

'And does Nietzsche he say *whose* blood? The artist you describe writes in other people's. The artist proper writes in his own. When did a beater ever have a good tale to tell? When did a beater ever hold his hand long enough to see the world around him? The stories we love are always written by, or from the point of view of, the beaten – we who wait and wonder, always in suspense, watching, wondering, with time forever on our hands, retelling and retelling the story of our ignominy—'

'And where is your art, Mr Pervert Artist, to prove this?'

'Here,' I said, extending my arms to take in the day, the sky, the time, the street, the table, us. 'Here, in the magnanimity of my feelings towards you, in the suspense of our narrative, in the not knowing where our story ends.'

'*We* don't have a story.'

'Oh, you can't be sure of that.'

'This isn't art you're describing, it's fantasy.'

I shrugged. 'And your art?' I asked. 'The art to which your temperament inclines you? Where is that?'

For the first time, our eyes met. So that was what women saw in him! An angry icy sadness, like a polar bear's. An ailment which, if they were fearless, if they dared get close enough, they might just be able to do something for.

Clearly he didn't like what he saw in my eyes either, though they felt to me, from the inside, as softly compliant as a Labrador's.

'My art,' he said at last, 'is in keeping you no further in suspense. Get lost! Just get up, leave the table and keep walking. I pay your bill, and you don't bother me again. How's that for an ending to our narrative?'

I rose from the table. *Just go to the fucking gallery*, I wanted to say. *Just go up the little stairs and see what's waiting for you. You won't believe your luck.* But I couldn't.

'Get lost!' he repeated.

And this time I did him the honour of believing that he meant it.

Fortune favours the brave. The following day, Marius was to be seen crossing Manchester Square, I assumed (for I was in a taxi myself and couldn't stop to make certain) on his way to the fucking gallery.

I can't prove it was our conversation that changed his mood. Logically, he might as soon have packed his bags and left the area forever. Who wanted to run into me on the High Street? And even if it hadn't affected him that way, there was nothing to say it had affected him the other. He might simply have woken up on a different side of the bed. Or looked out of his little window above the button shop and seen Marisa shopping at one of the boutiques opposite, or on her way to read to the blind man, wearing nothing under her coat. Just to have seen her at all would surely have reminded him, as his father's ghost reminded Hamlet, of his almost blunted purpose.

But what I like to think had happened was that I'd goaded him back to his desk. *And your art, Marius? Where is that?*

And of course reminded him of the existence of a beautiful woman.

Where was his art? Well, no doubt he thought he'd answer that – if only to himself – in the one way an artist could. He'd make some. Except he hadn't. That was my guess, anyway. It's art or women for some men, and Marius was definitely a man of that sort. Death, women, art. Art, women, death. Art, death, women. It didn't matter how he juggled them. One was always compensating for the other. He'd done death. Which left only the other two. And who would want to be making sentences when sentences didn't come easily and there was a luxuriant woman out there, his for the taking – quick, provocative, spiky, unsentimental, and married to another man.

The day Marius began belatedly to take up Marisa's challenge was the start of a new adventure for me too. I sat in the back of the taxi barely able to hear myself think, so loud was the lecherous chattering in my brain. 'Goats and monkeys!' I must have said aloud.

'I thought you wanted Paddington,' the driver said.

I told him I'd changed my mind. I was meant to visit a retired headmaster in Gloucester to give a valuation. But how could I concentrate on old books? 'Back to Marylebone,' I said. For I wanted to be close.

He was reading her note, or he soon would be. I read it again with him. It was some invitation. More than he had hoped for, all right. More than I had hoped for too. Marisa curled into the chest of the poet. Naked to her toes. And the water boy smirking.

God almighty!

He was as good as inside her.

He took her to her favourite restaurant (hitherto *our* favourite restaurant) where they sat as two cemented into one. They didn't notice what they ate. Afterwards they strolled out into the evening air, heavy that night with thunder, first arm in arm, then hand in hand, and then, a mere block from where we lived – Marisa and I – mouth to mouth, pausing to savour each other more – Marisa and he – under a street lamp that illuminated them as though from the glow of their hearts.

He looked more than usually handsome and very nearly in good temper in a tweedy suit that gave him the air of a country solicitor. He was the sort of man who excited romance in the hearts of farmers' wives and daughters, and of course the wives of red-brick university professors. But it goes down well with city women too, that suggestion of wind-blown provincial pitilessness. As though there are cruel country assurances of which soft men who work in international banks or inner city antiquarian bookshops are incapable.

Marisa, too, appeared animated. Conversation suited her. For conversation she wore her highest heels.

They ate out again, at the same restaurant, indeed at the same table – *our* table, naturally – until it became as much a tradition for them to eat there as it had been for us. Eventually – though this is to hurry anticipation forward – she invited him to the house we shared, and subsequently into her bed. Not *our* bed – she wouldn't permit confusions of that sort though she must have known I'd put up no objection. It was in the daytime and I was out at work. I'd been neglecting the business for Marius and was glad of the chance to get back to it. Sometimes I walked the streets, liking to walk where I knew they had walked.

It is highly romantic, haunting the place from which you've been removed. It is like living your life between mists and mirrors. I breathed with difficulty some days, but I put that down to elation. I didn't quite have what I wanted yet, but I was on the way. The ball was in their court. I'd done my bit for them, now they had to do the same for me.

I wasn't asking much. Only that they love each other.

PART FOUR

THE WIFE, THE LOVER

'. . . my heart dances;
But not for joy; not joy.'
William Shakespeare, *The Winter's Tale*

FOUR O CLOCK SUITED US ALL. L'APRÈS-MIDI D'UN FAUNE. SUITED THE FAUN, suited the nymph, suited the cuckold.

I liked him being in my house. There are men who would kill for less reason. They are in denial. Their funeral. They don't know what they're missing.

Marius was not of course aware whose house he was fauning it in, other than that it was half Marisa's. So I cannot accuse him of triumphing over me personally. That he enjoyed being in *some* man's house, though, I was certain. It sauced the afternoon up for him. He could throb to a woman for her looks and qualities alone, but he could throb to her to even greater effect if he was taking her from someone else. I'm not sure if that someone else had also to be someone older. But it wouldn't have surprised me. His track record suggested no less. And who's to say that we are not all cut from the same cloth? We cower before our virile fathers, like the boy in Turgenev's story, or – and it is only the same impulse reversed – we behead them. Marius was a beheader.

He hadn't wept at the funeral of the man whose wife he stole. He had picked up two underage girls instead.

Whatever their age, and whatever their bruising, girls had been his undoing. I have not been able to uncover categorical proof of why he left the university that employed him in a junior capacity not long after he'd eloped with Elspeth. Some whiff of scandal was in the air, but it was unlikely that Elspeth's husband had anything to do with it. He was too honourable and too doddery to bear a grudge. If anything it was probably him that got Marius the job in the first place. Professors like placing their students, whether or not they've run off with their wives. It satisfies a dynastic longing. Marius was gone, anyway, for whatever reason, before he'd made any lasting mark at least on the countenance of the university. The marks he'd made on the girls he taught was another matter. They idolised him, some of them. He was, as a teacher, as he'd been as a student – inspirational, brilliant, over-confidential, disposed to idealise and then despise. Where he thought he saw real aptitude, he brought it on. He liked winning unlikely converts to culture. When the grandiose mood was on him he thought, Pygmalionly, that he could animate what was lifeless and bring half humanity – the female half, that is – around to Baudelaire and Céline if he could only be granted sole access to it. No doubt he gave reading lists to the underage schoolgirls he had his way with in the cemetery before he found the loose change for their bus fares and packed them off home to their parents.

The shame – an especial shame for Elspeth – was that he couldn't leave it at converting his women students to culture. He had to convert them to him as well. There is reason to believe that he was whispered out of his job by campus feminists. I unearthed a couple of articles about him in the student newspaper, dated about the time of his resignation, which implied (careful of lawsuits) not only that he was the most lecherous member of a lecherous department (literature: it goes with the territory), but that women had been circulating letters among themselves and to freshers warning that he was the worst kind of teacher: not only a breaker of hearts but a rewarder of favourites, a teacher who starred your essays not for what you wrote for him on the page but for what you did for him in the bed. I doubt that. He had far too strict a sense of himself to go messing up the categories. If anything, he would have marked down any student he slept with to demonstrate his intellectual probity. And of course to show how little passion had moved him. So I take this to be a hysterical calumny of a sort that was rife on university campuses in those days. But a bounder is a bounder whatever the details and I presume him, on this account, to have been blackmailed out of his tenure.

Would he have brazened it out and dared the feminists to do their worst had it not been for Elspeth? Possibly. He could have lived with being the Lord Rochester of a West Midlands university. A bad reputation – particularly of that kind – never did a bachelor harm, no matter what warning letters circulate. But to Elspeth, who had once enjoyed the status of being married to a professor and had looked down sweetly on students as a species of orphan or foundling, it was humiliating. So they packed their things and left. For which – though this is only my theory – he was never able to forgive her.

Nor she him. To her friends – those that remained – she referred to him as the Dark Lord Morgoth. As a girl, she had sat on Tolkien's knee, had met him again in the company of her husband who trembled making the introduction, and subsequently read every word he'd written. So it's possible that the choice of Morgoth was tempered by her affection for the work; like Morgoth, Marius had fallen from airy grace into evil darkness, yet she still loved him. That she continued to call him Morgoth, however, knowing how much he despised her for confusing Tolkien with literature, suggests her anger towards him was real.

They rowed continuously, her temper all flounce and self-exposure, like the clothes she wore, his ice-cold and reserved, like water from a spring of scorn.

'If I'd known it was going to be like this,' she'd say to him, not finishing the sentence, her girlish puffball sleeves showing too much sway of slackened skin.

'How did you think it was going to be, Elspeth?' he'd ask. Hurting her with her name. Putting spit and spite into it.

'Lovely. Is there anything wrong with that?'

'*Lovely*. We tore at each other's flesh. Was that *lovely*?'

'We loved each other, Marius. We made promises.'

'That was in another country,' he'd say, leaving her to complete the quotation.

It was the mark of how bad things had got between them. Neither could finish what they'd started.

She didn't walk out on him, however dead to him she feared she had become. She'd left one man and saw no future for herself in leaving another. Presumably, too, she was unable to believe, having maddened him into desire once — he spoke the truth, he *had* torn at her flesh — that she couldn't do it a second time. Marius's turning niggardly where once he had been profligate served him well in his relations with women, at least in that they found it hard to drag themselves away from him until his profligacy returned. It's one of the cruellest laws of the erotic life that meanness in either sex, provided there's the remotest promise of generosity returning, never fails to be effective. We all cower in disgraced gratitude, like trained dogs, in anticipation of whatever scrap of love is going.

Even my mother, who knew perfectly well where my father had been, would welcome him back from his Grand Tour of the bordellos of France, Germany and the Low Countries provided he had Belgian chocolates for her.

And I am the same.

Behold Marius and Elspeth, anyway, in their peregrinations around the Welsh Marches, looking for something for Marius to do, the picture of marital unhappiness — though it was an unhappiness that transfixed Elspeth and kept her a sexual being, on edge and watchful, wanton even, when it might have served her better to notice she was ageing fast and make the appropriate adjustments of dress and expectation. 'He's "the great enemy" but he's good for me,' she told herself. Good for her erotically, she meant. Marius was a man who went deep into women, as though pursuing something not to be found on the surface, perhaps not to be found at all. With Elspeth when he bothered with her he went deep in the wounding as well as the exploratory sense. Out of a job and out of cash he kept his distance, looking at anything but her, but when he got work helping to put together a local newspaper in Ludlow, or driving a school bus from Stourport to Shrewsbury, or plastering cottages in Church Stretton where they finally settled — ironic work was how he thought of it, a joke against himself and all his early promise, a ludicrous life lived in a ludicrous part of the country – he returned to her with passionate vindictiveness, recalling how in their early days it had excited him to see her perfect *House and Garden* features screwed into a grimace, her wife-of-a-professor's mouth puckered as for a scream. And of course every time this happened, Elspeth believed that things were all right with them again, and would be until their ship at last reached the shores of the Uttermost West, dwelling place of the lords and queens of the Valar.

Marius was not all at once installed in my house after claiming his prize from Marisa – or, to speak plainer, his prize *of* Marisa. There was an intervening courtship period of several months – call it an interregnum – in the course of which all three of us had a number of adjustments to make.

I linger over this period perversely, though I hasten at the same time to get Marius under Marisa's sheets. Were my intentions sadistic, I'd have put them to bed together chez moi long ago; for the sadist hurries to the place of pain. As a masochist I obey a more complex and delicious chronology. It is always too soon to be there, for the masochist, no matter how long it's taken. There is always more of the run-up to torment to undergo before it can be enjoyed in its completeness.

So there are further details to be recorded of this 'interregnum' before Marius's cuckooing of me can be completed.

It was as it should be that Marisa took him to our favourite restaurant and sat him at our table. I'm not simply talking symmetry. By turning our haunt into their haunt, by allowing herself to be seen there in his company – ostentatiously and unapologetically *with* him – Marisa showed that she was a wife who attended conscientiously to her husband's needs. Humiliate me, I'd been mutely pleading since the Cuban had usurped my role, and had Marisa thrashed me in a public place she could not have humiliated me more.

One of those old family Italians, with pictures of Vesuvius and the Trevi Fountain on the walls, Madeira sauce over everything and caramelised oranges for dessert, Vico's had a been a home from home for me for years, first in my bachelor days, and later when I took Marisa there, as the conversation-starved wife of a man to whom I sold books. Though we frequented it less once we were married – you either went there on your own or you went there because you were up to no good, it seemed to me – I remained on the friendliest of terms with all the staff, in particular Rafaele the head waiter, a Pole pretending to be an Italian through whom confidences leaked as through a sieve. Marisa knew she could not go there with a man and not be reported the next time Rafaele saw me. Whenever I dined there alone – and the husband of a faithless wife dines alone often – he would roll his eyes into the back of his bald head and mention, if not in words then in looks, the coincidence of his having waited on her only the evening or the afternoon before . . . he had no idea in the company of whom . . . he assumed, for what else was there to assume, her brother or some other family member, so intimate was their conversation . . . A beautiful woman, your wife, Signore. Simpatica.

She was taking a risk, my beautiful, simpatica wife. A man might want his wife to be unfaithful without at the same time wanting all the world to know about it. In Dostoevsky, it is true, to be a cuckolded husband proper is to invite all society to be witness to your shame, but we were living in Marylebone not St Petersburg. For Marisa to have appropriated Vico's was a measure of her confidence in herself, but it also demonstrated her utter certainty of me. I was like a boxer who would hang on to the ropes and soak up every punch. Without fear of being hurt herself, she could circle me and hit as low and as often as she cared to. I'd double up but not go down.

As was proved by the Rumble in the Jungle, however, this kind of tactic can make things tough on the person doing all the punching. I never doubted that it was harder on Marisa than on me. A husband on the ropes is not every wife's ideal, no matter what the usual literature of cuckoldry proclaims. This is where the horn-mad Elizabethans had it wrong – a wife who will make a public fool of her husband is hard to find, because to have a fool of a husband is to be half a fool yourself. In facing that one out in public, Marisa showed herself to be a wife in a million.

But I was a husband in a million too, no matter that millions would have put themselves in my position had they been men enough.

Friday, the night Marisa manned the phones for the Samaritans, was the night I began to dine alone again at Vico's. On no other night of those first months they went out together could I be sure I wouldn't run into her on Marius's arm.

Because Fridays were busy, they were not the best evenings to get the attention of Rafaele, but in the shine of his officious, scandal-mongering face as he went scuttling by my table I saw everything I hoped to see. Pity was what he had decided to feel for me once it became obvious I intended to do nothing Italian (or Polish, come to that) to put an end to Marisa's affair, neither take a knife to her lover, nor throw Marisa herself out into the street. From the far end of the restaurant, even as he was dealing with other customers, he would shake his head in a dumb show of profound compassion, not unmixed with profound contempt. Once, when I made one of those skywriting squiggles in the air requesting the bill, he made one back to me. CUCU, I believe he wrote. And, if I wasn't mistaken, on those mornings when I called in for a coffee-fix on the way to work, something very like CUCU began to appear in chocolate on my cappuccino.

Then, after a particularly frantic evening, against all protocol he joined me at my table. He was sweating hard.

'I have come to the end of the line, Signor Quinn,' he said. 'I can take no more.'

I didn't know what to say to him. You forget when you are engrossed in the deviancy of your own desires what a profound effect your moral vagrancy might be having on other people. I reached out and put my hand on his. Mine cool and dry, his moist and fervid. 'I'm all right,' I said. 'In fact I'm more than all right. Everything is as I wish it. Here, drink some Brunello with me.'

Refusing the wine with a twist of his bear-like shoulder, he stared disbelievingly at me, then decided to go on as though I hadn't spoken. 'I have been waiter man and boy for forty years,' he said. 'It's enough. It's time to hang my hat. My legs are tired. Next week I go back to Umbria to be with my family.' He made a globe with his hands as though to suggest that though the world was now his oyster, the only world he cared about was Umbria. 'Sunshine, wine, salami,' he said.

No mention, I noted, of Polish sausage. But I was relieved not to be the reason he was hanging up his hat.

I shook his hand and told him I would miss him. He insisted that we kiss, as men, and then, perhaps as an association with men kissing as men, he said, 'Signor Quinn, in my country we have a saying – *Jestem człowiekiem i nic, co ludzkie, nie jest mi obce.*'

'That doesn't sound Italian to me, Rafaele.'

'It's Umbrian dialect. I come from a very remote village. But do you know what that saying means? "I'm human and nothing that is human is to me strange."'

'That's good,' I said.

'Good but not true. Some things are too strange for me to understand.'

'We are all made differently,' I said.

'And you are not unhappy, Signor Quinn?'

'I could skip out of my skin with happiness, Rafaele. I am alive to the tips of my fingers – feel! I only wish for you to be as happy in your native Umbria.'

He leaped to his feet. '*Dio ce ne scampi e liberi!*' he said. 'You know what that means?'

'"I should be so lucky"?'

He made a horror face and did something Polish with his thumbs, as though pointing pistols at his temple. 'It means, "God forbid!"'

I was sorry when he left. I missed the chocolate CUCU on my cappuccino.

But if I feared I'd lost my lifeline to the lovebirds, I was soon to get a better. You know when the gods of demented love are pleased with you: they shower you with gifts.

After Rafaele, Ernesto.

A real Italian this time, Ernesto was a tailor who had recently suffered a great tragedy and was looking for a change of scene. I had known him for many years from the small alterations business he ran above a shoe shop in Marylebone Lane, shortening trousers and moving buttons for Versace and Armani and whoever else happened to be passing. But he had lost his wife to a sudden heart attack, right there in the sewing rooms he had occupied for decades, and he couldn't bear to return to them. He wasn't looking for a new career. Just something to keep him busy and take his mind off what had happened. Really and truly he was waiting for a heart attack himself, so it didn't matter what he did.

He was a diminutive Roman with courtly manners and a kind, upsetting, crestfallen smile. I had always thought of him as a vigorous man, muscular in a compact way and delicately browned by the sun. But after the death of his wife the strength seemed to leave his body. He turned yellow.

I explained all this to the manager of Vico's, another old friend, adding that I thought Ernesto would recover his spirits after a while in their employment, that he wasn't looking for much money anyway, and would be happy just to go around pouring the San Pellegrino. I wasn't suggesting him as a replacement for Rafaele, simply a body who was willing to start at the bottom while everybody else moved up.

In fact, Ernesto never did get much beyond pouring the San Pellegrino, but he was grateful to me for the change of scenery. A gratitude on which I did not scruple to capitalise. To Ernesto, as a way of repaying the favour I had done him, I gave the Iago task of telling me what I was unable to see with my own eyes.

I didn't spare him. I'd meet him after he'd finished in the restaurant, order a taxi to take him home, and travel with him, sometimes keeping the taxi waiting an hour or more outside his wife-vacated house in Maida

Vale while I squeezed out the last drop of information. Initially his answers to my questions were the same: he had seen nothing really, he had only poured them water, his observations were not worth anything; but eventually he learned that his evasions hurt me more than his confidences. It's possible he made things up. It's possible Marisa wasn't even in the restaurant on some of the evenings he told me he had seen her holding hands across the table with a man who wasn't me. None of this mattered. It was an impression I was after in those early days. A sense of them, of how they were perceived as a couple, by a man who had been near them, leaned across them, refilled their glasses, and who therefore bore the warm impress of them on his person.

Had Mephistopheles himself appeared and offered me the opportunity to be at their table with them while they canoodled – not as an invisible presence but as an unwanted and ignored third party, a no one before whom they felt free to kiss without compunction – I'd have dared damnation for it. But in the absence of such a deal – and neither Marisa nor Marius was going to invite me to break bread with them of their own accord – I had to turn Ernesto into my eyes and ears and even lungs.

'Breathe them in,' I told him once, 'and then hold your breath until you can breathe them out again on me.'

'Hold my breath all night?'

'If you have to.'

He laughed his shrunken yellow laugh, all his Roman music gone. 'Then it will be my dying breath.'

'With luck it will be mine as well,' I said.

In the dark of the taxi I could tell that he was scrutinising me keenly. 'I thought you liked this.'

'I do. So tell me how it went tonight . . .'

No matter how forthcoming he was I always had to drag him back a stage. Between the restaurant and the bed there are, as the least curious men understand, questions to be asked. But between the water and the glass, between the bread and the buttering of it, between the menu and the ordering, is a host of dramatic detail not an item of which is to be forgone if you are me. Yes, Ernesto, but *before* she leaned forward to kiss him on the mouth, what had they said, had he asked for the kiss or did she give it gratis, had their conversation up until that point been animated, and who had done most of the talking, my wife or her lover, and would you have known from the way they inclined to each other, from the way they sat, that they were lovers, was there a consciousness of wrongdoing upon them, a self-conscious defying of the conventions, would you say, or a complete indifference to them, and of the two who looked the more delighted to see the other, did they arrive together or was one there first, which one, my wife or her lover, and did they kiss on meeting, a Continental cheek-on-cheek kiss, or French, mouth to mouth, and whose tongue . . .

Poor Ernesto. I had made him my Gyges as well as my Iago. By getting him to watch Marisa's every move I was showing her off to him, displaying her even more nakedly than Candaules had displayed his wife, because the Queen of Lydia, when all was said and done, had only disrobed for bed, whereas Marisa was Ernesto's to behold in flagrante delicto. But that was not all. As an ever-wakeful witness to the progress of Marisa's infidelity, he had become a sort of party to it, a parallel lover almost, privy to secrets he knew more about than I did; but further, he had become a parallel cuckold as well. Grown interested in Marisa at my instigation, grown to love her for all I knew, he had, like me, to suffer the torture of playing second fiddle to Marius. So when I asked him to open Marisa's mouth and describe – *lentamente*, Ernesto, *e con espressione* – the manner in which Marius slid his tongue into it, I was quite possibly putting him through agonies as unendurable as my own.

And at last he could endure them no longer. After three or four weeks of my interrogations he broke down.

'What you are asking I cannot any longer agree to,' he said before the taxi had come to a standstill outside his house.

I ordered the taxi driver to take us back to Marylebone. A look of weary pleading crossed Ernesto's face. 'It's all right,' I said. 'I'm not going to ask you more questions. I know they weren't there this evening anyway. Just come in and have a drink with me.'

Marisa was away. She'd told me she was meeting friends in the country – someone's birthday party, someone she had once worked with in the Samaritans – but I decided they were Marius's friends, hard as it was to imagine him having any. He had taken her to the Welsh Marches, I guessed. He was showing her off to people who remembered him when he was last there driving buses. Now the conqueror had returned, with another man's wife on his arm.

You could smell Marisa's absence. It was maudlin of me to let the house descend into melancholy the second she left it, to keep the lights dim, not to buy fresh flowers, not to wash up, but it was the upright version of the subspace into which I descended once there was no one left to talk to, no more information to screw out of anybody, just the silence of the house and her not in and I lying on our bed hearing her clothes coming off though she might have been a hundred miles away and the soft viscid sound for which there is no name of the porches of her body opening.

That's if her body had yet opened for Marius.

Rather than frighten Ernesto by taking him upstairs – who knows, he might have thought I had led him home in the spirit of Victor Gowan, to see my wife arranged indecently for his pleasure – I sat him down at the kitchen table and poured him wine. He asked for coffee. I made him coffee.

'It's hard to explain,' I began, but he held his hand up.

'It isn't hard to explain,' he said. 'I understand. Every man has some of these feelings. We deal with them differently. My wife had an affair soon after we married. With someone I knew. I wanted to kill her and to kill him. But one day he came to see me and cried in my arms. I cried too. Afterwards he went away and I was sorry for my wife. Some days I wanted to ask her why, what she had seen in him that she hadn't seen in me, but always I thought it would be cruel to her to ask. Her feelings were her feelings. They weren't to do with me.'

I listened quietly. 'You think I am being cruel to Marisa?' I asked.

He shrugged. 'That's not to do with me either. The person you are being cruel to is me.'

'I'm sorry,' I said.

'It is not easy for me. I am in mourning. I will be in mourning for the rest of my life. You have a wife. Why you are allowing or encouraging her to do this to you I do not understand. That's your business. But if she dies tomorrow you'll be sorry what you did. Anyway, I can't help you any more. I don't want these sexual feelings for myself. To you they are a kind of luxury. I cannot afford.'

'I'm sorry,' I said a second time. 'I won't ask any questions of you again.'

There followed a precarious period for me. Denied questions, I grew restive. If you don't ask questions you don't get answers, and where was the point of Marius and Marisa – for *me* – if my wondering about them went unconfided and unconfirmed?

There was too much I didn't know. For example, to start from the bottom, had they or hadn't they? Ask that of another pair spending as much time together as they were and they'd laugh lasciviously in your face. But Marius and Marisa had already taken an eternity to get this far. In their own way they were as hooked on suspense as I was. And at least one of them was a congenital holder-back. So it was entirely possible that as yet, no, they hadn't; that they were savouring each other still, saving themselves so that when at last they did it would be as the collision of planets.

But the not knowing was wrecking my nerves.

In the days before Marius, when Marisa wounded me with wounding doubt, there had always been scraps of intimated wrongdoing for me to chew on. She confided enigmatic thoughts to her diary, left ambiguously unfinished letters to her half-sisters lying around unfolded, allowed her expression to give away her feelings, spoke overexcitedly on the phone to callers I did not know. Now her diary was locked away, her eyes were always turned from mine and her phone had stopped ringing. Meaning, presumably, it was serious.

Leaving me with the question: How serious?

As for Marius, where once I had never let him out of my sight, delighting in apprehending him and ruining his four o'clock, now that he was squiring my wife around Marylebone I felt I had to keep out of his way. I still watched him, but from a greater distance. No more standing behind him at the cheese counter. No more sharing tin tables on the High Street. I didn't want him making connections if he saw me, nor did I want anything to happen that would cause Marisa to suspect we were acquainted. Though I longed to dine with them at Vico's and have them not notice I was there, it was essential they didn't notice I was there in actuality. Paradoxically, the very measure of my success was the care I had to take not to be seen enjoying it.

Thus it was as it always must be in a life dedicated to the twisted pleasures: with every gain I made there was a falling back.

Until at last I forced the issue. Not a word I associate with myself, force. But force was what I used.

'Samaritans, can I help you?'

The voice was gentle but not unctuous. And not Marisa's.

I had hoped for her but not expected her. You can't just dial up a Samaritan of your choice. You can't say, 'Put me through to Marisa, please.' You take your chance even if you're a regular. Who you get is who you get.

I'd discussed this with Marisa long ago, not knowing I'd have use for the information.

'So what happens,' I'd asked, 'if someone wants to talk to you and you alone?'

'They can't.'

'Why not?'

'Because relationships are frowned on. Not always, but usually if they want a particular person it's because they want the wrong sort of intimacy.'

'What's the right sort of intimacy?'

'When you don't hear heavy breathing at the other end.'

'But if they're not nutters or heavy-breathers, they can't ever get the same Samaritan twice?'

'I wouldn't say "not ever". It varies. But if you ring often enough you'll strike lucky eventually.'

'A bit of a lottery if you've got a gun in your mouth.'

'Mainly they don't have guns in their mouths, Felix.'

As did not I the day I rang. Though that all depends on what you mean by a gun in your mouth.

'I hope you can help me,' I said in answer to the impersonal greeting. 'I think my wife's having an affair.'

'What makes you think that?' the voice enquired, a trifle bored.

I could have put the phone down when it wasn't Marisa who answered, but I'd have felt pusillanimous. On the other hand I didn't want to pass for a heavy-breather either. *I fear my wife's having an affair, what colour brassiere are you wearing?* So I tried to sound like a perfectly normal man worrying about his wife's suspected infidelity, though it wasn't easy, for me, imagining what a perfectly normal man worrying about his wife's suspected infidelity sounded like.

'The usual signs,' I said, deciding I could do worse than try to sound like Marisa's first victim, Freddy – Radio Three, hurt, cultured, marginalised. 'She comes home at odd hours. The person I suspect, who is my best friend, has suddenly stopped joking with me. It's always the best friend, isn't it? Those are the thanks you get.'

'Have you spoken to your wife about this?'

'No, I haven't.'

'Don't you think you should? People are often wrong in their suspicions.'

'I never thought of that,' I said, seeing a quick way out. 'I'll talk to her when she comes home this evening. Thank you for your advice. You've been very helpful.' And I rang off.

This happened four or five times, with me thanking them sooner and sooner on each occasion. Once, when I thought I was back talking to the person I'd talked to first, I said, 'I just rang to let you know she hasn't been home yet,' and rang off again.

But then, as Marisa said would happen if I persisted, I struck lucky.

'Samaritans, can I help you?' The deep, *when I am laid in earth* contralto in which, only five years before, she had consented to be my wife. *Yes, she said, yes she will Yes*, only not like Molly Bloom. Not *then* like Molly Bloom.

Curiously, it wasn't the fact of my ringing her that seemed most duplicitous, but the fact of my ringing her from our house. I should be speaking from a phone box, I thought. I should be in the street. She would not be able to identify the street, but the silence of our house, what if it was obvious to her immediately? And wasn't it a sort of betrayal?

I pushed a paper handkerchief into each cheek as we'd done at school to change our voices. 'I'm having trouble with my marriage,' I said, sounding like Brando in *The Godfather*.

I could hear her listening hard. Much of your time, she'd said when talking to me about her work, is spent deciding whether anything the caller is telling you is true.

'What sort of trouble are you having with your marriage?' she asked after a decent period.

'I don't appear to have one.'

Again she waited. Then she said, 'In what sense don't you feel you have a marriage?'

I sounded so old she must have expected me to say, 'In the sense that my wife died sixty years ago.'

I moved the wads of paper with my tongue, trying to shed a few years. 'In the sense,' was what I finally did say, 'that people tell me by their looks I don't. Strangers regard me with compassion. The crueller of them laugh at me. And friends have started to enquire how the divorce is going, though I didn't know we were separating, let alone divorcing.'

Paranoid, I heard her thinking.

'I know what you're thinking,' I went on. 'You're thinking I'm paranoid. But I have the evidence of my own eyes. Yesterday I found an envelope containing two theatre tickets on the hall table.'

Three weeks before, I had found two ticket stubs for *Don Giovanni* on our hall table. Along with a credit card voucher in Marisa's name. It was not a performance to which she had invited me to accompany her.

'Theatre tickets don't necessarily prove anything.'

Now I was the one listening hard.

'They do to me,' I said. 'They prove fornication, adultery, betrayal – those sorts of things.'

I waited for her to slam the phone down. But there was only a long, deep silence. 'Felix,' she said to me at last, 'why are you doing this? You know you can't ring me here.'

'Can't I? Then where can I ring you?'

'Felix . . .'

'I'm ringing the Samaritans, not you. I have to talk to someone. I have a wife who is too sophisticated to communicate with me in the normal way of words. So I'll talk to whoever picks up the phone. You just happen to be the unlucky one.'

'Felix, we can't go on with this conversation here.'

'Then just tell me one thing –' I was astonished by how upset I'd suddenly become. My hands were shaking like an old man's. My eyes were wet. And I didn't recognise the place my tears or my words were coming from.

'No, Felix, not like this.'

'– have you fucked him yet?'

And this time, with the faintest of clicks, the phone did go down.

That night we talked.

I will not reproduce the conversation because I cannot. Though I'd begged her for words it's not the words that I remember. Even in extremis we were too good at talk, too slick, too oiled, for talk to have got us anywhere. Perhaps people who do not as a rule speak much to each other can use language to break through into candour. Not us. For all that I'd complained of the web of reticence she'd spun around me sexually, we were worded out. Silent or not, we suffered from a surfeit of articulation and literature. What we needed to help us break through into candour, Marisa and I, was not more Medea or Menelaus but raw emotion. We needed to weep awhile together. Throw things. Maybe do violence to each other.

It goes without saying that neither of us raised a hand or threw a plate. Though I – for reasons that were then and still partially remain inexplicable – shed tears.

Marisa cradled me like a mother. 'Hush, Felix,' that I do remember her saying. 'Hush, Felix.'

Where did it come from, all that emotion? What was I crying for?

Marisa was too good and intelligent a woman to point out to me that there was illogic in these tears, if true tears of regret they were. But it was palpable between us that I had rubbed the lamp in full knowledge of what would emerge from it, and been granted the first and maybe even the second of my three wishes.

'No going back on it now, Felix' – that, at least in so many words, she did not say.

But she did leave me with the sense that there was no going back on it for her. 'I did warn you about me,' she said, or something of the sort.

In fact Marisa had never been one of those women who present themselves as monsters of sexual volatility, warning men to beware that matrix of immoderation which is their heart. So her doing it now filled me with alarm. What was I to make of it – that she was lovesick? That Marius was for keeps now? That he had become, for her, unrelinquishable?

'I am not asking you to relinquish him,' was something else I didn't say.

But I was being cradled like a child, and like a child felt all of life's cruel opposites.

I took the opportunity, while I was on her breast, to tell her at last about the Cuban doctor. Maybe it would explain or extenuate me.

She laughed. 'The dirty devil,' she said.

'Him or me?'

'Both.'

'It's your fault for having a chest which is so beautiful.'

'Beautiful chests are ten a penny, Felix.'

'Beautiful ones, maybe, but yours is more than beautiful. Yours is eloquent. It announces you. Your chest is your prologue, Marisa.'

'Prologue to what?'

'To you. To the mystery of you. That's why you are so shocking to look at. You should enter a room backwards. Front on, you promise too much. You hurt my eyes. You always have.'

'Then close your eyes.'

'I've tried that. But all I see is the Cuban unlocking you. It's a sight, Marisa. Another man's hands . . .'

'Hush, Felix.'

'No, I won't hush. Once you've seen that sight you can't rest until you see it again.'

'Well you'll just have to use your imagination.'

Somehow or other we had it settled, before we went to sleep, that Marius would come to the house while I was at the shop. This was intended to answer the uncertainties from which we'd both been suffering. He would come to us and put both our minds at rest. But I would have to be sure I knew what I was doing.

'What *I* am doing?'

'Yes, Felix. What *you* are doing.'

'It's you, surely,' I said. Which, after a long and fearful pause, she took to mean that yes, I did know what I was doing.

Whether or not Marisa also intended it as a sort of parental assurance that I would not be left alone, that I'd know where she was, that she would remain as my wife, under my roof, I couldn't have said for certain. But that was how it felt. Like breaking a child in slowly to the fact of separation.

And yes, though it would have to be on her terms, subject to her restrictions and within the limits of what she considered permissible – 'What *I* consider permissible, Felix' – she would set aside a ritual time to include me, to the extent that language can ever be inclusive, in the progress of her feelings for Marius and of his feelings for her. Henceforth, she would be as wife to Marius, and as storyteller to me. We would stay married, but our conjugality would begin and end where her narrative began and ended.

We shed a final tear together and turned over. I was not proud of myself. I had hardly behaved like the revolutionary of sex I believed myself to me. But the means sometimes justify the ends. Looked at all round, I thought things had worked out pretty much the way I wanted them to. And I went to sleep anxious but exhilarated.

THUS OUR LITTLE FAMILY. MARIUS AND MARISA IN BED TOGETHER IN MY house, I – unless I had business to attend to, and I made sure I rarely did – out walking the streets of Marylebone, understanding what Marius meant by the hairspring hour, the day not yet spent, the wheels of evening just beginning to turn. People did look different at four o'clock once you knew what to look for, as anyone with that knowledge would have thought looking at me, a successful antiquarian bookseller by day but by afternoon a husband whose wife was lying naked with her lover.

Everything, at four o'clock in Marylebone, was in flux. There was an agitation in the shops I frequented that matched my own. The assistants were not as they had been earlier; what they weren't excited about, they dreaded. Their hearts fluttered. You couldn't get their attention. They were counting up or checking till rolls. At the fromagerie they were worrying about food going off. In the patisseries they were running out of cakes. Outside the restaurants the chefs and waiters were in the street, smoking their last cigarettes before the night's business began. I exchanged vaguely criminal looks with them as I passed. We were in something underhand together. Even the taxi drivers drove without looking for fares, reluctant to be flagged down in case someone mistook the hour and asked to be taken too far, or to the wrong part of the city. No one quite knew what it was they wanted – only that it wasn't this.

If the wind was right you could smell the park. A bitter, muddy smell as from a churned-up boating lake. Sometimes I thought about walking to the park but I never did. I wanted to remain hemmed in by buildings. When the days were short the lights were comforting, like a cage. I had never been a pub-goer but now I made a point of dropping in to one or other of them – I didn't bother to distinguish – for a glass of wine. I spoke to drinkers when they talked to me. But when I told them why I was there – 'I try to stay out of the house, as an act of decency, on those afternoons my wife entertains her lover' – they were inclined to leave me to my own company.

Once, sitting up at a bar, I fell into conversation with a businessman from Atlanta, visiting Marylebone to settle his daughter into the American InterContinental University which had a campus on the High Street. He'd have talked politics to me had I let him. Bush. Iraq. Guantanamo Bay. But I hadn't left Marisa in the arms of Marius to discuss America's policy on the Middle East. 'See her over there,' I said, pointing to a woman whom I took to be a producer at BBC London across the road – she had that bare-faced flirtatious manner undeterred by plain appearance and no dress sense I'd observed in women who worked for the BBC. She was in earnest conversation with a wild-haired man in a black T-shirt and leather jacket, presumably a presenter, and almost certainly married to someone else. Every now and then they leaned into each other and kissed with open mouths. 'She,' I said, 'is my wife.'

The businessman from Atlanta gripped my arm. 'You allow that?'

'I can't stop it.'

'Hey, I'll stop it for you.' And he would have been off his seat had I not held him back.

'It's what she wants,' I said.

'What about what you want?'

'I want what she wants.'

'Does the guy know you're the husband?'

'Doubt it. But it doesn't matter what he knows, does it?'

'It would to me. I'd hammer him.'

'What would you hammer him for? He's not doing anything you and I wouldn't do. She's the one that's putting out.'

He looked across at her and shook his head. She was leaning forward, her breasts resting on the table, offering up her mouth like a baby bird. 'And she can do that knowing you're watching?'

'She says she forgets I'm there.'

'Holy shit!'

'I know,' I said, getting up. 'She fucks him sometimes on the living-room floor, while I'm watching television.'

'Jesus!'

I shrugged and gave him my hand to shake. 'Thanks for talking to me,' I said. 'It helps.'

It hadn't helped actually, or it wouldn't have helped had help been what I was looking for. I wasn't sure what I was looking for. That little bit of humiliation extra, I suppose. Another witness to my ignominy. Another person on whom to try out an indignation I didn't quite feel. Always something more and someone else. But it wasn't working. The woman with her breasts on the table wasn't Marisa and I couldn't fake it. She was too obviously doing what it was natural for her to do. She wasn't acting against herself. Whereas whenever I thought of Marisa in the arms of Marius, I saw her at her most philosophically reflective, grave and distant, at odds with her own nudity, and therefore – because sex had to be shocking to her before she could enjoy it – at her most alarmed and most abandoned.

The pity was that I couldn't take the man from Atlanta home to show him that.

He came to my house three afternoons a week, my wife's lover, and stayed from four until seven. These hours suited them both, emotionally no less than practically. Each liked to keep a lid on things. From four until seven, Marius believed, he was in no danger of losing his head. And the idea of daylight robbery appealed to him. His life would have been different had he done that with Elspeth all those years ago. Had he gone to get the professor's assessment of his essay, and stayed to borrow the professor's wife. 'My turn, Professor,' it would have pleased him to say. 'You can have her back when I have finished with her.'

Instead of being stuck with her while she turned into an old lady.

As for the handover conceit, I malign him. It was mine not his.

Much of what I attributed to Marius was mine not his. They take your wives, these marauding melancholics, but they seldom give you the scurrilous vocabulary you long for in return. Which justified, I thought, the occasional ventriloquism. 'Watch it,' Marisa warned me when I let 'handover' slip one afternoon as I was putting on my coat. 'If you think you're playing pass the parcel, I ain't no parcel.' She was genuinely angry. I tried to explain that it was I who was being handed over, tossed out of my own house while my wife was wifed by another man, and then permitted to return when there was nothing she could want from me. But she was not so easily mollified. Any suggestion that I was playing push-me pull-me with Marius enraged her. What she now did, she did for herself. 'Pleasing you, Felix,' she shouted as I opened the front door, 'is a thing of the past.' Which terrifying thought warmed my insatiably topsy-turvy cuckold's heart as I walked the streets.

Otherwise the four o'clock slot fitted in well with Marisa's other arrangements. She didn't want to change her hours at Oxfam, and she would not have gone without getting her nails done or her feet massaged at the usual time. By four o'clock she was able clear her day for Marius, and by seven, when he left, she was ready to think about something else – dinner with one or other of her half-sisters, the theatre, the Samaritans, the Wallace, dancing. Or, if I was lucky, if I hadn't called her wrath down on me, she might re-enact her afternoon's abandonment for my unholy delectation, in language as graphic as she could bear to make it. My ear in such proximity to her mouth they might have been a single organ.

I won't pretend, as Marisa herself did not pretend, that this came easy to her. 'I find it embarrassing,' she told me, 'I find it ludicrous, I find it disloyal, and I find it upsetting.'

'Tell me, tell me slowly about disloyal,' I said.

'Good joke, Felix.'

I thought so, too. But I really did want her to tell me about disloyal.

'If it were you,' she said, 'you would not want to be talked about afterwards.'

'If it were me,' I said, 'I would not be going to another man's house three afternoons a week.'

'Does that absolve me of all obligation to respect his privacy?'

'Privacy! I am not asking you to describe his dick, Marisa.'

We were in bed – our bed. We had the lights off. And – my idea – we were burning incense. My back was turned to her, to minimise the embarrassment she'd spoken of. But I could sense her looking at me quizzically. They always wonder, women, whether it's the dick you're really interested in. Because they don't do jealousy as men do jealousy, because they take the Othello murder route themselves, and cannot imagine where the pleasure part comes in, they conclude it must be the deviancy they understand that explains it, rather than the deviancy they don't.

Leaving that, she said, 'Whatever I tell you is a violation of confidentiality.'

I agreed with her. 'It is,' I said. 'But sometimes a person loses the right to confidentiality. You climb over another man's wall, you take your chance what happens next.'

'I'm not your wall, Felix.'

'Wall, wife . . . He likes the transgressive element.'

'And you don't?'

'We're not talking about me.'

'We are, actually. What you ask of me violates you too, doesn't it.'

It was my turn now to say, 'Good joke.'

'A violation of your ear, was what I meant,' she said.

I told her she needn't worry about my ear. That it was a robust, inviolable organ.

'Don't dare me, Felix,' she said. And we lay there a long time, listening to her weighing up what she might do to me if I dared her.

But little by little, after a number of false starts, and bouts of nervous laughter – that salve to our conscience which we call a sense of the ridiculous, that spoiler of sin and sex and sensuality, that strategy for keeping our feet on the ground – we got around to it. But always – which was never the way when we danced, though this too was dancing of a sort – always with me leading. *And then and then and then . . . ?*

The questions, as in all ages and in all places, time-worn, tattered, tragicomic. *And then and then and then . . . ?* No matter whether the man is a metaphysician or an illiterate fool, the questions will be the same. *And then and then and then . . . ?* Thus does jealousy, like fear of death, iron out our differences. Some men are more exacting in their curiosity, that is all. They want the knife to cut a little deeper. *And then and then and then and did you look at him did you look into his eyes and did he look into your eyes and what did your eyes say and what did his eyes say and did you kiss him where did you kiss him how did you kiss him or did he kiss you who initiated it who kissed the first kiss and were your lips parted did you part them or did he part them with his tongue did you let him part them did you invite the parting or did he part them forcefully and then what were you thinking did you feel at that time did you feel what did you feel were you happy were you eager how eager were you how eager was he what did he say then and what did you say then or were you past words was there nothing more you wanted to say to him or he to you nothing you wanted to hear were you past hearing and then what did his hand caress your breast did it explore the roundness of you and did your nipple harden and did you say harder and did your hand what was your heart going like mad and yes did you say yes you would Yes?*

And did Marisa, in reply, orchestrate her re-enactments? Did she do to me what she had done to Marius?

I take that line of questioning, since we are being candid, to be no better than mine. Wherein lies the difference between the cuckold's transports of uncertain wondering – tell me tell me tell me tell me – and the reader's?

The wanting to know what happened next – *and then and then and then*: what is that but the spur to curiosity that drives us back, again and again, to our oldest and greatest stories?

Listen, Menelaus – what is Helen whispering to Paris? What Trojan promises lull her to her sleep, what Trojan laughter stirs her from her bed of shame?

What are her suitors, Odysseus – more suitors than she has ears to hear them with – saying to your wife Penelope while you dawdle on the high seas?

Thus literature, pandering to our unclean desires. And thus the reader, in his eternal wanting to be told – *what next what next* – as unclean as any cuckold.

As for what Marisa re-enacted, that is between her and me. Suffice it to say that I never loved her artistry more than when she swooned in Marius's arms while she swooned in mine. And never did I – a man who had read too much – approach any text with more attentiveness.

Soon, Marisa was saying such things to me, I couldn't be sure she remembered Marius had gone, or noticed that it was I who was lying beside her and not him. Such things I almost pitied Marius for missing out on.

This was a story, though, that couldn't end. One Thousand and One times One Thousand and One Nights, and always more to anticipate and dread. How long before Marisa would plunge her nails into my neck and whisper in my ear, like a lick of flame, 'Love me, Marius'? And then 'Fuck me, Marius'? And then, and then, 'Marius, I love you'?

How long before my bodice-ripper's reader's heart would crack asunder with the madcap all-consuming joy of it?

Go on – ask. *How long how long how long* . . .

And Marius?

If he was the loser by these violations, he was only the loser in someone else's eyes. Unaware, he grew more airily handsome the more four o'clocks he notched up.

It would have been cruel of me to have begrudged him this new lightsomeness. These are hard enough times for men already. Outside the never-neverwhere of celebrity, men are no longer permitted to fuck for the fun of it, though it is obvious that the activity brings out the best in many of them, as least as far as physical health and appearance go. And fucking my wife three times a week – allow me to say that again for the sheer unholy sweetness of it – *and fucking my wife three times a week* certainly brought out the best in Marius. Whenever I caught sight of him his hair was wet, either from showering before Marisa, or from showering afterwards. The look suited him. Men like me emerge from water blind and dripping like a rat that has gnawed itself out of a sack; Marius belonged to that class of amphibian mammal that rises glistening from the sea, shaking silver droplets from its torso, like Neptune. Or the Forsaken Merman, except that his forsaken appearance had left him entirely. His moustaches were clipped. His eyes had lost their ache. He was speaking audibly. And if I was not mistaken he had bought himself new clothes – a black corduroy jacket I had not seen before, a striped suit that played bohemianly, in much the same spirit as Marisa's suits, with the concept of the City, and a number of soft Italian shirts that buttoned high and added further arrogance to his already haughty head.

As I have explained, I wasn't watching him as much as I had before he became my house guest. This wasn't all precautionary. It was logistical too. If he was lying with my wife at four o'clock in the afternoon, he was not out on the High Street or pacing the floor above the button shop in frustrated creativity. He interested me no less now that I had him, so to speak. Nor did Marisa's late-night confidences diminish my curiosity. I by no means believed I knew all there was to know of him in report. But I had to be more vigilant than in the carefree past. We all had too much to lose if he discovered me now.

Nevertheless, he was never entirely out of my sight. Above the fray at the best of times, he barely saw where he was going now he had Marisa on his mind. So I could get a long view of him at the Sunday market, buying bread, or from the other side of the road collecting his *Financial Times*. Once I passed him coming out of the chiropractor's, and though I gasped, fearing the encounter, he strode on oblivious of me.

'Love her,' I said under my breath when I saw him. 'Love her, love her, love her.'

Did that show that my feelings toward him had softened? 'Fuck her,' was what I had always imagined saying to him in the course of our early meetings. 'Fuck her, fuck her, fuck her.'

Was 'Love her, love her, love her' the proof of my contention that you can love the man who fucks your wife, if only you are able to sort your mind out?

It might have been this new softening of husbandly feeling that made me start up a conversation with him, many months into the new arrange-ment, when we 'happened' – Fortune is a pimp and all that – to find ourselves in the travellers' bookshop on the High Street at four o'clock on a non-Marisa afternoon. But mischief can never be entirely ruled out of the motivation of a cuckold. It satisfied me to beard him in this way, he who knew nothing of me, I who knew everything of him. And then there was the frisson of seeing, close up, the aftermath of Marisa on his skin. What was it like to smell the breath of the man who was burgling your wife?

('What's this quasi-biblical talk of his "entering" me?' Marisa had enquired in the course of one of my earlier encouragements to her to describe her afternoon.

'I learned it from you. "The moment of entry is visually transfixing" – your words.'

'Oh, Felix.'

'What are you telling me, that entry isn't what he does?'

'Literally, I suppose he does.'

'You suppose so? Entry was good enough for me. Why is it too literal for him?'

'Because you make it sound like a burglary and that's not how it feels.'

'So how does it feel?'

'No, Felix. No you don't.'

I bit my lip. It isn't pleasant to be reprimanded at my age. And my question was reasonable enough. If it wasn't with him as it had been with me, how was it with him? But since she wasn't saying, I stuck at burglary. She might not have liked the word, but I — for reasons that were part onomatopoeic, part self-lacerating — did. Hence 'burgling my wife'.)

He was idling, the burglar of Marisa's body and affections, before the Africa section, not looking for anything in particular, I decided, but that didn't stop me wondering: was he thinking of fleeing, and if so was he thinking of fleeing alone or with my wife? He'd eloped before. Maybe it got easier each time.

'Off somewhere?' I asked.

He didn't know who I was at first. He never did. I didn't think it was personal. He just didn't know who anyone was at first, unless it was a woman or a girl in whom he had an interest. Part of me would have liked to reciprocate the insult — but it was a bit late for that.

'Oh Christ, you,' he said, when at last my face did swim back into his recollection. 'My Nemesis.'

I threw him a self-deprecating smile. I wasn't going to tell him he was mine.

'French Guinea,' I said.

'What about it?'

'I see you're planning a trip. French Guinea is said to be nice.'

'And what the hell has it got to do with you?'

'As your Nemesis, a great deal. It's important I know where you are every moment of the day. I can't have anyone else determining your fate.'

'I think you're taking me a trifle literally. Nemesis as in fucking nuisance was what I had in mind.'

'Not a usage I'm familiar with,' I said. 'But when we first talked and you described to me your four o'clock heartlands you never mentioned French Guinea.'

'I'm not mentioning it now. I don't owe you an atlas of my movements.'

'Of course you don't. But I wouldn't have picked you for an Africanophile.'

'I wouldn't have picked you for someone who had a right to an opinion.'

'I don't have an opinion. All I was going to do was recommend you further reading. Robbe-Grillet – you read him? I'd have thought he was up your street.'

He looked at me at last, or at least he looked at Robbe-Grillet. He was like me in this – he couldn't say no to an author or a title. It wouldn't have surprised me if in his mind's eye he could see the jacket of the first edition. Poor bookish bastards we both were.

'Robbe-Grillet? I don't know about up my street, but certainly of my persuasion in that he made objects more important than men. Which you'll forgive me saying – since you seem to want a man-to-man conversation – is precisely the ordering I favour at this very moment. I count on you to understand me when I say I would rather be talking to this bookcase than to you.'

'Absolutely follow you . . .'

'Yes, you do absolutely follow me, don't you. Is it just me, or are you following around other readers of Robbe-Grillet as well?'

'Ah, there are very few of us. As you don't need me to tell you, he's not in fashion. But honestly I'm not following anybody. I'm out and about a lot, that's all. I find it hard to stay inside. There is so much to see on the streets. Wasn't it Barthes who said that with Robbe-Grillet the novel becomes man's experience of what's around him without the protection of a metaphysic? Well that's me. I am that novel.'

'Oh, Christ yes, *The Voyeur*. You've tried to tell me this about your-self before, if I'm not mistaken, though why you think your voyeurism might interest me a second time when it didn't the first—'

'You remembered! I'm flattered. But I never told you I was a voyeur exactly. A general pervert was about as far as I was prepared to go with it to you, on the strength of a brief acquaintance and all that. Though now we know each other better . . .'

'No, please don't. General pervert is fine.'

'Haven't read *The Voyeur*, anyway,' I said. 'Though I will now you've recommended it. Is that set in French Guinea? I've always reckoned, you see, though I don't think we're ever really told, that French Guinea is where *Jealousy* is set. You know *Jealousy*, I don't doubt. It's the one where the main character – if you can call him a character – sits and counts the rows of banana trees between his house and the house he suspects his wife of carrying on in. The best novel about the banality of suspicion ever written. It's so authentically tedious in its minuteness of observation it's unreadable.'

'That saves me, then, the chore of having to read it.'

'But then again,' I said, as though he hadn't spoken, 'that's what it's like. You count the trees, you note the different heights of the trunks, you distinguish between the tangle of the fronds, you measure the unevenness of the rows, and then you start to count again, over and over because jealousy is the harshest taskmaster, demanding from its victims a punctiliousness that your average obsessional tap-twiddler would find deranging.'

'I think,' he said, 'that you've just put me off French Guinea.'

'But not, I hope, Robbe-Grillet.'

'Him too. You have a way about you of putting me off just about everything.'

'Jealousy as well?'

'I have never been *on* jealousy.'

'Never experienced it, or never approved of it?'

'Both. It's invariably an indulgence. We have the strength to walk away.'

'But one might not want to walk away.'

'Exactly, one might not. That, I think, is what indulgence means. You can but you won't.'

'You're a lucky man,' I said, 'to be able to exert so much self-control.'

'If this is a prelude to more pervert talk,' he said, 'I'll leave you to it.'

'I'm off perversion now. That was yesterday's interest. Today all I want to speak about is love.'

'Then I will definitely leave you to it.'

'Just one word before you do.' I was almost pulling at his jacket, so eager was I to continue the conversation. 'It is not of course my business but could the reason you do not feel jealousy be that you have never been in love? If there's no one you care about losing, then it stands to reason you won't care about losing her. Or him. Whereas when you are smitten

216

to your soul . . . but you're a reader, you must know all this from books. Don't you ever want it, though? Don't you ever envy those whom jealousy makes so alive that they register – well, like Robbe-Grillet himself – the minutest resonance of every object that is witness or confirmation of that which they suspect, every hair on the loved one's head, every button on the lover's jacket, every banana on every banana tree if we happened to be in French Guinea—'

'No,' he said, and without a further word of goodbye he strode out of the shop.

I offered an apology to Stefan, who managed the shop. We keep a friendly eye on each other across the book trade. 'Sorry, Stefan,' I said, 'I seem to have talked you out of a sale.'

'Well you'd have talked me into buying Robbe-Grillet. Which one should I start with? *Jealousy* or *The Voyeur*?'

'You were listening.'

'Felix, the whole shop was listening. You wouldn't pop in and do this on a regular basis?'

'What, and lose you a customer every time I do?'

But I decided, in the circumstances, that the least I could do was buy *The Rough Guide to West Africa*.

'Do you want it gift-wrapped?' Stefan asked.

'Of course,' I said. But didn't dare ask him to address it, much as I'd have loved to – for the pleasure of seeing the look on his face as much as anything, in order to suck on his pity for me – *To my wife's lover. In appreciation.*

'I'll pop round and buy a book from you one of these fine days,' Stefan said. Comical in his bookshop check suit and round David Hockney glasses.

'Not without an appointment, you won't,' I reminded him.

But the merriment of booksellers aside, what the hell did I think I'd been doing talking jealousy and banana trees to Marius?

Could it have been that I wanted him to know I knew?

And why had I bought him *The Rough Guide to West Africa*?

Did I just want to give him things?

Or did I want him to start making those associations I'd been so careful to blur? Discover me? Lose that fuzzy halo of happiness he carried above his head like a medieval saint? Feel used and cheated? Get the fuck out of my marriage?

I WASN'T ALWAYS OUT OF THE HOUSE WHEN THEY THOUGHT I WAS. THE FIRST time I stayed in when they were there was accidental. I'd been working in my office at home as I occasionally did even on workdays. I forgot it was a Marius afternoon. I realised when he rang the doorbell – a commanding, emasculating ring – that I couldn't escape without being noticed. So I quietly locked myself in. That was all. It wasn't as though I could hear anything, so I couldn't be accused of eavesdropping.

Though that's how I remember it, there is one thing wrong with this account. I would not have forgotten it was a Marius afternoon. I wore the almanac of his comings and goings in my flesh. So I must assume I lied to myself in order to be closer to them.

Thereafter I made a practice of it, by which I mean I did it about one visit out of six. Say once a fortnight. There was a queer comfort in it. Call that sinister if you will, but I meant them no harm. I simply wanted to occupy the same physical space they did. I would have preferred being alongside them in their bed, the same silent and ignored figure I'd have cut at their table had they let me, but as that was out of the question my study was the next best thing. I would lock my door, pull down the blinds, lie on the carpet at the time I calculated Marius would be lying himself beside Marisa, and remain there for the duration of his visit.

Subspace, but without the High Church ceremonials. Subspace pure and simple, subspace Calvinistical even, just me stretched out on my floor, gone from the world of the living, breathing only by courtesy of Marius and Marisa, so that had they stopped, I'd have stopped with them.

But once you've gone this far, only practicalities prevent your going further. It wasn't long before I made the decision to move up a floor. To one side of their adulterous bower was our bedroom, but it would have been impossible to conceal myself there in advance of their appointment without Marisa discovering me. To the other side, though, was a lumber room, full of computers I couldn't throw away, old photographs of the family, suitcases and ski clothes and ships' lamps from the thirties which I felt I ought to keep. Hidden in here, a room Marisa never penetrated, I believed I would be able to enjoy a greater proximity to the lovers, and on occasion maybe even hear them. I had thought about getting someone from the spy and surveillance shop on Baker Street to come along on a day Marisa was out and bug the house. Hidden cameras, too, seemed worth exploring, until I faced the fact that my needing to know contained an essential element of needing not to know. I wanted to think and feel myself between them, an altogether more active exercise for jealousy than merely looking on and listening in. Would that the general camp had tasted her sweet body, but not on closed-circuit television.

I was not, you see, your ordinary twopenny-halfpenny voyeur.

Anything I heard while concealed in the lumber room would by this reasoning have belonged to active not to passive jealousy, but I heard very little. Marisa had never been a noisy lover, and Marius at best mumbled his pleasures into his moustaches. Of the three of us I was the only one who bellowed, and I wasn't here to listen to myself. But I wasn't interested in hearing them moan anyway. I am not that kind of pervert. It's talk that does it for me – a single 'Fuck me, Marius' knocking the stereophony of fucking itself into a cocked hat. And if I couldn't hear the words I always had Marisa's narrative of the night before to remember and peruse. Humiliating though this is to report, I would flatten myself against the wall, not to hear the lovers but to be close to them, to feel, if nothing else, the vibration of their breathing, and then I would mentally run through all that Marisa had told me of their lovemaking the last time they were in the house. Thus, though I'd contrived to be at their elbow, I was always trailing in their wake – having to make do with the reported kisses of yesterday when I was only a few inches and a wall from the real kisses of today. Yet again, never quite laying hold on the thing I sought.

'There was always something wanting,' David Copperfield complained. There always is when you're slave to the adamantine in women. Though David Copperfield did not know that about himself until he matured into Philip Pirrip.

About four months into the new arrangement – I hiding in my own house while Marius helped himself to what he wanted from it – Marisa found me out. It was always a complex business, getting in before or after her, remembering whether to put the burglar alarm on or off, removing all incriminating trace of myself from the house, staying as silent as the grave, and eventually I made a dog's dinner of it, leaving a coat I should have been wearing to work on the bannister, and falling over a box of papers as I changed my position in the lumber room. Marius heard nothing. Marisa pretended to hear nothing but must have been a lot less fun to be with for what remained of the afternoon. After she'd let Marius out, she came looking for me. She was wearing a silk negligée I'd never seen before, black with the finest straps, and high-heeled, pubic, boudoir mules. I was surprised to see her looking so conventionally – she who chose her clothes with such meticulousness – the part of another man's mistress. Pleased, too. Words might have been my medium but the odd visual clue still helped. If I was not mistaken there was a bite mark, or at least a patch of broken skin, just inside the bodice of her negligée, above her right breast.

'Explain this,' she said.

'Explain *that*,' I felt like saying. But I feared the candour of real life. What if she'd stepped into the negligeé and painted on the bite mark the minute Marius left, in order to tighten the screws of jealousy? And what if, the moment I questioned her, she owned up to the deception – punitively – in order to loosen them again?

Besides, I was in no position to ask her to explain anything. I put my hands in the air. 'I surrender,' I said.

'I can't believe you'd stoop to this, Felix.'

I went to embrace her but she held me off. A great pity. I'd have loved to hold her still soft and nuzzled from Marius.

'I thought by now you knew I'd stoop to anything.'

'Are you recording us?'

'Of course not.'

'How do I know?'

'You can search me, or search the room for wires. I haven't been videoing you either. I just like being close to where you are. I love you.'

'You have a strange way of showing it.'

'The strangest. But you knew that.'

'I won't allow this, Felix. If you can't keep your side of the bargain I won't keep mine.'

'What does that mean?'

'I won't meet him here any longer. You said you were OK about him coming. You said it would make you feel safer. But you also said you'd be out. I can't have you both in the same house at the same time.'

There were a thousand retorts to that, and I rejected them all. 'I've said I surrender. I won't do it again. It was wrong of me. But it's hard, all this. So near to me, Marisa, and so far.'

'Is that a joke?'

'I don't do jokes within an hour either end of your lover.'

'Isn't it enough that I tell you all you want to know? That's hard, too. But I do it. Now it would appear that I don't do it well enough.'

'You couldn't do it better,' I said. 'I live to have you whisper your infidelities in my ear. It's what my ear is for. I ask for nothing else. Just every now and then, I wish I could be with you, that's all.'

'With me?'

'With you both.'

'You're mad.'

'Of course I'm mad.'

'With *us*? *Here?*'

'Here, in the restaurant, in the park. Anywhere. I'll take you both away for the weekend if you like. The seaside would be nice.'

'It's not appropriate, Felix.'

'Oh, *appropriate*! Do you call ours an appropriate household? What I propose – no, what I beg, Marisa – is as appropriate as you want it to be.'

'And I don't want it to be.'

'Then there's an end of it. But he doesn't have to know I'm your husband, if that's what's worrying you. I could just run into you. You could introduce me as your friend. I'd join you for a drink and then piss off.'

I watched the scene unfold before her eyes. She shuddered. I don't mean shook her head, or rolled her eyes, I mean shuddered.

'Why do you want this, Felix?'

'I'm lonely. I feel excluded.'

'I thought exclusion was what you sought.'

'I seek palpable exclusion.'

'Felix, there is no such thing.'

'There is. There is the exclusion of being there and not being there. The exclusion of your being oblivious to me. Allowing his hand access to your breasts, kissing without inhibition in my presence, as though I am beneath your notice.'

'Has it occurred to you that kissing without inhibition in your absence might be more fun?'

'For you.'

'Can't you consider yourself excluded by virtue of your exclusion – or is that too straightforward?'

'I want to be a witness to my ignominy. I want to suffer the sting of disregard.'

(I could have added, but decided it was unwise, that I wanted to be the water boy to their Horace and Lydia, a witness to their naked Roman revels, Marisa coiled into Marius's chest, naked to her toes.)

'Want, want, want.'

'Yes, want, want, want.'

She looked at me without pleasure. 'Then if the sting of disregard is what you want, you've got it. I disregard you. And if that's not enough, I don't know what to give you. Go get yourself whipped.'

So I did.

But not before a couple of odd events occurred, one on top of the other, neither of which improved my temper.

The first was the arrival of an anonymous communication. It was a postcard of Edvard Munch's *Self-Portrait, the Night Wanderer*, was addressed to me at the shop and said GET A LIFE. I was at my desk, going through mail, when I found it. I raised my eyes to Dulcie who was at that moment bringing me tea and biscuits. She shook her head. 'Nothing to do with me,' she said. Had she got to it first she would probably have destroyed it.

I should have destroyed it myself but I could not. Every ten minutes or so I would set aside what I was doing and reinspect it as though expecting to find a clue I'd missed. I didn't recognise the handwriting, but that meant nothing. Who sees anyone's handwriting any more? Marius was the obvious candidate in that he was the only person I could think of – given our last encounter – who might wish me ill, that's if telling me to get a life was wishing me ill. But Marius didn't know my name or my address, and Marisa sure as hell wasn't going to tell him. Besides, GET A LIFE wasn't his locution. Even when Marius told you to get lost he couldn't manage it in so few words.

So who then? Ernesto? Why would Ernesto tell me to get a life when I had recently given him back his? Rafaele? He was in Umbria, eating Polish sausage. Who else knew I had no life? Unless the whole of

Marylebone was witness to my cuckoldry – which I wouldn't of course have minded. I could think of a few of my more clubbable fellow anti-quarians who had grown lecherous over their brandies when I'd let them, offering it as their opinion that I was a lucky devil in my way to be married to a woman with a body as magnificent as her appetite to use it was unquenchable. Not what they could handle in a wife – not got the balls for it, old boy – but if I could, and I wanted it no other way, hats off to me. 'I'm bewitched,' I'd confessed to them, and they'd said she was a witch, all right, my wife, and in their orange eyes I'd seen the witch-yearning that lives in every man no matter what he tells you to the contrary.

But in that case it was they who needed to get a life, not me.

There was also something perplexingly incongruous about the choice of such a card for such a message. Munch in his self-portrait would get a life if he could, but life has been mislaid. It is a sympathetic, tormented study, painted sepulchrally, of a hounded, black-eyed man, barely daring to show himself to the night. Whoever chose that card could not have hated me.

Marisa?

My darling, get a life, get your life, get our life back. My dearest husband, do not end up looking as bleak and eyeless as Mr Munch.

Except that sending an anonymous card addressed in someone else's handwriting was not Marisa's style. Nor, when I'd last checked, was it her mood. GET A LIFE is not the same as GET A WHIPPING.

I would have gone on fretting about it had I not that same morning received an unexpected visit in the shop – unexpected by me, at least, because of some cock-up in our appointment system – from the most eminent of James Joyce's biographers, hot from the Oxford college where he resided in intellectual splendour, receiving lesser Joyce scholars as an emperor receives principalities. Professor X, as I will have to call him – for it would be a breach of professional etiquette to give his real name – had contacted me a month or two before regarding a number of Irish fairy stories signed W. B. Yeats (another of his subjects) which had appeared in our catalogue. I'd sent him the catalogue knowing they were his cup of tea. He was in a position now to inspect them if I still had them.

Of course, I told him, apologising for the cock-up, I still had them. I'd passed over several offers in the hope that Professor X would make his bid for them before too long. Who you sell to is not immaterial in this business. Besides, there was a question I was particularly anxious to put to him – as it were on behalf of the whole family – once our business was concluded. Joyce's wife Nora – was it true, as rumoured, that Joyce had encouraged her to . . .

'Put it about?' the professor obliged.

I bowed, as to his mastery of the vernacular. But blenched from the implicit suggestion that I'd been vulgarly intrusive. I was addressing a biographer, was I not? Isn't biography *ipso facto* vulgarly intrusive?

'You will be asking me next,' he went on, shaking his great woolly head at me, much like a sheep refusing to cross a ditch, 'whether Nora ever did what Joyce told her in a letter he would like her to do – sit in an armchair with her thighs apart, point her cane towards some imaginary misde-meanour for which he wished to be held responsible, pull him towards her in a simulacrum of rage, throw him face downwards in her lap, pull off his trousers, raise her cane . . .'

I waited. If I was vulgar I was vulgar.

'Who knows,' he said. Not a question but a statement, whereupon we both fell silent, listening to the words tumble like stones down a great, dark well.

It appeared he had nothing else to say, indeed I made to shake his hand, but quite suddenly, as though he felt he couldn't be done with me yet, he found one last stern remonstrance. 'You will be able to discover fetishism and anality or whatever else you want to call it in the life of any writer who is concerned, as Joyce was, to subject love to intense scrutiny, to break it down, reconstitute and crystallise it. A restless imagination will always be vulnerable to gossip.'

I couldn't, after that, say, 'And Nora's putting it about?'

My curiosity struck me, in the presence of the distinguished man, not just as bad form on the personal level but as an intellectual offence also. Quite how he squared his grand sniffiness with his profession of muck-raker I wasn't sure, but it was right of him, I thought – particularly as he knew nothing of my grandfather's shady encounter with Joyce and Nora in the Zunfthaus zur Zimmerleuten, and I certainly wasn't going to tell him now – to tick me off for an inquisitiveness that was inaesthetic. The life is not the work, the work is not the life. Joyce the novelist is Joyce the novelist, and Bloom the ex-blotting-paper salesman is Bloom the ex-blotting-paper salesman. But then Professor X didn't have to save either of them from me. I love a man, whether he is what he is in the name of art or not, who refuses to be in a permanent war over possession with other men, who prefers absorbency to power, who abdicates the imperiousness of his will and allows his wife to do with him as she pleases.

Which begs, I accept, a fairly large question. What if the thing she does with him is less what pleases her than what pleases him? Is his will, in that case, not so much abdicated as exerted in another form?

A row of this sort, I suspected, was brewing between Marisa and me, whether or not she was the one who had sent me the postcard of Munch's *Night Wanderer*, exhorting me to get a life. It is standard in the clinical literature on perversion that the masochist inscribes a tyrannical script, that wherever you find a submissive and a dominant entwined, it is the submissive who calls the shots. The bullied who does the bullying. The slave that dominates the mistress. A nice little paradox of the twisted life.

Much of this, I have to say, bores me profoundly. Anyone who has spent a moment considering the role of partners in a sadomasochistic relationship notices the topsy-turvy nature of their power exchange. But I am not interested in the person who has considered the subject for a moment; for the purposes of conversation, at least, I am interested only in the person who has studied it for a lifetime. So Professor X should have been my man. But the intense scrutiny of love he ascribed to Joyce seemed a touch abstract and yellow-bellied to me, an apology for unhusbandly behaviour when what one wanted was a celebration. Like so many biographers of the unconventional, he was too conventional adequately to do the job. Too conventional for me to jabber to, at least.

So much of what a pervert knows he cannot say because he cannot find anyone to say it to.

And yet I was the one they dared tell to get a life!

WHICH RETURNS ME, BUT AT A PERVERT'S PACE, TO THE WHIPPING.

As my father's son I knew about such things. All the men in our family my father's age had themselves whipped as a matter of course. Preferably on the Continent where the subtleties of temporary sexual metamorphosis were better understood. For whatever purposes he employed them, my father held British prostitutes in the highest contempt. They were a cause for national shame, he never tired of saying. He didn't mean for being prostitutes; he meant for being prostitutes with so little *joie de vivre* or *élan vital*. That he could express what they were lacking only in the French tongue was no accident: like his father before him, he packed a light bag and took himself off to France or Germany whenever he felt the rise of urges which marriage could not satisfy. 'You find a wife to clean your house this side of the Channel and a mistress to dirty your mind on the other,' he told me once when he was drunk. In this again, as a deliriously happy husband, have I broken with family tradition. I haven't needed to leave home to have my mind dirtied.

When my father and my uncles couldn't get away, however, they made do with what was round the corner.

I accompanied them once to a house on Baker Street, not far from Sherlock Holmes's address, as a sort of bonding exercise. It was my twenty-first birthday. 'You can have a thrashing or a cake,' my father had said.

'I'll have a cake,' I told him.

229

'That settles it,' he said, 'you'll have a thrashing.'

They viewed it as therapeutic, like going to the barber's for a hot towel or having a foot scrub.

We sat together on a long couch, all four of us, with crocheted anti-macassars behind our heads, and inspected the women who paraded before us. Anyone watching would have said we were auditioning kitchen maids, albeit unconventionally attired kitchen maids. Each of the women reeled off her specialism according to its geography of origin or practice – Greek, French, Moroccan, English – which my father decoded for me in the grossest terms. 'She'll piss in your mouth – do you want that? Supposed to be very good for your gums.' None of the girls was extraordinarily good-looking, but they weren't dogs either. I mentioned that fact to my father years later during one of his tirades against the condition of venery in England. 'That's because you've never been down the Reeperbahn,' he said.

I had actually, but it didn't seem worth making a row of it.

I don't know about my uncles but my father wasn't remotely interested in being beaten. He called it going to be thrashed but he liked to be the one who did the thrashing. Most Houses of Correction have submissives as well as dominatrices, and this House of Correction appeared to know already which of the submissives my father favoured. She was a pale Dickensian girl with big pleading eyes. The others wore towering show-girl's heels and variations of wicked-witch corsetry, but she was clothed in a yellowed slip, her hair cut straight and pulled off her face with a couple of spinsterish hairgrips, on her feet shoes such as I imagined were given to you when you entered an orphanage. Why my father paid for such a girl when we had any number of them working for us at home or in the shop, with each of whom he enjoyed whatever he wanted to enjoy, I only understood much later. It was the paying for them that constituted the excitement. Once he'd parted with his money he was pretty much ready to go home.

I chose a stringy, red-haired dominatrix who looked at me in a searching way I found arousing and who told me she was putting herself through psychology and sociology at Queen Mary, which aroused me even more. 'I'm at Oxford,' I told her.

'Nice,' she said, fastening a leather collar around my neck and leading me up and down a little dungeon that was so childishly make-believe, like a backdrop for an exhibit in Madame Tussaud's around the corner, that I would have laughed had laughter been appropriate.

'What's your subject?' she asked me.

'Classics.'

'Wow. I like an educated conversation.'

'Me too,' I said.

'You know Freud's problem,' she said. 'He thought that for sex to be normal it had to have a final aim. Anything that stopped short of that finality he considered perversion. Which would make both of us perverts.'

'Which we're not.'

'Dead right. Which we're not. Do you like this?'

'The collar? Quite.'

'Would you like it more if I led you by your cock?'

'Probably.'

'Well you'll have to be a good boy.'

'And if I'm not?'

'You'll get that,' she said, striking me across the cheek. She was wearing elbow-length black gloves, of the sort my mother wore for funerals, which compounded the insult.

'That hurt,' I said.

She struck me again.

'No, I mean that really hurt. I'll go if you hit me again.'

'There won't be any point, then, in me tying you to the whipping post?'

'None.'

She looked at me with her hands together. There was something of an El Greco Mater Dolorosa about her – washed-out and elongated in her sado-gear.

'All I can think in that case,' she said, 'is that you're a moral masochist.'

'As opposed to what?'

'A sexual masochist.'

'I didn't know I was a masochist at all.'

'So what are you doing here?'

'It was my father's idea.'

'And do you do everything your father tells you?'

'Only when's he's paying.'

'He's paying? Does your mother know?'

'My mother! God forbid.'

She cocked her head knowingly, like a great red scrawny parrot. 'Sounds to me,' she said, 'as though there's some idealisation of the mother going on here.'

'Not at all. I just know she wouldn't want my father brutalising me.'

'Brutalising, you say? Interesting word. Does he brutalise your mother?'

'Of course.'

'Does that hurt you?'

'Of course.'

'Did you ever want to make love to your mother?'

'Of course.'

'Did you hate your father for being able to?'

'Of course. But also for not bothering to.'

'So he didn't only have the woman you desired, he rejected her?'

'Does that make me a masochist?'

'It does if you identify with your mother.'

I thought about it. 'I still don't want you to hit me,' I said at last.

She laughed. 'We'll just have to try something else.'

But I didn't enjoy anything we tried. Not the crop, not the cat-o'-nine-tails, not the bullwhip, not the wheel, not the cage, not the manacles, not the ball lock, not the bit gag, not the cock ring, not the butt plug, not the separator, not the speculum, not the fisting sling, not the nipple clamps, not the bollock stocks, not the kneeling bench, not the hogtie bars, not the spanking horse, not the queening chair, and in the end not even her company. So presumably moral masochist was right, if that meant it was my mind I wanted someone to hurt, not my body.

My mind and in some unaccountable way my father.

I never again went to be whipped in Baker Street. The experience wasn't metaphorical enough for me. But on an impulse born out of idleness — the devil's time — I did once go to find my father's submissive. I was disappointed at first to learn she'd left, but when I thought further I decided it was for the best. You can't escape your psychology, but you can keep it under wraps. Another submissive, a touch prettier and less of a doormat than my father's, suited me just as well. I wasn't a chip off the old block. I could no more have raised my hand to her than I could have struck a child. But I'd decided after my last visit that the reason submitting to a dominant was no fun was that it was too predictable — what else are submissives and dominants meant to do? — whereas being a submissive to a submissive might have more of the excitement of unnaturalness. The submissive herself wasn't sure what she thought about the idea. She gave me the impression that she found it weird in the extreme. They are conventional people as a rule, prostitutes. She wasn't sure, either, whether she'd be seen to be taking work off the dominatrices. But when I told her I didn't want her to beat or whip me she relented.

'So what do you want?' she asked, leading me to her boudoir by the hand.

'To lie across your knee.'

'Is that all?'

'*All!* You call that all?'

'Men normally want more than that.'

'For me there is no more than that.'

So she put me over her cold knees.

After ten minutes of this, just lying there, my face in the rug, I said 'And now can we discuss it?'

233

'Discuss what?'

'This.'

'What *this*?'

'Me being a submissive's submissive.'

'What is there to discuss?'

'Just the words. Just say the words. Tell me what I am.'

She apprehended me in the end. 'You are a submissive's submissive.'

'Thank you. Now will you say, "Anyone can do whatever they like with me, but I can do whatever I like with you. Which makes you the abused of the abused."'

She didn't get it right the first or second time, but ultimately – at the cost of about fifty pounds – she was able to deliver the words in the order I'd requested them.

And?

And nothing. Have I not said that my life was one long sexual disappointment until I met Marisa?

For this reason, my single departure from utter fidelity to Marisa, the one and only time as Marisa's husband that my lips made contact with flesh that wasn't hers, must be reported in the third person. It wasn't me who did what I did.

Felix had of course – because he could not keep his nose out of any of her things – read Marisa's diary entry relating to the fetish club she'd been taken to in Walthamstow. The event was long ago, a betrayal of Freddy not of him, but he lived it as in present time and imagined taking himself to such a place – preferably not in Walthamstow – and meeting Marisa there, on the night she was supposed to be with the Samaritans, being felt up by strangers.

Other than that, a fetish club held no interest for him. He did not like dressing up and was not in need of a public whipping. Marisa's sleeping with Marius was flagellation of the heart enough. But she had dismissed him from her sight. Go get your sting elsewhere, she'd told him. In peevish response to which – to pay her back and hurt himself still more – he would allow some other woman to do her worst with him, since his wife had done her all.

He didn't know how to go about finding a fetish club but remembered seeing shops that advertised them while eating Indian street food with Marisa in Camden Lock. Thereafter it was easy. He collected fistfuls of flyers from a couple of those shops and made some discreet enquiries as to dress. He owned no leather shorts or chain-mail vests and was too embarrassed to try any on, but, yes, if that was all he had, a frilly Hamlet shirt and evening suit would do as well, depending of course on the signal he meant to send. A frilly Hamlet shirt and evening suit, he learned, might well be considered masterful. He flushed a little. Not on me they won't, he thought.

He found a club that promised more wildness than he believed he could handle, but at least it was in the City and therefore, he reasoned, likely to be classless and clean. In the taxi there he was suddenly overwhelmed by a desire to be taking Marius with him – a Virgil to his Dante, escorting him around an underworld he knew nothing of. Get a load of this, Marius, you narcissistic little cuckold-maker. Where are your underage Shropshire schoolgirls now?

Queer that he felt a denizen of the scene already, though all he'd done was pick up a flyer.

A bouncer made him open his coat to show he wasn't wearing street clothes, though they felt like street clothes to Felix. Behind a plastic-coated card table a woman in a nautical hat and with both her breasts exposed like party balloons looked surprised to see him, took his money and told him he was the first.

'The first what?' he asked.

'The first here.'

He consulted his watch irritably. It was eleven o'clock, for God's sake. In the action he saw what a toff he must have looked in his Burlington Bertie evening wear, amazed to discover that life had still not got going in some parts of town a full half-hour after the theatres had emptied in his.

'Shall I go away and come back, then?' he asked.

'Up to you,' she said. 'The bar's open. But it won't start to fill up until well after midnight.'

'Do I get a pass-out?'

'I'll recognise you,' the bouncer promised.

For an hour, he wandered the warren of streets that enclosed the Bank of England, cutely named to please Americans – Change Alley, St Swithin's Lane, Throgmorton Street, Austin Friars, King's Arms Yard – then stopped to buy himself a hamburger. Only unsavoury people were about. Which made him angry with Marisa. And her fucking lover. He read the headlines in the morning papers – LEADING LONDON BOOKSELLER MURDERED WHILE VACATING HOUSE FOR WIFE'S SEXY ROMP WITH UNEMPLOYED TOYBOY. He was flattering himself, he realised. Who'd care he was a bookseller? KINKY HUSBAND MURDERED, more like. KINKY CUCKOLD HUSBAND. In which event the consensus of opinion would be against him. Kinky cuckold husbands only get what they deserve.

Back at the club the bouncer asked him to open his coat.

'You promised you'd remember me,' he reminded him.

'I do remember you. I just don't remember what you were wearing.'

'It's getting going in there now,' the woman with the balloon breasts said.

Felix pushed open a tattered red curtain and almost fell over a shaven-headed man with no clothes on – just a gold bar, like an elongated cufflink, threaded through the eye of his penis – in the act of stepping into a kilt. There was a cloakroom but no changing room. People transformed themselves from librarians and telephone engineers into Egyptian goddesses and Nubian slaves wherever they could find a spare inch of space. Felix handed in his coat for which he was given a raffle ticket in return, straightened the frills on his shirt, and propelled himself – he'd been right to invoke Virgil and Dante in the taxi – into hell. Hell – no other word for it. He meant no criticism. There is a hell of the imagination that is simply a good time infinitely multiplied and unpoliced. And though these weren't Felix's good times, he felt a distant kinship with them, a fondness for the participants which was at one and the same time what an old man might feel for those learning a trade in which he's grown wise, and a timid deviant's admiration for perversions lived out to the full.

We think of Hogarth as the great painter of English debauch but only Bosch could have done justice to the sight that met his eyes – a Garden of Earthly Delights, no one vomiting or defecating, no one, in fact, behaving anything but civilly to everybody else, but otherwise that circus crush of flesh which we always imagine will presage or succeed the apocalypse, that grand carnival of the orifices which no English artist is capable of rendering for all the pride we take in our mastery of the grotesque.

Felix found room at the bar between a figure encased entirely in black rubber, with no means, that Felix could discern, to see or breathe through, and a man wearing one black and one white stocking under a dinner lady's apron. Why, Felix wondered.

He nodded at both of them, bought a German beer, and watched. Essentially the club was one large room with a dance area in the middle, and several side annexes, some no bigger than cubicles, created by screens and curtains. You could find privacy if you wanted it, but no one wanted it. Why come out to hide yourself away? The dungeon was periodically the main centre of attention, the extremity of the enacted scene determining the level of excitement. Felix wasn't sure at first what his rights to view were and stayed at the bar. The dance floor filled and emptied. Two transexuals, both modelled on ladies who took tea in the Brighton

Pavilion, circa 1922, danced in each other's arms. An old, head-masterish-looking man, completely naked but for a stout pair of sandals and a leather pouch strapped around his waist, danced alone. His penis, though apparently erect, was minuscule. Therapy, Felix thought. The cure for diffidence was exhibitionism, someone must have told the old man – perhaps Marisa if he'd rung the Samaritans – and now here he was without a care in the world, making a virtue of necessity and gifting his midget manhood to the room. No one made light of him, Felix noticed. Indeed, the only person noticing him was Felix.

The music was trance-inducing. The lighting low and acidic. A woman of Marisa's age, with an arrogant alabaster face, smooched with two men, one black, one white, kissing each of them in turn. She wore what Felix took to be a traffic warden's hat (why, Felix wondered). Just that and a gauze G-string which showed the outline of her vagina. Though the white man carried a whip he didn't use it on her. Once he turned her to face his companion and roughly thrust his fingers into her rectum. She arched into the pain while the black man kissed her face tenderly.

Watching them with interest was a person whose sex was diffi-cult to determine with confidence, in a plain white liberty-bodice and matching knee-length drawers, his face/her face covered with a stocking like a bank robber. Why, Felix wondered.

And why the couple dressed as Robin Hood and Maid Marian? The rubber nurse he thought he understood. And the Decline of the Empire centurion in a leather skirt and steel breastplate. And even the man with a wooden clothes peg on each nipple and a bouquet of wooden clothes pegs which appeared to spring like flowers from his testicles. But why the again-indeterminate person in a floor-length duffel coat and black scarf tied around his or her mouth like Tom Mix? Why, Felix wondered. Why, of all the places the sexual urge might arrest and fixate itself, why here?

At intervals, women whom Felix took to be professional whip-pers-in made their appearance and traversed the room. Some, in tight corsets and high-heeled boots, looked like the cartoon domi-natrices who had paraded before his father and his uncles in the House of Correction off Baker Street, but most – presumably because they were overweight – wore never-never Edwardian riding mistress habits that covered them from head to foot, or belle époque society dresses with feathers, veils and Merry Widow hats. Wherever a mistress was seated, a man was on the floor before her, kissing her feet, in one instance actually licking the soles of her lace-up ankle boots, an action of such concentrated intensity he must have wanted to lick up every impurity she had ever trodden in.

Sometimes these women took to the dance floor, dangling men on leather collars like the one with which Felix's red-haired Freudian had failed to make a sexual as opposed to a moral masochist out of him. As then, the conceit aroused him more than its execution. A woman leading a man around like a dog – it should have been exciting, but it wasn't. Some element was missing. What was it? A proper reduc-tion of man to animal, Felix decided. Had the woman gone on to geld the man, or have his throat cut in an abattoir, then yes, arousing.

He must have said some of this aloud to himself because an almost skinless man with a painted body and curved needles through his cheeks wondered if Felix was addressing him.

'I'm trying to make up my mind about dog leads,' Felix said, feeling that he knew the man and then realising that he did – he knew him from Moby Dick. Queequeg, the South Sea fetishist.

'What about them?'

'Whether they're a turn-on.'

'Not to me they're not. You?'

'Can't decide.'

'So what do you like?' He had the gentlest voice, and even a slight lisp, though Felix didn't know if that was an effect of the needles through his cheeks.

'I can't decide that either,' Felix said. 'Cuckoldage, I suppose.'

'What's that?'

'Submitting to your wife's infidelity.'

'How do you spell it?'

Felix spelled it for him.

'Is that a fetish?'

'I don't know. I suppose it must be.'

'Is that her?' He pointed to a woman encased in black rubber, dancing with the man encased in black rubber whom Felix had stood next to earlier. They were kissing – though through what aperture he could not tell – entwined about each other like a pair of black snakes copulating.

'No,' Felix said. 'Though if it were I'd be enjoying it.'

The man who reminded him of Queequeg adjusted one of the curved needles in his cheek and scratched his head in a bemusement he could not conceal. 'I think all this dancing spoils it,' he said, inconsequently. 'Too much posing, if you ask me. They're all just playing around.'

As opposed to what, Felix wondered. But then he noticed that a crowd had gathered in the dungeon and he decided this time to join it. A heavily made-up woman, Scandinavian in appearance, was dripping candle wax on to a man's penis. He was bound by leather straps into a sort of Bedlam chair. With every molten drop he winced, but could not move his hands to protect himself. Each time, the woman leaned towards him, her hair falling in his face. Felix assumed she was whispering something to him, asking if he was all right. But she was kissing him too. When it was all over they embraced. Felix was new here and had no measure other than his instincts, but other people surely must have known the difference between a transaction and a loving act. And they too, it seemed to him, saw this as a loving act.

There were many such. A beautiful, lithe girl with amber skin was rotated on a wheel by a young man in a leather waistcoat who

appeared to think the world of her. That the whipping he adminis-
tered answered more to her desire than to his Felix believed he could
tell from the tension in his shoulders. There were plenty of people
here who flogged without inhibition, their bodies at one with the
movement of the flogger. But the lover of the girl with the amber
skin flogged against himself. Now on her breasts, now on her belly,
now on her pubis, he struck, and with each blow he started, as she
did not. Perhaps she knew how beautiful she looked spinning naked
in the acid light. Perhaps she knew how much he loved her.

Felix fought against the sentimentality of his nature. Not every-
thing he saw was pretty. A man in chaps which bared his buttocks
made an occasional nuisance of himself, asking women if they
would piss on him. Another, dressed similarly, pushed himself too
close, in Felix's view, to other people's action and was eventually,
though with great politeness and discretion – for you must mind
your manners where you are otherwise vulnerable and abandoned
– removed from the premises. And often there was no knowing
where sentiment finished and opportunism began. A male equiv-
alent to the belle époque mistresses, haughty and preposterous in
tight riding trousers and a shirt not a million miles from Felix's,
attended a couple in their sixties in what was surely, though Felix
saw no money change hands, a professional capacity. The woman
was spread out on a version of a hospital trolley in an attitude
reminiscent of labour. In the intensity of his concentration, the
husband resembled a medical student, as painted by a Dutch master,
attending his first dissection of a corpse. With more flourish than
Felix thought necessary, the torturer raised the woman's skirts,
under which she was naked, spread her legs, patted her labia with
the handle of his crop which, when he thought she was ready, he
inserted, an inch at a time, into her vagina.

The woman made a sound like birdsong – not recognisably
human, perhaps the sound of however many thousand years of
shame leaving her body.

Had the world ended in flames that moment, the husband would not have drawn his eyes from his wife's vagina swallowing the crop.

What happened further Felix did not stay to find out. For him the world had already ended in flames. He was not disgusted. There is a magnanimity among perverts which is unknown to those who consider themselves straight. Freed from the fear of their own desires, they do not start in dread from other people's. But some acts are private whether you approve of them or not, and regardless of the actors' wishes. For Felix, this performance wasn't too cruel, it was, simply, too personal. Like the sight of a person at prayer, too devotional to intrude upon.

Much more in this vein did Felix see and think. What he did at last, he did because he thought he should do something. It was almost like showing solidarity, though it wasn't only that. He was also motivated by a boredom which had begun to creep over him. There is a monotony in flogging, for the viewer at least, no matter how outlandish the flogger, or how exquisite the flogged. Such beauty, such lewdness in the exposure, and yet how quickly the lewdness runs out of ways to express itself. In the end, only so much you can do with an anus or a vagina opened by an instrument of torture to the scrutiny of men and women who are beyond surprise or shock. But he was most motivated, of course, by his irritation with Marisa for refusing him so small a thing as he had asked, while out here in this netherworld of hellish passions, love showed itself as all-accommodating. He took off his shirt and tried a whipping, just for old times' sake as it were, but the woman he had approached, on account of her being built on a similar scale to Marisa, had no feeling for the subtleties of whipping as Felix understood them, chief among which was whipping him without hurting him. After that he joined the corpus of the sissy prostrate, waiting for a boot to lick. As it happened he struck lucky, finding a mistress of Mediterranean appearance who allowed him to kiss her ankles and then her legs and then her thighs, way up beyond her stockings until he reached a point he was not permitted to pass. She instructed him with her fingers – here, here, here! – then pulled his head back by the hair whenever his lips were guilty of trespass.

He enjoyed it not one bit. He found the pretence tedious and fatuous. In no real circumstance was he the servant of this girl. He resented her pulling his hair, telling him which parts of her body were forbidden to him, as though he gave a tinker's curse about her body. He hated her air of queenly complacency, never mind that it was assumed for his benefit. He hated the taste and odour of her. And finally he hated her for not being Marisa.

When they had finished with each other he went in search of a lavatory where he washed out his mouth. Not an act against the woman but against himself. He wanted his fetish back: he wanted to feel faithful again.

The last sight he saw before he left the club was the old headmaster with the penis the size of a pencil stub dancing rhapsodically with himself.

After his night in hell, Felix returned more than ever in love with his wife.

SOME ACTIONS IT IS WISE TO KEEP TO YOUR YOURSELF, NO MATTER WHAT your commitment to honesty. I decided against telling Marisa where I'd been. Now that she'd jerked the tears out of me once, I couldn't be certain she wouldn't jerk them out of me again. And yes, kissing the thighs of another woman struck me as a crying matter.

We didn't discuss the altercation that had precipitated my fall from grace. I didn't again ask to be the water boy at her Roman feast, didn't put a name to any of my wants, and was careful to be out of the house at Marius's appointed hour. For her part Marisa did not ask why I had returned home at four o'clock in the morning in a frilly shirt, smelling of smoke, and did not again reproach me for my neediness. Instead, we did what we were good at and changed the subject.

Normal life resumed. We were a happy family once more. The three of us.

Much talked about, no doubt, as time went on, but that was the way I liked it. Indeed, had the world turned into a sound box reverberating to our scandal, I could not have asked for more, so long as it reverberated, too, with admiration for Marisa. People were slow to understand I welcomed this, needed it even to counteract the conformism that will spread like suburban ivy over even the most outrageous *ménage*. I am not – apropos conformity – saying that we had settled into a serene imperturbability. Such a condition is impossible for a cuckold, who awaits in suspended agitation each new indignity. But with every passing week routine takes hold, until it is only through other people that you go on registering the strangeness of your life and the remarkable character of the woman who holds its continuance in her hand.

There was no shortage of concerned looks of the Dulcie sort, expressions of obscure compassion, or enquiries, from the more intrepid of my friends and business associates, as to the progress of my divorce since they assumed we must be separating. At the merest hint that I was ready for such opinions, some would assuredly have told me they had thought my marrying was unwise from the beginning, Marisa never striking them, if I wanted to know the truth, as a settling-down sort of person. Andrew was to be numbered among those who subtly let me know they had disapproved of Marisa from the start. But it's possible he was simply jealous of Marius for bagging the boss's wife just as he'd bagged the professor's. He left my employ, anyway, about six months into our arrangement. 'Sometimes you just have to know when to let go, Mr Quinn,' he said as we parted, though whether he was referring to me or to himself I couldn't decide.

Appreciation was far harder to come by. A writer of ecstatic tales who lived next door, well past her prime now but once a sort of bluestocking de Sade for women undergraduates – indeed, in her heyday a prolific buyer of eighteenth-century French pornography from us – made a prune of her face whenever we passed each other on the street.

'Your house!' she exclaimed one morning, as it were over the garden fence.

'What about my house?'

'Well you tell me what about your house.'

'I'm not sure I am obliged to. But since I think of us as coming from the same space erotically, Mariana, wouldn't you say my house exemplifies those freedoms your stories have always claimed for your sex? Is not Marisa one of yours?'

'Freedoms! Freedoms are taken, not given.'

'Ah, so you are privy to our negotiations.'

The word 'negotiations' caused her face to assume its prune shape again.

'"Fuck or be fucked" – wasn't that your exhortation to your readers? Well, my wife fucks. You should be fucking pleased for her. Unless you think she's thereby bringing down the tone of a respectable neighbourhood.'

'Well she's certainly not raising it,' she said. A high priestess of the sexual mysteries worrying about the value of her property.

I doubted that property was on the mind of the retired media lawyer who lived in widowered sadness the other side of us – a sweet man with broken veins in his cheeks who, when the sun shone, invited us into his garden for sherry he imported from Portugal. But he too, I thought, was watching Marius's comings and goings without knowing what to make or say of them.

'How's Marisa?' he would ask me some days. He was worried for her, he wanted me to see.

'Look,' I said to him one evening, sitting in his garden listening to the Marylebone bells striking six, the pair of us sipping sherry like a pair of old bees. I was without Marisa who was somewhere else. 'You're approaching this the wrong way. Imagine we're in Rome discussing Cleopatra. I'm Agrippa, who's never left the city, and you're the much-travelled Enobarbus impressing me with tales of the Nile. So . . . *the barge she sat in . . .*'

He tried, but lacked the amplitude of vocabulary. 'She's a peach,' he said, refilling my glass and blushing, 'there can be no two opinions about that.'

Leaving me to pine for descriptions of how she was adorned, what wild Asiatic scents came off her body, how sick with love for her the winds were.

At last it was Marisa's own sickness that began to cause me concern. Something, I could tell, was eating away at her. I hadn't noticed it coming on, but suddenly she was looking hollow-eyed. She left food on her plate, a thing she'd never done in the whole time I'd known her. She would stub out a cigarette barely before she'd drawn on it, then immediately light another. She started conversations she couldn't be bothered to finish. She missed appointments, two weeks running letting down the blind man and even failing to turn up to her precious dancing lessons, which I often thought she'd skip my funeral to attend. This latter omission I took to be especially significant with the summer coming round and London's open spaces getting ready for all those al fresco festivities Marisa loved – tea dances in Covent Garden, ballroom and old-time in front of the National Theatre, tangoing in Regent's Park.

As well, she stopped talking to me in the night about Marius.

I could have been the cause of it, however returned to husbandly compliance I now was. I was an oppression with my ever-waiting ear, I accepted that. But I didn't think it was me. If she looked anything, yes, she looked lovesick, and though I believed she was still in love with me, it wasn't any longer love of the sort that makes your eyes go black. So it was Marius. Things were not right between them.

I had several theories as to the cause of her distress. Chief among them being Marius's nature. Marius the Withholder doing what he did best – withholding. An unforgiving account of my part in their affair would see this as intrinsic to my intentions from the start. I had picked him for exactly this quality. If Marisa was suffering, was she not suffering exactly as I knew she would, indeed exactly as I meant her to?

It's hard for me to accept I wished Marisa harm. Where would the sense have been in that? I wanted her to fall for Marius in a big way, because that would hurt me, not her. But I see I may at some level have sought her degradation as the price or even the condition of mine. In which case I bore the blame for whatever Marius was doing, or not doing, to her now. Was this too, then, intrinsic to my intentions from the start – that I would have to save her from him?

'I know your game,' Elspeth told him once.

'I have no game,' he said.

'Oh, yes you do. You make women feel it's their fault you don't want them.'

'Women?'

'I'm not a fool, Marius.'

'My dear, I would never for one moment say you were.'

'Say it, no. But you look it, think it, communicate it every time I come near you.'

'You are hoping I'll say, "Then don't come near me," so I'll have proved your point.'

'It doesn't make you a pleasant or a kind man, Marius, to know your-self.'

'Self-knowledge isn't all it's cracked up to be, you say?'

'Not when it's you who's knowing you, no, it isn't.'

'Then who would you like me to know? Name a person you don't resent me knowing.'

The reference was to their previous argument when she'd accused him of seducing her godchild, a pretty girl with the eyes of Mata Hari who, like her godmother, had a soft spot for clever men. That Marius dared allude to this incident, however obliquely, damned him in Elspeth's eyes to just the criticism she'd been making. But she had no defences against its logic.

'You prick!' she said.

He curled his lip at her. 'And you wonder why I don't come near you.'

The godchild was called Arwen – the daughter of a woman Elspeth's husband had taught and who had formed a close union with Elspeth based on a shared enthusiasm for the Middle Earth. It had been in order to guar-antee a sort of continuity in Tolkien, should anything happen to her, that the mother had asked Elspeth to be godmother. Arwen had been staying with them in Church Stretton, recuperating from an unhappy affair with a famous poet. She had met the poet at a book signing in a London book-shop. He had apologised to her because his fountain pen had smudged his signature. 'It's running wet,' he said.

'Wet is how I like it,' Arwen had replied, and the next day the poet left his wife.

Six months later he left her.

She was more careful with Marius, who warned her against literary men in general but poets in particular.

'Was he dark-suited or did he sport a headband and two earrings?' he asked her.

'Are those the only options for a poet?'

'Yes.'

'He was dark-suited.'

'Ah, the worst kind. I guessed as much. And low-voiced?'

'How did you know?'

'And he chewed his words to make them digestible for you. But never quite audible. So you had to be forever inclining your head to hear him, like a beggar wanting alms.'

She laughed and flashed her eyes. 'How do you know this?'

'Because he's the fucking same himself,' Elspeth said.

They were in the garden, looking across towards the slumbering purple outline of the Long Mynd – Marius's least favourite sight on earth. Elspeth was serving them Pimm's. It was four o'clock and Marius felt that suffusion of irritated desire appropriate to the hour. His eyes met the girl's. He didn't need them to say anything. Elspeth had said it all for him. Always her mistake, to suppose she could discommend him as a bounder. All she did was pique the curiosity of the women she hoped to deter. For three days Marius held the girl in his eyes and let Elspeth do the talking.

'He's a bit of a poet himself, you know, *mon mari* Marius. And a potter when the verses stick. Never seen a poem or a pot come out, though, despite his all-night vigils *là*.' She pointed to the wooden shed which Marius had built, his bolt-hole from the trials of being a younger man manacled to an older woman grown desperate with insecurity.

'Do you work there every night?' Arwen asked.

'He does something there every night,' Elspeth went on. 'Would you call it work, Marius? Or do you go there just to imagine being out in the blackness with the foxes?'

Marius held Arwen's eyes in his.

On the third night of her stay, Arwen crept out into the garden and knocked on the shed. Marius opened the door. She put her mouth up to his and clawed at his neck.

'What's this?' Marius asked.

'You know what this is. Can I come in?'

'I like you at the door,' he said. 'The eternal visitor.'

'What does that mean?'

He mumbled something to himself then turned her around so that she could lean back into him. He took her weight and breathed in the fragrance of her hair. She relaxed against him, sighing. He put his hands under her jumper and held her breasts. She was just the smallest bit frightened, so tight was his grip on her. Not so much frightened of his strength but of what felt like sarcasm, if sarcasm is something a man can express in the way he holds your breasts.

'Smell the night,' he said. 'If you look hard you will at last make out the outline of the hills.'

'So beautiful,' she crooned.

'Beautiful? It's death out here.'

Then he pushed her back into the garden and closed the door of his shed.

How do I know what I know about Marius? One: I used my eyes. Two: I used my intuition (a masochist is not the inverse of a sadist but he knows him as a fly knows a spider). Three: Marisa told me.

There will be some who wonder why, over time, Marisa chose to tell me so much of what Marius told her. My question is more fundamental: what did Marius himself intend by telling her so much?

Her destabilisation, is my answer.

Love has strange ways of showing itself. Some lovers piss in each other's mouths. A wife scalds her husband's genitals with boiling wax; a husband arranges for a stranger in Marquis de Sade breeches to push a riding crop into his wife's vagina in a public place. These needn't always be, but often are, expressions of sincere devotion.

Your true sadist works in quiet and employs none of the clumping machinery of cruelty – his site of operation the mind, not the body.

Hence the mental unquiet I detected in Marisa.

But this was only a theory. It was also possible that Marisa was unhappy because she and Marius were so in love that neither of them knew what to do about it.

'Is everything all right?' I finally summoned up the courage to ask Marisa, a few weeks into her depression, if a depression it was.

I was, I knew, taking a risk. I hadn't alluded to Marius since our falling out and it was hard to ask if everything was all right without conjuring him into our bedroom, a place from which he was now conversationally banished.

'I'm fine,' she said. 'Woman's troubles.'

'Nothing I can do?'

'For woman's troubles?' She smiled. A wanner smile than I liked to see. 'What have you ever been able to do for woman's troubles?'

'Be a man?' I suggested, and no sooner suggested it than I wished I hadn't.

She kissed my cheek and continued getting dressed. A more private affair now than it had once been. Many of the rituals of our marriage more awkward now, or altered in some other way I regretted. The candour gone. The intimacy dimmed.

We left the house together. I didn't enquire where she was going. Something else that had changed. Once upon a time we knew the ins and outs of each other's days as though they were our own. It had been a matter of pride to me that on a Monday morning I could recite Marisa's week. No longer. Now we didn't know and didn't ask.

She walked with me to the shop – 'for the exercise' – then left me with the briefest of kisses. I watched her go. Another woman, feeling what I supposed she was feeling, would have shown it in her dress. Previous girlfriends of mine went lumpy when their spirits were lowered, almost as though they wanted the lines and straps and other indices of their underwear to show, to spite the world. Not Marisa. She might have been off to address a board meeting in the City, she looked so sharp. The slit in her sculpted skirt like a dagger, the man's jacket formidable with her fullness and authority, her coppery hair insolent with vitality. I smiled to myself, remembering her criticism that I always appraised her from the legs up. But today it was her legs that gave her away. In her stride she was not herself. She did not walk with her usual wide gait, attacking the paving stones with her heels. She was propelled by the momentum of her errand, but she did not, this morning, appear to propel herself.

Just for a moment I found it hard to breathe. Was she struggling to find ways of telling me she was going to leave me? Or was she coming to terms with Marius telling her he was leaving her?

Either way, her heart was torn and I saw that there was no fun left in this for either of us. Only sorrow.

If Marius had done this to her—

What? If Marius had done this to her, what?

What was it I proposed? What is it that a cuckold ever *can* propose?

Either way – I kept repeating that phrase to myself as though it denoted the only exits, both of which were locked. Either Marius had made her fall in love with him so that they could elope together and go and live in his rat-hole of frustrated ambition above the button shop. Or he had made her fall in love with him so that he could turn his back on her.

By whichever reading, Marisa was in love. And it was my doing. *Felix Vitrix* – my efforts garlanded with success. I had cuckolded myself to the limits of cuckoldom. I had sought palpable exclusion and exclusion didn't get more palpable than this. A thunderbolt had struck me and I was as though I'd never been.

Ruination was the only word for it. Ruination as promised to the irreligious and irresolute in the language of the great unforgiving Bible of the Hebrews . . .

Thou shalt betroth a wife, and another man shall lie with her . . . Thy sons

and thy daughters shall be given unto another people and thine eyes shall look,
and fail with longing for them all the day long: and there shall be no might
in thine hand.

That's telling them.

I made a fist of my right hand. A baby would have made a stronger.

A masochist seeks weakness and I had found it.

Those husbands of hot wives who set out to demean themselves to the bottom of all demeaning and suck the semen of their rivals out of their wives' vaginas couldn't hold a candle to me – I had nothing left to suck out semen with.

I didn't attempt to settle down to work that morning. I no sooner saw my desk than I knew I had to flee it. I walked the streets for an hour, unsure what to think or how I should proceed. Had I been a braver man I'd have walked into the path of a bus.

Eventually I decided that work would have to be good for me because outside Marisa work was all I had. I'd look at my appointments book, I'd talk to the invoice clerk, I'd check the progress of the new catalogue. I'd turn my mind from misery and when I next looked up maybe misery would be gone. But I wasn't allowed to do any of this, for sitting in the snug, obviously wanting to talk to me, was Dulcie.

'Two things,' she said when I joined her. 'Well three, actually.'

'Go on.'

'A friend of mine told me she's received one of those GET A LIFE cards. If you look carefully you'll see they're not handwritten at all. Apparently it's a PR campaign for a counselling service that's just opened in Devonshire Place. So you needn't have worried.'

To tell the truth, I had been so occupied with other matters I had clean forgot the postcard. GET A LIFE. It was sound advice whether it was directed personally at me or not. If anything I'd have preferred it had Dulcie not disabused me of its intent. But I wasn't going to tell her that.

'Indeed I needn't,' I said. 'Though that still leaves open the question of why they think I'm the one that could use a counselling service. Why, for example, didn't they tell you to get a life?'

'Because,' she said, raising her leg to show me that the gold chain was back becomingly around her ankle, 'I've *got* a life.'

'That's terrific, Dulcie,' I lied.

'You don't mind?'

'Why should *I* mind?'

'The firm's image and everything.'

'The firm has withstood greater scandal than this. If you're happy and Lionel's happy, Felix Quinn: Antiquarian Booksellers is happy.'

'And they're not the only ones,' she said, with an odd catch in her throat.

'Why? Who else is happy?'

'Guess.'

Not a day for guessing games. I shrugged.

'The electrician.'

'Dulcie, you haven't!'

'I have.' She looked uncomfortably pleased with herself, like someone who has just run her first marathon, but not in a very good time. A deep virginal blush began in her cheeks and spread down her chest.

'Dulcie!' I repeated.

'I know,' she said.

And this time the blush went all the way down to her ankle chain.

I did nothing for the rest of the morning. Clients came and went, none requiring my attention, Dulcie skipped about the office tinkling, and I sat in my chair and brooded like Electra for her father.

I'd pleaded Dulcie into the arms of her electrician and schemed Marisa into Marius's. Yet I was a man who, in the abstract and as it bore directly on me, attached the highest value to modesty in women. A cheap woman was to me a thing of horror. That might seem contradictory but it isn't. For where would have been the point of all I'd done had I regarded women cheaply?

So a Cuban doctor put his hands on my wife's breasts and kept them there – was that so big a deal? There must be parts of the world – maybe Cuba – where this is standard practice. But it wasn't standard practice for me. For me, any liberties taken with a woman's person, or any display of wantonness in women, have always been profoundly shocking.

I don't know how old I was when my father took me to see a production of Molière's *Le Misanthrope* at the Albery Theatre in St Martin's Lane, but I was old enough to be troubled and embarrassed when the actor playing Oronte placed his hands in the bosom of the actress playing Célimène. No wonder, I thought, that the fictional Alceste walked out on her shortly afterwards. You cannot love a woman who allows another man to touch her there. But what about the actress herself? How could she permit it, even in the name of art? What if her parents or her husband or her children were watching from the stalls? How would she explain it to them afterwards? And to herself what did she say? How could a woman depart, and in so public a way, from what womanly delicacy demanded?

Once, at a dinner party my parents threw, my mother's sister-in-law Agatha, who was rumoured to be even more unhappily married than my mother, exposed her breasts before all the company and screamed insults, first at her husband, then at another of my uncles, then at my father and then I thought at me, defying us to prove we had what men were supposed to have. 'Come on,' she shouted, 'come on, let's see what you can do when you're not with your tarts!' My mother quickly gathered me up and hid me away between *her* breasts, but not before the men had guffawed into their port. It was funny, they thought, to see a woman expose her breasts. But it wasn't in the slightest bit funny to me. I was never able to look my Aunt Agatha in the face again, ashamed for her for what I'd seen, and frightened by the animality of her distress. It had been a terrible thing, I thought, to witness a woman brought to such licentiousness.

This unease around any sign of promiscuity in a woman never left me, not even when I grew to be the age when boys maraud. I did not lust after the girls my friends pursued. I parted with the first girl I took out after Faith when I heard her laughing at dirty jokes. I hated overt sexiness, as I hate it now when women of all ages swing down Marylebone High Street with their navels jewelled and tattoos up and down their legs. A tattoo holds no seduction for me. I don't want a woman to look like a sailor. Where's the pleasure in coaxing wildness from a seven seas adventuress with a pimp in every port? Sex, for it to be worth throwing one's life away for, lives in surprise and dislocation. In geology the fault line marks the fracture in the vein of rock where movement has already occurred and where future trouble might be expected. Women, too, have fault lines – and no doubt men as well, but I do not study discontinuity in men – which carry the same promise of agitation. Only where there is discrepancy and equivocation in a woman does desire stir in me. Marisa crying 'Fuck me, Marius' on her lover's chest would not have been of interest were she a woman of easy virtue. It was the shattering of her reserve that made me gasp for air.

Perhaps in this way Marius and I shared a predilection. Wasn't that what drew him, in the aftermath of death, to girls young enough to be his daughters – the unblemish of them? The mark of Marius was the tick his fingers made on unused flesh, the bruised eyes he found, or left, on china faces. Youthfulness held no fascination for me, and I left no marks where I had been, but I too was a despoiler of sorts. The difference was that Marius did it, whereas I only watched or propagandised for it.

And now Lionel, presumably, the same, locating the fault line in Dulcie's nature.

Though I was hardly in a position to show it, I was shocked by what Dulcie had revealed to me. Dulcie back in ankle chains! Dulcie and the electrician! Dulcie having done the deed!

Yet again, she and Lionel had edged their lives uncomfortably close to mine.

So were we companioned, now, in this too – Lionel turning away from Dulcie in the night, sparing her the nakedness of eye to eye, but extracting from her no less insistently the compulsory oratory of the hot wife? *And then what did he do and then what did you do and then what did he say and then what did you say and then what happened and then how did you feel and then what did you say . . .*

And Dulcie, flushed from head to toe, lying in a pool of perspiration, shameless, wanton, crying 'Fuck me, Alec.'

Whereupon – whereupon in my meditations, that is – Dulcie popped her head around my door and asked to speak to me. But not here. The snug would be better.

'So what's the matter?' I asked.

'I did say there were three things I wanted to tell you,' she said. 'But in my excitement about myself I forgot the third.'

'You're allowed, Dulcie.'

'Well I shouldn't be. In fact I'm lying to you still. I didn't tell you what I was going to tell you because I was frightened to.'

'Why would you be frightened?'

'Because it's not my business, nor my place . . .'

'What isn't?'

'Mr Quinn, you'll probably never forgive me for this, and I know I shouldn't, but I couldn't live with myself if I didn't say something.'

'Say it, Dulcie.'

'That is not a good relationship Mrs Quinn is having with that man.'

Now it was my turn to flush down to my toes. I tried to make a joke of it. 'You mean your dentist.'

'You know I don't mean him.'

'How do you know I do know who you mean?'

'Mr Quinn.' She subjected me to such a scrutiny, as though she were a headmistress and I the worst liar in the school, that if I'd flushed before I was on fire now. 'Mr Quinn, how long have I worked for you?'

I lowered my head. 'What have you heard, Dulcie that you don't like?'

'Beyond the usual tittle-tattle, I haven't heard anything. It's what I've seen.'

I went from hot to cold in an instant. The sweat froze on my back. I truly believed Dulcie was going to tell me she'd seen Marius strike Marisa.

But that was the voice of my own deep apprehension talking.

'I've seen them twice now at the Wigmore Hall, once at an evening concert, the second time on a Sunday morning.'

'I know they go there, Dulcie.'

'It wasn't that they were there, it was *how* they were.'

'And how were they?'

'Together and not together. I wouldn't like to be in the company of such a man. He looks superior. He turns his head away when she is speaking. He looks at other women, and heaven knows, Mr Quinn, there aren't many of what you could call "other women" at the Wigmore Hall. He seems to exert some power over her.'

'Over Marisa? I doubt it. No one exerts power over Marisa. She'd be off if he displeased her.'

'The last time I saw her she was crying, Mr Quinn.'

'Crying? Marisa? Are you sure?'

'I'm certain, otherwise I would not be telling you. Real tears. And I'm sure she was aware that I was watching. So I think she'd have stopped them had she been able to. Real bitter tears.'

And her own eyes filled, describing them.

As did mine.

Love him, love him, love him!

That had been the mantra of my cuckoldom. Not have his baby. Not tell him how much bigger his cock was than mine. Not wear a hot wife ankle chain for all the world to see. But *love him. If he favours you, love him. If he wounds you, love him. If he tears your heart to pieces . . . love him, love him, love him!*

I don't know why. I am weary of trying to work out why. Because, that's why. Because it was. Because I did. Because because.

I know the theory – that it was *my* heart I wanted him to tear to pieces. Well, it was too late for theories, right or wrong. Had he torn my heart to pieces I'd have withstood the pain. My heart was made to be torn to pieces. Marisa's wasn't. I'm not saying she was more fragile than I was. Perhaps I'm saying the opposite. That she was built for better things. That it was a desecration of her to do to her what he was doing.

The details weren't important. I'd seen him operate. He'd fascinated her and then shown her he was not himself fascinated. He'd warned her enough times that he was a man who heard the end in the beginning, now he was letting her hear what he had. He'd turned cynic on her, as he'd always said he would. He'd shown her the cold curvature of his spine. But he hadn't walked out on her. He'd kept her just warm enough to wonder, in the same way that he'd kept Elspeth at the end of his tether, unable to move forward or move back, while the flesh fell off her bones.

Here he is, your four o'clock lover, he would have said, looking at his watch as she let him into the house, her sombre face lightening on seeing him as it had once lightened on seeing me – four o'clock, the hairspring handover hour, neither day nor night, four o'clock when a man of dreams and cynicism has no choice but to imagine himself in some other place. And of course, of course, the lovemaking would have been out of this world, sad, hectic, final, as the butterfly beat its wings for the last time in the moment before the hand of death closed over it.

Well he wasn't the only one who heard the last act in the overture.

'Tango with me, Marisa,' I said. 'Tango with me in the park.'

'Tango with you? You hate the tango.'

'Only because I can't do it. Teach me.'

'What's this about?'

'Just do it for me.'

'I'm out of practice.'

'I'm out of skill.'

'When is it?'

'This Sunday.'

'This Sunday! God, has it come around already?'

'Time flies when you're having fun, Marisa.'

She looked uneasy. 'We were planning to be out.'

We, we, we.

'Cancel it,' I said. 'Cancel it just this once, for me. You know you love dancing in the park. And the weather promises well.'

Marius, of course, was not a dancer. Too rational and nihilistic to be a dancer. You couldn't make a dance fall in love with you and then bruise its eyes. And he was not a park man, either. Parks reminded him of the Welsh Marches and the years he wasted there watching Elspeth fall to dust. So I felt confident he and Marisa were not planning to tango in Regent's Park together.

'Can I come back to you on this?'

'No. Just put off whatever else you were meant to be doing. I rarely ask anything of this sort of you, Marisa. You are not looking yourself. You need a dance.'

'You are not looking yourself, either,' she said. Kindly, I thought.

'You're right, I'm not. I'm feeling very much not myself. I need to dance with you.'

This time a long stare from her. Once upon a time a stare of that intensity would have propelled us into an embrace.

'OK, Felix,' she said.

This left me two days to sort out what needed sorting.

I thought immediately of Ernesto. No more questions, we'd agreed. But not necessarily no more favours. I didn't want to risk talking to him in Vico's in case Marisa and Marius were there, Marisa consoling Marius for the broken arrangement with a lobster linguini, the dish Vico's did better than any other restaurant in London, and whatever champagne the pair of them preferred. (Jacquesson Extra Brut 1996 – I knew which champagne the pair of them preferred.) So I took a cab to Maida Vale and waited outside his house for him to drag himself back on the Tube.

He didn't look particularly pleased to see me, but invited me inside. The house echoed to our voices. A house without a woman in it echoes.

There were plastic flowers on the hall table, undusted. A half-bottle of wine, not quite finished, was on the mantelpiece. A wedding photograph showed them laughing in front of a painted backdrop of a ship. Off on their great journey.

He was reluctant to help at first, fearing I was going to expose him to further sexual distress.

'Nothing is required of you,' I said, 'other than that you go over to this address tomorrow morning – it must be before ten when I know he's at home – and give him the book. No spying. No questions. Nothing. You just ring his bell, wait for him to come down the stairs and hand it over. He's bound to ask who it's from, so you tell him someone who approached you in Vico's. Say that the someone was anxious he received it. But don't under any circumstances mention my name, though I doubt he knows it. He might recognise you from the restaurant, he might not. He doesn't look at people. But if he does it's not a problem. In fact better that he does. It will lend conviction to your story about where the book came from. If he wants to know how you got his address, the person sending him the book gave it to you. If he invites you up, which he won't, refuse. You don't want to be interrogated. All I ask is that you put it in his hands, don't let him return it to you, and if he throws it at you and shuts his door, that you ring his bell again until he answers. And make sure the envelope doesn't fall out. The envelope contains important matter.'

'What if he's out?'

'At that time he is never out. He writes, or makes a gesture towards writing, until midday. Not a word published or ever likely to see the light of day, but that's what he does. Religiously. I assume you are a Catholic, Ernesto. Well Marius isn't, but this is how he expiates his sins.'

'And how do you expiate yours, Mr Quinn?'

'I give a book, Ernesto.'

The book I was giving Marius I had bought some months ago, not knowing at the time when or for what reason I would present it. *The Rough Guide to West Africa*. Maybe he would take the hint and go there. That's a joke.

I didn't want him out of the country quite yet. I inscribed it, as I always like to inscribe a book, though this time with a message I had not employed before. It would, however, be familiar to Marius on several counts. It went – 'There is no pleasure sweeter than surprising a man by giving him more than he had hoped for.' And was signed in initials he would not be able to distinguish. The surprise – assuming the book itself was not surprise enough – was contained in the long white envelope I had slipped inside its pages. It contained a letter advising him that the woman to whom he had formed an intense attachment and who he had reason to believe was no less attached to him, had – even now, now, very now – another lover coterminous with him. It was in order to be with this second lover that she had, at late notice, put off their Sunday date. If his curiosity extended to such a thing, he could find the two of them in Regent's Park that same Sunday afternoon – why not say four o'clock? – dancing, for all the world to see, that dance of port prostitutes, brothels, low dives and lechery: the tango.

And wasn't signed.

As though he'd be in the slightest doubt who'd sent it.

I gave myself a thirty per cent chance of success. First Ernesto had to get the book to Marius without a hitch. Had to deliver it to the right address, at the right time, and do and say exactly as I'd told him. Then Marius had to put himself to the bother of opening it, and go looking for an inscription, which there was every reason to believe he wouldn't, given that he'd know who sent it. Then he would have to admit, if only to himself, that he was sufficiently curious to read the contents of the envelope. How many opportunities were there here, between vicissitude and impulse, for him to throw the lot unopened in the bin? He had always made every effort to avoid me in person, why would he stay with me in print long enough for a poison that didn't disguise its toxic properties to get into his system? Leave Marius's opinion of me out of it – why would he trust anyone so transparently meaning to make mischief? A man cannot be straw to any wind that blows. We watch *Othello* and believe we would have acted differently. We owe trust to those we love. The smallest act of suspicion is a derogation of them. And a derogation of ourselves. And that's before we put on false moustaches and go sniffing out their secrets in the park.

Now add to these considerations the fact of Marius being Marius. A man in whom aloofness was a moral principle. A man who took pride in being beyond surprise or disappointment. A man who had been able to go for weeks knowing Marisa had secreted something for him among the inkstands and escritoires of the Wallace Collection without attempting to find it, and who in all likelihood would never have gone looking for it at all but for the intervention of yours truly.

What reason was there to suppose that he would take the bait?

Only this: whatever we say about suspicion, it is not in our natures to be above it. Honest Iago, false Iago – it doesn't matter who whispers in our ear: we are framed to listen. There is a template of falseness down there, in that place that can be reached only through the porches of our ears, that patiently awaits the confirmation of experience, so that every broken promise we hear of is a broken promise we've been expecting.

From which it had to follow that if Marius got as far as opening my envelope, I had him.

But why would he take even that risk? What I have just said is true only if we allow it to be true. Men and women of the tribe of Masoch cannot wait for it to be true. Best to get to the bottom of their fears and have done. Men and women of the tribe of de Sade – and we are all the heirs of one or the other, whether we are poets, painters, writers of unwritten books or just booksellers – know it to be true only in the sense that they know every baseness to be true. We are vile at every level, they say, which saves them from being curious. In effect, their cruelty is a mask to protect themselves from what they would otherwise be unable to bear. They are the cowards. The children of Masoch are the brave.

So, unless he loved Marisa as I had wanted him to love her – as I loved her, with that jealous desperation that must make everything it fears eventuate, and as I had wanted her to love him, blindly, with unquestioning devotion and submission – he would neither pick up the book I'd sent him nor bother with the envelope. He would simply put himself back to bed above the button shop.

As for his going to the park, there was as much hope of that as of his becoming my bosom friend.

FOR THE TANGO I WORE ALL BLACK — BLACK MULTI-PLEATED TROUSERS FOR easy moving, black silk shirt, and for the fun of it a black bandana. Some of the other men my age wore squashed pork-pie hats, in the style of Argentinian procurers. I envied their loucheness but knew it was beyond me. On me even a bandana was chancy. But it was a hot day in the park and a bandana could pass for a sweatband.

Latin American music was not my thing, but Marisa loved it and from the start I had aspired, however unsuccessfully, to love whatever Marisa loved. In fact, of all Latin American dances the tango pleased and suited her the least. Marisa danced to lose herself in movement, but the rhythms of the tango worked against the sort of self-abandonment she danced to experience. They demanded too many changes of direction. They were too abrupt. Too sardonic, perhaps, certainly too consciously deliberate for someone who loved to flow like water when she danced.

To me the steps made no real difference. I too liked to lose myself in music on the dance floor, but I'd have been just as happy to lose myself without moving my feet. If anything, the tango made immobility easier for me to get away with. At the highest reaches of achievement the male tango dancer has much to express, but down at the Regent's Park level most men found the steps so difficult they walked more than they danced and left the fancy footwork to the women. Besides, in my view — though I spoke without knowledge of Argentinian culture — it behoved the male tango dancer to simulate a raffish indifference to the woman who was just some common seaport slut anyway and whose job it was to lure her partner out of his cold machismo. As part of this ritual, not only must the man take his time responding, he must also put obstacles in the way of the woman, blocking her foot – a *parada*, this spiteful step is called – so that when she kicks and crooks her heels, she does so, as it were, in a half-imploring, half-skittish attempt to break free of his command.

I hadn't paid much attention during tango classes in our little church hall, mainly because I was more interested in watching Marisa pressed close to someone else, but I'd learned enough of the theory to understand it was a dance in celebration of sexual teasing and even cruelty, a choreographed invasion of intimate space, in which the woman hung on to the man in an embrace – an *abraẓo* – more desperate than it was always comfortable to observe if the woman was your wife and you were not the dancer – unless you happened to be a pain-chaser of my sort. In no other circumstance, outside the preliminaries to fornication, does a woman close her eyes, press her chest hard against a stranger's, hook her arm about his neck (sometimes even loop her fingers in his hair), and kick her feet in frustrated desire.

Not Marisa, though, for whom it lacked, as I have said, the prerequisite of dance. She was too masculine for it, was my guess. She would lose herself if she could but not at the say-so of some gaucho who blocked her feet for fun.

She had entered, though, into the urgency of my request, whatever it was about, and looked the part. I was even treated to a fashion show before we left the house, so that I could choose the part *I* wanted her to look. I chose predictably – a silvery grey leopard-skin skirt in a clingy material, smooth on the hips, and slashed on each side to show off her legs, one of those items of clothing that Marisa was somehow able to winkle out of a cheap high-street store but which looked expensive the minute it was on her. On her feet, steely-black strumpet high-heeled shoes – the highest I could persuade her into – with a strap around the ankle as the dance demanded. Above, a white shirt tied at the midriff. No point in that look if you're a girl with a cardboard stomach. But Marisa was just the right side of fleshy, and the tango is a fleshy dance. Trashy too, in token whereof she wore her trashiest white hoop plastic earrings.

No truly trashy woman ever did trashy as Marisa did. In trash, as in everything else, sophistication is the first essential.

Dancing with her as we had not danced for a long time, and she so voluptuous — her arm coiled about *my* neck, her chest hard against *mine* — I wondered how I'd ever persuaded myself to part with her. I pulled her closer to me, the still centre of her turning world, and let her kick her feet around me as she pleased. I was not sure which of us was keeping the other up. I knew her eyes were closed. I had heard them shut. I heard her heart. Heard its chambers open and close. What a fool I'd been! Never again. Sort this all out once and for all and then never again.

And then, as sure as fate, there rose up before me the Cuban doctor with his hungry horse's face. Not him, of course, or at least I assumed not him, but first one and then another of him, some in flattened pork-pie hats worn at jaunty angles, a couple in straw fedoras, one in a Stetson, one in a bandana just like mine, half of London's South American population come out to tango. Their dance. And as I hung on to Marisa I thought, as I had thought a thousand times before, their woman. Nothing in anything any of them said or in the way any of them looked at her, and certainly nothing in the way she looked at them, that's if she opened her eyes to look at all, but they no sooner shared a corner of the universe than I joined them in desire, gave her to them, gave them to her — regardless, yes, yes, regardless of *their* desire — and in the giving and the losing felt the sweetness of the rapture run again like honey down my gullet.

Once upon a time this would have been the moment I told Marisa I was tired and suggested she find another partner. But I hung on to her. It's possible that in the moment when jealousy liquefied my innards my feet discovered how to tango, because suddenly we were dancing. I don't say pivoting on our axes or performing *molinettes* or *giros*, but dancing. The music had changed — that had something to do with it. They were now playing Ástor Piazzolla's 'Libertango', the great Argentine musician creating the very beat and pain of the human heart itself, the bandoneón

– as agitated as breathing – elaborating on the jangle of the double bass, the violin, the piano, the electric guitar, while something unbearably percussive, I didn't know whether it was another instrument or the sum total of those I could make out, tore at our nerves, sarcastic and beautiful, brutal and exquisite, exhilarating and doomed.

I took advantage of Marisa being draped about my neck, and kissed her. Kissed her cheek, her neck, her ear. She raised her face, her eyes still closed and kissed me on the mouth. Time fell away from us. We were ourselves as we had been, not a hundred years ago, but yesterday.

Not exactly in the spirit of the occasion – on a laid wooden floor in the middle of Regent's Park, with children present, and a hundred dancers concentrating on their steps, tracing figures with their toes, as though in the dust of the callejuelas of Buenos Aires – to be kissing as voraciously as we kissed; but we couldn't stop and nobody, in all likelihood, noticed or cared. 'Libertango' for God's sake! When such music plays and pulls your chest apart, there is nothing you might not do. Indifferent, anyway, to what anyone thought, we devoured each other.

And when at last I did look up I saw Marius watching.

Given where he was standing when I saw him, and assuming he hadn't changed his position to get a better view, I calculate that Marius had entered the park from St Andrew's Gate, having walked along Wimpole Street with his ears roaring, past the specialists in back pain and throat infection and madness, crossing Marylebone Road where the traffic never stops and wondering, as I had wondered on my own behalf only days before, whether he wouldn't be better under its wheels. At St Andrew's Gate he must have paused, knowing it was run away now or proceed to ruin, and he had not run away. Then the Broad Walk, a stroll in the park at any other time but today like the last walk to the scaffold. Didn't King Charles I take a turn about a London park with his favourite dogs an hour or so before they removed his head? No less gravely, as I conceive him, Marius proceeded, a step at a time – for he was not a man to quicken his pace for anyone – the electric green of the grass after rain hurting his eyes, his overwrought senses offended by the fussy garden furniture: the overfilled urns and three-tier fountains, the troughs and beds of gaudy flowers, the plinths of coral geraniums, as violent as a migraine, held up by wild-faced griffins, the colours of everything that grew turning more vulgar, gross violets and psycho reds, the closer he got to the knot of dancers. On either side of him, under the lime trees, people sprawled on picnic blankets, odious, laughing, opening champagne. Not a bend in the path, nothing to shield the view or refract his wondering, just the undeviating walk in the direction of the mocking music, foredoomed, inexorable. And then the spectacle of us.

I didn't know how long he'd been there, but sometimes when you see a person in a crowd you know he's just arrived. At what early stage in his disordering perceptions was he, I wondered, as I met his eye. Had he seen Marisa yet, or just me, his nemesis and joker, just me tangoing innocently on a weakly sunny, threatening to be watery Sunday afternoon in the park, tormenting him, as I'd tormented him before, to no effect or end, with a woman he neither knew nor cared about? And in the moment of his recognising Marisa, what then, what horrid thoughts? He wouldn't, all at once, understand what he was seeing for there was too much to understand. That it was I who'd sent the letter he could never have entertained a single doubt; that for reasons of my own I wished him ill and hoped to hurt him with the spectacle of Marisa in the arms of someone else, that too all added up; but I could not *be* the 'someone else', not me and Marisa, not Marisa betraying him for me, unless, unless – and I would not have wanted to be inside Marius's head at that moment of *éclaircissement* – unless I was the one she had originally betrayed for him. The husband – me! The husband – that self-confessed pervert who had hung around him like a bad smell! But if I were the husband, a person with whose wife and in whose house he had made free, whose existence had never presented the slightest impediment to Marius's pleasure, nor to Marisa's come to that – if I were the faceless quiescent handover husband Marius had supposed him to be, whoever he was – why this intense embrace, why this deep, desperate kissing in the park as the 'Libertango' shook our hearts?

It does sometimes give me an advantage, my living as other men dare not. It enables me to confound rational explanation.

Whatever conclusion Marius reached, he reached quickly.

I had time for one profound regret as I saw him move away, and that was that Marisa would always think I'd staged our kiss for him. Whereas the absolute truth of it was that I'd never expected him to come and had forgotten him – all *but* forgotten him – under the influence of Marisa's closeness, the love I bore her, and the bandoneón, breathing as humans breathe when their lungs are fevered.

Did I want to tell him that, since I couldn't tell her? This was not for you, Marius, this was for us. Was that what made me release Marisa as though I'd suddenly seen my own death and go after him? Or was it another impulse entirely?

By the time I'd fought my way first through the dancers and then through the crowds of people watching – none of them pleased to be pushed aside while the music played – I'd lost him. Had he turned on his heel with the intention of going home, or was he determined to keep on walking in the same direction, as though seeing me and Marisa had been an incidental interruption to his journey and he would continue now without stopping until darkness fell and there was no road left to travel?

I looked this way and that, and even asked a couple of people if they'd seen him, a tall, parched man with walrus moustaches. When at last I did think I'd spotted him he was too far away for me to call his name, though I called it anyway. Then I ran. In a park full of strollers I was the only person breaking sweat. In fifteen seconds or so I caught up with him. He, long and aloofly handsome – for it became him to look drawn – like a plantation owner, in a pale, crushed colonial linen suit; I, puffing and impertinent, like his runaway slave, in a black bandana.

'I congratulate you,' I said. 'You are a man of your word. *We have the strength to walk away*, you said, and here you are, walking away.'

He did not slow his pace or turn to look at me. I had to hurry to keep up with him.

'But then,' I continued, 'it's not hard to walk away from jealousy when you don't feel it.'

I thought he hesitated a fraction. Would he seize me by the throat? Would he fall into my arms?

'I'm surprised,' I said, 'that you haven't stopped to say hello to my wife. But given the hour of the day I presume your mind is already somewhere else. I'll convey your greetings to her, shall I, and tell her not to be concerned, for you are a man indifferent to anything that jealousy can throw at him. Same time as usual next week?'

I'm not sure if he did pause at that moment, or whether his blow was the more effective for being delivered on the move. But without quite knowing how, I was on one knee holding the side of my face. It hadn't been a punch, more a lunge with the elbow, as when you are shooing away a pickpocket. And I'd say it was the surprise of it, as much as the force, that knocked me off balance.

A man playing football with a dog smaller than the ball stopped to see if I was all right. 'Shit, what did you say to *him*?' he asked.

'Just a domestic. I'm fine, thank you.'

But I did act on his suggestion and sit down on a bench.

I could not say how long afterwards – minutes? hours? days? – Marisa appeared, holding her shoes.

'What happened?' she asked. Though from her expression I believed she knew. Some events you dream in advance of their happening, so inevitable are they.

'Marius,' I said, assuming that would be enough. But as it was not enough, I added, 'I thought he might like to see how well we dance together. It would appear he didn't.'

She put her fingers to her temples. 'Felix,' she said, 'don't come home tonight.'

I nodded.

She began to say something else, but changed her mind. She had turned

271

quite white, the planes of her face giving her a monumental gravity, like one of Picasso's demoiselles. For a moment I thought she was going to faint, but it could just have been the music still pumping blood too quickly through her body. She seemed distraught, like a woman who might tear her hair, or scream. I couldn't tell, from the way she was moving her head, whether she was trying to rid herself of all memory of the day, or looking for Marius.

'He went that way,' I told her.

My words seemed to help her gather her wits. Without looking at me she put on her shoes, then went in the other direction to which I'd pointed.

I stayed on the bench for about an hour, regardless of the light rain that had begun to fall. A bird hopped out of the tree above me. A magpie – what else could it have been but a magpie! 'Hello, Mr Magpie,' I said. 'How's Mrs Magpie?'

Which could have finished me off had the man with the football-playing dog not reappeared that very moment. I smiled at the dog. Nothing beats having a dog to smile at when you don't have a woman. He was a dachs-hund or something like. Though he had no legs to speak of, he kept the ball under perfect control. No doubt he thought he was kicking a badger.

'That dog of yours sure can dribble,' I said to his owner.

'You think that's good? You should see him in goal.'

I laughed until the tears ran down my cheeks.

PART FIVE

THE HUSBAND

I am the wound, and yet the blade!
The smack, and yet the cheek that takes it!
The limb, and yet the wheel that breaks it,
The torturer, and he who's flayed!

Roy Campbell, *Poems of Baudelaire*

Isn't that meant to be the way of it? After the wrongdoing the retribution. Anna Karenina must throw herself beneath a train. Don Giovanni
must go to hell. Vengeance is mine, saith the Lord, though in fact the Lord
couldn't give two hoots. What we ascribe to moral justice is merely the
guilty conscience of the reader, the viewer, the observer, the eternal voyeur
of art, demanding payback to justify the salaciousness that's kept him
curious. In reality, punishment if it comes at all is usually more prosaic.
Anna Karenina is as likely to find herself another civil-servant husband
who makes her no happier than the first, and Don Giovanni, bald now
and without his teeth, will go through his address book on the longest
night of the year and discover that of those still alive none wants to come
out and play. But we haven't asked *and then what and then what* only to
learn that sex runs out of steam. It is on the condition that indecency must
await a grand and terrible finale that we turn the pages, pornographers in
the early chapters on the strict understanding that it's as puritans that we'll
read the last. In this way the good citizen is every bit as apocalyptically
dirty-minded as the deviant – each imagining sex to be so consuming it
will leave not a wrack behind.

So here's a scene to warm the hearts of puritans and pornographers
both: a man much like me, in a cemetery again – for it was in a cemetery
that his sordid tale began – standing by an open grave, grieving for the
wife he's lost, knowing he will never be able to forgive himself for ignoring

what she tried to tell him, because he had ears only for something else. Another man, too, bent over the grave – another haunter of cemeteries, he too with a taste for death – the pair of them joined in a remorse that must stay forever mute.

Neat. And I won't say a million miles away from truth. But not what happened.

Depending on your point of view, what happened was worse. But I will not have it that anyone got his or her comeuppance. Whether our desires are foul or fair, it is mortality itself that thwarts them, because our bodies are frailer than our fantasies.

I did as Marisa told me, and stayed away from the house that night. In fact I stayed away for two nights to be on the safe side. I'd remembered there was a hotel near the park in Primrose Hill. Not much of a place but I didn't care to be seen anywhere better. Not feeling as I felt. And not in my tango clothes. I had them bring me food up and never left the room.

Extremity has its consolations. There was nothing I could think because every thought was too terrible. It was like being a schoolboy again on the eve of his examinations. I had prepared all I could: now what would be would be. Such moments, when we can do no more for ourselves, are among the calmest we enjoy. We pass or we fail – it's in someone else's hands.

But for the occasional, intense descent into sleep out of which I awoke in sheer terror, not remembering where I was or how I'd got there – but for these black amnesic interludes that must have lasted only ten or fifteen minutes but felt like days, I lay wide awake. Not in subspace. Subspace was a festival compared to this. Those nights when Marisa left me without a word, sometimes appearing briefly to show me what she wore – a silent twirl for my approval when the situation amused her, a smile and then gone – were sumptuous, a feast of smell and colour, my every nerve alive to the subtle music of abandonment: the sound of her not there, the sound of her adventuring in the world, the sound of her returning, full of traveller's tales, which I awaited as amazed as Adam in the moments before the creation of Eve. The hours lying awake in the Primrose Hill dosshouse were a cruel parody of this – austere, odourless and bleak.

The worst of it, when, in the taxi back, thought insisted itself upon me finally, was knowing that Marisa must have supposed me to have arranged it all, to have arranged *her* – and in that way to have abused every last feeling we had for each other – in order to get at Marius. Unless worse still was knowing I would never be able to convince her this was not the case, not if we crept back into what passes for a normal marriage and lived to be a thousand.

Marisa was not there when I got home. I can't say that surprised me. I went to her wardrobes to see if she'd cleared herself out completely. She hadn't. But much of her make-up was gone from the bathroom. I checked the suitcases. Had she taken an overnight bag or something bigger? She had taken something bigger.

There was no note. No message on my phones. I went into work, avoiding everybody, not because I was capable of work but because I wanted to be where Marisa knew she would be able to find me on a Tuesday morning. No message from her there. I made no attempt to contact her for another twenty-four hours. This might or might not have been the right thing to do. I didn't go looking for her shape in the windows above the button shop either. That *was* the right thing to do. At last I decided I had to know, at least, that she was all right. I rang her mobile but she didn't answer it. I composed a simple, non-committal text – *r u safe?* The uncharacteristic r u from me – she knew I hated text abbreviations – denoting a bare urgency that didn't intend to trap her into a conversation she didn't want to have. And who could say? – perhaps denoting a changed and much-improved personality as well.

Later that night I got my reply. *I am.* Well, that was something. But I was disappointed. I had hoped she would tell me where she was, and perhaps thank me for not bothering her. *Safe* had its own exquisite tact, I thought. A husband who had forgotten to keep his distance remembering to keep it now. But then, as I consoled myself with thinking, so had her reply. Tactful of her not to reproach me for what I'd done. Tactful not to tell me I could go to hell for all she cared. It was only after brooding on it further in the dark that I realised she hadn't reciprocated my concern and asked if I was safe.

So was that to be the way she paid me back? Of the man who asked too many questions, not a question would be asked?

The following evening at about seven o'clock the doorbell rang. I was sitting in my study drinking blood-red wine and listening to lieder. The bell startled me. Seven o'clock was not a time when people rang our bell. Too late for tradesmen or deliveries, and in London friends don't call on you without at least a fortnight's warning. So it was good news or bad. My first excited thought was Marisa, ringing rather than letting herself in as a way of signalling she did not live here any more. I did not check my appearance before I opened the door. Let her see me looking rough, whether it inspired pity or satisfaction. Just let her see me.

But it wasn't Marisa. It was Marius.

'This is not your usual time,' I said.

His fingers rose to his moustaches. 'I know that.'

'Marisa isn't here,' I said.

'I know that too.'

How did he know that? Did he know it because she was with him?

He read what I was thinking. 'She is not with me,' he added.

But that still implied they'd been in touch and that he knew more about her whereabouts than I did. I was not, though, going to ask him what he knew.

'So what can I do for you?' I said.

He looked me up and down. 'So you're the bookseller,' he said. 'You mentioned artist and pervert. But you said nothing about selling books. I should have put the three together.'

'If you're here on book business our office hours are ten to six. I believe you are familiar with our shop. But I remind you that an appointment is necessary.'

'I am not here on book business. Can I come inside?'

I laughed. 'Do you want me to show you through or will you make your own way? I assume you know where everything is.'

'I don't know why you're acting the aggrieved husband,' he said.

'Could it be because I'm aggrieved?'

'You have no more right to act the aggrieved husband than I have to act the aggrieved lover. Less, if you want the truth.'

Incorrigible, the thing I called my heart. Even at such a time I had only to hear him call himself my wife's lover and I was aflame all over again. Had he called her his mistress I'd have combusted.

I regarded him from the higher step, eyeball to eyeball. Did I want to see what Marisa saw? He eyeballed me back. Did he want to see the same? This close, of course, you don't see anything in another person's eyes except the depths of your own looking. For a few seconds we were in a staring competition, like schoolboys. But it was my instinct, still, to let him win. 'Come in,' I said, releasing him. 'We'll sit in my study.'

He had the tact not to comment on the decor in my study being different from the rest of the house. Apart from stuffing it with technology I had barely touched the room since it was my father's study, and he had barely touched it after his father died. We liked a little continuity in our family, though no earlier Quinn, I suspected, ever entertained his wife's lover here. The women in our family might have had a better time of it if only one had.

I poured him wine which he sipped with an unsteady hand. Whatever he wanted, I didn't think he was here to throw his weight around.

His attention rested on a photograph on my desk of an elderly gentleman on a couch eyeing off a woman's legs with an intensity which the photographer clearly found both comical and touching. Heroical as well, I thought – hence my owning it – on account of its obsessiveness. If it was an erotic photograph it was so partly in despite and partly by virtue of its domestic setting: a normal bourgeois sitting room, the man in pyjamas and dressing gown, the woman – not in the first flush of youth herself and somewhat manly in appearance – dressed like a secretary (think Dulcie without the ankle chain, though an ankle chain would not have been amiss) and, with the knowingness of a practised secretary, raising her black skirt infinitesimally, no more than to show a suggestion of knee, but that can be enough to keep the right sort of man enthralled. Whether he is looking at the knee itself or the action of lifting the skirt it is impossible and probably pointless to determine. What the photograph celebrates is the heat which can be generated by a marriage, even a marriage of some duration, when the husband is sexually uxorious to the point of madness, and the wife indulges him.

'Takes one uxuriator to know another, wouldn't you say?' I said.

A guest in my house, Marius deferred to my greater knowledge of the subject. 'I don't know what I'm looking at,' he admitted.

'Helmut Newton. The subjects are the artist Pierre Klossowski and his wife Denise. You are obviously not familiar with Klossowski's work or you would recognise Mrs Klossowski. She was the model for many of her husband's most obsessive paintings and sculptures and for the heroine of his philosophical and pornographic novel *Roberte Ce Soir*, the story of a wife who obeys the oldest laws of hospitality, as adumbrated by her husband, and offers her body to any house guest who cuts the mustard.'

'I think I can see why the photograph is of interest to you,' Marius said.

'And not to you?'

'Well I have never myself been married.'

'No, but you are not indifferent to the appeal of a wife.'

'That's true, but only as it concerns the wife in question and myself.'

'You like to keep what you have found entirely to yourself, is that what you are saying?'

'I do. Am I to apologise for that? I don't think I am unusual in my preference.'

'You might not be, but one never knows what people really think. It is a taboo subject still, wife-sharing, for reasons to do with economics, machismo and the equivocal nature of jealousy. That aside, you are in fact unusual in one regard, and that is in the amount of cooperation you have received from husbands.'

He did not reply to this at once. He was deciding, I could only imagine, on the heat of his response.

'In another place I would challenge your use of the word cooperation,' he said at last, keeping his eye firmly on the worn but still beautiful bestiary carpet that had once covered the floor of a state room on the *Queen Mary* and which I wouldn't have put it past my grandfather to have stolen and smuggled back from New York in his luggage.

'How's assistance then?' I helped out. 'Or aid, or abetment. Abetment has a nice ring.'

'Call it what you like – I never sought it. But you speak of husbands as though there were more than one. Who else am I to discover has been palming his wife off on me?'

Now it was my turn to be annoyed. 'Palming, as I understand *your* use of the word, implies unwanted. Let me assure you there has never been anything unwanted about Marisa.'

'Indeed there hasn't. And I am more than willing to be educated in the appropriate vocabulary for an activity to which until recently I have been a stranger. But who are these other magnanimous husbands you claim to know something about?'

'I once did a little book business with a Shropshire professor,' I said. 'It was what took me to his funeral some years ago, and subsequently brought you to my shop. We are, you see, joined in books, you and I.'

We were back where we had been, and where no doubt we should always have remained, with him loathing me to death.

'You were at Jim Hanley's funeral?'

'I do funerals.'

'Why? Are they a happy hunting ground for you?'

'For what?'

'For whatever it is you hunt?'

'I don't hunt anything. I would rather say, if we must stay with your metaphor, that I am the hunted. They find me.'

'I didn't find you.'

'Well you did, by virtue of your attractiveness. "I have it," you as good as shouted. I was there to mourn a nice old man, nothing else, and there you were, shouting that you had it.'

'Had what?'

I laughed. When one man tells another what he 'has', laughter is a necessary accompaniment. Unless he is meaning to take the tragic route, which I wasn't.

'The sacred terror,' I said.

'And what's that when it's at home?'

'You don't know the sacred terror? I must say I'm surprised. But maybe you don't need the term seeing as you have the thing. It's how Henry James describes what every kindly, mild-mannered and perhaps impotent man wishes he had – the wherewithal to make a woman tremble.'

'Oh, for God's sake.'

'I know. Sounds pouffy. But a husband such as I am has to try to see the way a woman sees.'

'And you think Henry James will help you do that?'

'Well he didn't lead me far astray on this occasion,' I said.

So where is Marisa, I suddenly found myself wanting to say. Where is she? And in the end, though I would rather have asked any man than Marius, I couldn't help myself. 'Where is she?'

'I don't know.'

'You really don't know?'

'I really don't know, though it surprises me that you'd think I'd tell you if I did.'

'Just an ordinary expectation of candour,' I said. 'I'm used to people telling me everything. I have always hated secrecy. Marisa too.'

Silence between us as I made to refill his wine glass, an offer he declined. My father's motto: never trust a man who doesn't drink as much wine as he is offered.

I watched him think hard about how he phrased his next question because it was *the* question, when all was said and done, that had brought him to my front door. But he took too long about it for my taste. I had things I needed to get off my chest, since he'd called. 'So did Marisa tell me *absolutely* everything, you are wondering. Well, some wondering we must take with us unanswered into hell. If I were to tell you all Marisa told me I would be betraying her confidence, and that would jeopardise your future happiness together. Which is not something I would want. Not for you, not for Marisa, and least of all for me. I have enjoyed myself since you and she finally . . .'

My smile, as I let it hang there, was Mephistophelean in all it encompassed. Beneath our feet a bestiary carpet in lurid colours, and in my eyes the bestiary of Marius's wild afternoons in my house, he and my wife locked like animals in each other's embrace. I kept my gaze on him so he could drink it in, my possession of their coupling, until he choked on it.

'I will,' he said at last, 'accept another glass of your wine.' I hesitated, worrying for the rug. Would he throw wine at me? I decided not. He had struck me once. Attacking me twice would, for Marius, have been to make himself predictable. Instead, he raised his filled glass to me. 'I drink to you,' he said. 'I have never met a man who disgusts me more.'

I raised my glass in return. 'Not for the first time,' I said, 'you have made my day. From the moment I clapped eyes on you all I ever wanted – no, not *all* I ever wanted, but much of what I wanted, was to turn your stomach. My only fear now is that like Othello my occupation's gone.'

He put his wine down and rubbed his face with his hands, almost as though he were washing me off him. 'What the fuck have I ever done to you?' he said.

It was a fair question and I gave it the consideration it deserved. I covered my face. Maybe we had to do this blind.

'"Done"? Nothing,' I said. 'But nor have I acted as though you had. After all, to put this at its crudest, what have I "done" to you but given you my wife? I know, I know, Marisa was not mine to give. Any more than you were mine to give to her. But I laboured, when you were getting nowhere with each other, to bring you forth. Without me you would both be still discussing Baudelaire on the High Street. So I have nothing to apologise to you for. But yes, it pleased me, man to man, to think I was doing what would appal you to your soul, and you a man without a soul. A thoroughgoing masochist will always be an affront to a sadist. He takes away the sadist's *raison d'être*.'

'I'm at a loss to understand why you have me figured as a sadist. This isn't the first time you've accused me of a brutality I must tell you I don't find in myself.'

'That's because you're looking in the wrong place. Your brutality is the brutality of the rationalist. You've said you are not unusual and indeed I see you as very much a man of our time. Nothing surprises or disappoints you, you boast. You have seen through to the bottom of human nature. And then a respectably dressed husband with a quiet manner hands you his wife and you're disgusted. One night you must let me take you to a club I know. That will test the strength of your world-weariness. What you don't seem to understand is that I like you. I feel we have something in common. We are both trying to survive the death of God. Only I think I survive it better. I don't pretend to disillusion. I say, when there is nothing else left to believe in, believe in the erotic life. If you've truly nowhere else to go, then let it take you on a journey of its choosing.'

'If you're telling me this is a contest between belief systems, you've been fighting with yourself. In relation to your wife I never knew of your existence until the other day.'

'Your incuriosity does you no credit.'

'And you think your obscene curiosity does you any? In all your nosing about your wife's life and mine, did it ever occur to you we might feel sincerely for each other?'

'All the time. It was what I wanted.'

'Why? So that you could rub your itch?'

'So that I could love her better.'

'You can only love a woman beloved of someone else?'

'I could ask the very same question of you. I said we had much in common. But no – I loved Marisa fine when there was no one else, not you or those who preceded you. Since you, however, yes, I have loved her more.'

'You are hooked on loss, my friend.'

'And you are hooked on victory. We both know that love will die at last, turn tepid and perfunctory, decline into mere companionship and affection, if there is not cruelty in it. Not physical harm or violence, but cruelty. The cruelty of loss. Of dread. Of jealousy. Whatever the counselling professions tell us about trust, where we are not jealous we are not in love at all. Othello was within his rights, though it is not fashionable to say so, to claim he loved too well. His mistake was not to see that suffocating his wife was not the best way to express it. Inviting Cassio to his bed would have been the infinitely preferable option for all parties.'

'Provided he could watch?'

'Maybe. He was a simple soldier. But being told, as Iago very nearly taught him, is more rewarding. Words excite far more than mere vision ever can.'

He looked at me evenly. Had circumstance been otherwise I would have said with compassion.

'Words can deceive,' he said.

'Are you saying Marisa deceived me? Perhaps I've disgusted you enough for one day, but I must tell you that ours has always been a highly verbal marriage. When she deceives me, she tells me.'

'Now it's my turn to express philosophic disappointment in you. Words aren't always, as you know as well as anybody, messengers of truth. Even when they mean to be honest they are bound by the crookedness of their nature. I'm surprised it has never occurred to you that Marisa might have deceived you in her deceptions.'

'You are too subtle for me.'

He shrugged and rose. 'Then let's agree we have out-subtilised each other.'

I scrutinised him. A host's prerogative – to take a long, insolent and uncontested look at an unbidden guest. A handsome man without a doubt, Marius, but dry. Squeeze him and nothing would come out. Just a little dust. And he was more haggard when one really looked. Had they always been there, those dark impermeable circles round his eyes, each like the rim of an eclipsed moon? Mustn't it have made Marisa sad, looking into those?

'So why did you come here?' I asked him.

'Old times' sake.'

'I see you intend to leave on a victorious note. Well I'm not hard to vanquish, as you know.'

'I'll let you into a secret. I don't feel victorious. And I never felt victorious over poor Jim Hanley, though that is your view of me. *Amor vincit omnia*. Love ruins us all.'

'Only if we let it.'

'It's a dice with death, and you know it.'

'Better to say a dance with death. Enjoy the dance, is my view.'

'Well that's your lewd romance.'

'And, don't forget, Klossowski's,' I said, noticing that he had given Helmut Newton's photograph a final glance. 'In fact I think you'll find that half the men in the world are of my party – the half that's not of yours. There's no other way to be. Your way or my way. The hammer or the anvil. Finito.'

'And who's having the better time, would you say?'

'Depends how you measure. But if we're talking rapture, the anvil. The hammer strikes, the anvil feels the blow. The hammer does, the anvil feels. Hammers don't paint paintings or write novels.'

'Of the Henry James type?'

'Of any type. Art happens on the anvil, beneath the hammer.'

'Look,' he said suddenly, as if he didn't want to get into any of that, his voice finding another key entirely, 'forgive this intrusion into your marriage—'

I could have snorted, but I didn't. I too was suddenly in another mood. 'That,' I said, 'since we are being candid, is if I have a marriage.'

He looked away momentarily. Not a subject for him to enter into. Funny how a man can sleep with your wife and still be nice about whether you do or do not have a marriage.

'What I was going to say,' he said, 'was just this. My reputation might be of no concern to you, but Marisa's well-being surely is. Punch me on the nose if you like – no doubt you believe you owe me one – but I think – and as the subject of your conversations I have a right to think – that you should listen less to what you want her to tell you, and more to what she wishes to say.'

'What is that supposed to mean?'

He extended his hand to me and then held mine a moment longer than was necessary. A shocking act, I thought. It made me catch my breath. So this was what Marius felt like. Would he kiss me next? Had he come on an ironic mission, to fill me in on the few things I didn't know about him that Marisa did? Such as the fleshly texture of him?

But if so, that was all he intended to fill me in on. He offered no answer to my question.

'Words deceive,' he said again. And then was gone.

I sat a long time wondering what, if anything, he'd been trying to tell me.

The next time we met – if I may put it fancifully – was in a cemetery.

The following afternoon – I took the timing to be coincidental – I received a call from Flops saying that she and Rowlie were on their way to me from Richmond to collect some of Marisa's belongings and would I arrange to be at the house for them.

'So she's with you,' I said. 'Is she all right?'

'We'll talk when we see you, Felix.'

'So is she all right?' I asked again when I opened the door to them.

Rowlie looked away. Flops stared at me with what I thought was loathing. 'Of course she's not all right,' she said.

I took that to refer to the degree of upset I'd caused Marisa, the nature of which she might well have conveyed to her half-sister. Once the family is involved, the pursuit of sexual ecstasy by whatever means can never be made to sound good. Perversion never travels well across the in-laws.

'I'll get some things together for her then,' I said in quasi-shame.

'No, Felix. She asked me to do it. Please make this easy for us all.'

'Us all?'

'She's given me a list of what she wants and where I'll find them. She said you wouldn't object.'

'Object! Of course I won't object. What do you think I am?'

She didn't answer.

Rowlie stayed in the kitchen with me. We barely spoke. It was almost as though he was there to keep an eye on me, to be sure I made it easy for them all. I offered him tea. He shook his head.

'Something stronger?'

'I'm driving,' he said.

And then, emboldened by the sound of his own voice, he said, 'It's not good, old man.'

'What's not good?'

'Marisa.'

'What about Marisa isn't good?'

'Her health.' He put his hand on my shoulder. 'Sorry.'

And that was how I learned the doctors had found a malignant tumour in Marisa's breast.

She had half promised me this once, not long after I'd come clean about the Cuban. We were both exhausted after a night of narrative – I exhausted into exaltation, she into the grey remorseful sleeplessness of second thoughts.

'What will become of us?' she said.

'We will grow old and love each other forever.'

'Will we? When my flesh falls into folds and my knees have gone?'

'I'm not him. The ageing of the body doesn't repel me.'

'Doesn't now.'

'Won't ever.'

'How do you know it won't?'

'I'm not a man who changes with the seasons.'

'That's just what frightens me, Felix. You'll still be you, lying here waiting for me to come hobbling home in the early morning with stories of men falling at my feet. But I won't still be me. The men won't go on falling, Felix.'

'They'll always go on falling, Marisa. You possess the secret of eternal beauty.'

'I don't,' she cried, sitting up in bed, 'I don't possess the secret of eternal anything.' She took her breasts in her hands, exactly as my Aunt Agatha had done when I was a boy, to shame every man who bore the name of Quinn. 'It won't be the men that fall, Felix, it will be these. That's what they do. If you're lucky that's *all* they do. You must face that. Anything can happen. And where are we then? How will you be when the surgeon's finished with me?'

'Don't start invoking surgeons.'

'How will you be, Felix?'

'I will be concerned for you. That's all.'

She shivered as though an icy blast had blown through her. 'Easy to say. But you need me whole for what you like. It's a tyranny, Felix. I don't deny it has its compensations. And it must speak to something in me otherwise I'd have walked away from you long ago. You have influenced me too much. Men always have. I'm like my mother. I don't blame you. You could have influenced me in other ways. You could have painted a different picture of me. Mother Teresa, say. I'd have been good as her. But what I do *I* do. I don't complain. But I'd be insane not to worry where it will end.'

'Not with a surgeon. Don't wish surgeons on us.'

'There you are! Don't wish surgeons on *us*. It would be me he'd be chopping up, not you. But already it's you who's being mutilated.'

'I'm speaking about my feelings for you, Marisa.'

'Yes, you might be. But you are also thinking about your desire for me.'

'Any husband or wife must learn to deal with what the surgeon does to desire.'

'But your desires are not the desires of any husband, Felix. You'd be

289

dealing with what the surgeon does to every other man's desire for me as well. I can't say it is isn't flattering sometimes to be the mistress of the world in your eyes. I go with the pretence. But what follows is that I'll be the hag or amputee of the world in the end.'

'Marisa, what is this? You're a young woman. The world will have melted or blown itself up long before that time.'

'*That* time, Felix, could be any time.'

But I was sleepy now, wiped out by all she'd told me of the afternoon she'd spent with Marius, her untainted limbs entwined with his, her eyes rolling in her head like a bacchante's, her breasts bathed in a cold quick-silver sweat.

And now here it was, from the mouth of Rowlie – my comeuppance. Symmetrical and jeering: the Cuban doctor by Marisa's bedside again, only this time wielding a surgeon's blade. Except – and this is the trouble with comeuppance – it was Marisa's comeuppance too, indeed far more Marisa's comeuppance than mine, and what had she done to call down so terrible a retribution?

I got no more out of Rowlie. When Flops descended, in a cloud of bags and cases, she refused to speak to me. I followed her out of the house and watched her load up the car. 'So what now?' I asked. 'What's happening next?'

'To you, I suppose you mean,' she said, her head in the boot of the car.

'To Marisa. To Marisa. What's happening? How do I see her?'

'You don't.'

'Excuse me,' I said, 'she's my wife.'

A sardonic laugh from Flops. I was absolutely certain she said beneath her breath, 'And how many other men's, thanks to you,' but she didn't say it loud enough for me to challenge her.

Rowlie was already in the driving seat. 'Text her, old man,' he said confidentially, as though assisting in our elopement.

'Text her! Fucking text her!'

But I was shouting at a car that had driven away.

I tried ringing Marisa's mobile but it was off. I rang Flops's home number, but if Marisa was there she wasn't answering. I thought about getting a cab to Richmond then changed my mind; a seriously ill Marisa would not appreciate my making a scene. So text her was what I did. *Darling, what can I do?* I wrote.

An hour later a text came back. *Darling, nothing.*

With the words, it was as though a sheet of tears had fallen. I did not even try to blink their sting away. I succumbed to them as though they had been foretold, tears waiting for me from another life. I lay down on our bed and closed my eyes. Subspace with a vengeance. When I next opened my eyes it was dark outside. I wanted to read the text again but didn't dare. She had called me darling which was something, more than something, but she had told me I could do nothing, which was less than nothing.

Darling, nothing. Nothing in the sense that there was nothing she wanted from me? Nothing in the sense that there was nothing *I* could do, whether she would have welcomed my help or not? Or nothing in the sense that there was nothing anyone could do? It was too final to bear, however I read it.

Death came two-tiered for me. There was the death of men and then there was the death of women, and the death of women was immeasurably more painful. I wept over my mother long after my father forgot her name. 'Pull yourself together,' he told me when he could stand the sight and sound of me no more, 'you'll need some grief left over for me.'

'You're just a man,' I told him.

'I'm your father.'

'A father's not a mother.'

'That won't stop me dying.'

'No, but it will stop me caring.'

I had always known I would not handle my mother's dying well. I had been preparing for it too long. As far back as I could remember I had been possessed of the utter sadness of it – not just my mother's death, whenever it happened, but the death of women, full stop. And later there was not a woman I encountered whose death I did not foresee and grieve for in advance of its occurring. There are women out there in the world today, rosy-cheeked and blooming who have no idea that I broke down before their coffins years ago.

No doubt it goes with my condition. Freud understood the passive-masochistic state as one in which the son takes the place of the mother and desires to be loved by the father. Hard to credit with a father like mine, but that's the unconscious for you. If Freud was right then I was grieving for the woman I had already killed or intended to kill.

But there must have been another stage, too, in which I disavowed my mother not by killing her but by denigrating her. Grieve for her, prostitute her. Prostitute her, grieve for her. Who's to say which comes first or where the causation is?

All I know, whether I wanted to be the mother, or wanted to defile her, was that desire had always been imbued with sadness for me. I no sooner fell in love with a woman than I imagined her dead.

IN THE WEEKS THAT FOLLOWED I LIVED BEHIND THE SHEET OF TEARS THAT had fallen with Marisa's text. I did not go into work. I barely left the house. I rang Richmond ten times a day but always got the answer-machine. I left messages but they weren't answered. I dreaded ringing Marisa's mobile because I knew that if I heard her voice I'd break down. And how would that help her? Texts, too, I feared, because another like the last and I'd be a dead man myself.

Finally she did text me. *Going into hospital today. Expect to live. Love, M.*

Which hospital? I texted back.

No need for you to know.

I'm your husband. I must be with you.

You wouldn't cope.

Cope??

Cope!!

Isn't that for me to decide?

Nope.

For myself, I could have gone on with this. I even punched in *Nope???* before thinking better of it. A sick woman on the point of going into hospital could only do so much texting.

I let half the day go by in morbid self-indulgence – going through the things of hers that still remained, looking at old photographs and letters, blaming myself, imagining life without her, exactly as I had imagined life without my mother and every other woman I had ever cared for, then retreating again behind the sheet of tears. In the afternoon I pulled myself together and began going through the phone book, systematically ringing every hospital in London to find which one had admitted her. Eventually I located her in a private hospital in Kingston. By then it was almost midnight. They were surprised, when I told them I was Marisa Quinn's husband, that I didn't know her operation wasn't scheduled until the day after next. 'I'm away,' I explained, which surprised them more.

I asked if I could speak to her but they said she would be sleeping. I was pleased about that. She would not have wanted to hear my voice. And I would not have made a manly job of hearing hers.

But in the morning I sent a taxiload of flowers to the ward. No sooner did the taxi leave than I jumped into a second taxi and told him to follow it. By the time I reached Putney I realised my mistake and got the driver to turn round. What would I do at the hospital if she wouldn't see me, and I knew she wouldn't see me? Hang around the waiting room? Run into Flops? Sit with my head between my knees, smelling death?

Marisa was right about me. I couldn't cope.

We'd had the conversation many times. 'You entertain me but God knows how you'd be in an emergency,' she'd said.

'Right behind you,' I'd replied.

'Exactly,' she said. Only she wasn't laughing.

She half severed a finger once, chopping vegetables. 'Ring an ambulance,' she said calmly. When I saw what she'd done I fainted. So she rang her own ambulance.

Couldn't cope.

Not coping, of course, was part of my condition – no one knew that better than I did. Like all masochists, I called pain down on myself in order to bring it under my control. My whole life was a protest against the blind chance and malevolence of real cruelty which strikes where and how it chooses. Let those who accuse me of cruelty to Marisa remember this: I sought to shield her, too, from the harsh contingencies of living.

And yes, when those harsh contingencies eluded the art I made of them, I couldn't cope.

Such high ambition for us I'd had. So grand an adventure I'd thought to take us on, far from the timidities of the ordinary marriage. And now here I was, unable to cope with the commonest contingency of all. Years before, sitting in a café in San Francisco reading Charles Bukowski's slapdash, drink-sodden, fag-end novel *Notes of a Dirty Old Man*, I'd been struck by Bukowski's great tragicomical barroom wail of masculinist frustration – 'I could not as one man change the course of sexual history, I just didn't have it.' What had struck me about it? I don't know. I wasn't, when I read it, planning to change the course of sexual history myself. That ambition only devolved upon me when I set eyes, or when I set eyes on someone else setting eyes, on Marisa. But the lines of your failure are always waiting for you if you know where to look. And those were mine. *I just didn't have it.*

Wasn't ever going to change the course of sexual history and wasn't ever going to help Marisa with her half-severed finger. Wasn't ever going to cope.

But you have to cope, don't you, when your wife has what Marisa had?

On an impulse that surprised and disgusted me, I went looking for Marius. Not because – not *consciously* because – I wanted him to do the coping for me, but because he should be told. That was my reasoning, anyway.

But what if he *had* been told? What if he was sitting by Marisa's bed right now, as my flowers arrived? What if he was telling her about our conversation, or planning where they'd run off to when she was well?

I didn't welcome these wonderings. I held them to be inappropriate to the occasion. Death and desire might have been closely bound in me, as they are bound in any pervert, but death had a right to clear a space for itself too. Death deserves to be left alone sometimes.

Marius didn't answer his door and when I asked after him at the button shop they said he'd gone.

'Gone out?'

'No, gone. Left. There were estate agents taking photographs of the flat yesterday.'

I thought my heart would stop.

'Do you know gone where?' I asked. If they said Richmond – well, if they said Richmond, I didn't know what I'd do. I held on to one of the tables, fearing for the buttons if I fainted.

I had not previously seen the girl who was answering my questions. New here. Everyone in London was new there. She called into the back of the shop. A voice called out in return, 'Shropshire, I think. He said back to where he was before. I'm sure Shropshire. Shropshire, yes. He's left us a forwarding address if you want it. Are you a friend?'

A friend? Absurdly, I felt like the last rat left on a sinking ship.

I became a recluse.

I closed my windows, shut the blinds and waited for news. Had I been waiting for instructions I could not have behaved more passively.

All memory of desire vanished. And with it all anticipation of desire. Cuckoldry bequeaths one this: after it, nothing. Sad and sacrilegious to remember what I had felt for Marisa at the height of my irreligious rapture, when the bloom of health was on her, and sadder and more sacrilegious still to want her well so that she might do it to me all over again. And if not her, who? Who else could I possibly desire now? What other eroticism was there that could hold a candle to what ours had been?

Yes, I thought too much about myself. But every day began with my thinking about her. My first impulse every morning took the shape of a resolve – I would go to Richmond and climb the gates of my half-sister-in-law's house, or I would attempt a sea-assault from the Thames. Flops's house enjoyed a river frontage: what was to stop me hiring a barge or motorboat and calling to Marisa from a loudhailer? Or even scaling the walls of the house and rescuing her by force? But I never got past making the resolution. The fact that I imagined such intervention absurdly only showed how absurd all action felt to me. Everything I thought of doing ended in farce. The great comic heroes of literature, I had always believed, were of necessity of the school of Masoch. No comedy ever flowed from de Sade or the sadistic impulse. Cruel satire, perhaps; but satire isn't comedy. Wasn't the proof of a novel's expansiveness (speaking of the classic novels I cared about) the author's willingness to let his hero be a clown? Not to punish him with his clowning but to luxuriate in it. Of all great clowns not a one isn't a masochist to his soul, and very few aren't cuckolds as a consequence. So why wasn't I prepared to live out the logic of my nature and risk whatever foolishness might befall me? Why wasn't I shinning up the drainpipes of Marisa's hospital and pulling her from her bed? Why wasn't I climbing dripping from the Thames and chancing fisticuffs with Flops and Rowlie, and possibly their children, on their lawn? So I fell off the drainpipe, broke every bone in my body and had to be admitted to hospital myself! So Flops's youngest child laid me out with a blow to my kidneys! So what?

I had turned too passive even to be a clown, that was what kept me at home with my blinds drawn. I had cuckolded myself out of the grand folly of my calling. I was reduced to standing on the dignity of my sadness.

A little late for that, Felix, I thought. But it was a little late for everything.

Marisa's operation went as well as such operations could be expected to go and she was recuperating in Richmond. Rowlie was good enough to ring me with the details but I failed, or chose not to grasp them. I did not want to think of Marisa as other than she'd always been. Complete and dangerous. So she had me figured out again. 'How will you be when the surgeon's finished with me?' she had asked long before there was any surgeon in our life. 'Fine,' I'd answered. But she'd been right not to believe me. I was fine so long as I didn't know.

She texted me a couple of times.

All OKish, was the first.

Please don't, was the second. This in response to my text to her – *This ridiculous. Coming to see you.*

And once she phoned me. We both cried a little during that. No, I cried a lot. Who knew, was the gist. Who knew how well she was or how well she would go on being. But she wasn't who she'd been. She felt terrible and looked worse.

'I bet you don't,' I said.

'I do. But what about you? Are you looking after yourself?'

'Of course I'm not. There isn't a me to look after if you're not here. When are you coming home?'

'Don't ask me that, Felix.'

'Well when can I come to see you?'

'Don't ask me that either.'

My punishment. *Don't ask me that.*

Was it a test? Was it a trial of my resolution? Exert your will, Felix. Exert it over mine. If it was a test, I failed it. What she asked me to do I did. Passive. The old failing. A passive husband when what she needed was an active one.

The only thing I took like a man was my punishment.

I told her of course that I loved her and missed her. That I would never forgive myself for not being by her when she needed me. She told me not to reproach myself with that. The decision was hers. And yes, she loved me. But she never said she missed me. Which I took to mean she didn't.

'How long are you going to insist on this?' I asked her.

'Don't ask me that.'

'Don't ask you because you don't know, or don't ask you because you think I will not be able to bear the answer?'

'Don't ask.'

I wondered if it was up to me to tell her Marius had upped sticks and returned to Shropshire, scene of the most miserable time of his life. But I had to work on the assumption that she knew.

'Heard from anyone else?' I said inconsequentially.

But she wasn't going to be fooled by that. There was silence in the course of which I fancied she was holding the phone away from her, letting its toxins fall where they could do no harm to her already poisoned body. 'This,' she said after a moment or two, 'is why I can't consider coming home.'

I couldn't change – that was why she wasn't coming back to me. I was stuck in who I was. Marius, I believed, was stuck in four o'clock, and I, Marisa believed, was stuck in Marius. I wasn't but I could see it looked that way. I was just stuck in myself, and myself needed a Marius, which was not quite the same thing.

I wished I could have cried 'I'll change, Marisa' and meant it. But a pervert worth his salt knows that that's where his perversion really lies – not in chasing underage schoolgirls or inviting other men to have congress with his wife and give her babies, preferably black, but in his unchangingness. Not in the menace posed by his obsession, but in its monotony.

'I might as well be a hermit, Marisa,' I told her, 'if I can't see you. Or at least know how soon I can start looking forward to seeing you.'

'You wouldn't enjoy seeing me right now. You wouldn't cope. I can't imagine how you'll cope with being a hermit either. You enjoy talk too much.'

'Then ring me up and talk to me.'

'No, Felix. You'll have to try to do without. You'll fail, but you'll have to try.'

'Then I'll show you you're wrong,' I said.

And I did. I locked myself away and exchanged words with no one.

Dulcie excepted. She came over to the house a couple of times a week with mail.

'I'm worried,' she said.

'For the business or for me?'

'Both. But mainly you.'

'Don't. I'm serving out my time.'

'Until when?'

'Don't ask.'

She invited me over to dinner but I refused. 'I don't want to have to talk,' I said.

Once only I accepted one of her suggestions. A Sunday Schubert sherry morning at the Wigmore Hall. Not lieder. I couldn't have risked that in a public place. Just wordless chamber music. She had a ticket for me. 'Are you going?' I asked. She was. 'Then if you see me don't speak to me. I've stopped conversing.'

I'd stopped listening to music as well. And reading. Art is good for softening a hard heart, but when you are already pulp, art is not what you need. Silence is what you need. A wordless dark . . .

So probably not a smart move, risking Schubert's String Quintet in C, even if there were no words. One too many cellos in it for a man reduced as I was. I sat with my head in my hands and wept through every movement. Dulcie, I recalled, had seen Marisa and Marius both tearful in this very room. The thought of which only made me weep the more. I wept with jealousy, because it is unbearable to imagine your wife weeping for another man, far more unbearable than imagining him enjoying every of inch of her sweet body. But I wept with plain old grief still more. The grief that remains when jealousy has no more flesh to feed on.

I did not intend to stay for sherry afterwards. But on the way out I caught sight of Dulcie, Lionel and I assumed the electrician, queuing for theirs. It's possible I would not have recognised them had they not given off something I recognised. Euphoria, if I must give it a name.

Anyone else observing them would have said the electrician was the husband and Lionel was the friend, but I knew what to look for. No 'friend' hovers in quite the way Lionel did. No friend pays such careful attention to the glances that pass between the married couple, the smallest bodily pressures they exchange, no friend could tell you the temperature of the air that passes to and fro between their faces. Lionel hung back and watched, and I hung back and watched Lionel. I couldn't say whether Dulcie had her chain around her ankle because she was wearing black boots with her sensible woollen coat, but she was a hot wife in actuality now and didn't need the symbolism. She was laughing and looked loved. When the electrician handed her her sherry she raised it as in a toast. Not to anyone in particular. To the world.

The electrician must have been a pleasant surprise to her when she met him because he had the air of a gentleman farmer, slightly ruddy, enthusiastic, loyal like his dogs. Between the men there appeared to be no tensions. They were as two friends out enjoying a picnic. Dulcie was the picnic. And other than helping himself to the contents of the hamper first, the electrician insisted on no privileges that were denied to Lionel. If Lionel hung back, that was up to Lionel.

On Lionel there was that milky wash of defencelessness which people had noticed on me in those early days when I lived not knowing what Marisa might do. You didn't expect to see so plain a man as Lionel transfigured, but there was no other word for it: the light of angelic visitation was upon him, he had passed from man to vapour, freed of his will he floated around Dulcie and her lover like a spirit guiding them from another dimension. I watched them lose themselves among the throng of music lovers, oblivious to them all.

They did not, I think notice me. Had they done so they would have thought they'd seen a ghost.

TWO YEARS WENT BY. I DID NOT IN THAT TIME SEE MARISA. SHE CALLED me occasionally, but each call was more painful than the last. Not least as we realised we were growing accustomed to our estrangement. One day we would simply accept that we would never set eyes on each other again.

'Do you know what I dread most?' I said once. 'That it's so long since I've seen you that should I pass you in the street I won't recognise you.'

'You won't,' she said.

'Won't pass you in the street?'

'Won't recognise me.'

She went into hospital on two further occasions. I begged her to allow me to visit but she begged me not to. And her beg was stronger and more just than mine.

OKish, she texted me both times. *Ta for flowers.*

But she wouldn't answer any of my questions about how well she really was because she insisted I couldn't cope with knowing.

Tell me, tell me . . . But she wouldn't tell me anything.

I just knew that she was tired. You can hear tiredness and I heard Marisa's.

It rained at the funeral. A sunken, sodden, better to be dead than alive in morning. Whether a wet funeral is preferable to a warm funeral I've never been able to decide. For the dead, sun is crueller by far than rain, but for the mourners you could argue either way, depending on what hopes for a new life they entertain.

There were few people there and of those I recognised only two or three. I held myself together remarkably well, I thought, for someone who'd been brimful of tears for two years. But then Marius had never exactly been dear to me.

He had died walking in the Brecon Beacons. He had lost his way and suffered a heart attack. He had been dead three days when he was found. That was the official version. His heart had never been sound, it seemed, and fatigue and exposure had done the rest. My own view, based on no evidence, was that he'd walked out one afternoon when there was less than usual to live for and willed himself to death. I had no doubt that on whatever day he did this, it would have been four o'clock, the light not yet spent, the wheels of evening just beginning to turn. The hour when men dream of being somewhere else.

Marisa was informed of the place and date of his funeral by a close friend she didn't know he had but who knew of her. Marius, he explained, had been very fond of her. She had been his second and he said his last big adventure. Marisa then rang me.

'Christ!' I said.

'I know.'

'Jesus Christ!'

I meant Jesus Christ that he had died, but also Jesus Christ about everything else – Jesus Christ that he had died like that, Jesus Christ that he had become a walker, Jesus Christ that his heart had never been sound, Jesus Christ that he was to be buried in the same churchyard that held Elspeth and her husband. Whose idea was that, I wondered. Had Marius left a will expressing his desire to be buried close to them? There was much I wanted to ask Marisa, but accepted it was not my place to ask anything. Just as, for the same reason, I accepted it was not my place to ask how badly the news had affected her.

We fell silent with each other. 'You don't have to come,' she said at last, 'and in some ways I don't think you should, but then again . . .'

'Then again what?'

'Well it draws a line under something between us.'

'I thought we'd already drawn a line under something between us.'

'Then don't come.'

'No, I'll come.'

'Good. But just one thing, Felix.'

'Don't come over and talk to you? Don't act as if I know you? Don't ask any questions?'

'Don't be shocked by how I look.'

We didn't travel up to Shropshire together, though I knew the way to the churchyard. But I did warn her that the Wrekin heaved and advised her to take galoshes.

When I say I held myself together remarkably well I am referring only to my demeanour by the graveside. The moment I saw Marisa my legs gave way beneath me. I must have turned the colour of poor Marius.

She was standing with someone I took to be the old friend Marius had never mentioned, an unexpectedly red-faced man with a nautical expression. Who knew who Marius knew? She waved to me – a hesitant, fragile, fluttering gesture I was unable to read, almost like the action of someone troubled by summer flies, though there were no summer flies here. I couldn't decipher its meaning – stay away, come here, meet me at four o'clock behind the headstones? I waved back. It was impossible to tell how she looked. She was wearing a long black coat, a black hat, a black veil. Did anyone wear a veil for funerals any more? Did anyone wear black even? Had Elspeth worn a veil at her husband's funeral, I tried to remember. I thought not. But I recalled how like a fallen woman in a Victorian novel she had looked, conscious of an ancient and never to be repaired wrong, and Marisa, to my eye, appeared even more the mistress whom everyone in this superstitious place would obscurely blame for Marius's death.

After it was all over, the dirt thrown in, the last dread word spoken, we made a halting move towards each other.

'Some place to meet,' I said.

What else was there to say? I couldn't ask how hard this was for her. I couldn't lower my voice and say *My dear, I am so sorry.*

'Don't look at me,' she said.

I shook my head and smiled. 'Marisa, for God's sake. You are beautiful. You are always beautiful.'

But I was uncertain how to embrace her. I was afraid to take her in my arms. I didn't know how much of her was left, where she was in pain, what part of her she didn't want me to touch or didn't want to be touched.

She lifted her veil and gave me her lips. Cold in the rain. Her face had changed, though I couldn't quite explain to myself how. A little thinner, maybe. The grey beneath her eyes more pronounced, as though the tragedy which her face had always appeared to be anticipating was on her at last. That, I think, was the biggest shock – her being of her time now, no longer playing catch-up or saving herself for another day. She had taken possession of her life.

But perhaps this was exactly how she'd looked the last time I saw her and I hadn't noticed. It was so long since I'd seen her.

'Come home,' I said.

She made a clicking noise in her throat. 'You look well,' she said.

'I look like a recluse.'

'You do a bit. But it suits you.' She took my arm. 'Walk with me,' she said.

I looked down at her feet. She had not taken my advice about sensible shoes and galoshes but wore black patent high heels instead. For which I would have cheered her had I dared. And asked her to raise her coat so I could see her legs.

'You'll sink into the mud in those,' was all I could manage.

'Then I'll have to hold on to you.' She squeezed my arm. 'It's nice to feel you again.'

'Is it?'

'Very.'

'Then come home.'

'Elspeth's stone must be here somewhere,' she said.

'Do you want to look for it?'

'No, I don't think so. Apparently he wanted to be buried near her but there was no space.'

I said nothing.

'You have strange loyalties, you men,' she went on.

'Do we?'

'There is one thing I have always thought I would tell you, but maybe now I think I shouldn't.'

'And what's that?'

'I think I shouldn't.'

'Why shouldn't you?'

'It will spoil it for you.'

'Spoil what?'

'He never got over Elspeth, that's all.'

'*Marius* never got over Elspeth?'

'Never.'

'Meaning?'

'Meaning he wasn't . . . No, forget it.'

'Wasn't what, Marisa?'

'This isn't the place.'

'Then where *is* the place?'

She paused as though to catch her breath. Did it hurt her, I wondered.

'Felix, I told him better than he was.'

I turned to look at her. If I could have scraped her meaning off her soul I would have, however great the pain it caused her.

I remembered what Marius had said to me as he was leaving my house. 'Words deceive.'

'When you say better . . . ?'

'Better, other . . . I gave you the Marius you wanted.'

'*I* wanted!'

'I told you this would spoil it. Leave it, Felix. Let it lie. Let *him* lie.'

But *she* hadn't left it. Whatever the 'it' was, *she* hadn't wanted it to lie unspoiled.

'What are we talking here, Marisa,' I persisted, 'hyperbole or invention? Are you telling me we've buried a man who never lived?'

'In a sense that's what I'm telling you, yes.'

'In a sense? So who was that who rang our doorbell three times a week? Who shared your bed, Marisa?'

She shook her head and sighed. 'Ah, Felix, Felix, you are impossible. Foolish of me ever to have worried. No one can ever spoil it for you, can they? I think I probably envy you that. It's a gift I don't have. Or if I had it, I don't have it now. Come on, it's getting wetter. Let's walk.'

There are some things you know you must postpone. At least in the presence of death. However bewildering or sensational, they are not for now, they are for later. And maybe not even for then. So we walked, and I was glad to.

I had always loved having her on my arm. I liked bearing her weight, the husbandly sensation of supporting her. This was at odds sometimes with the pleasure I took in watching her from a distance, whether approaching or receding. It would have pleased me, for example, to see another man bearing her weight, enjoying the husbandly sensation of supporting her, if somehow she could still have hung on to me as well. The old, unsolvable conundrum – how to be with her and not with her, how to be me and someone else.

Now become another unsolvable conundrum, left to me to mull over unanswered in the lonely hours ahead: had that someone else been there at all, ever really been with Marisa in all the senses that mattered to me?

The rain began to fall more heavily. As though to show it mattered not a jot to him, a fat sleek crow flew out of the trees and crossed our path, bursting with greedy life, uncaring of the rain which slid from his body. I put up an umbrella, careful of Marisa, gently pulling her close to me, but ignorant of what I was supporting, of how she really was, sure only that I was not to ask.

'Come home,' I said again, feeling her weight on my arm.

'And do what?'

We walked on, picking our way between the rows of long-buried bones.

Occasionally we stopped to read an inscription. Prose, poetry, a line of Bible, a scrap of doggerel – what difference? Wouldn't that have been Marius's thought as, presumably upon these very stones, he helped himself to girls below the age of lawful taking? *What difference?* I longed to ask Marisa her opinion, whether she thought the what difference question had presented itself to him just once too often on the Beacons, before he lay down in the damp and closed his eyes – or before he left his flat above the button shop come to that, before he left *her*, that's if he'd ever been with her – but I knew that that too I couldn't ask.

'Well?' she said.

'Well what?'

'You haven't answered me. Come home and do what?'

And terrible to say I was unable to give her an answer, because I didn't have one.